PELLE THE CONQUEROR

M. Andersen Nexö"

Pelle the Conqueror

VOLUME 2: APPRENTICESHIP

Martin Andersen Nexø

Translated from the Danish by
Steven T. Murray & Tiina Nunnally

With an Afterword by
Niels Ingwersen

Fjord Modern Classics No. 4

Fjord Press
Seattle
1991

Special thanks to Inge Rifbjerg

Title of Danish edition: *Pelle Erobreren, Første Bog: Læreår*
Originally published in 1907 by Gyldendalske Boghandel, Nordisk Forlag,
Copenhagen

Published and distributed by:
Fjord Press
P.O. Box 16501
Seattle, Washington 98116
(206) 625-9363

Book design: Fjord Press
Typesetting: Nete Leth, Fjord Press
Cover design: Jane Fleming
Title typography: Art Chantry
Front cover photograph: Bornholms Museum, Rønne
Frontispiece & back cover photograph: The Royal Library, Copenhagen
Printed by Thomson-Shore, Dexter, Michigan

Library of Congress Cataloging in Publication Data:
(Revised for vol. 2)

Andersen Nexø, Martin, 1869 –1954.
    Pelle the Conqueror.

    Translation of: Pelle Erobreren.
    Vol. 2 translated by Steven T. Murray & Tiina Nunnally ; with an afterword
by Niels Ingwersen.
    Vol. 1 based on the 1913 translation by Jessie Muir.
    Vol. 2 in series: Fjord modern classics no. 4.
    Contents: v. 1. Childhood — v. 2. Apprenticeship.
    I. Murray, Steven T. II. Nunnally, Tiina. III. Series: Fjord modern classics ;
no. 4.
PT8175.N4P413   1989   839.8'1372   89-7837
ISBN 0-940242-41-9 (v. 1 : alk. paper)
ISBN 0-940242-40-0 (pbk. : v. 1 : alk. paper)
ISBN 0-940242-49-4 (v. 2 : alk. paper)
ISBN 0-940242-48-6 (pbk. : v. 2 : alk. paper)

Printed on acid-free recycled paper with soy-based ink   ∞

Printed in the United States of America
First edition, 1991

PELLE
THE
CONQUEROR

VOLUME TWO
APPRENTICESHIP

I

On that brilliant May day when Pelle cast himself out of the nest, old Klaus Herman came bumping along just then in his manure wagon on his way to town to take away some manure. This coincidence came to determine the boy's lot in life. There was no time to waste on the question of what Pelle was going to be.

Pelle had not even asked himself this question—he was just setting out that day with his mind open to the bright world. Whatever he would be when he got out there was something so unimaginable that it was simply crazy to guess at it. So he just kept walking straight ahead.

Now he had reached the top of the ridge. He lay down on the side of the ditch to catch his breath after the long walk, tired and hungry but in a splendid mood. Down at his feet, only a couple of miles away, the town was shining cheerfully, and from hundreds of hearths the smoke of dinnertime curled up into the blue sky, and the red roofs laughed roguishly into the happy face of the day. Pelle started counting the buildings right away; he had estimated them at no more than a million so as not to exaggerate, and he was already well past a hundred.

In the middle of his count he broke off—what would they be eating for dinner down there? They probably lived well. He wondered whether it was good manners to keep eating until you were completely full, or were you supposed to put down your spoon halfway through—like the Kongstrups did when they were at a party? For someone who was always hungry this was a very serious question.

There was heavy traffic on the highway. People passed by both driving and on foot, some with a trunk in the back of the wagon, others carrying their things in a sack on their back just as he did. Pelle knew some of them and nodded with a smile; he knew something about each one of them. They were people who were heading for town—his town. Some of them would continue on, far across the sea: to America, or over to serve the King; you could see it by their outfits and their stony faces. Others were just going in to squander their wages and celebrate turn-over time—they came singing in large groups, carrying no bundles and in a devil-may-care mood. But the real ones were those bringing their trunk with them on a wheelbarrow or carrying it with one person at each handle. Their cheeks were red and their movements feverish; they

9

were people who had given up the countryside and the way of life they were used to and had chosen the town, just as he had.

A farmer came along rolling his wheelbarrow with a little green chest that was wide at the bottom and had nice handpainted flowers on it. Beside him walked his daughter; her cheeks were flushed and she was staring off into the unknown. Her father spoke, but she didn't seem to hear him. "Well, now you're going to be taking responsibility for yourself, remember that, and don't throw yourself away. The town is good enough for someone who wants to get ahead and can stand on her own two feet, but it doesn't mind so much if someone is trodden down. And don't trust anyone too much—people in town are practiced at the art of seduction. But you must be friendly and polite!" She didn't reply; she was probably more concerned with trying not to wear down the heels of her new shoes.

A stream of people was coming out of the town too; all day he had passed Swedes who had arrived with the steamship that morning and were heading out to the countryside to look for work. There were old, worn-out people and little boys, girls as beautiful as Fair Marie, and young workmen with the strength of the whole world in their loins and muscles. It was life streaming in from somewhere else, to fill up the vacuum left by the hordes who were leaving—but it had nothing to do with Pelle. It was seven years since he had gone through everything that was now filling their faces with apprehension. He was done with the cycle they were now beginning. There was no reason to look back.

But here came the foreman from Kåse Farm walking along, all decked out for America with his valise and silk scarf and papers sticking out of the inside pocket of his open coat. So he had finally decided to go, after his sweetheart had already been there for three years.

"Hey!" shouted Pelle. "Is it time?"

The young man came over and set down his valise by the ditch.

"Yes, now's the time," he said. "Laura won't wait for me any longer. So the old folks will just have to see about getting along without a son. I've been doing everything for them for three years now. I hope they can manage by themselves."

"I'm sure they can," said Pelle with the voice of experience. "Otherwise they'll have to hire some help. There's no future for young folks in that house." He had heard the older people say that, and he struck the grass self-confidently with his walking stick.

"No, there isn't, and Laura doesn't want to be a farmer's wife either. Well, goodbye to you!" He held out his hand to Pelle and attempted a smile, but his features went their own way, and it only turned into a grimace. He stood there a while looking down at his boots, and his thumb fumbled across his face as if he wanted to wipe away the embarrassment. Then he took his valise and left. There was probably not much to him.

"I'd be glad to take over your ticket and your sweetheart!" shouted Pelle hilariously, stretching like a grownup. He was in a fantastically good mood.

Today the whole world was moving in the direction Pelle's own blood was urging him: every young man with a little get-up-and-go, every girl who was good-looking. The road was not free of traffic for a moment. It was like a great exodus—away from the places where everyone knew he was doomed to die at the exact spot where he was born, and out into the excitement of uncertainty. The little brick houses that lay strewn across the hill above the town, or stood in two single files along the road running into town, were the little huts of the farming country that had broken free of everything out there, dressed themselves in town clothes, and started down the hill. And down by the beach the houses were shoved together in bunches around the church. You couldn't tell where anything was, they were so tightly packed together. So these were the hordes who had been on their journey outward, driven by their longing to leave—and then the sea had stopped them.

But Pelle was in no mood to let himself be stopped by anything. Maybe he wouldn't like it in town, but would go to sea instead. Then one day he would find a coast that he liked, go ashore, and take up gold-mining. Over there the girls went around naked, after all, hiding their shame with blue tattoos; but Pelle would have a sweetheart sitting at home, waiting faithfully. She would be more beautiful than Bodil and Fair Marie put together, and there would always be men running after her. But she would sit faithfully and sing the lover's lament:

> A lover I had who then went away,
> He sailed o'er the waves so cruel.
> Three years it is since I spoke to him,
> And still not one letter I've seen!

And even as she sang, a letter would come in through the door. But a 10-krone note would fall out of each letter that Lasse received, and one day there would be tickets for both of them too. Then the words of the folk songs would no longer come true, because in the songs they always perished on the journey across the ocean, and the poor youth would stand on the beach for the rest of his days, staring out to sea in the blackness of his madness after every ship with billowing sails. But she and Lasse would arrive safely—after many tribulations, of course—and Pelle would be standing on the beach to greet them. He would just dress up like a savage and pretend he was going to eat them before he told them who he was.

Watch out! Pelle sprang to his feet. From up the road there was a rattling sound, as if at least a thousand scythes had fallen afoul of each other, and a buckboard was rocking slowly down toward him, pulled by the sorriest two heath-nags he had ever seen. On the seat-board sat an old farmer, dangling just as precariously as everything else. Whether it was the wagon itself or the two bony hacks in front that were making such a huge racket out of their slow progress, Pelle wasn't quite sure. But when the vehicle finally reached him and the old farmer drew to a stop, he couldn't resist the invitation to climb aboard. His shoulders were still aching from the sack.

"I suppose you're on your way to town?" said old Klaus, poking at his belongings.

To town, of course! It went straight to Pelle's overflowing heart, and before he knew it he had spilled out everything about himself and his entire proud future to the old farmer.

"Well, yes... you don't say... and that too, naturally!" Klaus agreed, nodding, as Pelle rushed along. "Yes, that's for sure! Less than that wouldn't help at all! And what did you intend to be—a government official or a king?" he drawled, looking up. "Yes, to town, that's the way everybody goes, all those who feel called to do something. As soon as a puppy gets a little strength in his limbs or a *skilling* in his pocket, he has to go to town and lay it down. And what comes out of the town? Crap and nothing else! I've never been able to find anything else there, and I'm sixty-five now. But what good does it do to talk? No more than turning your backside to the wind and farting into it. It comes over them just like the colic over baby calves, and zip, off they go, in to do something great. Then Klaus Herman gets to drive in and fetch them again! They have no place to stay, and no relatives to seek shelter with either; but what's waiting for them is always great. Because in town the beds are made up and waiting for them on the streets, and the gutters are overflowing with food and money. Or what did *you* have in mind? Let's hear it."

Pelle turned fiery red. He hadn't even reached the beginning, and he was already revealed for the codfish he was.

"Now, now," said Klaus goodnaturedly, "you're no bigger fool than all the rest. But if you'll take my advice, then apprentice yourself to shoemaker Jeppe Kofod. I'm just on my way down to his place to pick up some manure, and I know he's looking for a boy. Then you won't have to float around in uncertainty, and you'll be driven right up to the door—like all the other aristocrats."

It gave Pelle a start—if there was something he could never imagine being, it was a shoemaker. Even out in the countryside where they looked up to craftsmen, they always said when a boy was born deformed: well, you can always make a shoemaker or tailor out of him! But Pelle was no cripple who had to find a sedentary job in order to get by. He was strong and well-built. What he was going to be ... well, it lay in the good hands of fortune. But he was sure of one thing, that it would be something lively with a lot of vigor to it. Anyway, he had an excellent idea of what he did *not* want to be.

But as they rattled through town, and Pelle, receptive to the big world, doffed his cap to everyone although no one returned the greeting, his courage fell and a feeling of his own unimportance sneaked into him. The wretched wagon, which the people of the town pointed their fingers at, laughing, probably contributed to this as well.

"There's no reason to take off your cap to that rabble," sneered Klaus. "Just look how puffed-up they act, and they've stolen everything they own from the rest of us. Don't you think? —Can you see whether they've got the spring seed into the ground yet?" He stared scornfully down the street.

No, there was nothing growing on the cobblestones, and all these little houses squeezing each other every which way gradually took the wind out of Pelle's sails. Here there were people by the thousands, or maybe more, and all blind faith had to yield to the simple question of where they got their food from. With that he was back again in his familiar, impoverished world, where it was ecstasy enough just to acquire a pair of socks. All at once he felt sincerely humble and realized that it might be hard enough for him to earn his keep here among these stones, where people didn't grow their food from the earth in a natural way but got it—well, how?

The streets were full of serving folk. The girls stood in bunches with their arms around each other's waists, staring bright-eyed at the cotton goods on display. They rocked gently back and forth as if they were dreaming. A servant boy about Pelle's age with a blotchy red face was walking down the middle of the street eating a big loaf of wheat bread that he held in both hands; he had scabs on his ears, and his hands were swollen from the cold. The farm hands arrived toting red bundles in their hands, their overcoats flapping against their legs. They would stop short at a streetcorner, look around warily, and then dart down a side street.

Outside the shops, the merchants were walking back and forth bareheaded. When someone stopped at their window, they invited them inside with the most courteous turns of phrase—and winked across the street at each other.

"Today the merchants have really got their wares put out," said Pelle.

Klaus nodded. "That's right, today they've got everything put out they can't get rid of—because today the fools come to market. Down there are the innkeepers," he said, pointing down the side streets. "They're looking up this way mournfully, but their turn will come soon enough. Wait until tonight, and then go around and ask people how much they have left of last year's wages. Yes, the town is a wonderful place—fie on the Evil One!" Klaus spat, disgusted.

Pelle had lost all his blind courage. He didn't see one person doing anything that he could earn his keep with. And no matter how much courage he had to be a part of this new world, to dare to do something that, maybe without his knowing it, might help pull the clothes from his old companions' backs, he couldn't do it. Stripped of all his skill and with a miserable feeling that even his only wealth, his hands, were worthless here in town, he let himself bump listlessly along to Master Jeppe Kofod's workshop.

II

The doors were open from the front room out to the alley where people were coming and going: Madam Rasmussen, who was always busy, old skipper Elleby, the comptroller's girl in a white cloak, old tenant farmers who took their life's savings from the farm and ate them up here in town, captains weak with rheumatism who had said farewell to the sea. The sparrows were making an awful din out there on the bumpy cobblestones. They sat there with puffed-up feathers, luxuriating in the horse droppings, fighting so the feathers flew, and cheeping giddily.

The door to the courtyard stood open too. All four windows were open, and the green light seeped in and fell across the faces inside. But none of this helped at all. There was not the slightest breeze—and besides, Pelle's heat came from inside him. It was fear that made him sweat.

All the same, he kept pulling hard at the cobbler's wax—except when something outside seized his tormented mind and drew it out into the sunshine.

Everything out there was literally splashed with sunlight. From inside the murky workshop it looked like a golden stream flowing past between the rows of houses, always in the same direction, down toward the sea. A scrap of white fluff came sailing in the light, and grayish-white thistledown, whole swarms of mosquitoes, and a great bumble-bee, broad and hovering. They swirled brilliantly past the doorway and kept on going, as if they were all running toward something: an accident, or maybe a party.

"Asleep, you rascal?" said the journeyman sharply. Pelle gave a start and kept on working the cobbler's wax, holding it in the hot water and kneading it.

Over at the baker's (the old master's brother) they were busy hoisting up the flour sacks. The pulley screeched pitifully, and once in a while you could hear Master Jørgen Kofod bullying his son in a high falsetto. "You're an ass, Søren, a blasted idiot! What's going to become of you? Don't you think we have anything better to do than run off to prayer meetings in the middle of a workday? Does that bring in any bread? Now you stay here—or God help me, I'll beat you into a cripple." Then his wife started jabbering too, and suddenly there was silence. And a little while later Søren came darting like a shadow along the wall across the street with his hymnbook in his hand. He looked like Blubbering Per, creeping along the wall, his knees buckling when anyone gave him a sharp look. He was twenty-five years old and took beatings from his father without a murmur. But when it came to religious gatherings, he defied gossip and beatings and his father's wrath.

"Asleep, you rascal? You want me to come and put some life into you?"

No one else spoke in the workshop; since the journeyman was silent, the others had to keep quiet too. Everyone bent over their work, and Pelle stretched out the cobbler's wax as far as he could, kneaded fat into it, and pulled some more. Outside in the sunshine occasional street urchins would slouch past. Catching sight of Pelle, they would put a clenched fist under their nose, nod tauntingly, and sing:

> See the cobbler with his waxy snout,
> the more he wipes it, the worse he pouts!

Pelle pretended not to see them, but privately he took note of every single one of them. He honestly intended to obliterate them all from the face of the earth.

Suddenly they set off at a run up the street, which was filled by a mighty droning voice. It was the crazy clockmaker standing at the top of his stairs, shouting curses of damnation out at the world in general.

Pelle knew quite well that the man was mad; the words he cast out so authoritatively over the town didn't mean a thing. But that didn't make them sound any less strange, and the "cord test" loomed over him with the feeling of Judgment Day. He would involuntarily start to shiver at that admonishing voice which measured out the words with such gravity that they held no meaning at all, like the powerful words in the Bible. This was quite simply *the voice.* How terrifying it could sound coming out of the cloud, so that both Moses and Paul quaked—as fateful as Pelle himself once heard it in the darkness of Stone Farm, when the judgment was at hand.

Only the thought of Little Nikas's strap kept him from jumping straight up in the air and collapsing just like Paul. It was a bit of inescapable reality in the midst of all the fantasies; in two months it had taught him never to forget completely where or who he was. Now he pulled himself together and had to settle for putting all his sadness into the working of this wax, which it might be so tempting to compare with the wax pool in hell where he was to be martyred. But then he heard Young Master's cheerful voice out in the courtyard, and it all receded. The test couldn't be that dangerous, since all the others here had passed it. He had seen more formidable fellows in his day!

Jens sat with his head down as if expecting a blow; it was the curse of the house that constantly hung over him. He was so slow that Pelle could already outwork him; there was something obstructive inside him, like a spell. But Peter and Emil were hardy fellows—they just liked to fight.

Beneath the apple trees the early summer was playing, and right up against the workshop windows the pig stood slobbering in his trough. This sound was like a warm caress to his heart; from the day Klaus Herman shook the squealing piglet out of the sack, Pelle had begun to put down roots. It had cried so disconsolately at first that some of his own feeling of desolation was carried away with its whines. Now it just screeched because it didn't get enough to eat, and Pelle got quite angry at this disgrace. A pig should eat heartily, that was half of what it needed to thrive. You couldn't be running back and forth dumping in more and more slop every five minutes—when it got really hot the pig would have a sour stomach. But there was no common sense in these city dwellers.

"Doing anything, you rascal? Sounds like you're snoring."

Young Master came hobbling in, took a drink, and buried himself in his book. As he read he whistled softly in time with the others' hammering. Little Nikas began to whistle along, and the two oldest boys pounding leather started hammering in time; they beat in counterpoint so it sounded like a stick stuck in the spokes of a wheel. The journeyman's trills grew louder and louder in order to keep up, one driving the other. And Master Andrès raised his head from his book, listening. He sat and gazed into the distance; veiled visions from his reading hung in his eyes. And then with a start he was back in the present and in the midst of everything. His eyes played roguishly over all of them; he stood up, his cane supporting his bad hip. The master's hands danced loosely in the air, his head and his whole body writhing foolishly under the force of the rhythm.

His dancing hands swooped down over the shoemaker's butt knife, and Master lashed out the notes on the sharp edge with his head tilted and his eyes closed, his whole expression lost in inward listening. But then his face suddenly lit up with happiness, his entire body crept around with idiotic pleasure, and one of his feet flailed desperately at the air as if he were playing the harp with his toes—Master Andrès was both a musical fool and a musical clown. And with a clatter the knife lay on the floor, and he had the big tin lid in his hand: tim-da-da, tim-da-da! As if by magic the whistling had been transformed into drums and cymbals.

Pelle laughed so hard he almost burst. He looked in terror at the strap, and then laughed again, but no one paid any attention to him. Master's fingers and wrists were dancing the Devil's dance on the tin lid, and suddenly his elbow joined in and banged at it so the lid jumped—*had* to jump—quick as lightning down against the master's knee, around toward his high wooden heel that stuck out behind, right at Pelle's head, around to the most impossible places, bam, bam, wildly possessed by the journeyman's whistling. He couldn't help himself: the indentured apprentice boldly began to whistle, at first cautiously and then, when nothing flew at his head, with full force. And the next youngest boy, Jens (the music devil, as Master called him, because everything turned into tunes in his hands), grabbed so clumsily at the shoemaker's cord he was stroking that it started running and humming under everything, rising and falling on two or three notes, like a contented droning that carried it all. Outside the birds came hopping onto the branches of the apple tree. They tilted their heads inquisitively, puffed out their feathers crazily from their bodies, and threw themselves into this orgy of joy caused by a scrap of blinding blue sky. But then Young Master had a coughing fit, and everything came to a halt of its own accord.

Pelle slaved over the wax, kneading it and adding fat. When the black mass was on the verge of hardening, he shoved both hands into the hot water so his fingertips cracked. Old Jeppe tottered in from the street, and in a flash Master Andrès placed the cutting board over his book and sliced industriously with his knife.

"That's right," said Jeppe, "put the wax in the heat and it will hold better."

Pelle had rolled the wax into balls and thrown them in the basin to soak. Now he stood there in silence; he didn't have the courage to tell them he was ready. The others had blown up the cord test into something enormous. All sorts of terrors grew out of this mysterious thing awaiting him. And if he hadn't known inside that he was a strong lad—well, he would have run away from the whole thing. But now he *wanted* to take his turn, no matter how badly things went; he just needed time to swallow first. Then he would have the peasant burned out of him for good, and the trade would lie open with its songs and itinerant life and smart journeyman's clothes. The workshop here was no more than a stuffy cave where you sat and slaved over stinking oiled boots, but he understood that he had to get through it in order to make it out into the wide world where the journeymen wore patent leather shoes every day and sewed shoes for the King himself. In the meantime the little town had given Pelle an inkling of how almost insurmountably huge the world was, and this inkling filled him with impatience. It was his intention to surmount it all!

"I'm ready now," he said resolutely. Now it would be determined whether he and the trade were suited to each other.

"Then you can make a shoemaker's cord—but as long as a month of Sundays!" said the journeyman.

The old master was all fired up. He watched over Pelle with his tongue hanging out. His step was practically youthful, and he expounded on his own apprentice days sixty years ago in the King's Copenhagen. Those were the days! Boys didn't lie around snoozing until six in the morning then, or put aside their work as soon as it was eight o'clock, just to get out and fool around. No, up at four a.m. and keep at it as long as there was work to do. In those days people could work. And you really learned something; everything was said only once and then—the strap. That's when the trades were respected; even royalty had to learn a trade back then. It wasn't like now: botched work and cheap goods and shirking from everything!

The boys winked at each other; Master Andrès and the journeyman were silent. You might just as well start bickering with the closing machine because it was buzzing. Jeppe was allowed to run down by himself.

"You're waxing it good, aren't you?" said Little Nikas. "It's for pigskin."

The others laughed, but Pelle stroked the cobbler's cord with the feeling that he was building his own scaffold.

"I'm ready now," he said in a low voice.

The biggest pair of men's lasts was taken down from the shelf, tied to the end of the cord, and placed all the way out on the pavement. Outside, people stopped and stood there staring. Pelle had to get all the way up on the platform in back and bend way over. Emil, as the oldest boy, placed the cord on the back of Pelle's neck. They were all standing up except Young Master; he didn't participate in the fun.

"Pull!" commanded the journeyman, who was leading the solemn ritual. "That's it—all the way down to your feet!"

Pelle pulled, and the heavy lasts bumped forward across the cobblestones. But he came to a halt with a gasp—the cord had grown hot on the back of his neck. He stood and stamped like an animal that's been kicked and doesn't understand the reason for it; he cautiously lifted his feet and looked at them anxiously.

"Pull, pull!" ordered Jeppe. "You have to keep it moving or it'll stick!" But it was too late. The wax had hardened in the fine hairs on the back of Pelle's neck—the ones Papa Lasse had called "pig's luck" and because of which he had prophesied such a great future for Pelle—and there he stood and couldn't budge the cord no matter how he worked at it. He grimaced idiotically in pain, and humiliating drool ran out of his mouth.

"Ha, he can't even tumble a couple of lasts," said Jeppe scornfully. "It'd be best for him to go back to the country and wipe the cows' behinds again."

Then Pelle tugged in anger; he had to close his eyes and writhe as it broke loose. Something sticky passed through his fingers along with the cord, probably bloody hair, and across the back of his neck the cord burned its way in a groove of bloody fluid and molten wax. But Pelle no longer felt any pain, his head was in a bitter turmoil, he felt a strange, vague urge to take a hammer and strike them all down, run down the street hitting everyone he met on the skull. But then the journeyman took the lasts off him and the pain was there again, and all his wretched-ness. He heard Jeppe's cackling voice and saw Young Master sitting there huddled up, not daring to speak his mind—and suddenly Pelle felt so sorry for himself.

"That's right," growled Jeppe, "a shoemaker mustn't be afraid of waxing his hide a little. What's this? I do believe it's drawn water from your eyes! No, when I was young, there were *real* cord tests—we had to wind the cord twice around our necks before we were allowed to pull. Our heads hung and dangled by a thin thread by the time we were done. Those were the days!"

Pelle stood there stamping to fight his tears, but he had to chuckle out of sheer malice at the thought of Jeppe's dangling head.

"So now let's see if he can take one on the snoot," said the journey-man, putting up his fists.

"No, let that wait until he's earned it," intervened Master Andrès hastily. "The occasion will surely come up."

"Well, he managed the cord," said Jeppe, "but can he sit? There are some who never master that art, you know."

"That will have to be tested before he can be accepted," replied Little Nikas in utter seriousness.

"Aren't you through with your pranks yet?" asked Young Master angrily and walked out.

But Jeppe was lost in his own thoughts. He had his head full of youthful memories—a whole chain of little devilish ideas for making the initiation a solemn one. In the old days the trade was burned indel-ibly into the boys; they never ran away from it, but regarded it with respect as long as they drew breath. But times were soft now and full of foolishness: one boy couldn't tolerate one thing, another boy something else. There was leather colic and sitting sickness and God knows what else. Every other day they were running in with certificates for sitting boils, and then you had to start all over. "No, in my day we proceeded in a different manner—the lad naked across a three-legged stool and two men going at it with the strap! It was leather against leather, and they learned damn well to tolerate the seat of a chair!"

The journeyman made a sign.

"Now they lecture about the seat of a chair—all right, you can sit down now."

Pelle listlessly took his place. He didn't care anymore. But he leapt up with a cry of fright and looked around hostilely. He had a hammer in his hand. It dropped from his hand again, and now the floodgates burst and he started to cry.

"What the devil are you doing to him?" Young Master came rushing in from the cutting room. "What kind of dirty tricks have you thought up now?" He moved his hand over the seat of the chair; it was covered with broken awl points. "You're all damned barbarians. You'd think we were among savages."

"What a lot of pampering nonsense," snarled Jeppe. "Now we aren't even allowed to apprentice a boy properly and inoculate him a bit against boils. I suppose they have to be rubbed with honey both front and back like the kings of Israel? Or maybe you're a freethinker?"

"Father must leave now!" shouted Master Andrès, beside himself. "Father must leave!" He was shaking and quite gray in the face. Then Old Master shuffled out, without giving Pelle the slap on the back and welcoming him properly into the trade.

Pelle sat and pulled himself together; he was almost ashamed. Out of all the ambiguous innuendoes there had grown something terrible—but also impressive. He had envisioned the test as one of those things that mark a great turning point in life, so that you come out on the other side a totally different person; something in the line of the Bible's mysterious circumcision—an initiation into the new. But it was all nothing but a maliciously planned torture!

Young Master tossed a pair of children's soles over to him. He had been accepted into the trade and could no longer get by with making cobbler's cord for the others. But this realization brought no joy. He sat and wrestled with something meaningless that kept welling up from deep within him. When no one was looking he moistened his fingers with spit and rubbed them across the back of his neck. He felt like a half-drowned cat that had twisted out of the noose and was now sitting and licking its whiskers dry.

Outside beneath the apple trees the sunshine swam golden and green, and far away—over in the skipper's garden—three girls in white dresses were playing. They looked like creatures from another world: happy children on sun-bright shores, as the ballad went. Now and then a rat appeared behind the pigsty and rummaged around, clattering in the great heap of glass shards. And the pig stood there gobbling up rotten potatoes with the desperate sound that made Pelle abandon all proud dreams of the future and yearn—oh so unreasonably.

And then all kinds of things flooded over him too in that moment when he really ought to feel like a victor: all the adversities here at the workshop during his probation, the street urchins, the apprentices who wouldn't accept him, all his own thoughts that were constantly taking in ideas from this unfamiliar world. And then this dingy workshop itself where there was never a ray of sun—and respect! The respect that he never got.

When the masters weren't present Little Nikas would sometimes condescend to talk with the oldest boys. Then remarks might be made that would open new horizons for Pelle—and he had to ask questions. Or they would talk about the countryside out there that Pelle knew better than all of them put together—and he would burst out with a correction. Smack came the box on the ear, so that he rolled into the corner; he was supposed to keep his mouth shut unless they spoke to him. But Pelle, who used his eyes and ears and had gone around chattering to Papa Lasse about everything between heaven and earth, *could not* learn to keep quiet.

With a heavy hand each of them collected his quota of respect, from the boys to Old Master, who was bursting with pride in his trade. Pelle was the only one who couldn't demand anything, he had to pay tribute to them all. Young Master was the only one who didn't lower himself like a yoke onto the boy's childish soul. Cheerful as he was, he would feign indifference to the journeyman and everything else and decide to flop down next to Pelle as he sat there feeling small.

Outside the sunshine broke through the trees in a special way. The chirping of the birds took on a singular tone—it was nearing the time when the animals awoke from the afternoon's ruminations. And a boy appeared out of the little gray clouds, crowing a song at the top of his lungs and lustily cracking the cattle whip: Pelle, the general of everything, who didn't have a living soul above him. And that figure that came tottering across the fields to move the cows—that was Lasse.

Papa Lasse—yes it was!

He couldn't help it, a sob burst from him, it took him so ridiculously by surprise. "Shut up!" exclaimed the journeyman menacingly. But then it was too much for Pelle, and he didn't even try to hold back.

Young Master came over and took something down from the shelf above his head. He leaned familiarly on Pelle's shoulder, his weak leg hanging free, dangling. He stood there a moment, staring out into space, lingering; and the warmth of his hand on the boy's shoulder was comforting.

But there was no question of him being happy now that he clearly realized that it was all about Papa Lasse—such a terrible longing. He had not seen his father since that bright morning when he set out and left the old man to sink back into loneliness; he had not heard from him either, or hardly even thought about him. The main thing was to make it through the day in one piece and to fit in; there was a whole new world to explore and adjust to. Pelle simply had not had time. The town had swallowed him up.

Yet at that moment it rose up before him as the greatest treachery the world had ever known. And the back of his neck kept hurting—he had to get away where no one would see him. On some pretext he went out into the courtyard, all the way behind the washhouse, and curled up in the firewood bin next to the well.

There he lay, cringing in dark despair because he had abandoned Papa Lasse so disgracefully for all that was new and strange. Yes, and even when they had been together, he hadn't been as good or attentive as he should have been. Instead it was Lasse, old as he was, who had sacrificed himself for Pelle, had eased his work, and had taken the burdens upon himself, although Pelle had the younger shoulders. And he had been a little too harsh that time when the affair with Madam Olsen had collapsed for his father. He had had so little patience with his familiar old man's chatter then, which Pelle now would have given body and soul to listen to. He remembered all too clearly one incident after another when he had snapped at Lasse—made him come to a halt with a sigh. Papa Lasse never snapped back, but merely fell silent and sad.

Oh, it was so terrible! Pelle threw aside all his swaggering and surrendered himself to despair. What was he doing here when old Lasse was walking among strangers, lonely and unable to take care of himself? There was no solace, no getting around it; bawling, Pelle acknowledged that this was a betrayal. And as he lay there, tearing at things in despair and crying his eyes out, a quite manly decision took form in him: he had to give up everything of his own—his future and the great world and everything—and dedicate his life to making life comfortable for the old man. He had to go back home to Stone Farm! He forgot that he was only a child and could barely manage to earn enough to feed himself. Take care of decrepit old Lasse in every way and make his life easy— that's what he would do. In the midst of his breakdown he shouldered all the responsibilities of a strong man.

As he lay there wearily toying with some kindling, the elder bush behind the well parted and a pair of big eyes stared at him in amazement. It was only Manna!

"Did they hit you—or why are you crying?" she asked gravely.

Pelle turned his face away.

Manna tossed her curls and gazed at him intently.

"Well, did they? Did they hit you? Because then I'll go over there and yell at them."

"It's none of your business."

"You shouldn't say that—it's not civilized."

"Oh, be quiet!"

Then he was left alone. Over in the back of the garden Manna and her two younger sisters were climbing in the trellis; there they hung, staring uncomprehendingly over toward him. But what did he care? He wasn't about to be pitied by skirts and have them as his defenders. They were a bunch of impudent girls, even though their father sailed on the great oceans and earned a lot of money. If they had been over here with him, he would have given them a thrashing or two! Now he had to settle for sticking out his tongue.

He heard their horrified exclamations—but so what? He wasn't going to play with them anymore in the garden over there with the great conch shells and blocks of coral. He was going to go to the country and take care of his old father. Later, when it was all over, he would set sail himself to get those things—whole shiploads full!

Over from the workshop window someone was calling: "What on earth has become of the beast?" he heard them say. He gave a start—he had completely forgotten that he was an apprentice shoemaker. But now he hastened to his feet and went inside.

Pelle had finished clearing up quickly at the end of the workday. The others had taken off to have some fun. He was alone up in the garret room, gathering his belongings in a sack. There was a whole collection of delights: steamboats made of tin, a train, and horses that were hollow inside—all he had been able to acquire of the town's irresistible wonders for five shiny kroner. He put them inside his linen so they wouldn't be harmed. He tossed the sack through the garret window down into the narrow alleyway. Then he only had to sneak down through the kitchen without Jeppe's old woman suspecting anything. She had the eyes of a witch, and Pelle thought anyone would be able to tell what he was up to.

But he managed it. He strolled as calmly as possible up to the nearest streetcorner so that everyone would think he was carrying his wash. Then he took off at a run—the urge toward home was in him. A couple of street urchins hooted and threw rocks at him, but Pelle didn't mind as long as he got away. He was numb to everything else; remorse and longing had taken a heavy toll on his mind.

It was past midnight by the time he stood among the outbuildings of

Stone Farm, out of breath and with a stitch in his side. He leaned against the dilapidated smithy and closed his eyes to calm himself. As soon as he had caught his breath, he went in the back door of the cow stable and over to the herdsman's room. The floor of the feed alley felt so familiar beneath his feet, and there he went past the big bull in the dark. It sniffed at his body and exhaled deeply—did it still know him? But the smell from the herdsman's room was unfamiliar to him. Papa Lasse certainly seems to be neglecting himself, Pelle thought, pulling the quilt off the sleeping man's head. A strange voice began to curse.

"Isn't it Lasse?" said Pelle, his knees shaking under him.

"Lasse?" exclaimed the new herdsman, sitting up. "Did you say Lasse? Is it that child of God you're looking for, you devil? They've already been here from hell to get him, and carried him off alive. He was too good for this world, you see. Old Man Satan was here himself and measured him for a wench; so look for him there. Go straight ahead until you meet the Devil's great-grandmother, then just ask your way till you find the Evil One."

Pelle stood in the lower courtyard for a while, thinking. So, Papa Lasse had taken off! And was going to be married, or maybe he was already. And to Karna, from what he understood! He stood stock still and fell into nostalgia. The big courtyard lay immersed in moonlight, in a deep sleep. And all around the memories purred cozily in their sleep, with that familiar purring from his childhood when the kittens slept on his bedstead and he lay his cheek against their soft, quivering bodies.

Pelle's senses had deep roots. One time at Uncle Kalle's he had lain down in the big twin cradle and let the other children rock him—he must have been nine at the time. After they had rocked him for a while, the situation took control over him: he saw a sooty timbered ceiling that was not Kalle's ceiling swaying high up over his head, and he had the impression that a bundled-up older woman was sitting like a shadow behind the headboard and rocking the cradle with her foot. The cradle lurched with forceful jerks, and every time her foot slipped off the rocker, it would strike the floor with the sound of a cracked wooden shoe. Pelle leapt up. "It's lurching," he said in confusion.

"It is? Then you must have been dreaming." Laughing, Kalle peered under the rockers.

"Lurching," said Lasse. "That was something for you, all right! When you were little you couldn't sleep unless the cradle lurched—we had to make the rockers practically square. It was almost impossible to rock. Bengta ruined many a fine pair of wooden shoes rocking your cradle just to humor you and your ideas."

The courtyard here was also like a great cradle that rocked and rocked in the waning moonlight, and as soon as Pelle surrendered to it, there was no end to everything rising up from his childhood. His whole life had to come forth and reel over his head as it did in the past, and the earth had to open up to abysses wherever there was merely a dark spot. And the tears gushed out, fatefully, and drenched everything so that Kongstrup slunk away like a wet dog, and the others cursed and cringed. And Lasse—well, where was Papa Lasse?

Pelle suddenly found himself in the laundry room, pounding on the door to the maids' room.

"Is that you, Anders?" someone whispered inside. Then the door opened and a pair of arms wrapped warmly around him and pulled him inside. Pelle pushed away, his hands sinking into a naked bosom—it must be Fair Marie!

"Is Karna still here?" he asked. "Can I talk to Karna?"

They were glad to see him again. Fair Marie patted his cheeks warmly; she was almost about to kiss him too. Karna couldn't get over her surprise, he had such a city air about him. "So now you're a shoemaker in the biggest workshop in town. Yes, we asked about you, butcher Jensen found out about it at the marketplace. And you've grown so tall—and so city-fine! You carry yourself well!" Karna tugged at his clothes.

"Where's Papa Lasse?" was all Pelle said. His throat felt tight when he mentioned his father.

"Yes, yes, just a minute and I'll go with you a ways. You look so gallant in those clothes, I wouldn't have recognized you. What do you think, Marie?"

"He's a sweet boy... he always was," said Marie, nudging him with one of her swinging feet. She was in bed again.

"These are the same clothes I've always had," said Pelle.

"Yes, but you carry yourself differently. Down in town they all act like noblemen. Shall we go?"

Pelle said a friendly farewell to Fair Marie. He remembered that he had much to thank her for. She looked at him strangely and wanted to pull his hand under her quilt.

"What about Father?" he said impatiently as soon as they were outside.

Yes, Lasse had run off, all right. He couldn't stand it after Pelle left; and the work was too hard for one person as well. Karna didn't know exactly where he was at the moment. "He's running around looking at property," she said proudly. "Maybe he'll be in to visit you in town someday."

"How are things here otherwise?" asked Pelle.

"Well, Erik has gotten his speech back and is starting to be a human being again—he makes himself heard. And Kongstrup and his wife are trying to outdrink each other."

"Do they drink together? Like the clog-maker and his old lady?"

"Yes, and sometimes they lie around in the house up there and can't see each other through the haze of booze. Everything is going to hell here, as you can see—'no master, no protection,' as the old proverb says. But what can you say about it? They have nothing else in common! Because they can't do the *best* thing together anymore. But I don't care, because as soon as Lasse finds something, I'm taking off."

Pelle could understand that—he had nothing against it.

Karna looked him up and down with amazement as they walked. "So you're living a fine life in town?"

"Sure, really sour gruel and rancid pork. We lived much better here."

She flinched—that sounded much too ludicrous. "But what about everything they have in the shops in the way of food and baked goods and sweets? Where does it all go?"

"I don't know," replied Pelle sullenly. He had wondered about that himself. "I get what I need to eat; but I have to take care of my own wash and clothes."

Karna had a hard time getting over her astonishment. She had probably imagined that it was as though Pelle had been taken up to heaven alive. "But then... things must be pretty hard for you," she said, worried. "Well, well, as soon as we get our feet under our own table, we'll help out the little we can."

Up at the main road they parted, and Pelle walked back wearily and with a discouraged step. It was almost daylight when he arrived, and he managed to sneak inside and get into bed without anyone discovering his attempt to escape.

III

Little Nikas had rubbed the blacking from his face and was in his nice errand-running clothes. He was supposed to go down to the market square with a bundle of wash that the butcher from Åker had to take home to his mother, and Pelle walked behind him carrying the bundle. Little Nikas said hello to a lot of nice servant girls up in the windows all around them, and Pelle found that it was more fun to walk beside him than behind him—there were two of them so they could keep each other company, after all. But each time he moved up next to the apprentice, Little Nikas would push him into the gutter. At last Pelle tripped over a gutter board and gave it up.

Up the street the crazy clockmaker stood on the edge of his high steps swinging a plumb-bob around. It was hanging on the end of a long cord, and with his finger he followed the oscillations of the pendulum as though counting the time. It was exciting, but there was a chance that the apprentice wouldn't notice it.

"The clockmaker's probably just experimenting," he said briskly.

"Shut up!" snapped Little Nikas. Then Pelle remembered that he wasn't supposed to speak, and shut his mouth tight.

He walked along squeezing the bundle, trying to get an idea of its contents. He had his eyes on all the windows and down the side streets. He kept moving his palm to his mouth as though he were yawning—and swallowing bits of rye bread he had stolen from the kitchen. His suspenders were broken, and he had to keep sticking out his stomach. There were hundreds of things to watch out for—like the coal dealer's dog, who had to have a kick in the rear as it stood sniffing innocently at a cornerstone.

A funeral procession was coming toward them. The apprentice passed it with his head bare, and Pelle did the same. At the end of the procession came Bjerregrav the tailor on his crutches; he went along to all the funerals and was always last, because the way he walked required plenty of leeway. He would stand still and look down at the ground, while the rest of the party moved on a few steps; then he would move his crutches forward, move a step—and stop again. That's how he made progress on his bad legs, just by standing and looking at the others and taking a step now and then. He looked like a slowly moving pair of calipers measuring the path the others took.

But the funniest thing was that he had forgotten to button the bib of his black funeral trousers; it hung down over his knees like a leather apron. Pelle wasn't quite sure if the apprentice had noticed it.

"Bjerregrav has forgotten—"

"Shut up!" Little Nikas took a swing backwards at him, and Pelle ducked his head and pressed his hand tight to his mouth.

Up on Stålegade there was a big commotion: an enormously fat woman stood arguing with two sailors. She was in a nightcap and petticoat, and Pelle recognized her.

"It's the Sow," he said excitedly. "She's a real terror! At Stone Farm—"

Bam, Little Nikas was on him with a punch that made him sit down on the woodcarver's steps. "One, two, three, four—come on!" He counted off ten paces and started off again. "But God help you if you don't keep your distance!"

Pelle conscientiously kept his distance. But he was angry and soon discovered that Little Nikas, just like old Jeppe, had much too large a behind. That came from sitting so much—you got bent in the pipes! He stuck out his behind a ways and tucked a fold of his sweater across his loins, raised himself coquettishly on the balls of his feet, and sashayed off with one hand on his chest. When the apprentice scratched himself, Pelle did too, and made the same grandiose swings with his body. His cheeks were burning, but he was heartily satisfied with himself.

As soon as he was his own master, he went around to the country butchers to ask for news of Lasse, but none of them had heard anything. He went and asked from one wagon to another. "Lasse Karlsson?" one of them said. "Oh, that was the herdsman from Stone Farm!" Then he called to another man and asked about Lasse—the old Stone Farm herdsman! And then *he* would shout to a third; they all came over to the wagon to discuss the matter. They were people who were always traveling all over the countryside buying up livestock. They knew God and everybody, but had no information to give about Lasse.

"So he must not be in the country," said the first man, quite convinced. "You'll have to get yourself another father, my boy."

Pelle was in no mood for joking and sneaked away from the wagon. Besides, he had to go home and work; the tradesmen, who were darting from one wagon to the next and feeling the meat, were already looking askance at him. They stuck together like pea straw when it came to keeping the apprentices in line, though they were usually envious of each other.

Bjerregrav's crutches stood behind the door. He sat inside by the platform in his stiffest funeral finery; he had a white folded handkerchief in his clasped hands and kept drying his eyes.

"Was it one of your relatives, Bjerregrav?" asked Young Master genially.

"No, but it's so sad for those who are left behind—wife and children. There's always someone who grieves and pines. People lead a strange existence, Andrès!"

"Yes, and the potatoes are bad this year, Bjerregrav."

Neighbor Jørgen filled the entire doorway. "Well, there we have the blessed Bjerregrav!" he exclaimed. "And in the stiffest finery. What's up with you today—are you after a woman?"

"I was at the funeral," replied Bjerregrav softly.

The big baker made an involuntary gesture; he didn't like being continually reminded of death. "You ought to be a hearse driver, Bjerregrav—then you wouldn't be working for nothing!"

"I'm not working for nothing just because they're dead," stammered Bjerregrav. "I'm not good for much, poor man that I am, and I have no one close to me. It doesn't hurt any of the living if I follow along after those who have died. And I know them all anyway and have followed them in my thoughts ever since they were born," he added by way of excuse.

"If you were even invited to the wake and got to eat some of the good food, then I could understand it," the baker went on.

"To eat the food of a poor widow left with four little children, who doesn't know how she'll be able to feed them—no, I would never do that! She had to go 300 kroner into debt just to have a decent burial for her husband."

"That ought to be forbidden by law," said Master Andrès. "A woman like that with little children has no right to throw away money on the dead."

"She is showing her husband the final honor," said Jeppe reprovingly. "It's the duty of every good wife."

"Of course it is," replied Master Andrès, "something has to be done! Like over on the other side of the world: there the wife even throws herself on the bonfire when her husband is being cremated."

Baker Jørgen slapped his thighs and laughed. "Now that's a good lie you told, Andrès. They'd never get any woman to do that, if I know anything about them."

But Bjerregrav knew that Young Master wasn't lying, and he waved his thin hands in the air as if trying to ward off something invisible. "Thank God someone has seen the light here on this island," he said softly. "Only familiar things happen here, no matter how wrong they might be."

"I wonder where she got the money from?" said the baker.

"Probably borrowed it," said Bjerregrav in a tone as though wanting the matter dropped.

Jeppe hooted, "Well, who would loan a poor first mate's widow 300 kroner? That's just like throwing the money into the sea."

Baker Jørgen went right for Bjerregrav's gut. "You gave it to her, didn't you? No one else would be such a stupid ass!" he said hostilely.

"Leave me alone," stammered Bjerregrav. "I didn't do anything to you. And she has one happy day in the midst of all the grief." His hands were shaking.

"You're a codfish."

"What do you think, Bjerregrav, when you stand there looking down into the grave?" asked Young Master to change the subject.

"I think, now you're going someplace where you'll be much better off than here!" said the old tailor ingenuously.

"Yes, because Bjerregrav only follows the poor wretches, he does," exclaimed Jeppe with a hint of reproach.

"I just can't help thinking... what if he's been fooled," Master Andrès went on. "What if he arrives, expecting a great deal—and then there's nothing there! That's why I don't like seeing dead bodies."

"Well, see, that's just the point. What if there's nothing?" Baker Jørgen twisted his fat body. "Because here we go around imagining lots of things; but what if the whole thing is a lie?"

"*That* is the spirit of heresy," said Jeppe, stamping hard on the floor.

"God preserve my mouth from speaking heresy," replied brother Jørgen, passing his hand ceremoniously across his mouth. "But you just can't help thinking. And what do you see all around you? Sickness and death and hallelujah. We live and we live, I have to tell you, brother Jeppe—and we live in order to live! But I say 'Lord Jesus' for the poor things that haven't been born yet!" Then he fell into thought—about Little Jørgen, as usual, who wouldn't come to earth and take his name and the likeness of his person and carry it on for him. That was where his belief in things lay; there was nothing to be done about it. And the others started talking softly so that they wouldn't disturb him in his reverie.

Pelle grappled with everything between heaven and earth, and he kept his protruding ears open for every word that was spoken, but when the talk turned to death he yawned. He had never been seriously ill himself;

and since Mama Bengta passed away, death had made no impact on his world. Fortunately, because in that case it would be all or nothing: Papa Lasse was all Pelle had. For Pelle, hard-handed death didn't even exist. He couldn't understand how people could lie down with their nose in the air, there was so much to do here. The town gave *him* enough to do anyway.

Even on the first evening he ran out looking for other boys, right where the swarm was the thickest. There was no use waiting. Pelle was used to taking the bull by the horns—and he longed to make his mark.

"What kind of a sissy is this?" they said, crowding around him.

"I'm Pelle," he said, standing right in the middle of the group and staring at them all. "I've been at Stone Farm since I was eight years old, and that's the biggest farm in the north country." He spat nonchalantly with his hands in his pockets, because this was nothing compared to what he usually had to face.

"So you're a farmer, are you?" said one of them, and the others laughed. Rud was among them.

"Yes," said Pelle, "and I've done plowing and fed grain to the calves."

They blinked at each other: "You mean you *are* a farmer?"

"Sure, of course I am," answered Pelle, confused. They said the word in a peculiar tone of voice, he now discovered.

Then they all burst out laughing. "He admits it himself. And he's from the biggest farm—he's the biggest farmer in the country."

"No, the farmer was named Kongstrup," said Pelle modestly. "I was just the cowherd!"

They roared with laughter. "He doesn't even get it—he's the biggest hick there is!"

Pelle didn't lose his head; he had heavier artillery, and now he was going to strike. "And on the farm there was a hired hand named Erik. He was so strong that he could beat up three men. But the foreman was even stronger, because he beat Erik into an idiot!"

"Oh yeah, how did he go about doing that?"

"Can a farmer be beaten into an idiot?"

"Who beat you into an idiot, I wonder?"

The questions rained down over him.

Pelle went right up to the one who asked the last question, eye to eye. But the boy shrank back. "Watch out for your good clothes," he said, laughing, "and don't wrinkle your cuffs."

Pelle had on a clean blue tunic under his vest, with neck- and wrist-bands serving as collar and cuffs; he knew he was neat and clean. And now that's just what they latched on to!

"And what a pair of platters he's got on, geez, they're covering half the Harbor Square!" They were Kongstrup's shoes, which Pelle had squirmed about wearing on a weeknight.

"When did you have the moving party?" asked a third—this was directed at Pelle's plump red cheeks.

Now he was about to jump out of his skin. His eyes darted around for something to hit them with, because this would probably end up in a fight with the whole gang. Well, Pelle had had everyone against him before.

But then a tall, thin boy stepped forward. "Have you got a pretty sister?" he asked.

"I haven't got any brothers or sisters," Pelle snapped back.

"That's too bad. Do you know how to play hide-and-seek?"

Yes, that was something Pelle knew how to do!

"All right, now you can be It!" The tall boy put his cap over Pelle's eyes and turned him around to face the fence. "You count to a hundred... and no cheating, or else."

No, Pelle wasn't going to cheat—he wouldn't peek or skip numbers—there was too much riding on this beginning. But he made himself a solemn promise to use his legs; they were going to be tagged, each and every one. He finished counting and took the cap away from his eyes—not a sound. "Ready or not, here I come!" he called, but no one answered. Pelle searched for half an hour through piles of lumber and storage sheds; then he slunk home to bed. But that night he dreamed that he caught them all, and they elected him to be leader forever...

The town was not the open embrace he could just throw himself into with his childish trust in being borne forward all at once. Here people kept quiet about all the deeds that gave people support in other places; here they only aroused scornful laughter. He tried over and over again, always with something new. But the reply was always: Farmer! His whole little body was bristling with good will—and he was unceremoniously rejected.

Pelle could already see the whole fortune he had saved up slipping away between his fingers. All the respect he had fought for back home at the farm by his boldness and good will—here it all turned to nothing. Here other actions and a new jargon applied; the clothes were different, and people placed their feet differently. Everything he had valued highly was ridiculed, even the beautiful cap with the sheaves and harvest implements on it. He arrived so securely confident in himself, only to make the painful discovery that he was a ridiculous phenomenon. Every time he wanted to be included he was pushed aside; he had no right to speak—to the back of the line, please!

There was nothing to do but strike back along the whole line, until you wound up at the bottom of it all. And no matter how hard it was for a healthy boy who was burning with the desire to put *his* mark on everything, Pelle did it and cheerfully got ready to crawl back up again. No matter how much they picked on him, he still retained a hardheaded feeling of his own worth; no one could take that away from him.

He was convinced that it wasn't him, but all the different things about him that were the trouble, and he restlessly set out to discover the new values and wage a war of extermination against himself. With every defeat he pursued himself doggedly, and the next evening he would dash out again, enriched with so much new knowledge, and accept his defeat on yet another point. He was *determined* to triumph—no matter what the sacrifice! He knew of nothing more magnificent than to march thundering down the street, with his pants stuffed into the tops of Lasse's old boots—that was the epitome of manliness. But he was man enough to stop doing it too, since here it was regarded as peasant-like. It was harder to swallow his past; it was so indivisible from Papa Lasse that he had a feeling of betrayal! But there was no way around it; if he wanted to get on in the world he would have to immerse himself in all of it, both opinions and prejudices. On the other hand, he promised himself to rub their noses in it as soon as he got on top.

What oppressed him the most was the shoemaker's trade. There was so little respect attached to it. No matter how much he set himself to accomplish, a shoemaker was and remained a poor wretch with a waxy snout and a behind that was much too big. Here his personal effort was of no use, and he had to see about saving his own skin and taking up something else as soon as possible!

But he was in town now, and one of its inhabitants; nothing could change that. And the town had a grand and festive effect on him, even though it didn't measure up to the fairytale impressions he had from the time he and his father had come ashore here. Most people went around in their Sunday clothes, and many sat earning a lot of money, though he couldn't imagine how. Here all the roads came to an end too, and the town sucked everything into itself: pigs and grain and people—everything would wind up here sooner or later! The Sow lived here with Rud, who was apprenticed to a painter, and the twins were here. And one day Pelle saw a big boy stand sobbing against a courtyard gate with his arms in front of his face while some little boys pounded away at him. It was Blubbering Per, who was sailing as a galley boy on a coastal ketch. *Everybody* was heading this way.

But Papa Lasse was not here!

IV

There was one thing about the town: it was hard to go to bed and hard to get up. Down here there was no dawn to climb shivering over the earth and wake everything up; the houses blocked the open face of the morning. And the waning day did not pour its evening weariness heavily into the limbs and drive them toward bed. Life here moved in the opposite direction, and people turned lively toward nightfall.

At half past five the master, who slept downstairs, would pound on the ceiling with his stick. Pelle, who was the one responsible, mechanically rolled out of bed and pounded on the side of the bed with his fist. Then he fell back again, still asleep. A little later the whole thing was repeated. But then the master would lose his patience. "Damn it all, aren't you boys getting up at all today!" he roared. "Do I have to bring you coffee in bed?"

Drunk with sleep, Pelle tumbled onto the floor. "Get up, get up!" he shouted, shaking the others. Jens got to his feet easily, he always woke up with a terrified expression on his face and covered his head. But Emil and Peter, who ran around with girls, were impossible to shake any life into.

Pelle hurried down and got things ready, filled the softening basin and put out a pile of sand on the platform for the master to spit into. He was no longer surprised at the others anymore, he was in a bad mood in the morning himself. On days when he had to crawl right onto his three-legged stool without running the morning errands first, it took him hours to wake up.

He checked to see whether he had made a chalk cross in any obvious spot the night before, because then there was something that he definitely had to remember—that's why he had come up with this clever idea. Then all he had to do was not forget what the crosses meant, because then he'd be no better off.

When the workshop was straightened up he ran to the baker's for the mistress to get bread "for themselves." He got a rusk for his coffee and drank it out in the kitchen while the old woman went around grumbling. She was as dried-up as a mummy and moved bent way over, and when she wasn't using her hands she went around with her forearm pressed against her abdomen. She was unhappy with everything and talked incessantly about the grave. "My two oldest are across the sea—

in America and Australia. I'll never see them again. And here at home two grown men go parading around doing nothing and have to be waited on. Poor Andrès is sick, and Jeppe is no good for anything anymore, he can't even stay warm in bed. But they know how to make quiet demands, and they let me run to and fro with no help and do everything myself. I'm really going to thank God, the day I lie in my grave. — What are you standing there yawning for? Let's get going!" Then Pelle carried the coffee with the brown sugar out to the workshop window.

They didn't feel much like working in the morning as long as the master wasn't up. They were sleepy and looking forward to a long, surly day. The journeyman didn't work very hard; he had to make sure there was something left for him to do. Then they sat and fiddled around, banging their hammers once in a while, pretending to work, while some of them slept on, leaning on the workbench. They jumped when the three blows sounded on the wall next to Pelle.

"What are you doing? It sounds pretty dead out there to me," the master might ask, staring suspiciously at Pelle. But Pelle had marked down what each of them was supposed to be working on, and told him.

"What is it today, Thursday? Hell and damnation, tell Jens that he has to stop working on Manna's galoshes and start in on the pilot's boots — they were promised for last Monday." The master sighed sadly. "Oh, I had a bad night, Pelle, a really disgusting night, hot and with a rushing in my ears. The new blood is so damned uncontrollable, it keeps on boiling inside my head, like soda water. But it's good that I get it, or else I'd be a goner before long, damn it all. Do you believe in hell? Heaven is a bunch of nonsense, of course; what good should we expect somewhere else when we can't even organize things properly down here? But do you believe in hell? I dreamed that I spit up my last piece of lungs and went to hell. 'What in Satan's name are you here for, Andrès?' they asked me. 'You've still got your heart in one piece' — they wouldn't have me. But what good does that do? You can't breathe with your heart; I'm going to croak all the same. And what's going to become of me, will you please tell me that? There's something called going back into your mother . . . if I could just do that, and then come into the world a new man with two good legs. Then you'd see me take off across the sea in a flash — whoosh! I sure wouldn't be hanging around here for long. Have you looked at your bellybutton today? Oh, you're laughing, you beast, but I'm serious! Not much can go wrong for you if you start each day by looking at your bellybutton."

Master was half serious and half joking. "Well, you can bring me my port wine then, it's on the shelf behind the box of laces—I'm so beastly cold."

Pelle came back and announced that the bottle was empty. The master looked at it goodnaturedly.

"Then get hold of another one! But I don't have any money, I must tell you. You figure out something—you're not stupid." Master gave him that look that tugged at his heartstrings, so he was about to burst into tears at any moment. Pelle's world had been quite straightforward; he didn't understand this play of wit and misery, joking and deathly seriousness. But he felt something of the good Lord's face, and it made him shiver inside. He would risk death for the master.

When there was sleet, Master had a hard time getting out of bed. The cold crippled him. When he finally came out to the workshop, freshly washed, his hair wet, he would take up his position by the cold wood-stove and stand with his teeth chattering, his cheeks quite hollow. "My blood is so thin these days," he would say, "but new blood is on the way, it sings in my ears every night." Then he would have a coughing fit. "Upon my soul, there we have a piece of lung again." He showed a jellylike clump to Pelle, who was standing by the stove polishing shoes. "But a new one will grow back!"

"Master will soon be thirty years old," said the journeyman, "then the dangerous period will be over."

"Yes, damn it, I ought to be able to hang on that long—only half a year more," said Master eagerly, looking at Pelle as if it were in *his* power. "Only six more months! Then the whole cadaver will be rejuvenated—new lungs, new everything. But I'll never get a new leg, by God."

A special, secret understanding arose between Pelle and the master that was not built on words or anything spoken, but was felt through glances and tone of voice and their very beings. It was as if Master's leather vest itself emanated warmth whenever Pelle stood behind him. Pelle's eyes sought out the master whenever and wherever they could, and Master treated him differently from anyone else.

When Pelle came home from running errands in town and turned the corner, there was the happy sight of Young Master standing in the doorway. With his lame leg in repose and his hand clutching his cane, he would stand there, his gaze shifting with his longing for faraway places. That was his spot whenever he wasn't sitting indoors and reading his adventure books. But Pelle always wished that he would be standing there. And when he slipped past, he would duck shyly, because quite often Master would squeeze Pelle's shoulder so hard that it stung, shaking him back and forth, and say fervently, "You little devil!" That was the only caress that life had left over for Pelle, and he basked in it.

Pelle didn't understand Master—he didn't understand the slightest thing about him. Master never went out. Only once in a while, when his strength was good, would he limp over to Beer Hansen's and have a game. Usually his journeys took him no farther than out to the street door. There he would stand and look around a little, and then come limping inside with his contagious good humor that transformed the dim workshop into a meadow filled with chirping birds. He had never been abroad, nor did he feel the urge for it; yet the wide world came and went in his being and his speech so that Pelle would feel completely sick with longing for the world. Master asked nothing more than good health from the future, and there was an aura of fantasy around him. He gave the impression that all happiness would drift down and settle on him. Pelle idolized him and did not understand him. Master, who could make fun of his lame leg and in the next second completely forget about it, or make jokes about his poverty as if he were tossing joyous gold coins about—it was beyond comprehension. And Pelle was none the wiser when he sneaked a look at the books that took Master Andrès's breath away. He would settle for less than the North Pole and the center of the earth if only he were allowed to take part.

He didn't have the chance to sit and indulge in fantasies. Every second it was: "Run, Pelle!" Everything was bought in small amounts, even though it was done on credit. "Then it won't add up so fast," said Jeppe. Master Andrès couldn't care less.

The shop foreman's maid came rushing in, and she absolutely had to have those shoes for her mistress—they had been promised for Monday. Master had forgotten about them. "We're working on them," he would say undaunted. "Jens, damn it all!" And Jens would get busy putting lasts in the shoes while Master Andrès accompanied the maid out to the hallway and flirted with her to put her in a better mood. "Just give them a box on the ear so they'll hang together," Master said to Jens. And then: "Pelle, take off with them as fast as you can! Tell them we'll pick them up tomorrow morning and fix them properly. But run like the Devil's at your heels!"

Pelle ran, and just as soon as he had come back and slipped into his apron, he would have to be off again. "Pelle, go over and borrow a few brass tacks, then we won't have to buy any today. Go over to Klausen's. No, go to Blom's instead. You were at Klausen's this morning."

"Blom is mad about that shoetree," said Pelle.

"That's right, hell and damnation! We'd better see about fixing that—and taking it back. Remember to take it over to the blacksmith! So what on earth are we going to do?" Young Master stared helplessly from one to the other.

"Shoemaker Marker," suggested Little Nikas.

"We don't borrow from Marker," said the master, frowning. "He's a louse!" Marker had weaseled his way in with one of the workshop's oldest customers. "He doesn't even own enough salt for an egg!"

"Well, what then?" asked Pelle a little impatiently.

Master sat in silence for a moment. "So take it!" he exclaimed remorsefully, tossing a krone to Pelle. "I'll get no peace as long as I have an øre—you beast! Buy a box of tacks and then give Klausen and Blom what we borrowed from them."

"But then they'll see we have a whole box," said Pelle, who could also act sensibly. "Besides, they owe us so many other things they've borrowed."

"What a scoundrel," said Master, sitting down to read. "Good gracious, what a rogue!" He looked pleased.

And again, a little while later: "Run, Pelle!"

The day was spent running errands, and Pelle was not one to do them any quicker than he had to—he felt no longing for that dim workshop with the three-legged stool. There were so many things that had to be investigated. He practically regarded it as his duty to be everywhere he had no business being; he wandered around like a puppy and had his nose in everything. Already the town had almost no secrets from him.

Pelle had a genuine urge to conquer it all. But for the time being, he had only defeats to show for it. He had sacrificed and sacrificed what *he* possessed without getting anything in return. He had sloughed off his shyness and distrust here in town, where the important thing was to open yourself to all sides; he was in the process of sacrificing his sturdy traits on the altar of the town as being too peasantlike. But he gained in dauntlessness—the less cover he possessed, the more fearlessly he kept at it. The town *would* be taken. He had been lured out of his secure shell, and would be easy to devour.

The town has cast him out of his secure nest; and by the way, he is still that same splendid fellow. Most people would not notice any difference, except that he has shot up in the air. But Papa Lasse would certainly weep blood if he caught sight of the boy, popping up in the street, full of insecurity and the urge to imitate; wearing his best shirt on a weekday—and yet with his clothes in disarray.

He's walking along, flinging a pair of boots, his fingers in the straps, and whistling jauntily. Every now and then he grimaces and walks more cautiously, whenever his pants rub the tender stripes on his thighs.

It has been a hot day for him, just because he went past a smithy in the morning and was stopped by the wonderful display of strength in there in the dimness and the light of the forge. The flames and the ringing of the metal—all that energetic banging of real work—seized him, and he had to go inside and ask whether they needed a boy. He wasn't so stupid as to say where he belonged, but when he got home, Jeppe had already heard and... Well, now it's forgotten—except whenever his pants touch his thighs. Then he remembers that here in this world there is no backing out. Once you've gotten into something, you have to eat your way right through, like the boy in the fairytale. And this discovery is actually not a terribly new one for him.

As usual, he has chosen the longest detour, ferreting around in courtyards and side streets where there's a chance of experiencing something, and he dashed in to see Albinus, who is a clerk for a grocer. Albinus was not much fun. He didn't have anything to do and was out in the warehouse as usual, hanging around, intently preoccupied with making a short ladder stand straight up in the air as he climbed up it. You could never get a word out of him when he was sweating over something like that, so Pelle stole a handful of raisins and took off.

Down at the harbor he goes aboard a Swedish schooner that has just come in with a load of staves. "Anything you need help with?" he shouts, holding one hand behind where his pants have a hole in them.

"Klausen's boy was just here and got what there was," replies the skipper.

"That was dumb—you should have let us have it! Have you got a clay pipe?"

"Sure, come over here!"

The skipper grabs the end of a rope, but Pelle manages to jump ashore. "Are you going to give me that thrashing soon?" he shouts, teasing him.

"I'll give you a clay pipe if you'll run and get me 5 øre's worth of tobacco."

"What's it supposed to cost?" asks Pelle innocently. The skipper reaches for the end of the rope, but Pelle is already gone.

"Five øre's worth of shag," he shouts even before he gets inside the door. "But make it the best, because it's for a sick person." He slams the *skilling* down on the counter and puts on a haughty face.

Old skipper Lau pulls himself up with his two canes and hands him the tobacco, his jaw working like a rolling mill, all his limbs crooked with rheumatism. "I suppose it's for a patient in labor?" he asks jokingly.

Pelle snaps off the stem of the clay pipe so that it won't break in his pocket, boards the salvage steamer and disappears forward. A little while later he reappears from beneath the canvas covering with a pair of huge sea boots and a piece of chewing tobacco in his hand. Behind the steamer's cabin he takes an enormous bite of the brown quid and stalwartly chews away—he is bursting with manliness. But over by the boiler where the ships' planks are bent he has to empty his stomach; all his guts turn inside out, as if by sheer force they want to see what it's like to hang on the outside. He drags himself onward, sick as a dog, his temples pounding. But somewhere inside him there's a little scrap of satisfaction about this too, just waiting for the worst side effects to be over before being transformed into a mighty deed.

Otherwise the harbor, with its stacks of timber and ships in drydock, is just as exciting as the time he lay and crawled in the wood shavings and kept an eye on Lasse's sack. The black man with the two baying dogs is still sticking up from the roof of the harbor shed—it's incomprehensible that he had once been afraid of him. But Pelle is busy.

He runs on a few paces, but over by the old slipway he has to stop, for there stands "the Power" chopping the tops off some blocks of granite—copper brown from the sun and wind. In his beautiful black hair hang chips of stone. A shirt and canvas pants—he has nothing else on. The shirt is shoved back from his powerful chest, but it's stretched tight across his back, showing the play of his muscles. When he takes a swing, the air goes "whoosh!" and there is a sighing all around in the stacks of wood and bulwarks. People come scurrying; they stop some distance away and stand there staring at him. There is always a little crowd standing there gaping—and taking each other's place as if by the lion's den. Something might happen: one of those sudden outbursts that shake everything and induce terror in decent people.

Pelle goes up close. The Power is the father of Jens, after all, the next-to-youngest boy at the workshop. "Hello!" he says fearlessly, stepping right into the giant's shadow. But the stonecutter brushes him aside without investigating who he is, and keeps on chopping, whoosh, whoosh!

"It's a long time since he really let loose," says an older citizen. "Do you think he's settling down?"

"Someday he'll have to get it out of his system," says someone else. "The town should soon see about getting rid of him." Then they leave, and Pelle has to move on too, someplace where no one can see him.

Shoester come fooster, put gruel in your meat!
A lash on your back will taste so sweet!

It's three cursed street boys. Pelle is not at all in a fighting mood; he pretends not to see them. But they walk right behind him and step on his heels: "Footy, footy, footy, fie!"—and before he knows it, he's fighting with them. He doesn't realize it until he's lying on his back in the gutter with all three of them on top of him. He's stretched out lengthwise along the gutter and can't move. And he's weak after that damned strong tobacco. The two biggest boys spread his arms out on the cobblestones and press down on them; the smallest one gets to practice on his face. It's a well-placed revenge: all Pelle can do is turn his head away from the blows—but it still hurts because of his ignominious plump cheeks.

A dazzling sight appears before him in his need: over in the doorway stands a white-clad baker's boy enjoying himself royally. It's Nilen, that wonderful confounded little Nilen from his school days who went after everybody like a rat terrier and always held his own. Pelle closes his eyes and feels ashamed, even though he knows quite well that it's only a kind of vision.

But then the miraculous happens, and the vision steps down to him in the gutter, tosses the boys aside, and pulls him to his feet. Pelle recognizes that grip; even in school it felt like an iron claw.

Then they sit indoors behind the oven on Nilen's dirty bed. "So you've become a shoemaker's brat?" he says over and over, sympathetically. He looks damned healthy in his white clothes with bare arms crossed on his bare chest. Pelle is feeling quite comfortable; he has a Napoleon cake and thinks the world is getting more and more interesting. Nilen chews manfully and spits out black across the floor.

"You chew quid?" asks Pelle, and rushes to give him the chewing tobacco as a present.

"Yes, we all do. You have to when you work at night."

Pelle couldn't understand how anyone could manage to turn day and night upside down.

"That's what all the bakers do over in Copenhagen—so people can have fresh bread in the morning. And now Master wants to try it here. But it's not something everybody can do, it means turning your whole cadaver upside down. Midnight is the worst—when everything is transformed. Then the trick is to watch the clock, and right when it strikes twelve, we all hold our breath—then nothing can get in or out. Master himself can't stand the night shift. The tobacco turns sour in his mouth, so he has to put it on the table. When he wakes up again, he thinks it's a raisin and slaps it into the dough. What's your girlfriend's name?"

For a moment Pelle's thoughts consider the skipper's three girls, but he can't sacrifice them. No, he doesn't have a girlfriend!

"Hey, listen here, that's no good. I've taken up with the master's daughter lately, and she's awfully sweet—and she's fully developed, believe me! But we have to watch out for the old man."

"Are you going to get married when you get to be a journeyman?" asked Pelle.

"And drag around with a wife and kids? You're a dope, Pelle, but don't worry about that! No, women, they're just for when you're bored, know what I mean?" He stretches, yawning.

Nilen has become a handsome fellow, but his expression is a little cruel; he sits there staring down at Pelle with a strange gleam in his eye. "Shoemaker's brat!" he says snidely, sticking his tongue in his cheek. Pelle doesn't answer; he knows he can't fight Nilen.

Nilen has lit his pipe and is lying on his back on the bed—with his filthy shoes on—and keeps on jabbering. "What's your journeyman like? Ours is a snooty one. The other day I had to give him a licking; he was so stuck up. I've learned to bang heads Copenhagen style; so it's easy to get by. But it takes a strong forehead." He's a hell of a fellow. Pelle feels smaller and smaller.

But suddenly Nilen is in a rush to get up—there's the sound of a sharp voice out in the bakery. "Out the window, damn it," he hisses, "it's the journeyman." So Pelle has to tumble out the window, tall as he is, and his boots are tossed out after him. As he takes off, he hears the familiar sound of a smacking box on the ear.

When Pelle returned home from his roaming, he was tired and sluggish; the dim workshop was not enticing. He was crestfallen too, because the clockmaker's clock showed that he had been gone for three hours. He couldn't understand it.

Young Master was standing in the doorway surveying the street, dressed in a leather vest and apron of green billiard cloth. He was whistling softly, and he looked like a baby bird that didn't dare venture out of its nest. His curious eyes were often full of amazement at the world.

"Were you down at the harbor again, you little devil?" he asked, fastening his claw on Pelle.

"Yes," said Pelle, ashamed of himself.

"Well, what about it? Is there anything new?"

So Pelle had to report, standing there on the steps: about a Swedish cargo ship loaded with timber, and the skipper's wife had given birth on the open sea and the cook had served as midwife; about a Russian ship that had put into port with a mutiny on board—and about lots of other things. Today there was only the pair of boots. "They're from the salvage ship. They need to be resoled."

"I see," Master gave them a look of indifference. "Is the schooner *Andreas* ready to sail?"

Pelle didn't know about that.

"What kind of idiot are you? Don't you have eyes in your head? Oh well, can you go get me three beers? But put them under your shirt and don't let Father see them—you little beast!" Master's good humor quickly returned.

Later Pelle pulled on his apron and tightened the belt across his knee. Each man was busy with his work, and Master Andrès was reading. No sound was audible except the sound of their work, and every so often a mumbled reproof from the journeyman.

Every other day around five o'clock the door to the workshop would open slightly and a naked, floury arm would put the newspaper on the table. It was the baker's son, Søren, but he never showed himself; he preferred to move about like a thief in the night. Whenever the master happened to catch him and haul him into the workshop, he was like a frightened forest demon who wandered out of the thickets. He would stand with head bowed, hiding his eyes, and it was impossible to get a word out of him. And when he saw his chance he would slip away.

The arrival of the newspaper gave their work new appeal. When the master was in the mood, he would read aloud: about calves with two heads and four pairs of legs, about a squash that weighed 50 pounds, and the world's fattest man, and hunting accidents, and the snakes on Martinique. All the brilliant wonders of the world trooped up and filled the dark workshop—he skipped over the political nonsense. Whenever he was in one of his desperate moods his reading would be totally crazy: about the burning of the Atlantic Ocean so that people ate themselves to death on fried cod; or when the sky had torn open over America so that angels fell right down into people's soup plates. Things you knew full well were lies—and godforsaken gibberish that might bring perdition down upon him at any moment. Yelling at anyone was not Master's style; he felt sick if there was discord in the air. But he had his own way of commanding respect. In the middle of his reading there would suddenly be a reprimand for someone, which would make the man wince and believe that all of his faults were printed in the paper.

Toward evening a softer sound always came over their work. The long workday was drawing to an end, and their minds would throw off the fatigue and boredom of the day and rush outward—toward the dunes or the grove, in the direction where happiness shone. Sometimes a neighbor would stop by and shorten the time with his talk; this or that happened, and Master Andrès, who was so clever, had to put his seal on it. Sounds that were usually swallowed up by the day now reached in to them and made them part of the town's life. It was as if the walls had fallen.

Around seven o'clock a weird sound would grow louder up in the street and head down toward them at a deliberate tempo: a hollow thump and two crashes, and then again that thud as if from a mighty foot wrapped in cloth—and the crashes. It was old Bjerregrav hurling himself toward the workshop on his crutches, Bjerregrav who moved slower than other people but made faster headway. Whenever Master Andrès was in one of his bad moods, he would limp inside so he wouldn't have to be in the same room with a cripple; but normally he liked Bjerregrav.

"What kind of rare birds are these?" he would shout when Bjerregrav pulled up to the stairs and poled himself in sideways. The old man would laugh—he had been coming here every day for years. Master took no further notice of him either, but kept on reading, and Bjerregrav slipped into his silent ruminations. His pale hands fumbled over one thing after another as if he didn't recognize the most ordinary things. He touched everything with such naiveté that they had to smile and let him sit there, puttering around like the child that he was.

It was impossible trying to keep a conversation going with him, because when he finally made some remark, it was usually a non sequitur. Bjerregrav most often got stuck on details that no one else felt like dwelling on.

When he sat there like that, pondering some quite ordinary object, people would say: "Now Bjerregrav's curiosity has got hold of him!" And Bjerregrav *was* curious; he went around addressing questions to everyone and everything, even to the food he ate. He would ask about the most ridiculous things, things that everybody else took for granted: Why is a stone hard, and why does water put out a fire? People didn't answer him either, they just shrugged indulgently. "He's smart enough," they would say. "There's nothing wrong with his brain. But he looks at things the wrong way!"

Young Master looked up from his book. "Am I going to inherit your money, Bjerregrav?" he asked in jest.

"No, you've never done anything bad to me. I don't want to cause you any harm!"

"Worse things could happen to me. Don't you think so, Bjerregrav?"

"No, because you have a passable livelihood. And no one is entitled to more than that, as long as most other people are in need."

"But some people have money stashed at the bottom of their chests," Master Andrès insinuated.

"No, that's all over now," replied the old man happily. "I'm just as rich as you are—precisely."

"What the devil? Have you squandered it all, Bjerregrav?" Master swung round in his chair.

"You and your 'squandered'! All of you are always reproaching and accusing me. I'm not aware of any wrongdoing, but it's true that the need increases every winter. It's a burden to have money, Andrès, when people are sitting around you starving. If you help them, you're told that you're just doing more harm. They say that themselves, so it must be true. But I've given my money to the charity association, so now I suppose it will go to the right places."

"Five thousand kroner," said the master dreamily. "There'll be some happy people among the poor this winter."

"Well, they won't get the money directly for food and fuel," said Bjerregrav, "but it should benefit them in other ways. Because when I made my offer to the association, the chairman—shipowner Monsen, as you know—came over and asked if he could borrow the money for a year. He was going to go bankrupt if he didn't get it, and he was miserable at the thought of all those people who would lose their jobs if his vast enterprise fell apart. So that responsibility fell on my shoulders. But the money is safe enough, and this way it will benefit the poor twice over."

Master Andrès shook his head. "I just hope you haven't stepped in the nettles, Bjerregrav."

"What do you mean? Now what have I done wrong?" said the old man in fright.

"He isn't on the verge of bankruptcy—he's a scoundrel," muttered the master. "Did you get collateral on the loan, Bjerregrav?"

The old man nodded; he was quite proud of himself.

"And interest—5 percent?"

"No, no interest. I don't like it when money begets money. Because they have to absorb the percentage from somewhere, and it would probably come from the poor too. Interest is blood money, Andrès. And it's a newfangled invention, too. In my youth no one ever heard of drawing interest on money."

"Well, well. He who gives until he's a beggar will be whipped until he's a goner," said Master and went back to his reading.

Bjerregrav sat there, sinking down into himself. Suddenly he looked up.

"You who are so well-read, can't you tell me what holds up the moon? I was lying in bed pondering that last night when I couldn't sleep. It wanders and wanders; and you can clearly see that there's nothing but air underneath it."

"Darned if I know," replied Master Andrès, cogitating. "It must hold itself up by its own power."

"That's what I thought—because duty wouldn't be strong enough. The rest of us go trudging and trudging along where we've been put, but we have the earth to support us. And you're still studying! You must have read all the books in the world by now, haven't you?" Bjerregrav picked up the master's book and examined it thoroughly. "This is a good book," he said, striking his knuckle against the binding and holding the book up to his ear, listening intently. "There's good material in it. Is it a tall tale—literature—or a history book?"

"It's a travel book. They're up at the North Pole, snowed in. They don't know whether they'll ever reach home alive."

"But that's terrible! To think that people dare venture out like that. I've often speculated about what might be at the ends of the earth, but I don't dare make the trip to see for myself. Never to come home again!" Bjerregrav turned his tormented gaze from one to the other.

"And they have frostbite on their feet, so their toes will have to be cut off—the whole foot on some of them."

"Oh, don't tell me that. They're going to be cripples, those poor men. I don't want to hear any more about it." The old man sat there, rocking, as if in pain. "Did the King send them up there to fight a war?" he asked a little later.

"No, they're out there to look for the Garden of Eden. One of the people who studies the Scriptures has probably discovered that it's supposed to be up there beyond the ice," explained the master in a solemn voice.

"The Garden of Eden, also called Paradise! But it lay where the two rivers flow into a third one, in the East! That's what is written. So what you're reading is false teachings."

"It probably was located at the North Pole," said Master, who had a tendency toward freethinking. "By God, it was! Anything else is just stupid superstition."

Bjerregrav sat in dejected silence. His shoulders drooped and his gaze was fixed on someplace where no one else could go. "Well, well," he said softly, "everyone thinks up something new to make himself noticed, but no one can change the grave."

Master Andrès shifted impatiently; he could change his mood like a woman. Bjerregrav's presence was bothering him. "I've just learned how to conjure—do you want to try, Bjerregrav?" he said suddenly.

"No, not on your life!" the old man smiled uncertainly.

Master pointed at his blinking eyes with two fingers and fixed him with a stare. "In the name of blood, in the name of juices, in the name of all fluids—good as well as bad—and the oceans too," he muttered, creeping around like a cat.

"I said stop it! Stop it! I don't like it!" Bjerregrav hung there bewildered, swinging between his crutches. He stole a glance at the door but couldn't tear himself away from the spell. Then he struck desperately at the master's conjuring hand and made use of the pause in the magic to slip away.

Master sat there blowing on his hand. "Damn, he really hit me," exclaimed the master in surprise and showed them his red hand.

Little Nikas didn't say a thing. He wasn't superstitious, but he didn't like anyone making fun of the nature of things.

"What should I do?" asked Pelle.

"Are First Mate Jessen's boots ready?" Master looked at the clock. "Then you can gnaw on your shinbones."

The workday was over. Master took his hat and cane and limped away to Beer Hansen's to play a game of billiards, the journeyman changed his clothes and left, and the older boys scrubbed their necks in the basin used for softening leather. Then they were going out to have a good time.

Pelle gazed after them. He felt a consuming need to shake off the tedious day and set out too, but his socks were nothing but holes and his tunic had to be washed so it would dry by morning. And his shirt—his ears grew hot—was it only two weeks, or was it the fourth week? Alas, time had grabbed him by the nose! A couple of evenings he had pushed the unpleasant washing aside, and now it had added up to two weeks! There was a nasty, creeping feeling all over his body. Was he already being punished because he had turned a deaf ear to his conscience and ignored Papa Lasse's words about the disgrace that would befall anyone who didn't keep himself clean?

No, thank God! But Pelle had had a real fright, his ears were still burning as he scrubbed his shirt and tunic out in the yard. It was probably best to regard it as a warning from on high!

Then the shirt and tunic hung spread out on the fence as if they wanted to embrace the sky out of joy over their cleanliness. But Pelle sat despondently up in the window of the boys' room, sewing—with one leg hanging out so it was out in the air, at least. The elaborate darning that his father had taught him was not put to use here; you could take one hole and put it together with another one! Pelle sewed—and Papa Lasse would have died of shame. After a while Pelle crept all the way out on the roof. Down in the skipper's yard the three girls were hanging around. They were bored and gazing over at the workshop.

Then they caught sight of him and changed completely. Manna came over and stood pressing her stomach against the stone wall impatiently, moving her lips at him. She tossed her head angrily and stamped her foot on the ground, but there was no sound. The two others crept around stifling their laughter.

Pelle understood quite well what the silent language was about, but bravely held out a little longer. Then he couldn't do it anymore; he threw everything aside and was down there with them.

All of Pelle's dreams and vague longings were out in the places that men frequented; nothing was as ridiculous to him as running after skirts. Women were almost something contemptible: they had no strength and not much of a brain either. The only thing they knew how to do was make themselves pretty. But Manna and her sisters were different; he was still enough of a child to play, and they were excellent playmates.

Manna—the wildcat—was afraid of nothing. With her short skirts and her braid and her jumping around she reminded him of a frisky, inquisitive bird flitting in and out of a thicket. She could climb like a boy and ride on Pelle's back all around the yard; it seemed almost a mistake that she was wearing skirts. Clothes didn't last long on her; every other minute she would come rushing into the workshop with something broken on her shoes. Then she would turn everything upside down, take the master's cane away from him so that he couldn't move, and get her hands on the journeyman's new American tools!

On his very first day she threw herself at Pelle. "Who's the new one?" she said, pounding him on the back. Pelle laughed and looked straight back at her, with the self-confidence that is the secret of the very young. There was no trace of shyness between them; they had known each other forever, and at any time could continue their playing right where they had left off. In the evening Pelle would stand by the wall and look at them; a second later he was over there playing.

Manna was no crybaby who blubbered at the consequences of every-thing. If she got herself into a fight, she never begged for mercy, no matter how fierce it got. But there was one thing about her that Pelle made allowances for because of her skirts. You had to admit that she could have been a little stronger!

But she did have courage, and Pelle would playfully return the blow — except in the workshop where they kept a close eye on him. When she sneaked up on him there and put something down his back or knocked him off his three-legged stool, he would control himself and quietly pick himself up.

All his happy days were spent over there in the skipper's garden; and what a peculiar world it was that captured his imagination. The girls had foreign names that their father had brought home from his voyages abroad: Aina, Dolores, Shermanna! They wore heavy red coral around their necks and in their ears. And scattered around the garden lay giant conch shells in which you could hear the boiling of the ocean itself, tortoise shells as big as a 16-pound loaf of bread, and entire blocks of coral.

All this was new to Pelle, but he didn't let it intimidate him. He incorporated it as fast as possible into his everyday world and kept himself ready at all times to encounter something even greater and stranger.

In the evening he would disappoint them and take off for town where the important things were going on — to the dunes and the harbor. Then the girls would stand by the wall, drooping and bored and peevish. But on Sundays he would show up faithfully as soon as he was done at the workshop, and they would expand their playing, conscious of having a long day ahead of them. There were hundreds of games, and Pelle was at the center of them all. He could be used for everything: husbands and cannibals and slaves. He was like a tame bear in their hands; they rode on him, trampled him, and sometimes all three would throw themselves at him and "murder" him. And then he had to lie still and put up with them burying the body and erasing all traces. Authenticity demanded that he be completely covered with dirt, only his face was spared — since that was unavoidable — and allowed to make do with a few withered leaves. If he complained afterwards about his nice confirmation clothes, their hands could be so gentle while brushing him off. And if he refused to be comforted, all three of them would give him a kiss. Among the girls he was never called anything except "Manna's husband."

That's how the days passed for Pelle. He was more jaunty than happy; he was dimly aware that things were going backwards, and he had no one to turn to. But undismayed he kept on fighting with the town. It was on his mind day and night; he fought with it in his sleep.

"If you need anything, you always have Alfred and Albinus—they'll help you out," Uncle Kalle had said when Pelle paid his farewell visit; and Pelle wasn't slow about seeking them out. But the twins were the same sly, shifty fellows they had been out in the fields. They never risked their hides, either for themselves or for anyone else.

Other than that, there was plenty of ambition in them. They had come to town from the country in order to better themselves, and they started out by taking jobs as servants, just until they saved enough so they could find something more respectable. Albinus had gotten stuck there, because he didn't want to learn a trade. He was a goodnatured fellow who was content to leave everything to other people as long as he was allowed to practice his acrobatic arts. He was always juggling something or other and balancing things on end in the most impossible ways. He had no understanding of the order of nature; he went around twisting his limbs into all kinds of positions, and when he hoisted something up into the air, he demanded that it stay up there while he did something else. "Things should be able to be trained just like animals," he said and continued on, undaunted. Pelle laughed; he liked him, but he didn't count him for much.

Alfred had taken a completely different direction. He had nothing to do with turning cartwheels anymore. He walked properly on his two legs, was constantly tugging at his collar and cuffs, and was always anxious about his clothes. He was a painter's apprentice now, but he wore his hair parted like a shop clerk and bought things at the pharmacy to rub into his hair. Whenever Pelle fell in with him on the street, Alfred always looked for some excuse to get rid of him. His only companions were shop clerks, and he was always busy greeting people left and right—people who were a cut above him. Alfred was quite simply a conceited ass, and Pelle would give him a licking someday!

In one respect the twins resembled each other: there was no help to be found from either one of them. They gladly exposed themselves to laughter, and when anyone ridiculed Pelle, they laughed too.

It wasn't easy to get by. Pelle had emphatically sent the farmer in himself packing, but now there was trouble with poverty itself. He had cheerfully apprenticed himself for room and board; he had a few clothes on his back, and he knew of no other needs if you didn't drink or run after girls. But then the town came and demanded that he re-outfit himself. His Sunday best was not too good for everyday wear here. He had to see about getting himself a rubber collar—the advantage was that you could wash it yourself—and cuffs were a distant goal. He needed money, and the vast sum of 5 kroner that he possessed when he arrived to take everything by storm, or in the worst case, buy it—that money the town had wheedled away from him before he could turn around.

Up until now Papa Lasse had taken all the worries upon himself, but now Pelle had to take care of everything alone. Now it was him and life, and Pelle managed quite a lot, considering he was such a greenhorn. But occasionally he would break down, and this inhibited all his childish expressions of life.

At the workshop he made himself useful and tried to stay on good terms with all of them. He won over Little Nikas by making a drawing of his sweetheart in enlarged format from a photograph. Her face wouldn't really come out right; it looked as if someone had stepped on it, but her dress and brooch were beautiful. The drawing hung in the workshop for a week and brought much joy. Karlsen, who was a delivery boy for the stone quarry, ordered two large pictures of himself and his wife for 25 øre apiece. "But you have to put some curls in my hair," said Karlsen, "because Mother always wanted me to have curly hair."

Pelle couldn't promise the pictures for a couple of months; it was late-night work if it was going to be done right.

"That's all right. I won't have the money for them before then anyway. This month we have to pay the lottery ticket, and next month the rent is due." Pelle understood quite well, because Karlsen earned 8 kroner a week and had nine children. But he didn't think he could reduce the price any more than that.

Money certainly didn't flow like water in town. And if he did get his hands on a *skilling*, it would jump right out of his grasp just as he was walking around wracking his brain about how he could spend it most wisely—like the time he discovered an irresistible pipe shaped like a boot in the window of a little shop.

Whenever the three girls called him from over the wall, his child's soul would have its way; then he would forget about struggles and sorrows for a moment. He was a little embarrassed if anyone noticed him slipping over there. Pelle didn't feel honored by their fine company—and they were girls, after all. He just felt happy over there, where the oddest things were used to play with: Chinese cups and weapons from the South Sea islands. Manna had a necklace of white teeth, sharp and bumpy; she maintained that they were human teeth and she dared to wear them on her bare skin. And the garden was full of wondrous plants: corn, tobacco, and lots of other kinds that supposedly grew in other parts of the world as densely as wheat did in Denmark!

The three girls had finer complexions than other people, and they smelled of the most exotic corners of the world. And he played with them. They looked up to him with admiration, mended his clothes when there was a rip, made him the center of their games—even when he wasn't present. There was a hidden compensation in this, even though he took it for granted: it was part of everything that fate and good fortune had reserved for him, a little advance on life's unlimited adventures. He insisted on ruling over them without restrictions, and when they were stubborn, he would get into such a temper that they gave in. He knew quite well that every real man subjugates woman.

Early summer dragged along this way, and the dead period drew closer. By Whitsuntide the town's residents had already supplied themselves with what they needed for the summer, and people out in the country had other things to think about than going into town with work for the craftsmen; the approaching harvest occupied everyone's mind. It was felt everywhere, even in corners where they didn't do anything for the farmer—how dependent the little town was on the countryside. It was as if the town had suddenly forgotten all its superiority; the craftsmen no longer looked down on the farmland but stood and gazed far out across the fields, talking about the weather and prospects for the harvest, and had forgotten all about town interests. If, on rare occasion, a farm wagon rolled through the streets, everyone ran to the window to have a look. And when the harvest was imminent it was as if old memories made all of them lift their heads; everyone who could sloughed off town life and went back to the country to help with the harvest. From the workshop the journeyman and the two oldest boys went out. Jens and Pelle could easily handle the work.

Pelle didn't notice the deadness. He was completely preoccupied with looking after himself and getting the most possible out of life. There were thousands of contradictory impressions of good and bad that had to be collected and united into a whole—into this peculiar thing called *the town,* which Pelle never knew whether to bless or curse, because it always kept him oscillating.

And in the midst of his preoccupation, the figure of Lasse would appear and make him lonely in the whirlwind. Where was Papa Lasse? Would he ever hear from him again? Any day he had expected to see him tottering in the door, on the strength of Karna's words; and whenever someone fumbled at the door handle, Pelle was sure that it was him. It became a quiet sorrow in the boy's soul, a tone running through everything he did.

V

One Saturday as Pelle was running along Østergade a cart loaded with furniture came jolting in from the countryside. He was in a hurry but he had to see what was going on. The driver was sitting in front of the furniture, all the way forward between the horses. He was big and ruddy-cheeked and securely bundled up in spite of the heat. Hey, that was cousin Due, Kalle's son-in-law! And up in the middle of all the junk sat Anna and the children, their legs dangling. "Hello!" Pelle waved his cap and with a leap he had his foot up on the shaft and was sitting next to Due, who was laughing heartily at the meeting.

"Well, now we're tired of farm country and we're going to see if things will be better here in town," said Due in his quiet way. "And here you're rushing around like a native!" There was admiration in his voice.

Anna crept forward over the furniture and laughed down at them.

"Do you have any news of Papa Lasse?" Pelle asked her. This was his perpetual question whenever he met acquaintances.

"Yes, we do—he's in the process of buying a farm out on the heath. Will you behave yourself, you little devil!" Anna swatted behind her and a child began to cry. Then she came forward again. "And we're supposed to bring you many greetings from Mother and Father and everybody."

But Pelle had no interest in Uncle Kalle's family.

"Is it up by Stone Farm?" he asked.

"No, it's more to the east, out toward Troll Rocks," said Due. "It's a large plot, but there's not much of anything but stones. If only he doesn't work himself to death on it—I hear there were two men before him. He's set up housekeeping with Karna, you know."

"Uncle Lasse knows what he's doing," said Anna. "I guess it's Karna who put up the money. She had some put away at the bottom of her chest."

Pelle had to jump off—his heart had leapt at this news. Gone were all the uncertainty and all the terrifying possibilities. He had gotten his father back! And Lasse had had his life's dream fulfilled and was now sitting with his feet under his own table! And he had become a landowner too, if you didn't look too closely at things. And Pelle himself— well, he was a farmer's son now.

By nine o'clock at night he had finished everything and was ready to head out on the road; his blood pounded with excitement. Were there any horses? Yes, of course, but would there be workers too? Had Lasse become a landowner who paid out wages on turnover day and came driving into the town on Saturday with his fur collar up around his ears? Pelle could clearly see them come up the steps, one after the other, take off their wooden shoes, and knock on the office door. They were going to ask for an advance on their wages. And Lasse would scratch the back of his neck, look at them thoughtfully, and say: "No, I don't think so, you'll just drink it all up!" But he would give it to them anyway, when it came right down to it. "A man's too softhearted!" he would say to Pelle.

For Pelle had said goodbye to shoemaking and had come home as a farmer's son. In fact he was the one who actually ran things—only he didn't say so. And at the Christmas banquets he would dance with the farmers' plump daughters. There was whispering in the corners when Pelle came in. But he walked right up and asked the pastor's daughter for a swing around the floor, so she lost her breath, and more than that, and asked him to marry her right away.

He ran and he dreamed; his longing drove him onward, and before he knew it he had put the twelve miles of the main highway behind him. The parish road he now turned onto led through the heath-covered hills and conifer forests. The houses were poorer here and there was more distance between them.

Pelle took a guess and turned down a side road a little way up ahead, and ran with his senses alert. The summer night only let him glimpse everything partially, but it was all as familiar as the mended places on the back of Papa Lasse's vest, even though he had never been here before. The impoverished landscape spoke to him with a mother's voice; there was no other place in the world as secure as here among these mud-built huts where the poverty-stricken pioneers struggled with the rock for a handful of topsoil. All of this belonged to him down through many generations, right down to the rags stuffed around the windows and the old junk that had been hauled up onto the thatched roof to hold it in place. There was nothing here to wrack your brain about like other places in the world—you could lie here securely and rest. But he wanted no part of building and settling among all this. He had grown away from it, the way you grow away from your mother's skirts.

The side road gradually turned into a deep wagon rut twisting its way through rocks and marshes. Pelle knew he should keep heading east, but this road kept turning, first toward the south, then north. He grew tired of it, carefully took his bearings, and started off cross-country.

He had a hard time making his way. The moonlight fooled his eye so that he stumbled and fell into holes; heather and junipers reached up to his waist and hindered every movement. And then he grew stubborn and refused to turn back to the wheel ruts, but pushed on so hard he steamed, crawling up over the steep faces of cliffs slippery with dew on the moss, and tumbling over the edge every which way. A little too late he noticed the depths beneath him; an icy wind seemed to pass through his stomach and made him clutch wildly in the air for support. "Papa Lasse!" he cried, and at that very moment he was caught by the vast blackberry brambles, and he sank slowly down through the interwoven branches, and vine after vine slapped a thousand claws into him and reluctantly passed him on until he was carefully released deep down among the sharp stones at the bottom of a ravine. Shivering, he had to thank his good graces for all those thorns, which had mercifully flayed his hide so that he wouldn't split his skull open. Then he had to feel his way through the darkness and the noise of the sea down below until he found a tree and could climb up to the top of the cliff.

By this time he had lost his bearings, and when he realized this he lost his head too. There was nothing left of the confident Pelle. He ran blindly onward to make it to high ground. And when he jumped up to the top, free, to take his bearings from the cliffs, the ground broke and closed around him in a terrifying tempest. The air turned black and full of noise; he couldn't see his hand in front of his face. It was like a gigantic explosion—created by his joyful stomping on the cliff. The land was flung up into the air and dissolved into darkness, and the darkness itself screamed with terror and swirled around. Pelle's heart leapt in his breast and robbed him of his remaining senses; he leapt with uncontrollable terror and howled as if possessed. Above his head the black masses gathered so he had to duck down, gashes of light appeared and disappeared. It roared like the surf up there and shrieked incessantly in a hellish chaos of sound. Then it suddenly flung itself aside, headed northward, and fell. And Pelle realized that he had stepped into the middle of a rookery.

He found himself behind a large rock. He had no idea how he had gotten there, but he knew that he was a complete fool. How easily he could have crushed fifty rooks just by throwing some stones in the air!

He followed the ridge, enormously brave in his determination but weak in the knees. Far off on a stone a fox sat and barked wanly in the moonlight, and off to the north and south he caught glimpses of the sea. It was up here that the subterranean goblins lived; when you took a step on the rock it rumbled with a hollow sound. Pelle started to walk softly.

To the south the sea lay in the silvery gleam of the moon, but when he looked down that way again, it was gone; the lowland down there had vanished in whiteness. On all sides the land was disappearing. Pelle saw with amazement that the sea was slowly rising and filling all the hollows. It took the small hills too—each one in a mouthful—and it took the long ridge to the east so that only the tops of the pine trees were sticking up. But he did not give himself up for lost; behind all his terrifying thoughts lay a vague vision of Mt. Ararat and kept him going. Then it turned strangely cold, and his pants clung to his body. "It's the *waters*," he thought and looked around with fear: the mountain had been transformed into a tiny island that was floating with him in the ocean.

Pelle was a robust little realist who had been through a lot. But now terror had saturated his blood, and he accepted the supernatural without protest. The earth had simply gone under and he was adrift, out in the horrible cold universe! Papa Lasse and the workshop, Manna and Young Master's bright eyes—all of them were gone. He did not grieve but he felt terribly alone. Where would this take him? And was this death? Had he been killed before when he fell down the cliff? And was he now on the journey to the land of the blessed? Or was this the end of the world that he had heard people talk of so alarmingly for as long as he could remember? Maybe he was floating on the last fragment and he was the only one left alive. It wouldn't surprise Pelle if he managed to survive when everything else perished; even in that moment of despondency, deep inside him he found it quite natural.

He stood still without breathing, listening toward infinity; he was listening so hard that he heard the piston strokes of his pulse. And then he heard something else. Far away in the singing nothingness that was boiling against his ears he caught the inkling of a sound, the humming of something alive. Even though it was so infinitely distant and faint, Pelle felt as if it were rolling right through him. It was a cow fettered and chewing her cud; he could hear the way she was rubbing her neck up and down along the stake.

He ran down over the rocks, fell, and got to his feet again—and kept on going. He didn't notice the mist swallowing him up. Then he was down in the clearing and out in something that felt like familiar ridges under his feet—land that had once been plowed and had turned into heath again. The sound grew and turned into all the homey night sounds from an open cow stable, and a dilapidated farmhouse appeared in the fog. It wasn't the one Pelle was looking for; Papa Lasse's was a real farm with four buildings! But he went inside all the same.

Out in the country people didn't anxiously lock up everything the
way they did in town: he could walk right in. As soon as he opened the
door to the main room, joy flooded over him. He was met by the most
familiar smell he knew, the very basis of all smells—Papa Lasse's smell!

It was dark in the room; the evening light couldn't penetrate the low
windows. He heard the deep breathing of people asleep and knew that
they hadn't awakened—so the day hadn't changed yet! "Good evening," he said.

Then a hand started fumbling with some matches. "Is someone
there?" asked a sleepy female voice.

"Good evening!" he exclaimed again, stepping into the room. "It's
Pelle!" He said the name like a song.

"Ah . . . is it you, lad?" Lasse's voice was shaking, and his hands
couldn't manage the matches; but Pelle went forward by the sound and
took hold of his wrist. "And how did you find your way all the way up
here in the wilderness—at night and everything? All right, now I'll have
to get up," he said, trying with a moan to sit up.

"No, you just lie there, and I'll get up," said Karna, who was lying
next to the wall. She had kept quiet while her man was speaking. "He's
got this pain in his lower back, that's why," she said, and climbed over
him onto the floor.

"Well, I've been going at it a little too hard out here. That's what can
happen when you get something of your own to take care of. It's not
easy to know when to quit. But it gets better after I get going—work is
good grease for a sore back. So, how are you doing? I was just about to
start thinking you died down there in town."

Pelle had to sit down on the edge of the bed and tell about everything in town: the workshop and the master's lame leg and everything.
But he skipped telling about his troubles; that was nothing for men to
dwell on.

"So you're getting along well out there in the big world!" said Lasse,
delighted. "And you're well respected?"

"Well, yes . . ." Pelle was a little hesitant. For the time being, respect
was not the thing he had acquired the most of. But why sing about his
misery? "Yes, the young master likes me; he talks to me a lot over the
head of the journeyman himself."

"Well—there you have it! I've often wondered how you were
doing, and whether we wouldn't soon hear some big news from you;
but everything takes time, of course. And as you see, I've changed a
lot."

"Yes, you've turned into a great farmer!" said Pelle with a laugh.

"Damn it all, I have to admit it!" Lasse laughed but winced at the pain in his back. "In the daytime when I'm working I feel well enough, but as soon as I go and lie down it comes back. And it's truly the Devil's work—just like the wheels of a heavily loaded wagon rolling to and fro across my back, or something like that. Well, anyway, it's still a pleasure to have your own place! It's come over me so strangely that plain bread at my own table tastes better than . . . well, upon my soul, I might even say roast chicken at someone else's table. And then to be able to stand on your own two feet and spit in whatever direction you feel like without having to ask permission first. And the land here isn't that bad, even though most of it has never been under a human hand. It's been lying here storing up fertility since the beginning of time. But what about the people who live in town, are they high and mighty?"

Oh, Pelle had nothing to complain about. "When did you get married?" he asked suddenly.

"Well, it's like this . . ." Lasse started stammering. He had been waiting for just this question from the boy. "Married in that sense we're not, because it costs money, and the farm is more important than anything. But we intend to, of course . . . as soon as we can afford it and the opportunity arises." Lasse's honest opinion was that you might as well save the expense, at any rate until children were on the way and needed to be born legitimately. But he could see in Pelle's face that this wouldn't satisfy him. The boy was the same meticulous devil as always when it came to honor. "As soon as we get the harvest in, we'll invite you to a big party," he said resolutely.

Pelle nodded eagerly. Now he was the son of a landowner, and he could use it against those stuck-up town boys. But he didn't want to be punched in the nose because his father was living with a woman.

Karna came in with the food. She gave the boy such a kind look. "Please accept our poor food, son," she said, touching his arm gently; and Pelle wolfed down the food with a healthy appetite. Lasse hung halfway out of the sleeping alcove, full of joy.

"You haven't lost your appetite down there," he said. "Do you get decent food? Karna thought it might be rather skimpy."

"It's all right," replied Pelle stubbornly. Now he regretted that he had blabbed to Karna that evening when he was feeling melancholy.

Lasse began to get hungry; little by little he crept out of the alcove. "You're sitting here so alone," he said and sat down at the table dressed in his underwear and nightcap. He had acquired a knitted nightcap—the tip fell so nicely over one ear. He looked like a real old farmer, one with money under the bed straw. And Karna, who went back and forth as the menfolk ate, had a plump stomach and a big bread knife in her hand. She looked as solid as any farmer's wife.

A bed was made up for Pelle on the bench along the wall. He put out the fire before he got undressed, and stuck his clothes under the pillow.

He woke up late. The sun had already left the eastern sky. There was the most blissful smell of coffee in the room. Pelle got up quickly to put his clothes on before Karna came in and saw their condition. He put his hand under the pillow—his shirt was gone! And on the chair lay his socks, darned.

When Karna came in, he was lying motionless and silent with spite; he didn't reply to her morning greeting and didn't take his eyes off the wall cupboard. She shouldn't go around sniffing at his things!

"I took your shirt and washed it," she said calmly, "but you'll get it back tonight. Maybe you'd like to wear this one in the meantime." She placed one of Lasse's shirts on the comforter for him.

Pelle lay there for a moment as if he hadn't heard her, then he sat up sullenly and pulled on the shirt. "No, stay there in bed while you drink your coffee," said Karna when he tried to get up, and she set things out for him on the chair. So Pelle had coffee in bed, the way he had dreamed it would be when Papa Lasse got married again, and his bad humor had to pass. But the shame continued to burn inside him and made him taciturn.

That morning Lasse and Pelle went out to inspect the property.

"Don't you think it's best if we walk around it first, so you can get an idea where the boundaries are?" said Lasse, who knew it was the size that would make the biggest impression. It was a walk through heather and vines and brambles, down into swamps and up along steep cliff walls. It took several hours to make their way around it.

"It's an awfully big property," Pelle kept saying.

And Lasse would answer proudly: "Yes, ha! There are over fifty acres of land here. If only it were cultivated!"

It lay there like virgin soil, overgrown with heather and juniper thickets that were intertwined with blackberry bushes and honeysuckle. In the middle of the sheer cliff faces hung wild cherry and ash trees, clinging to the naked wall with expanses of roots that looked like deformed hands. Crab trees, blackthorn bushes, and wild roses formed impenetrable thickets that already bore the mark of Lasse's axe. And in the midst of this luxuriance the bedrock thrust forth its determined brow, or came so close to the surface that the sun burned off any vegetation.

"It's a whole little paradise," said Lasse. "You can hardly set your foot anywhere without crushing berries. But it has to be cleared, of course, if a man is going to make it."

"Don't you think it's poor soil?" said Pelle.

"Poor? When all this can thrive and flourish?" Lasse pointed toward where the aspen and birch stood swaying delightedly with their shiny leaves in the breeze. "No, but it'll be beastly hard work to get it under cultivation. I'm sorry that you're not at home now."

Lasse had mentioned this same thing several times, but Pelle ignored it. This was not what he had imagined, after all. He felt no urge to stay home as the farmer's son in this situation.

"It'll be tough to raise food here," he said, oddly wise for his years.

"Oh, it won't be hard to get food out of it—though it won't be banquet food every day," said Lasse, offended. "And here you can straighten your back without having a foreman come yapping. Even if I work myself to death here, at least I'm out of slavery. And you'll never forget the joy there is in watching the earth come under control from day to day and produce something instead of just lying fallow. It is, after all, the foremost task of human beings to conquer the earth and make it fertile—I can't think of anything better! But I suppose you've lost the pull of the land down there in town?"

Pelle didn't answer. But if it was supposed to be something good and great to work yourself to death on a plot of heath, just so that it would grow something else someday, then he was glad he didn't feel the pull of the land.

"My father, and his father before him, and everyone I've known in our family—we've all had it in us: the need to improve the earth without paying any heed to our own comfort! But it probably never occurred to any of them that someday we'd be criticized for it—and by one of our own, to boot." Lasse spoke with his face turned away, like God the Father when He was irate with His people. Pelle felt like an ugly changeling who took after the very worst. But still he wouldn't give in.

"I don't think I'm cut out to stay here," he said apologetically, peering off toward the sea. "I don't think so."

"No, you've broken away from everything, haven't you?" replied Lasse bitterly. "But maybe you'll regret it someday. Life out there in the unknown probably isn't all happiness and delight either."

Pelle said nothing; at that moment he was too much a man to let one word prompt another. He kept himself in check, and they plodded along in silence. "Well, it's not exactly an estate, of course," Lasse said suddenly to take the sting out of any further criticism. Pelle was simply silent.

Over by the house the land was under cultivation, and beyond the cultivated land the surface of the abundant heath revealed a vanishing remnant of field backs and furrows. "This was probably a grain field once," said Pelle.

"Oh, so you can see that too!" exclaimed Lasse, half jeering, half in admiration. "What a devil of an eye you have. I wouldn't have noticed anything special about that heath myself if I hadn't known about it. Yes, it was under cultivation, but the heath has taken it over again. It was during the time of my predecessor; he took on more than he could handle, and he cracked under it. But here you can see that it *can* produce something!" Lasse pointed at a section of rye that Pelle had to agree looked quite good.

But running through the entire length of the fields were high crests of broken stones that warned him of what terrible work this earth demanded to be put into cultivation. Over beyond the rye lay newly broken ground—it looked like chunks of ice. The plow had wandered through nothing but rock shards. Pelle saw everything and felt despair on his father's behalf.

Lasse was undaunted. "That's the way things are, you see. It takes two of us to hold the plow. Karna is plenty strong, and even so it feels like your arms are being pulled right out of your body, for every inch the plow goes forward. And most of it has to be broken up with hoes and crowbars—it even takes a little sneeze once in a while! I use dynamite, though it's more dangerous than gunpowder. It breaks up the bedrock better," he said proudly.

"How much has been plowed now?" asked Pelle.

"Including the meadow and the garden, about ten acres; but there will be more before the year is out."

"And on those ten acres two families have gone under," said Karna, who had come out to call them to dinner.

"Yes, yes, may God make it easy for them. It's because of their toil that we're now going to succeed. The parish won't be coming back to take over from the two of us." Lasse said this with confidence; Pelle had never seen him stand so straight.

"I'm not completely happy about it all the time," Karna rushed in. "It's like the earth of a churchyard we're cultivating. The first one the parish had out here hanged himself, they say."

"Yes, he had a sod hut over there where you can still see the elder trees. It's collapsed since then. But I'm glad it didn't happen here in the house." Lasse shuddered with horror. "They say that he walks again when anything bad is about to happen to his successors."

"This house was built later on?" asked Pelle with amazement. He thought it seemed so dilapidated.

"Yes, my predecessor built it. The parish gave him the plot free for twenty years provided that he build on it and put one acre of land under the plow each year—so those weren't the worst conditions. But he took on too much all at once. He was the kind of man who works himself ragged in the morning and is worn out before noon. But he built the house well," Lasse slapped the thin walls filled in with mud, "and the timber is first-rate. I think I'll break up some stones when winter comes; they have to be moved anyway, and it wouldn't be a bad idea to take in a few hundred kroner. Then in two or three years we'll turn the old house into a barn and build us a new farmhouse, Karna—maybe with a cellar under the whole thing and a steep stairway like at Stone Farm. It'll be made out of chipped granite. I can put up the walls myself."

Karna glowed with happiness, but Pelle couldn't really join in. He was disappointed; the fall from his fantasies to this naked reality was too great. And there was something stirring within him, a dull defiance against this endless toil with the earth; as inexperienced as he was, it had settled inside him over ten or twenty generations. He had not done the harsh work in the earth himself, but from the time he could crawl he had naturally understood everything that had to do with cultivation; every kind of agricultural tool felt comfortable in his hand. The only thing he had not inherited was joy in the land. His mind had taken a new direction! And the endless toil with the earth lay settled inside him with a rancor that gave him the perspective Lasse lacked. In this respect he was pragmatic; he didn't lose his head over fifty acres of land, but asked what they contained. He wasn't conscious of any of this, but his whole being bristled with opposition to putting his strength into that futile labor. And his expression was so experienced that he could have been Lasse's father.

"Wouldn't you have done better to buy a house on ten acres of land that were in good shape?" he said.

Lasse squirmed impatiently. "Sure, then you could waste all your time going around in circles and never get anywhere, cut off the front pieces to patch the back, and preferably chew everything twice. Hell, then I could have stayed where I was. This place does take more work and trouble, but there's a future in it. As soon as I get it under the plow, it'll be a farm that beats most of the others hands down!" Lasse's gaze swept over his property. In his mind it billowed with grain and was full of first-rate livestock.

"It could easily support six horses and a couple of dozen cows," he said aloud. "Now, that's prosperity, isn't it? Or what do you think, Karna?"

"I think the food's getting cold," said Karna, smiling. She was very happy.

At the table Lasse suggested that Pelle send his clothes home to be washed and mended. "You must have enough to do without that too," he said cautiously. "Butcher Jensen goes in to market every Saturday; if you got him to take your clothes along and leave them by the church, I'd be surprised if there wasn't someone at church on Sunday who lives out here in the heath who could bring your clothes out to us."

But Pelle grew suddenly taciturn and would not reply.

"I just thought that you might be tired of washing and mending for yourself," said Lasse meekly. "There are probably other things for you to think about in town, and besides, it's not proper work for a man."

"I can do it myself," muttered Pelle truculently. Now he would *show* them that he could keep himself neat. Saying no to this offer was also a kind of revenge on himself for his slovenliness.

"All right," said Lasse gently, "I was just asking. I hope you don't take offense."

Even though Karna was strong and willing to help with everything, Lasse was still in great need of a man's hand. Work had piled up that required two, and Pelle gladly lent a hand. They spent most of the day heaving big stones out of their places and towing them away. Lasse had hammered together a sled and hitched up the two heath-nags to it.

"Well, you shouldn't look at them too closely right now," he said, running his hand lovingly over the two bags of bones. "Just wait a couple of months, then you'll see! They don't lack spirit either."

There was plenty to do, and the sweat poured off them; but they were in good humor. Lasse was astonished at the boy's strength—here was finally some help. But he would need two or three boys like this to turn over the whole wilderness. He regularly had to vent his feelings with a sigh that he didn't have Pelle at home; but Pelle was steadfastly deaf in that ear. Before they knew it, Karna appeared again and called them to supper.

"I'm thinking about hitching up and driving Pelle halfway to town . . . as payment for his work," said Lasse grandly. "And the two of us could use a pleasure ride." So they hitched up the nags to the buckboard.

It was amusing to watch Lasse. He was an alert driver, and you couldn't imagine that he was driving anything but a couple of thorough-breds. Whenever they met anyone, Lasse would carefully gather up the reins, to be prepared in case the horses spooked. "It's so easy for them to take control," he said solemnly. And if he managed to work them up into a slight trot, he was delighted. "They're stubborn!" he would say, pretending that it took a lot of effort. "Damn, I think I'm going to have to get a new bit!" He had to brace both feet against the front of the wagon and yank on the reins.

When they had driven halfway, Lasse decided to go a little bit farther, and a little bit more, and then to hell with it, just as far as that farm! He had completely forgotten that another day would come tomorrow with hard labor for him and the horses. Finally Pelle jumped down.

"Well, shall we make arrangements for your clothes?" Lasse asked again.

"No!" Pelle turned his face away. They could just as well stop harping on it.

"All right, all right, goodbye, son—and thanks for lending a hand! You'll come home for a visit as soon as you can, won't you?"

Pelle smiled at them but said nothing; he didn't dare open his mouth for fear of the cowardice he could feel way up in his throat. Silently he gave them his hand and set off at a run toward town.

VI

The other apprentices bought their clothes by working for themselves in their free time; they got work from friends and sometimes even stole customers from Master by secretly underbidding him. They kept their own work hidden under the counter. When Master wasn't home they would take it out and work like mad. "I'm going out to meet a girl tonight," they said, laughing. Little Nikas said nothing.

Pelle had no friends who could give him work, and he didn't know very much yet either. When the others were busy after hours or on Sunday, he had to help them, but not much of it rubbed off. But he had taken in Nilen's shoes to mend—for the sake of old acquaintance.

Jeppe had talked on and on about tips the day Pelle apprenticed himself. Citizens often dwelled on them as an oppressive expense and spoke out strongly about limiting or completely abolishing this burden on trade. But that was just something they got from the newspapers over there—so they wouldn't seem more backward than in Copenhagen!

And they would always mention the word whenever he brought their shoes and rummage around in their coin purses. If they found a *skilling*, they would cover it up with a finger and look unhappy; Pelle would get it next time, he should remind them himself! At first he did remind them — they had told him to. But Jeppe got word that his new boy had better stop pressing for money. Pelle didn't understand, but an emerging antagonism began to grow in him toward these people who could go through such shameless contortions just to make a 10-øre piece disappear — which they didn't even have to account for.

Pelle, who felt that he had had enough of his poor-man's world and ought to see about attaining some other level in society, learned once again to count on poor people, and he was cheered by every pair of those proletarian shoes that Master cursed because they were worn so thin. The poor were not afraid of giving him a *skilling* when they had one. Sometimes it hurt him to watch them scrambling in every corner and emptying the children's piggy banks to scrape together a couple of øre, while the children stood in silence, watching with sad eyes. And if he said "No, thank you," they would be insulted. The little he received he owed to people who were just as impoverished as he was.

Down here coins were no longer the same round, indifferent objects that were piled on top of each other in whole stacks higher up in society. Here, every *skilling* was so much worry or joy; a little dirty coin could contain both the raging curses of a man and the despairing cries of a child for food. Widow Høst gave him 10 øre, and he had to tell himself: She just gave away her dinner for two days!

One day as he passed the wretched hovels out by the northern dunes, a poor young woman appeared in a doorway and called to him. She was holding the remains of a pair of elastic-sided shoes in her hand. "Hey, you, shoemaker's brat, couldn't you be nice and mend these a little for me?" she asked. "Just put a few stitches in them so they'll stay on my feet for half an afternoon. The stonecutters are having a barn dance on Thursday, and I want to go so badly." Pelle looked at the shoes; there wasn't much that could be done with them. But he took them along and worked on them in his free time. From Jens he found out that the woman was the widow of a stonecutter who lost his life in an explosion right after they were married. The shoes were quite nice-looking when he delivered them.

"Well, I don't have any money, but I'm truly grateful," she said, looking at her shoes with delight. "So pretty they are. And God bless you for it."

"Thanks is what the smith's cat died from," said Pelle, laughing. Her joy was contagious.

"Yes, and it's God's blessing that comes from two poor people going to bed together," replied the young woman, teasing him. "But I still want to wish you well in return—now I can have myself a dance!"

Pelle felt quite satisfied with himself as he left. But a couple of houses down, another woman waylaid him. She had probably heard about the first woman's luck, and she was standing there with a pair of dirty children's shoes, which she begged him so earnestly to mend. He took the shoes and repaired them, even though he grew even poorer by doing so; he knew too much about need to say no. It was the first time that anyone here in town acknowledged him, counted him among their own at first glance. Pelle puzzled over this a great deal; he didn't know yet that poverty is international.

When he went out after finishing his day's work, he would keep to the periphery, associate with the poorest boys, and make himself as inconspicuous as possible. But a kind of desperation had come over him, and sometimes he could make himself noticed through actions that would have made Lasse cry—such as when he aggressively sat down on a newly tarred mooring post. That made him the hero of the evening; but as soon as he was alone, he went behind a fence and, crestfallen, pulled off his pants to determine the extent of the damage. During the day he ran errands in his best clothes. That was no joke. Lasse had imprinted his frugality deep inside Pelle and taught him a meticulousness about things that practically approached devotion to God. But Pelle felt himself abandoned by all gods, and now he was challenging them.

The poorest housewives on the street were the only people that paid any attention to him. "Just look at that boy, now he's running around, ruining his confirmation shirt on a weekday!" they said and called him inside to give him a good tongue-lashing—which usually ended with them doing a bit of mending for him. But Pelle didn't care; he was just doing what the town did when he wore his best clothes outdoors. At least he had a shirt, no matter how coarse it was! But the new barber's journeyman, who showed off in a frock coat and top hat and was the ideal of every apprentice, he didn't even have a shirt on. Pelle noticed this one time when the journeyman barber was pushing some ladies on a swing. Back home in the country, where a man's esteem was based on the number of shirts he owned, this man would have been impossible! But here in town, life was lived in the shorter term.

Now he was no longer astonished by all these people—sober-minded people as well—who had no permanent place but slipped from one workplace to another the year round, by sheer chance. They looked happy, nevertheless, had a wife and children and went out and had fun on Sunday. Why should you carry on as if the world were collapsing because you didn't have a tub of pork and a heap of potatoes to face the winter with? A carefree attitude was ultimately an escape for Pelle too. Wherever any bright future seemed dead, it would seize upon the fairy tale once more and lend excitement to naked poverty. There was suspense in starvation itself: were you going to die of it, or weren't you?

Pelle was poor enough that everything lay ahead of him, and he possessed the poor man's wide-open spirit. *The wide world and the fairy tale* were the forces that bore him through the emptiness, they were the very melody of life that was never silent but followed murmuring behind good cheer and sorrows. He knew very well what the world was like: it was something inconceivably huge that ran back into itself. In eighty days you could go around the whole thing—around to where they walked with their heads pointing down, and back again—and experience all its wonders. He had also set off into the incomprehensible and had landed in this little town where there wasn't a scrap of food for a hungry imagination; it was filled only with petty worries. You could feel the cold draft from out there, and the dizziness. When the little newspaper arrived, the tradesmen would run excitedly across the street with spectacles on their noses and talk with sweeping gestures about the events out there. "China," they would say, "America!" and pretend that they were in the midst of the world's tumult. But Pelle wished hard that a little of the great world would find its way over here—since *he* was stuck here! It would be quite nice to have a little volcano underfoot, so the buildings began to tilt toward each other; or a little flood, so the ships drifted over to the town and had to be moored to the weathervane on the church spire. He had such an unreasonable need for something to happen here, something that chased your blood out of its hiding places and set the hair on your head on end. But for the time being he had enough to contend with; the world would have to take care of itself until times were better.

It was harder to give up the fairy tale; it had been sung into his soul by poverty itself, and carried there by Lasse's quavering voice. "There's often a rich child in a poor woman's womb," his father would frequently repeat when he was reading the omens of his son's future, and the words sank into the boy like a refrain. But this much he had learned: that there were no elephants whose necks an agile boy could straddle and ride the

tiger to death, just as it was about to tear apart the King of the Hima-
layas! And then, of course, win the daughter and half the kingdom for
his deed. Pelle spent a lot of time at the harbor, but he never found any
elegantly dressed little girl in the water so he could rescue her and marry
her when she grew up. And if it did happen, he now knew quite well
that her parents would cheat him out of a tip. He had also totally given
up waiting for a golden carriage to drive over him so that the two
terrified women dressed in mourning would put him into the carriage
and take him to a castle with six ballrooms! And always keep him with
them, of course, in place of the son they had recently lost, who—
amazingly enough—was exactly the same age he was. There weren't
any golden carriages here!

Out in the wide world the poorest boy had the greatest prospects.
All the great men in his primer had been poor boys like himself who had
prospered through luck and their own boldness. But the people who
owned anything here in town had come into their possessions by bullying their way to the top and putting the squeeze on poor people. Even
now they sat there brooding and miserly, not tossing out anything for
the fortunate one to grab—or leaving anything behind for a poor fellow
to come and pick up! And none of them thought they were too good to
pry an old pants button out of the cobblestones and wear it in good
health.

One evening Pelle ran off to buy half a pound of tobacco for Jeppe.
Outside the coalman's store the big dog came rushing at his legs as
usual, and he dropped the 25-øre piece. While he was looking for it, an
elderly man came over to him. Pelle knew him well; it was shipowner
Monsen, the wealthiest man in town.

"Did you lose something, my boy?" he asked and started to help
him search.

Now he'll ask me questions, thought Pelle, so I'll answer him
smartly, and then he'll look at me attentively and say... Pelle was
always hoping for these mystical events from above that would unex-
pectedly take a clever boy and pull him up into good fortune.

But the shipowner didn't ask him anything like that, he just searched
eagerly and said, "Where were you walking? Was it here? Are you
sure?"

In any case, he'll probably give me another 25-øre, thought Pelle.
It's certainly strange how eager he is... Pelle was bored with looking,
but he couldn't very well stop before the other man did.

"Well, well," said the shipowner finally, "you're probably just pretending that you dropped something. What kind of clumsy oaf are you,

anyway?" And then he left. Pelle gazed after him for a long time before he reached into his own coin purse.

Later, when he came by again, there was a man bending over and lighting matches close to the cobblestones. It was the shipowner. Pelle felt a peculiar hollowness in his stomach. "Did you lose something?" he asked maliciously. He was prepared to run in case it looked like he'd get a beating.

"Yes, yes, a 25-øre piece," gasped the shipowner without straightening up. "Can you help me look for it, my boy?"

Pelle already knew that Monsen had become the richest man in town by storing spoiled foodstuffs and rigging out old leaky tubs that he kept heavily insured. He also knew who was a thief and who was bankrupt, and that grocer Lau only associated with the tradesmen because his daughter had gotten into trouble. Pelle knew "The Full Sail," the woman who was the town's secret pride and singlehandedly represented the corruption of the big cities, and the two con men and the councilor with the ravaging disease. This was altogether satisfying knowledge for an outcast to have.

He had no intention of letting the town retain any of the delights with which he had once endowed it; with his constant scurrying around he stripped it to the skin. There lay the houses along the street, staggered and decorative, with quaint old doors and flowers in all the windows. They glistened with shiny tar on the half-timbered frames and had a fresh plaster color: yellow ocher or blinding white, sea-green or blue like the sky. On sunny days they gave an impression of celebration and flags flying. But Pelle had investigated the back side of every house, and there were the water spouts with long slimy beards, stinking pig troughs, and a big manure bin with a scraggly elder bush handing over it. The pavement was covered with herring gills and codfish innards, and the walls were scaly with green moss along the bottom.

The bookbinder and his wife walked hand in hand when they went to prayer meetings. But at home they fought, and when they sat in the meeting house and sang from the hymnal, they would pinch each other on the leg. "Look," people would say, "what a handsome couple." But the town couldn't hide anything from Pelle; he knew all about it. If only he had been just as sure about where he was going to get a new tunic!

One thing did not allow itself to be unmasked but continued to retain some of its fairytale quality—credit! At first it took his breath away, that people in town got everything they needed without money. "Would you charge it!" said people when he brought their shoes. "Put it on our account!" he said himself whenever he did the shopping for

Master. Everybody said the same magic formula, and Pelle had to think of Papa Lasse, who would count his *skillings* twenty times before he'd dare spend them. He had great expectations from this discovery. He intended to use this magic formula liberally when his own means had run out.

Of course, he was a little smarter than that. He had seen that in particular the poorest people always had to stand with their money in their fist, and besides, a day of reckoning would come for the others too. Master was already speaking with dread about New Year's. The business was being held back by the fact that he was in the leather dealer's pocket and couldn't buy his materials where they were the cheapest. All the small tradesmen suffered under this.

But this did not ruin the fairy tale—here was a way to draw on the happiness that was long in coming, and on the future that would pay all the bills. Credit was a splash of fantasy amid all the petty scrambling. Here people were as poor as churchmice and yet walked around pretending to be nobility. Alfred was born lucky that way. He didn't earn a red øre, but his clothes were as fine as a shop clerk's and he never denied himself anything. If he wanted something he just went right in and got it on credit. He was never turned down. His friends envied him and looked up to him as if he were born under a lucky star.

Pelle and good fortune also had a score to settle. One day he stepped boldly into a shop to buy himself some underwear. When he demanded credit, they looked at him as if there were something wrong with him—he had to leave without completing his business.

There must be some secret I don't know about, thought Pelle. He had a dim memory of another boy who couldn't get the pot to cook the porridge or the tablecloth to cover the table—because he didn't know the *word*. He sought out Alfred at once for an explanation.

Alfred was wearing new suspenders, knotting his tie. On his feet he wore slippers with a fleecy edge; they looked like curled-up doves. "I got these from the master's daughter," he said, wiggling his feet coquettishly. "She's completely crazy about me. She's damned nice—but there's no money."

Pelle told him about his needs.

"Shirts! Shirts!" crowed Alfred, slapping his head. "God in heaven, if he doesn't want to get shirts on credit! If only he wanted shirts with French cuffs!" He was about to die laughing.

Pelle went back to the shop. As the farmer that he was, he had thought of shirts first; but now he wanted to get a summer coat and rubber cuffs.

"But why do you want credit?" asked the shopkeeper reluctantly. "Are you expecting money from somewhere? Or is there someone who can vouch for you?"

No, Pelle would vouch for himself—but just at the moment he didn't have any money.

"So wait until you get some," grumbled the shopkeeper. "We're not accustomed to outfitting poor boys!" Pelle had to slink off like a wet dog.

"You're a codfish," said Alfred curtly. "You're just like Albinus. He never learns either."

"So how do *you* do it, then?" asked Pelle in a low voice.

Do it? Do it?—Alfred didn't know of any specific way to *do* it; it came quite naturally. "But I don't tell them that I'm poor. Well, you might as well not even try. It won't work for you!"

"Why are you sitting like that and pinching your lip?" asked Pelle suspiciously.

"Pinching? I'm twirling my mustache, you fool!"

VII

Pelle was sweeping the street on a Saturday afternoon. It was getting on toward evening, and fires had already been lit in the hearths of the little houses. You could hear a sizzling at bricklayer Rasmussen's and at Anders the Swede's house, and the smell of fried herring filled the street. The housewives were making a little something extra to give their husbands since they would be coming home soon with the week's wages. Then the women scurried off to the grocer's for aquavit and beer, letting the doors stand wide open—they had just that half a minute while the herring was finishing up on one side in the frying pan. Pelle poked his nose inside. So, now Mrs. Rasmussen had fallen into conversation at the grocer's! "Mrs. Rasmussen, your herring is burning!" shrieked a voice, and then she came running, her skirts gathered up, turning her head shamefully from house to house as she raced across the street and inside. The blue smoke settled down among the houses; the rays of the sun slanted in and filled the street with golden dust.

All along the road people were sweeping the street: baker Jørgen, the washerwoman, and the comptroller's maid. The heavy mulberry trees drooped over the wall on the other side of the street and offered the last ripe berries to anyone who wanted to pick them. Behind the wall, rich grocer Hans (the man who had married the nanny) was probably puttering around in his garden. He never went out, and the rumor was that he was being held prisoner by his wife and her family. But Pelle had had his ear to the wall, and heard the murmuring voice of an old man repeating the same terms of endearment over and over, so that it sounded like one of those love ballads that never end. And at dusk, when Pelle sneaked out of his garret window and crept up on the roof to take a look at the world, he would see a tiny little white-haired man walking down there with his arm around a younger woman's waist. They looked like ambling young people, and every other second they had to stop and give each other a peck. The wildest myths circulated about grocer Hans and his money—the fortune that was once founded on a paper of pins and now was so large that a curse had to be attatched to it.

Søren came sneaking out of the bakery with the holy hymnbook in his hand. He went right over to the wall and raced off. Old Jørgen stood there chuckling at him, leaning on his broom with his hands folded.

"Now there's a man for you!" he called over to Jeppe, who was sitting just inside the window, shaving himself in the milk dish. "Look how he's dashing off! Now he's going to ask God's forgiveness for his courting."

Jeppe came to the window and told him to hush. Brother Jørgen's falsetto could be heard all down the street. "Is he courting? How did you get him to venture out?" he asked eagerly.

"Oh, it was when we were eating . . . I had an attack of melancholy because I happened to think about Little Jørgen. There won't ever be any Little Jørgen to carry on my name, I said to myself, because Søren is a dishrag and I don't have anyone else to fall back on! And any day I might be lying there with my nose in the air—and then it's all blown away and in vain. I think about things like that, you know, when that sort of thought comes over me. I sat there looking spitefully at Søren, I did; because there sits a splendid, real woman right across from him, and he doesn't even see her. Then suddenly I slam my fist on the table and say: 'Now, Søren, you take Marie's hand and ask her if she'll be your wife—because I want to see once and for all what you're good for!' Søren winced and stuck out his hand, and Marie's not half bad. 'Yes, I will!' she replied quickly, before he had time to think twice. So now we'll be having a wedding soon."

"If only she can make a silk purse out of that sow's ear," said Jeppe.

"Oh, she's hot—the way she's built! She'll get him warmed up. Women know what to do. He won't freeze in bed." Old Jørgen laughed contentedly and went back to work. "Yes, they even know how to shake life into the dead, they sure do," he repeated out on the street.

The others dashed off in their best clothes, but Pelle didn't feel like it. He wasn't happy during that time: he hadn't been able to fulfill his stubborn decision to prove that he could keep himself neat, and the awareness of his defeat gnawed at him. And those holes in his socks, which were now so big that they could no longer be darned, made themselves felt against his skin in a particularly hideous way, so he felt disgusted with himself.

Now his youth was pulling him outward. He caught glimpses of the sea down at the end of the street; it lay completely still, catching the colors of the sunset. Then he felt pulled toward the harbor or the dunes. There was going to be dancing out in the open, maybe even fights over girls! And boys Pelle's age were playing highwaymen among the small fir trees. But he wouldn't stand for being laughed out of the group like a mangy dog—he'd turn his back on the lot of them!

He tore off his apron and settled down on the beer keg just outside the gate. Over on the bench the old men of the street sat smoking their pipes, chatting about this and that. Now it was the sabbath evening, and the bells were ringing it in. Madam Rasmussen was scolding and spanking her child in time to the bells. Suddenly it all stopped and the child's sobs remained like a gentle evening song.

Jeppe mentioned Málaga—"the time I was in Málaga!"—but baker Jørgen was still caught up in his melancholy, and he sighed: "Oh yes, oh yes . . . if only you could see into the future." Then he suddenly started talking about the Mormons. "It still might be fun to try out what they have to offer."

"But I thought Uncle Jørgen really was a Mormon," said Master Andrès. The old man laughed.

"I've experienced a thing or two in my day," he said, staring out into space.

Farther up the street the clockmaker was standing on his stone steps. He turned his face to the sky, flinging out his insane cry. "The new age! I'm asking you about the new age, O God the Father!" He repeated it over and over.

Two weary dock workers walked past. "He wants to erase poverty from the face of the earth and create a new life for all of us—that's what his madness is struggling with," said one of them with a dull smile.

"It must be the Millennium he has in mind," replied the other.

"No, he's just barking at the moon," old Jørgen shouted after them. "There's going to be a change in the weather."

"He's not feeling well right now—poor man," said Bjerregrav, shivering. "It was this time of year when he lost his mind."

Something inside Pelle was urging him: Don't sit there with your hands in your lap, go up and take care of your clothes! But he couldn't make himself do it; it had become insurmountable. Tomorrow Manna and the other girls would call him, and he wouldn't be able to jump over the wall to them; they had begun to wrinkle their noses critically. He understood why—he had become an outcast, someone who didn't even feel like washing himself properly anymore. But what good would it do? He couldn't keep on fighting the insurmountable! No one had warned him in time, and now the town had spun him into its web and left the rest up to him. He was left to flounder through life alone!

Not a single person paid any attention to him. When the washing was done in the master's house, it never occurred to Jeppe's wife to do any of Pelle's clothes at the same time, and Pelle was not one to ask. The washerwoman was more thoughtful—she did some of his wash whenever she had a chance, even though it meant more work for her. But she was poor herself—the others just wanted to *use* him! Here in town there wasn't a single person who thought unselfishly enough about Pelle's welfare that they would open their mouth and tell him the truth. This was the feeling that could make a man weak in the knees—even if he was fifteen years old and dared take on the wildest bull! More than anything else, it was the feeling of being abandoned that broke down his resistance. He was helplessly alone among these people, a child who, as long as he was useful, was left to figure out how to defend himself from all that assaulted him on every side.

Pelle sat there watching sorrow come and go at will inside him while he listened to the life around him with half an ear. But suddenly he felt something in his vest pocket—money! He felt tremendously relieved, but he didn't jump up; he tiptoed inside the gate and counted it. One and a half kroner! He was just about to regard it as a gift from above, something Our Lord, in His mercy, had slipped him—but then he realized that it was Master's money. He had gotten it for the soles on a pair of women's shoes yesterday and hadn't remembered to turn it in, and Master had strangely enough forgotten to ask for it.

Pelle dunked his head in a basin out by the well, scrubbing himself so his blood burned. Then he pulled on his best clothes and stuck his bare feet into his shoes to avoid the embarrassing feeling of socks full of holes. He buttoned the rubber collar, for the last time, onto his collarless shirt. A little while later he stood in a shop looking at some big collars that were the latest thing and had four different sides that could be turned up. They covered the entire front so the shirt wasn't visible. Now his humiliation was over! For a moment he ran back and forth, taking big gulps of air; then he took his bearings and dashed off toward the dunes, where youth was playing in the summer night above the pale sea.

It was only a loan, after all! Pelle had a pair of shoes that needed resoling from a baker's boy who worked with Nilen. As soon as they were done, he would pay the money back. He could put the money in Master's room under the cutting board. Master would find it there, look at it with an amused expression, and say: "What the devil is this?" Then he would knock on the wall, deliver a long lecture to Pelle about his magical talents, and in high spirits send him off to get half a bottle of port.

But Pelle didn't get any money for the resoling. He had gotten half in advance for the leather, and it would be a long time before he got the rest because the baker's boy was a drunkard. But Pelle didn't question his own honesty; Master could feel as secure about his money as if it were in a bank. A couple of other times Pelle forgot to return the change—whenever some pressing need hung over him. They were all loans . . . until the golden time arrived. And that was never far off.

One day when he came home, Young Master was standing in the doorway, gazing out at the scudding clouds. He gave Pelle's shoulder a familiar squeeze as he reproached him: "Well, what happened, didn't the town treasurer pay for his shoes yesterday?"

Pelle turned bright red and his hand flew to his vest pocket. "I forgot all about it," he said in a low voice.

"Well, well, well," Master shook him goodnaturedly, "it's not that I mistrust you. But just for the sake of good order!"

Pelle's heart pounded wildly; he had been just about to spend the money on a pair of socks on the way home. Now what? And Master's good faith in him! All at once his behavior became apparent to him, with all its shameful betrayal. He was so upset that his innards felt like they were going to turn inside out. Up until now, through everything, he had guarded the feeling of his own worth. Now it collapsed; he couldn't imagine a more contemptible person on earth than himself! No one would ever be able to believe him after this, and he wouldn't be able to look anyone in the eye—not unless he went straight to Master and surrendered himself and his shame to Master's mercy or displeasure. He knew that no other redemption was possible.

But he wasn't sure that Master would be broad-minded and turn everything to the good; he had given up fairy tales, after all. Then he would just be chased off, maybe whipped in front of the courthouse— and then it would be all over for him.

Pelle decided to keep it to himself; for days he went about suffering under his own wretchedness. But then need seized him by the throat and pushed aside everything else. In order to get the most necessary things for himself he had to take the dangerous route: when Master gave him money for something or other, he would ask the merchant to put it on account.

And then one day everything collapsed on top of him. The others were about to tear down the house; they heaved his things out the window and called him a dirty animal. Pelle cried; he was sure that it wasn't him. It was Peter, who always kept company with the filthiest females—but no one would listen to him. Then he ran away, determined never to come back.

Emil and Peter caught up with him out on the dunes. Old Jeppe had sent them out after him, so that Pelle wouldn't do himself harm. He didn't want to go back with them, so they knocked him out and carried him, one at his head and the other at his feet. People stood in their doorways laughing and asking questions. The two boys explained, and it was a shameful journey for Pelle.

Then he fell ill. He lay under the tile roof reeling with fever—that's where they had flung his bed. "What, isn't he up yet?" said Jeppe in astonishment when he came out to the workshop. "Oh, he'll get up when he gets hungry." It wasn't the custom to give sick boys food in bed. But Pelle did not come downstairs.

One day Young Master excused himself and took some food up to him. "You're making a fool of yourself," snarled Jeppe. "You'll never keep anyone on that way." And his mother scolded him. But Master Andrès kept on whistling until he was out of their range.

Little Pelle lay there reveling in delirium. His little head couldn't stand so much; now it had gone into reverse, and he lay there taking in all that he had been deprived of.

Young Master sat with him up there a great deal and found out a thing or two. He wasn't very good at getting things done, but he had it arranged so that Pelle's wash would be done in the house. And he saw to it that word was sent to Lasse.

VIII

Jeppe was related to practically half the island, but he wasn't always equally interested in declaring his family ties. It was easy for him to start all the way back with the patriarch of his family and trace it down two hundred years, following individuals from country to town, across the sea, and back again, demonstrating that Andrès and the judge must be second cousins. But when some more humble person said: "Now how was it? Weren't my father and Master Jeppe cousins?" Jeppe would answer curtly: "That might be, but that relationship has gotten rather thin over the years."

"Well, what do you know! Then you and I are second cousins — and you're related to the judge too!" said Master Andrès, who liked to make other people happy. The poor man would look at him gratefully and think he had such kind eyes; it was a shame that he wouldn't have a chance to live.

Jeppe was also the oldest master craftsman in town, and the shoemaker with the biggest workshop. He was very skilled too — or rather, had been. He possessed old-fashioned skills in difficult areas, which progress was busy circumventing or eliminating altogether with new inventions. Elastic-sided boots and boots with tongues had made fulling unnecessary; but people still talked about this ancient art. And when some eccentric old codger came to the masters and demanded oiled boots without any newfangled nonsense, then they had to go to Jeppe — no one could full an instep the way he could. And when it came to treating the heavy greased leather for sea boots, Jeppe was the man. He was stubborn too, and would put his foot down obstinately against anything new when all the others were letting themselves be seduced by it. Thus he became even more the bearer of knowledge from the olden days, and there was great respect for him.

The boys were the only ones who didn't respect him; they did everything to bother the life out of him in return for his iron hand in the craft. Everything was aimed at teasing him, and they did the most ordinary things in a covert way just to make old Jeppe suspicious. So when he spied them and caught them doing something that turned out to be nothing at all, they had a great day.

"What's this? Where are you going without permission?" asked Jeppe when one of them got up to go out in the courtyard. He was always forgetting that times had changed. They didn't answer, and then he flew into a rage. "Respect here!" he shouted, stamping on the floor so hard that he almost had a fit.

Master Andrès slowly raised his head. "Now what's going on with Father?" he asked wearily. Then Jeppe spilled out all his rage against the new times.

When Master Andrès and the journeyman weren't present, the boys amused themselves by getting the old man's goat; that was easy enough, since he saw insubordination everywhere. Then he would grab a strap and start whacking away at them, while the sinner made the weirdest faces and emitted a peculiar clucking sound. "Take that, even though it pains me to resort to harsh measures!" Jeppe gasped. "And take that! And that! Because that's what it takes for the craft to survive." Then he planted something that might be vaguely reminiscent of a kick on the boy and stood there gasping for breath. "You're a difficult boy—will you admit it?"

"Yes, my mother used to break a broomstick to smithereens on me every day," replied Peter the scoundrel, sniffling.

"So, you see? But he can still be saved—the foundation is good!" Jeppe paced back and forth with his hands behind his back. The rest of the day he was in a solemn mood and did little things to wipe out permanent traces of the punishment. "It was for your own good!" he said in conciliation.

Jeppe was the first cousin of Crazy Anker, but preferred to ignore it. If the man was crazy that was his own affair, but he lived humbly by going around selling sand—a skilled citizen. Every day Anker's tall, thin figure could be seen on the street with a sack on the back of his flat neck; he wore blue denim clothes and white woolen stockings, and his face was as yellow as a corpse. There wasn't a scrap of meat on him. "That comes from thinking too much," people said. "Just look at the schoolmaster!"

At the workshop he never showed up with his sack of sand; he was afraid of Jeppe, who *was* the eldest in the family. But normally he went in and out of all the houses in his clunking clogs, and people bought from him, since they needed sand for their floors anyway and his was just as good as anyone else's. He spent almost nothing on his expenses; people claimed that he never ate a thing, but was nourished from within. For the few *skillings* he took in he bought paraphernalia for *the new age*; and what was left over he scattered from his high stairway during his grandiose moments. The boys always came running when his shout announced that the madness of the new age had come over him again.

He and Bjerregrav were childhood friends. As children they were together night and day, and neither of them wanted to do his duty and get married, although both could afford to support a wife and children. At the age when others are engrossed in pleasing women, those two went around with their heads full of nonsense: freedom and progress, and more of that deviltry that made people crazy. In those days a loathsome rabble-rouser lived with Bjerregrav's brother; he had been in prison on Christiansø for many years, but now the government had given him permission to spend the rest of his sentence here. His name was Dampe. Jeppe knew him from his school days in Copenhagen; he had set himself the goal of overthrowing God and the King. But it didn't work, because he was cast down like some Lucifer, and only out of sheer mercy was he allowed to retain his head. The two boys latched on to him, and he turned their heads with his poisonous words, so they started thinking about things that normal people ought to stay away from. Bjerregrav escaped from it with his skin more or less intact, but Anker had to pay for it with his sanity. Although they both enjoyed an ample income, it was poverty in particular that they brooded about—as if *that* could teach them anything special!

This was all at least forty years ago, of course. It was during the time when the mania for freedom flourished all over in many countries, with revolution and fratricide. It didn't turn out that badly here, though, because neither Anker nor Bjerregrav was very belligerent, but anyone could see that this town was far behind other places in the world. His town pride always ran away with Master Jeppe, though normally he had nothing but condemnation for the whole business. Still, it was easy for him to jump on Bjerregrav when talk turned to Anker's malady.

"Dampe, yes," said Jeppe testily, "he's the one who turned both your heads."

"You're wrong there," stammered Bjerregrav. "Anker only got his later—after King Frederik had granted us freedom. And though my abilities may be modest, I still have my reason, thanks and praise be to God!" Bjerregrav solemnly moved the fingers of his right hand to his lips; it seemed an almost invisible vestige of the sign of the cross.

"You and your reason!" Jeppe countered. "You throw your money away on the first tramp who comes down the road! And defend a disgusting rabble-rouser who never even went out in the daytime like normal people but only came out at night."

"Sure, because he was ashamed of human beings—he wanted the world to be made more beautiful!" Bjerregrav blushed with shyness at having said this.

But Jeppe went right through the roof with scorn. "So, potential convicts are ashamed of us decent people now, are they? Is that why he took his promenade at night? The world would certainly be beautiful, all right, if it was filled with people like you and Dampe."

The sad thing about Anker was that he was a fine craftsman. He had inherited the clockmaking trade from his father and grandfather, and the Bornholm grandfather clocks he made were probably known all over the world—orders arrived both from the island of Fyn and from Copenhagen. Back when the Constitution was first granted by the King, he behaved like a little child—as if we haven't always had freedom here on this island! It was *the new age,* he said, and in his frenzied glee he wanted to make an ingenious clock in honor of the new age: it would show the phase of the moon, the date, and what year and month you were in. He was skillful, and it all fell into place easily for him; but then he got the idea that the clock should show the weather too. Like so many others to whom God has given talents for safekeeping, he ventured too far out and wanted to compete with Our Lord Himself. But that was where he was stopped—the whole thing almost fell apart on him. For a long time he took it greatly to heart, but when the work was done he was happy anyway. He was offered a large sum of money for his masterpiece, and Jeppe advised him to strike while the iron was hot. But hysterical as he was, he still replied: "This can't be paid for with money. Everything else I make has a monetary value, but not this. Do you think somebody can buy *me*?"

He was long in doubt about what he ought to do with his clock, but then one day he went to Jeppe and said: "Now I know. The best shall have it—I'll send it to the King. He gave us the new age that the clock was made to show!" Anker sent the clock, and some time later he received 400 kroner paid out through the county treasury.

It was a great deal of money for that work, but Anker wasn't satisfied. He was probably expecting a letter of thanks in the King's own hand. He acted so oddly, and everything seemed to go wrong for him; little by little the derangement took up residence in his mind. He gave the money to the poor and went around grieving that the new age hadn't come after all. In this way he went and worked himself deeper and deeper into his madness; no matter how Jeppe scolded him and appealed to his reason, it did no good. Finally he went so far that he started imagining that *he* was the one who was supposed to create the new age—then he was happy once more.

There were three or four families in town who were utterly poverty-stricken, so far gone that even the sects didn't want anything to do with them. They gathered around Anker and heard God's voice in his shouts. "They have nothing to lose by seeking shelter with a madman," said Jeppe in scorn. But Anker didn't suspect a thing; he went his own way. Soon he was a prince in disguise and was betrothed to the King's eldest daughter—then the new age would surely come! Or when he was feeling more balanced, he would sit and work on an infallible clock that wouldn't just *show* the time but *be* time itself—the new age!

Now and then he would come to the workshop to show Master Andrès the progress he had made on his invention; he had developed a blind devotion to the master. Every New Year's, Young Master had to write a letter for him, proposing marriage to the King's eldest daughter, and see to it that it was placed in the proper hands. At long intervals Anker would come running over to hear whether there had been a reply, and at New Year's another proposal letter was sent off. Master Andrès had them all in his desk.

One evening just after the work was done, someone pounded on the workshop door, and the sound of someone marching in place could be heard out in the foyer. "Open up!" cried an official voice. "The prince is here!"

"Pelle, hurry up and open the door!" said Master.

Pelle threw the door open wide, and Anker marched in. He was wearing a paper hat with a waving plume on it, and epaulettes of paper fringe. His face was shining as he stood saluting and waited for the marching to die out. Young Master stood up in high spirits and shouldered arms with his cane.

"Your Royal Highness," he said, "how's it going with the new age?"

"It's not going at all," replied Anker, turning serious. "I'm missing the weights to keep the whole thing running." He stood looking at the floor; his brain was working mysteriously.

"They have to be gold, don't they?" Master's eyes were flashing, but he was all seriousness.

"They have to be made of *eternal material*," replied Anker reluctantly, "and it has to be invented first."

He stood there for a long time, his gray eyes staring into space, without saying a word. He didn't move; only behind his temples did he keep working, as if some worm were gnawing inside and wanted to get out. At last it became quite ominous; Anker's silence might be like the darkness that comes alive all around you. Pelle sat there with his heart pounding hard.

Then the madman went over and bent down to Young Master's ear. "Has there been a reply from the King?" he asked in a penetrating whisper.

"No, not yet, but I'm expecting one any day now. Anker may rest assured on that," Master whispered back. Anker stood there for a moment. It looked as if he was thinking too, but in his own way. Then he did an about-face and marched out.

"Go after him, Pelle, and see that he gets home all right," said Master. His voice sounded sad now. Pelle followed the clockmaker down the street.

It was Saturday evening, and the workers were on their way home from the big stone quarries and clay works that lay a few miles north of town. They arrived in ponderous groups, with their lunchbox on their back and a beer bottle in front to keep their balance. Their walking sticks banged hard on the cobblestones, and sparks flew from the iron cleats on their wooden clogs. Pelle recognized this weary gait, which looked as if the weight and weariness of the rock itself was engulfing the town. And he knew the sounds from the silent ranks, these rumbling sounds when one of them made an involuntary movement with his stiff limbs and had to groan in pain. But this evening they were tossing remarks to each other, and something that resembled a smile broke the crusty stone dust on their faces—it was the reflection of the shiny kroner that lay in their pockets after the week's toil. Some of the workers were on their way to the post office to renew their lottery ticket or ask to postpone payment; a few wanted to drop into a tavern, but would be caught at the last moment by a woman holding a child by the hand.

Anker stood still on the sidewalk with his face turned toward them as they passed by. He had removed his hat, and the huge plume hung down to the ground. He looked moved, and something seemed to well up in him that couldn't be expressed in words, but only emerged as stray incomprehensible sounds. The workers shook their heads sadly as they trudged on. One young man tossed off a flippant remark. "Keep your hat on, it's not a funeral!"

A few unfamiliar sailors came sauntering up the harbor hill. They zigzagged back and forth across the street, spitting into every street door and laughing uproariously. One of them walked straight ahead with his arms stretched out, knocked off Anker's hat, and kept going with his arm out in the air as though nothing had happened. But suddenly he whirled around.

"So, you want to make trouble?" he said, walking straight up to the madman, who cowered in fright. Then another sailor came running up and hit Anker behind the knees so he fell over. He lay screaming and kicking in terror, and the whole gang jumped on him.

The boys rushed in every direction to gather rocks and help Anker. Pelle stood jumping up and down as though the old fit were going to come over him again. Time after time he sprang forward, but something gave way inside him—the illness had taken away his blind courage.

There was one pale, skinny boy who was not afraid. He plunged into the middle of the sailors to drag them off the crazy man, who had turned quite wild beneath them. "Leave him alone, he's out of his mind!" shouted the boy, but he was tossed aside with his face bleeding. It was Morten, the brother of Jens at the workshop. He was so furious that he was crying.

A big man came lurching out of the darkness, muttering to himself as he walked. "Hurray!" yelled the boys, "here comes the Power!" But the man didn't hear a thing; he stopped next to the fighting men and stood there muttering, his giant form swaying back and forth over them.

"Father, help him!" shouted Morten. The man gave a foolish smile and slowly started pulling off his sweater. "Help him, please!" bawled the boy, beside himself, tugging at his father's arm. Jørgensen reached out his hand to pat his boy on the cheek, and then he saw that he had blood on his face. "Beat them up!" screeched the boy, possessed. A shudder went through the giant, almost as if a heavy burden was set in motion. Then he bent down, wobbling a little, and started tossing the sailors aside. One after another they stood for a moment, feeling the place where he had grabbed them—and then took off at a run down to the harbor.

Jørgensen managed to get the madman onto his feet and accompanied him home; Pelle and Morten followed behind holding hands. A current of strange satisfaction flowed through Pelle—he had seen the Power himself in action, and he had gained a friend!

From that day on the two boys were inseparable. Their friendship didn't need to gather strength at first; it stood there looming mightily over them, magically conjured out of their hearts. In Morten's pale, handsome face there was something nameless that could make Pelle's heart pound, and everyone lowered their voice when they talked to him. Pelle honestly didn't understand what could be attractive about himself, but he basked in this friendship, which fell like a refreshing rain over his harried mind.

Morten would show up at the workshop as soon as work was over, or else he would stand and wait up at the corner—they always ran when they were going to meet. When Pelle had to work late, Morten didn't go outside at all, but sat in the workshop and entertained him. He was devoted to reading and told Pelle all about what happened in his books.

Through Morten, Pelle also got closer to Jens and discovered that he had a lot of good qualities underneath his cowed exterior. Jens had that timid, broken spirit from which children could instinctively sense that he despised his home. Pelle had actually thought they were on the dole; he couldn't understand how a boy could suffer because his father was a giant the whole town was afraid of. Jens had a thick, wide nose, and he looked hard of hearing when anyone spoke to him. "He's gotten so many beatings from Father," said Morten. "Father doesn't like him because he's stupid." True, he wasn't intelligent, but he could whistle the most wonderful songs using only his lips, so that people would stop and listen as he passed by.

Pelle was on the alert for everything after his illness. He no longer indifferently let the breakers crash over him the way a child would, but exercised a selective capacity—he was looking for something. Everything had taken much too simple a form for him, and his dream of happiness had been constructed too palpably. It was bound to break easily, and then there would be nothing behind it that would endure. Now he needed to have a better foundation, he needed nourishment from farther away, and his soul was about to venture outward. He let his threads drift far out into the unknown, seeking a foothold. He had to set the goal of his yearning farther out into the boundless; he now took his awe away from the great mystical *out there*, where the contours of the mysterious face of God lay concealed.

For Pelle the God of the Bible stories and the sects had been merely a human being equipped with beard and justice, grace and all that; He was all right, but the Power was capable of being stronger. Until now Pelle had needed no god, but had participated dimly in the compassion that rises from the stinking heaps of rags and overshadows the heavens—in the lunatic dreams of the impoverished, which from a thousand bitter privations create a pilgrimage toward the promised land. But now he sought for what cannot be expressed—the word "millennium" had a strange sound in his ears.

Anker was indeed insane, since the others said so. When they laughed, Pelle laughed with them—but something was left over. Mainly, it rankled that he had laughed. Pelle himself also wanted to throw money from his tall stairway for people to scramble for when he got rich. And if Anker talked strangely about a time of happiness for all the poor—Papa Lasse's sighs had resounded with the same thing, as far back as he could remember. The depths of the boy's being were also stirred by the holy shudder that forbade Lasse and the others out there in the country from laughing at crazy people: because God's finger had touched them, so that their souls frequented places no one else could ever reach. Pelle felt the face of the unknown God staring at him from the fog.

He had changed since his illness; his movements had acquired more reflection, and pronounced features had sprung forth on his rounded face. The two weeks he was sick in bed had driven the worries from him but had buried them inside his character for good. He went about quietly, surrounding himself with solitude—and watched Young Master in an oddly persistent way. He had the impression that Master was testing him somehow, and that hurt him. Inside he knew that what had preceded the illness could never repeat itself, and he squirmed terribly under the suspicion.

One day he couldn't stand it any longer. He took the 10 kroner that Lasse had given him for a used winter coat and went in to Master in the cutting room and put the money on the table. Master looked at him with his astonished face, but in his eyes a light glimmered.

"What the hell is this?" he asked slowly.

"It's Master's money," said Pelle with his face turned away.

Master Andrès stared at him with his dreamy gaze. It was already coming as if from another world, and all at once Pelle understood what everyone said: that Young Master was going to die. Then he burst into tears.

But Master didn't realize it himself.

"What the devil—it doesn't matter at all!" he said, waving the bill in the air. "Oh, almighty God—so much money! You certainly aren't cheap!" He stood not knowing what to do, his hand resting on Pelle's shoulder.

"It *is* correct," whispered Pelle, "I've figured it out exactly. And Master mustn't mistrust . . . I'll never—"

Master Andrès made a deprecating gesture; he wanted to say something but suddenly had a coughing fit. "You little devil," he groaned, leaning heavily on Pelle; he was purple in the face. Then the vomiting started, and the sweat beaded up on his brow. He stood there a while, gasping, letting the life run back into him, and then handed Pelle the bill and shoved him out the door.

Pelle was crestfallen. Justice had not taken its course, and what would become of the atonement? He had looked forward eagerly to being rid of all the shame. But that afternoon Master called him in to the cutting room. "You know, Pelle," he said confidentially, "I was supposed to have my lottery ticket renewed but don't have any money. Do you think you could lend me that 10 kroner for a week?" So it went the way it should, after all; it was now his intention to shed all disgrace.

Jens and Morten helped him with it; there were three of them now, and Pelle felt as if he had a whole army backing him up. The world hadn't become smaller since his illness, or any less enticing because of the endless defeats of the past year. From the depths all the way up to his present station in life, Pelle had his certain knowledge—and it was bitter enough. Down there nothing lay in fog; the bubbles that occasionally rose up to the surface and burst did not imbue him with any mystical wonder about the depths. But he didn't feel oppressed either— what was in the depths didn't concern him. And above him the other hemisphere of the world arched in bright blue wonder and once again sounded its merry "Go ahead!"

IX

In his solitude Pelle had often wandered out to the little house by the churchyard where the Due family lived in two tiny rooms. There was always a kind of consolation in seeing familiar faces, but they were no help to him otherwise. Due was nice enough, but Anna thought only of herself and how they could best succeed. Due had a job as a driver for a teamster, and they seemed to have the basic necessities.

"We don't intend to be content with driving other people's horses," said Anna, "but you have to crawl before you can walk." She didn't long for the countryside.

"There's nothing out there for people of modest means who want a little more than gruel in their stomachs and a few rags on their backs. People treat you worse than the dirt they walk on, and there's no future at all. I'll never regret leaving the countryside."

Due did miss it, though. He was used to having a mile to his nearest neighbor, and here he could hear right through the thin wall when the neighbors kissed and argued and counted their *skillings*. "It's so cramped here too, and I miss the soil; the cobblestones are so hard."

"He misses some manure to tread into the house," joked Anna, "because it was the only thing there was plenty of out in the country. Here in town it's better for the children too. Out in the country, poor people's children don't have a chance to learn anything and get ahead, because they have to help earn the bread. It's wretched to be poor in the country."

"It's probably worse here," said Pelle bitterly, "because here only people who wear fancy clothes are important!"

"But here there are so many ways to make a living; if one thing doesn't work out, you can go try something else. Many a man has set off for town with his behind hanging out of his pants and is now a well-respected citizen! As long as you have the will and the desire! I've been thinking, the two boys ought to go to private school when they get older; knowledge is nothing to sneeze at."

"Why not Marie too?" asked Pelle.

"Her? Phooey! She's no good at learning anything. And after all, she's a female!"

Anna had set her sights high just like her brother Alfred. Her eyes flashed when she talked about it, and she probably didn't intend to let anything stand in her way. She was the one who made the decisions and the big speeches, she spoke her mind and was clever; Due just sat there smiling and looking good-natured. But it was said that deep inside he knew what he wanted. He never boozed, but came straight home from work. In the evening he would let all three children crawl all over him without making a distinction between his own two little boys and six-year-old Marie, who was Anna's dowry.

Pelle also liked little Marie a lot. She had thrived in the care of her grandparents, who loved children, but now she was skinny and stunted and had eyes that were much too experienced. She could look at you like a poverty-stricken mother who goes around grieving, and he felt sorry for her. When her mother was hard on her, he always remembered that evening at Christmas the first time they visited Kalle, when Anna came sneaking home limp and worn-out from crying, in a terrible state. Little Anna with the joyful, child-loving soul that everyone couldn't help liking: what had become of her?

One evening when Morten was busy, Pelle ran out there. Just as he was about to knock on the door he heard Anna shouting inside. Suddenly the door flew open and little Marie was dragged out into the hall. The child was crying pitifully.

"What's the matter now?" asked Pelle in his brisk way.

"What's the matter? Only that the child is sassy and won't eat, just because she doesn't get exactly the same food the others do. You have to go around weighing and measuring—for a brat like that—or else she sulks and refuses to eat anything. Is it any of her business what the others get? Is she going to start comparing? She is and will always be nothing more than illegitimate, no matter how much you try to hide it."

"She can't help that, can she?" said Pelle angrily.

"Help it? So maybe I can help it, eh? Is it my fault that she didn't become a farmer's daughter but had to settle for being illegitimate? You'd better believe that the neighbor women rub my nose in it. 'That one there doesn't have her father's eyes, does she?' they say, looking as friendly as cats. So I suppose I'll have to be punished for all my days because I wanted to get ahead a little and let myself be tempted onto a path that was a dead end. Oh, that little monster!" She clenched her fists toward the hallway, where the child's weeping could still be heard. "Here I go slaving away to keep the house nice and be like decent people, and then no one gives you a chance—all because once you were too gullible!" She was completely beside herself.

"If you're not nice to little Marie, then I'll tell Uncle Kalle," said Pelle threateningly.

She snorted with scorn. "Tell him? I wish to God you would! Then maybe he'd come and get her, and I'd sure be happy."

Then they heard Due stamping on the threshold and saying comforting words to the child. He came in holding the little one by the hand, flashed a warning glance at his wife, but said nothing. "There, there, it's all over now," he repeated to stop the child from sniffling, and dried the dirty tears from her cheeks with his big glove.

Anna coldly put out his food, muttering out in the kitchen. As he ate his supper, cold pork belly and rye bread, the child stayed between his knees and stared at him with her big eyes. "Knight," she said, smiling persuasively, "Knight!" Due placed a cube of pork belly on a piece of bread.

> There came a knight a-riding
> All on his snow-white mare mare mare!

he sang softly, making the food ride slowly down toward her mouth. "And then what?"

"Then"—chomp—"he rode in through the gate!" said the little girl, eating both horse and rider. As she chewed she kept her eyes riveted on him with that pitiful seriousness that was so sad to watch. But sometimes the rider would ride all the way down to her mouth, flail about with a jump, and vanish at a full gallop between Due's white teeth. Then she would laugh for a moment.

"It's no use feeding her bits and pieces," said Anna as she came in with coffee in honor of the visit. "She certainly gets all she can eat—she's not starving."

"She's hungry anyway," mumbled Due.

"Sure, because she's fussy—it's not good enough for her, our poor food. She's got big ideas, let me tell you. And whatever's wrong now will just get worse when she finds out you're backing her up!"

Due didn't reply. "So, you're all better now?" he said, turning to Pelle.

"What did you do today?" asked Anna, stuffing the long pipe for her husband.

"I went around in the heath with a planter from up top. I made a krone and a half tip."

"Let me have it right away!"

Due handed over the money and she put it in an old coffee can. "You have to muck out the stalls for the inspector tonight," she said.

Due moved wearily. "I've been on my feet since 3:30 this morning!"

"But I promised them, so we can't back out of it. And then I thought you could take care of the fall digging for them; now that the moon is out you'll be able to see all right—and then on Sunday too. If we don't take it, someone else will get the job. And they pay well."

Due said nothing.

"In a year or two, I'm thinking, you'll have your own horses and won't have to scrape together a living from strangers," she said, placing her hand on his shoulder. "Don't you think you ought to go and take care of the mucking out right away? Then it'll be over with. I also need a few logs chopped up before you go to bed."

Due sat and blinked his eyes wearily; now that he had eaten, the fatigue came over him. He could hardly see, he was so sleepy. Marie handed him his cap, and finally he got to his feet. He and Pelle went out together.

The house the Dues lived in was at the top of a long alley that dropped quite abruptly toward the sea. It was an old watercourse; during a heavy rainshower, the water would still run like a straight creek down between the hovels.

Down by the path to the beach they met a group of men setting out with lanterns in their hands; they were armed with heavy cudgels, and one carried a mace and wore an old leather hat—it was the night watchman. He went first, but behind the whole group walked the new daytime officer, Pihl, in his shiny uniform. He kept behind the others in order to protect his uniform and make sure that none of the watch crew fell behind. They were half drunk and were taking their time; every time they met someone they would stop and give a longwinded account of the reason why they were setting out.

The Power was at it again. All day he had been boozing, and the town constable gave orders to keep an eye on him. And quite rightly too; in his stupor he encountered shipowner Monsen on the church hill and started abusing him with both invective and blows: "Are you the one who's taking the bread out of a widow's mouth, eh? You tell her that the *Three Sisters* has shipwrecked and then take over her shareholdings for next to nothing? Out of pure sympathy, of course . . . What about it, you scoundrel? And all that was wrong with the ship was that it had sailed too well and would make too much profit. So you did the poor widow that favor, eh?" A scoundrel he called him, and with every question he struck the shipowner so he stumbled.

"We're all witnesses to it, and now he's going in the hole. No raggedy stonecutter is going to go around acting like the law of the land! Come along and help us, Due—you're strong!"

"I have no quarrel with him," said Due.

"The smartest thing for you to do would be to keep out of it," said one of the men sarcastically, "or else you might wind up feeling his paws." Then they trudged on with a scornful laugh.

"They're not happy about the job they've got to do," said Due smiling. "That's why they drank a tall *snaps* to get their courage up. The Power is a pig, but I wouldn't want to be the one he takes a swing at."

"Just so they don't catch him," said Pelle eagerly.

Due laughed. "They'll make sure to be everywhere he isn't. But he could pay attention to his work and stop making so much trouble. Let him drink himself into a stupor and sleep it off at home. He's a poor devil, after all, and ought to leave it to the big shots to act crazy!"

But Pelle had a different opinion about that. A poor man, yes, he had to walk quietly down the street and take off his cap for everyone, tradesmen and all. If anyone returned his greeting, then he felt proud and had to tell his wife about the great event when they went to bed: "The clerk even doffed his hat to me today—he really did!" But stonecutter Jørgensen only looked straight ahead when he was sober—and in his cups he would stomp with his big feet right through everything.

Pelle didn't care about the grubby judgment of the town. Out where he came from, strength was everything, and here was someone who could take Strong Erik and put him in his pocket. Pelle went around secretly measuring his wrists and lifting things that were much too heavy. He had nothing against being like the Power someday—a man who held the town's attention singlehandedly, both when he was in a rage and when he was out like a light. Pelle got dizzy at the thought that he was a friend of Jens and Morten, and he couldn't understand why they submitted so humbly to the town's judgment, when it wasn't the poorhouse that people could rub their noses in, but only the fact that their father was a man of strength. Jens cringed when he kept hearing his father's name on everyone's lips and refused to look them in the eye; in Morten's open expression it sat like a nameless pain.

One evening in the midst of the worst of it, they took Pelle home with them. They lived east of town by the big clay quarry where the town's garbage was dumped. Their mother warmed up supper in the wood-stove, and in the corner by the stove a wrinkled old woman sat knitting. It was a very poor household.

"Oh, I thought it was Father," said their mother, shivering. "Have any of you heard where he is?"

The boys told her the little they had heard; someone had seen him one place, another somewhere else. "People are so willing to keep us informed," said Jens bitterly.

"This is the fourth evening I've warmed up his supper in vain," their mother went on. "He usually looks in at home once in a while, even when he's in the worst condition—but he may show up yet." She tried to smile encouragingly but suddenly buried her face in her apron and broke into tears. Jens went around with his head bowed and didn't know what to do with himself. Morten put his arm around his weary mother's shoulders and spoke to her softly: "There, there, it's no worse than it's been so many times before," and he stroked her across her bony shoulder blades.

"No, but I had been looking forward to the day it would be over. For almost a whole year he hasn't made a move, but eats his food in silence when he comes home from work and then crawls into bed. He hasn't broken anything in all that time; he just sleeps and keeps sleeping. Finally I thought he had turned into an idiot, and for his sake I was happy; then he'd be free of those terrible thoughts. I really thought he had calmed down after all his defeats and wanted to take life as it came—just like the others, his peers. And now he rises up again in all his spite, and the whole thing starts all over again!" She wept miserably.

The old woman sat there shifting her sharp gaze from one to another; she resembled a wise bird of prey that has been put in a cage. Then she began to mumble, monotonously and without passion.

"You're a fine fool, here you go making an omelette on the fourth evening in a row for a boozing mate, and you're always content with a kiss and a hug. I wouldn't be the one to sweeten my husband's sleep if he treated my house and home so shamefully. I'd send him to bed dry-mouthed and hungry and let him get up the same way—then maybe he'd learn how to act properly. But there's no bite to you, that's the thing. You actually believe in his generosity."

"Should I put stones in his way, then? Who's going to be good to him when his poor head needs a soft pillow? Grandmother should realize how he needs a person who believes in him. And I have no other gift to give him."

"All right, you just get to work and wear yourself out so there can be something for Big Boy to wreck when the spirit comes over him! But now you should go to bed, and I'll take care of Peter and give him supper if he shows up. You must be exhausted, you poor thing."

"It's an old proverb that a man's mother isn't good to her son's wife—but it's not true of you, Grandma," the boys' mother said kindly. "You always take my side even though it isn't necessary. But now *you* should go to bed! It's long past your bedtime, and I'll take care of Peter. He's so easy, as long as he knows it's someone who means him well."

The old woman acted as if she hadn't heard that and went on knitting. The boys remembered that they had something in their pockets: a paper cone of beans, a little rock candy, and some rolls.

"You always go and fritter away your precious *skillings* on me," said their mother reproachfully, and put on water for coffee as her eyes shone with gratitude.

"They probably don't have any sweethearts to waste them on yet," said the old woman dryly.

"Grandma is so peevish tonight," said Morten. He had taken off her glasses and was looking into her gray eyes, smiling.

"Peevish—you can be sure of that! But time flies, I can tell you, and here a person sits on the edge of the grave and waits for her own offspring to step forth and do something great, but nothing ever happens! My powers are squandered and run like creek water into the sea, and the years are wasted—or is what I'm saying a lie? Everyone wants to be the boss, and no one wants to carry the sack; then they twist and climb on each other's backs to get higher up that fir tree. And here in town it's supposed to be elegant, but poverty and filth are in every nook and cranny. I think the good Lord will soon say He's had enough of this! Not an hour goes by that I don't curse the day I let myself be lured away from the peasant land. Out there the food grew in the fields for poor folks too, as long as they took it as it fell. But here a poor man has to show up with his *skilling* in his fist just so he can put a little greenery in his soup. If you've got money, you can have it; if you don't, you can hoof it! Yes, that's the way it is. But I had to come to town—to share in Peter's good fortune! Things looked so promising, and fool that I am, I've always assumed that I'd see my own blood prevail. And now I sit here like some beggar princess. Things have turned out so well, since I'm the mother of the biggest drunkard in town."

"Grandmother shouldn't talk that way," said the boys' mother.

"All right, all right, but I *am* tired of everything, yet I don't dare think about dying! I hardly dare go to bed, because who will keep Peter in check? The Power!" she said in scorn.

"Grandmother can go to bed in peace. I can handle Peter best when I'm alone with him," said the wife. But the old woman didn't budge.

"Get her to leave, Morten," whispered the mother, "you're the only one she listens to." Morten talked with the old woman for a long time, until he persuaded her to go; he had to promise to go along and tuck the bedclothes around her feet.

"So we got her out of here at last," said the mother with relief. "I'm so afraid that Father will forget someday that she's his mother. He doesn't notice anything when he gets like that, and she has no intention of yielding—it's force against force. But now I think you two should go out where the young people are and not hang around here!"

"We're going to stay and see if Father shows up," declared Morten.

"What's gotten into you? You can say hello to him anytime. Now go, do you hear? Father would rather see me alone when he comes home happy like this. Then maybe he'll take me in his arms and swing me around, strong as he is, so I swoon like a young girl. 'Whoopee, girl, here comes the Power!' he'll say, laughing out loud the way he did in his roaring youth. Yes, when he's got enough in his head, he often gets so strong and merry again like when he was in his prime. It makes me happy, no matter how briefly it lasts. But it's not something for you to see—you should go." She gave them a pleading look, and jumped when she heard the door rattle. Outside it was terrible weather.

It was only her youngest coming home from work. She couldn't be more than ten or eleven years old and quite tiny, although she looked older. Her voice was hard and rasping, her little body already coarse and etched with toil. Not a spot on her reflected any light; she looked like some dirt-covered creature that has wandered up to the surface of the earth. She walked across the room like a dead person and dropped into Grandmother's chair, and there she sat drooping to one side, her face twitching now and then.

"She's got that back problem, you know," said the mother, stroking her thin, filthy hair. "She got it from carrying around the doctor's little boy, he's so big and fat. But as long as the doctor himself doesn't say anything, there can't be any danger. —Well, you've had to go out working early in life, my child, but at least you're getting good meals and learning something. —And she's clever too, she takes care of the doctor's three children all by herself! The oldest one, who's as old as she is, has to be dressed and undressed too. Those rich folks never learn to take care of themselves."

Pelle stared at her with curiosity. He had been subjected to a good deal himself; but to turn himself into a cripple by dragging around children that were even heavier than he was—no one was going to make him do that. "Why does she have to carry around those overfed kids?" he asked.

"They have to be taken care of," replied the woman, "and their mother, who you'd think would do it, doesn't seem to want to! At least they're paying for it."

"If it was me, I'd let the kids fall—I'd probably drop them," said Pelle briskly.

The girl turned wearily to look at him, and a spark of interest seemed to glow in her gaze. But her face retained its ironclad indifference. It was impossible to say what she was thinking, her expression was so hard and experienced.

"You shouldn't be teaching her bad things," said the mother. "She's going to have enough to struggle with; she has a tough spirit.—And now you should go to bed, Karen." She caressed her again. "Father won't want to see you like this if he comes home with a headful... He loves you so much," she added helplessly.

Karen shrank away from the caresses with no change in her expression; silently she went up to the attic where she had her bed. Pelle hadn't heard a word out of her.

"That's the way she is," said the mother, shivering. "Not even a good night. Nothing affects her anymore, good or bad. She's become wise to the world too soon. And I have to watch out not to let Father see her when he's in that mood. He can act like a wild animal, both to himself and others, when he gets an eyeful of how disfigured she's become." She looked nervously at the clock. "Now go, do you hear! It would really make me happy if you all went." She was just about to cry.

Morten got up reluctantly, and the others followed his example. "Now put your collars up around your ears and run!" said their mother, buttoning them up. The October storm was thumping against the house and lashing hard rain on the windowpanes.

As they said goodbye there was a new noise outside as the outer door banged against the wall; they heard the storm come in and fill the entryway. "Oh, now it's too late," the mother complained reproachfully. "Why didn't you leave before?" They could hear a vague rustling out there, like a huge animal sniffing up and down the chinks in the door and searching for the door handle with its wet paws. Jens wanted to run over and open the door. "No, don't!" shouted his mother in despair, shoving in the bolt—she stood straight, shaking all over. Pelle started shivering too; he felt as though the storm was lying in wait out in the hallway like an enormous, shapeless creature, panting with heavy satisfaction, licking itself dry as it waited for them.

The wife stood bent forward, listening in tense distraction. "What's he going to come up with now?" she mumbled distantly. "He's such a rogue!" She sobbed it out. She seemed to have forgotten the boys for the moment.

Then the outer door was slammed and the monster pulled itself up onto all fours with wet slapping sounds and started calling, with a familiar roar. The wife writhed in distress, waving her hands before her in confusion, then she slapped them to her face. But now the giant beast became impatient, banging sharply on the door and growling in warning. The wife cringed as though she wanted to throw herself down on all fours and reply. "Oh no, no!" she wailed, and then checked herself. Then the door burst in at his heavy blow, and the bear tumbled in across the threshold and fumbled for her in his clumsy way. He held his head back in astonishment that his little friend didn't leap toward him, barking hotheadedly in greeting. "Peter, Peter—the boys!" she whispered, bending down over him, but he slapped her to the floor and lay a heavy paw on her, growling. She tore herself loose from him and got up onto a chair.

"Who am I?" he asked in a thick, troll-like voice, getting up to face her.

"The great Power!" She still had to smile at the way he made himself so big and gruff.

"And you?"

"The happiest woman in the world." But then her voice turned to sobbing again.

"And where is the Power going to sleep tonight?" He grabbed for her breast.

She jumped up with burning eyes. "You animal, oh, you animal!" she shouted and hit him in the face, red with shame.

The Power wiped his face in astonishment with every blow. "We're just playing," he said. Then he gave a start as he caught sight of the boys, who were cowering in a corner. "So, is that you standing there?" he said, laughing idiotically. "Well, Mother and I are just playing a little, aren't we, Mother?"

But his wife had run outside; she was standing under the thatched eaves, sobbing.

Jørgensen paced restlessly back and forth. "She's crying!" he muttered. "There's no gumption to her—she should have married a farm boy. What the devil—it's got to come out! It's sitting inside my head and pressing just like somebody was clamping the ferrule down on my brain. Let go, Power! Just let go, then you'll be freed of it, that's what I say every day. No, let me be! is what I say. You've got to control yourself or else she'll go and cry. And she's never done anything but good! But damn it, it's got to come out! Then you go to bed and say: Thank God that day's over with . . . and that day, and that one! They stand there staring, waiting. But let them wait, nothing's going to happen—because now the Power has got hold of himself! And then all of a sudden it sneaks up behind you: Lash out! Right in the midst of them! Tell that rabble to go to hell! It's no wonder a man's got to drink—to keep his powers in check . . . So, there you sit—can't any of you lend me a krone?"

"I can't," replied Jens.

"No, not you. Only a real blockhead would expect anything from you. Haven't I always said: He takes after the wrong side of the family, he's like his mother? You've all got the heart, but you don't have the talents. What do you know how to do anyway, Jens? You get nice clothes from the master and you're treated like a son—and maybe you'll end up taking over the business as his son-in-law. And why not, if I might ask? Your father is probably as well respected as Morten's, isn't he?"

"Morten isn't going to be any son-in-law either—since his master doesn't have a daughter," muttered Jens.

"Oh, really? But he could have had a daughter, couldn't he? So there we have it. It's obvious from your answer—you're not sharp. Morten's got it up here!" He tapped his brow.

"So why don't you stop hitting me in the head?" replied Jens
sullenly.

"In the head? Of course! But intelligence dwells in the head; that's
probably where you have to put it in. What good does it do, I ask you,
if you make a fool of yourself with your head and I start hitting you
from behind? You don't need any intelligence for that, do you? But I
think it's helped anyway—you've gotten a lot smarter. For instance,
it wasn't dumb at all to say: 'Why don't you stop hitting me in the
head?' " He nodded in acknowledgment. "No, here's a head that can
make things complicated—there are knots of intelligence in that wood,
eh?" The boys had to feel the top of his head.

He stood like a swaying tree and listened with shifting expressions to
his wife's sniffling subsiding; she was sitting on the stove just outside
the door now. "She's just crying," he said sympathetically. "That's only
women's way of having fun. Life has been hard on us, and she hasn't
gotten used to the adversity, poor thing. I can tell you that it makes me
want to smash the woodstove to smithereens"—he grabbed a heavy
chair and swung it around in the air—"whenever she starts bawling.
She blubbers about everything. But when my ship comes in I'm going to
take another wife too—one who knows how to entertain—because this
is a bunch of crap. Could she have elegant strangers to dinner and speak
in a genteel way? Phooey! What the hell good does it do for me to raise
us out of the mud? But I'm leaving—it's no fun here."

His wife came in quickly. "Oh, don't go, Peter! Stay here!" she
begged him.

"Am I supposed to stay here and listen to your blubbering?" he said
sullenly, twitching his shoulder away. He looked like a big, good-
natured boy being difficult.

"I'm not blubbering, I'm happy—if only you'll stay!" she clung to
him and smiled through her tears. "Look at me—don't I love you? Stay
with me, Power . . ." She breathed hotly in his ear. She had to wipe
away her worry and straighten up, flushing prettily.

The Power looked at her affectionately, gave a silly laugh as if he
were being tickled, and let her pull him back and forth; he imitated her
whisper and was sparkling with good humor. Then he sneaked up to her
ear with his lips, and as she listened he tooted right into her ear so she
jumped with a little shriek. "Stay now, you big boy," she said, laughing.
"I won't let you go, because I can still hold on to you." But he smiled
and squirmed away from her and ran off without his hat.

For a moment it looked as though she was going to run after him,
but then her hands dropped to her sides. "Let him go," she said wearily,

"then whatever happens will happen. There's nothing to do about it anyway; I've never seen him so dead drunk before. I know, you're looking at me, but remember that liquor has a different effect on him— he's got so much to worry about!" She said it with a kind of pride. "And he laid a hand on the shipowner to punish him—even the constable doesn't dare touch that man. The dear Lord Himself couldn't be more honorable than he is."

X

The dark evenings had arrived with the long hours of work by lamp-light. The journeyman had left by dusk; there wasn't much for him to do. In November the indentured apprentice finished his training. He was placed alone in the master's room. There he sat for a whole week, working on his journeyman's piece: a pair of sea boots. No one was allowed to disturb him, and it was all very exciting. When the boots were done and had been inspected by several masters, they were filled with water and hung up from the ceiling. There they hung for a few days, to test whether they were watertight. Then Emil was solemnly declared a journeyman and had to pay for a round at the workshop. He drank a toast with Little Nikas so they would be on a first-name basis, and in the evening he went out on a binge with the other journeymen of the town—and came home dead drunk. Everything went the way it was supposed to.

The next day Jeppe came out to the workshop. "Well, Emil, now that you're a journeyman, what are your plans? You're going out on the road, aren't you? It's good for a new-baked journeyman to get out and take a look around and learn something."

Emil didn't answer but began to gather his things. "All right, it's not important, we're not throwing you out, you know. You can come and get shelter and warmth here at the workshop until you find something else; those are generous terms, believe me. No, things were different when I finished *my* apprenticeship—then it was a kick in the behind and out the door you go! And that's good for young people—that's good for them."

He could sit in the workshop and list all the masters on the island who had journeymen working for them. But it was practically a joke;

new journeymen were never hired. On the other hand, he and the others knew exactly how many new-baked journeymen would be put out on the streets this fall.

Emil wasn't disheartened. Two evenings later they accompanied him down to the steamer bound for Copenhagen. "There's plenty of work there!" he said, beaming with joy.

"You have to promise to send for me in a year's time," said Peter, who would be finished with his apprenticeship by then. Yes, Emil promised he would.

But before the month was out, they heard that Emil was back again. He was probably too embarrassed to show himself. Then one morning he came slinking into the workshop, full of shame. Yes, he had found work—several places, but he'd been fired at once. "I hadn't learned a thing," he said despondently. He wandered aimlessly for a while, came and got shelter and warmth at the workshop, and was allowed to sit there with some repair work he had managed to get hold of. He kept himself afloat in this way until Christmas, but then he gave up everything and brought shame upon his craft by taking an ordinary laborer's job at the harbor.

"I've wasted five years of my life," he was quick to repeat whenever they ran into him. "Get out while there's still time. Otherwise it will go the same for you." He didn't come to the workshop anymore, out of fear of Jeppe, who was mad at him because he had disgraced the craft.

It was cozy in the workshop when the fire was crackling in the stove and the dark was tearing fiercely at the naked black windows. The workbench had been moved in from the window so there was room for all four of them: Master with his book and the three boys, each with his repair work. The smoking lamp hung over the middle of the workbench, just managing to make a slight dent in the darkness. The scant light it gave was sucked in by the big glass globes, which gathered it up and spread it out over their work. The lamp swayed slightly, and the spot of light floated like a jellyfish, back and forth, so that every other second their work would be in darkness. Then the master would swear and stare painfully into the light.

It just made the others' eyes ache, but the master grew sick from the dark. He kept pulling himself up with a shudder. "Ugh! How disgustingly dark it is in here. It's like being in the grave! Can't we get any light tonight?" Then Pelle would fiddle with the lamp, but it didn't get any brighter.

When old Jeppe came shuffling in, Master Andrès would look up without hiding his book; that meant he was in a fighting mood. "Who is it?" he asked, straining to see in the darkness. "Oh, is that you, Father?"

"Is something wrong with your eyes?" asked the old man sarcastically. "Do you need some eyewash?"

"Father's eyewash . . . no, thanks anyway. But this damned lighting! You can't even see your hand in front of your face."

"Yawn and your teeth will light things up," Jeppe sneered. They were forever fighting about the light.

"I'll be damned if we're not the only ones on the whole island who sew with such miserable lighting—just so Father knows that."

"I never heard complaints about the lamp in my day," replied Jeppe. "And better work was done by the light of a glass globe than they do now with their artificial inventions. But they have to waste money. Youth today knows no greater pleasure than to throw money away on modern junk."

"Yes, in Father's day—everything was *so* lovely," said Master Andrès. "That was when the angels walked around invisible."

During the course of the evening one person after another would drop by to bring news and ask for the latest gossip. And when Young Master was in a good mood, they would stick around. He was fire and soul incarnate, as old Bjerregrav would say—he could explain so many mysteries from his reading.

Whenever Pelle lifted his eyes from his work he would be blinded. Down there on the floor of the workshop where baker Jørgen and the others sat and talked, he saw only dancing spots of light with his own work hovering in the middle, and he saw only the laps of his colleagues. But inside the glass globe the light moved like playful fire; inside there was a whole world in endless flux.

"Well, tonight it's shining just fine," said Jeppe when one of them glanced at the lamp.

"It is, is it?" replied Master Andrès indignantly.

But one day the boy from the dry-goods store brought something in a big basket—a hanging lamp with a circular burner. And when it was dark the dry-goods shopkeeper himself came over to perform the first lighting and show Pelle how to handle this wonder. He proceeded very cautiously and meticulously. "Because it *could* explode, you know," he said, "but you'd have to be turning the mechanism pretty hard. As long as you treat it sensibly and with care, there's no danger."

Pelle stood by and held the glass while the others pulled back their heads from the workbench, and Young Master stood down on the floor, fidgeting. "Damned if I want to shoot up to heaven alive," he said with his amusing turn of phrase. "How the devil do you dare, Pelle? You're a gutsy fellow!" And he looked at him with his big, astonished eyes with their double layer of jest and seriousness.

Finally the light shone from the lamp; on even the farthest shelf up toward the ceiling you could count all the lasts. "It's like an enormous sun," said Young Master, putting his hands to his cheeks. "Upon my soul, I think it's warming up the air." He was quite flushed and his eyes glittered.

Old Master kept his distance until the shopkeeper had left. Then he came rushing up. "So, you haven't gone up in smoke yet?" he asked in great amazement. "That's a hideous light it makes—a really ugly light, disgusting! It doesn't shine properly; it cuts into your eyes. Well, go ahead and ruin them!"

But for the others the lamp meant an influx of life. Master Andrès basked in its rays. He was like a bird drunk with the sun; sitting there he would suddenly burst into cheers. And to the neighbors who came to see the lamp and discuss its merits he would wax expansive in great speeches, so the light multiplied many times over for them. They came often and were quick to stay. Master shone and the lamp shone; like insects people were drawn to the light—the lovely light!

Twenty times a day Young Master would be out in the doorway to the street, but he would come right back inside and sit down to read on the platform, his boot with the high wooden heel sticking out behind him. He spat a great deal; Pelle had to change the sand next to him every day.

"It must be some kind of animal that's sitting and gnawing in your chest, don't you think?" said Uncle Jørgen when Andrès's cough was bad. "You look so healthy otherwise. You'll get over it before we know it."

"Yes, by God!" Master laughed merrily between two attacks.

"Just give it a rough filing, then it'll croak for sure. It's now, when you're almost thirty, that you should be able to beat it. Even if you gave it cognac!"

Jørgen Kofod often came tramping over in his big wooden clogs, and Jeppe would complain. "You wouldn't think you had a shoemaker for a brother," he snapped. "We get all our rye bread from you."

"But when I can't keep my feet warm in those cursed leather shoes! And I'm full of rheumatism—it's sheer hell." The big baker squirmed pitifully.

"That rheumatism must be awful," said Bjerregrav. "I've never had any myself."

"Tailors don't get rheumatism," replied baker Jørgen scornfully. "A tailor's body would be too cramped to take up lodgings in. It takes twelve tailors to make a pound as far as I know."

Bjerregrav didn't answer.

"Tailors have their own backwards world," continued the baker. "I wouldn't dare compare myself to them. A deformed tailor is one who has all his faculties intact."

"Oh, tailors have always been just as good as rye-bread bakers," stammered Bjerregrav feverishly. "Any farmer's wife can bake rye bread."

"Ha, just as good—I'll be damned if I believe that. When a tailor sews a cap he has cloth left over for a pair of pants for himself; that's why tailors are always dressed so fancy." The baker was talking off the top of his head.

"It's millers and bakers who are known for their cheating." Old Bjerregrav appealed to Master Andrès, shaking with fury. But Young Master stood and looked cheerfully from one to the other, his lame leg swinging freely.

"Nothing is enough for a tailor. 'I take up too much space!' said the tailor as he suffocated inside a pea. As the saying goes: 'It takes no more space than a tailor in hell!' Those are some men! We've all heard about the woman who gave birth to a full-grown tailor without even realizing that she was in the family way."

Jeppe laughed. "All right, now stop, both of you, if neither one of you has anything sensible to say."

"No, and I have no intention of trampling a tailor to death if it can be avoided. They're not easy to see." Baker Jørgen cautiously lifted his big wooden clogs. "But they're not real men—or are there any tailors in town who have been across the sea? There weren't any men present either when the tailors were created: a woman was standing in the draft of a street door, and she got pregnant with a tailor." The baker just couldn't stop once he got started teasing someone; now that Søren had gotten married his good humor had returned.

Bjerregrav couldn't stand it. "Say whatever you like about tailors," he finally managed to put in, "but rye-bread bakers aren't considered craftsmen—no more than washerwomen are! Tailors and shoemakers, now those are proper trades—with professional tests and everything."

"Well now, a shoemaker, that's something entirely different," Jeppe opined.

"There are just as many sayings about you as about us." Bjerregrav blinked his eyes miserably.

"Is that so? Well, it can't be more than a year ago that Master Klausen got married to a carpenter's daughter! But who can a tailor take for a wife? His own maid."

"To think that Father bothers," sighed Master Andrès. "One person is just as good as the next."

"Now you're turning everything upside down! But I want my craft respected. Now there are vagrant agents and woolen merchants and other rabble setting up shop in town and talking big, but in the old days craftsmen were the backbone of the country. Even kings had to learn a craft then. I did my apprenticeship in Copenhagen itself, and at that workshop a prince had learned the trade. But the devil take me if I've ever heard of any king that went in for tailoring."

They could keep on like that. But just as they were sitting there squabbling, the door opened and Wooden-Leg Larsen clumped inside and filled the workshop with fresh air. He was wearing his knit hat and blue pea jacket. "Good evening, children!" he said cheerfully, heaving a pile of leather holsters and mismatched boots onto the platform.

They all grew lively. "Here we have the music man! Welcome home! Did you make any money this summer?"

Jeppe examined the five boots, all for the right foot, one by one, pulling the upper leather away from the edge and holding the heel and sole up to eye level. "A bungler got hold of these," he grumbled and then started in on the holsters for the wooden leg. "So, is the layer of felt working?" Larsen had a tendency to freeze on his amputated foot.

"I haven't felt any foot-chill since."

"Foot-chill!" The baker slapped his thigh and laughed.

"Yes, say what you like, but every time my wooden leg got wet, I caught a cold."

"Well, I'll be damned," exclaimed Jørgen, rolling his enormous chest like a hippopotamus, "that's amazing."

"There are many amazing things on this earth," stammered Bjerregrav. "The time my brother died, my watch stopped at the very same instant. He had given it to me."

Wooden-Leg Larsen had been all over the kingdom with his barrel organ and had tales to tell. About the railroad trains that drove so fast that the countryside ran in circles around itself, about the huge shops in the capital, and about the amusement parks.

"I don't care about anything else, but this summer I'm taking a trip to Copenhagen to work!" said Master Andrès.

"Jutland—they have so many shipwrecks there!" said the baker. "It's supposed to be nothing but sand, the whole place. I've heard tell that the land shifts eastward—right under their feet. Is it true that they have a post you have to scratch yourself on before you get to sit down?"

"My sister has a son who's married and lives with the Jutlanders," said Bjerregrav. "You didn't run into him, did you?"

The baker laughed. "Tailors are so big—they go around with the whole world in their vest pocket! What about the land of Fyn? Were you there too? That's where the women are so accommodating! I was anchored off Svendborg once to take on water, but there wasn't any time to go ashore." It sounded like a sigh.

"Can you really stand to travel around so much?" asked Bjerregrav anxiously.

Wooden-Leg Larsen looked with contempt at the club foot Bjerregrav had been born with—he had gotten his own infirmity near Helgoland with an honest bullet. "When a man has his faculties," he said, spitting out across the platform.

Then the others had to tell him about what had happened in town during the summer, about the Finnish three-masted bark that had run aground up north, and about the Power who had gone on a rampage. "But now he's sitting and twiddling his thumbs behind lock and key."

Bjerregrav latched onto the name and called it blasphemous. "There is only one Power—as it is written, and woe to us if He came down upon our heads."

But Wooden-Leg Larsen didn't think that power had anything to do with God but was made of earthly material. Over there it was used to pull machines—instead of horses.

"It's my opinion that power means females," said baker Jørgen, "because they damn well control the world. And God help anyone when *they* get going! But what do you think, Andrès, since you have so much book-learning?"

"The power is the sun," said Master Andrès. "It rules all life, and science has discovered that all power emanates from it. If it fell into the sea and was cooled off, the whole earth would turn into a clump of ice."

"That's right, because it's the sea that is the power," declared Jeppe triumphantly. "Or do you know anything else that can break down and pull everything to it the way the sea can? And from the sea we receive everything back again. That time I was in Málaga—"

"Well, that's true too," agreed Bjerregrav, "because most people find nourishment in the sea, and many find death too. And the wealthy men we have—they've gotten their money from the sea."

Jeppe straightened up and his glasses flashed. "The sea can carry whatever it likes, stones and iron, even though it's soft itself! The heaviest burdens can travel on its back. And then all of a sudden it can suck everything in. I've seen ships sail their prow straight into the waves and disappear, when it was so commanded."

"I'd like to know whether all the countries are floating or whether they're standing on the bottom of the sea. Don't you know that, Andrès?" asked Bjerregrav.

Master Andrès thought they were standing on the sea bottom, but Uncle Jørgen didn't think so. "Because the sea is so enormous," he said.

"Yes, it's big all right, because now I've been over the whole island," said Bjerregrav matter-of-factly. "But I've never found a single place where I couldn't see the ocean. All the parishes of Bornholm border on the sea too! But it doesn't have any power over the farmers, does it? Since they belong to the soil?"

"The sea has power over all of us," said Larsen. "Some people, who have traveled it for years, deny it; then they suddenly become seasick in their old age, and that's a warning. That's why skipper Andersen retired. And it attracts some people all the way from up top in the farming country! I went to sea with some men like that who spent their whole lives up there looking at the sea but had never been down to it. And then one day the Devil seized them; they dropped the plow and ran down to the sea and hired on. They weren't the worst sailors, either."

"That's right," said baker Jørgen, "and everybody in this country has traveled by sea. There are Bornholmers on every ocean as far as the vessels can sail. I've also met those who had never been near the sea before, and yet they were so at home on it. While I was sailing the brig *Klara* for skipper Andersen I had a man like that as my navigating apprentice. He had never been swimming; but one day as we lay at anchor and the others were out swimming, God help me if he didn't throw himself out there as if into his mother's arms—he thought that swimming would just come naturally. He went straight to the bottom of the sea and was half dead before we pulled him out."

"Only the Devil understands the sea," exclaimed Master Andrès, short of breath. "It circles around incessantly, and it can rise up onto its hind legs and stand there like a wall, even though it's liquid! And I also read in a book that there's so much silver in the sea that every person on earth could be rich."

"Oh, good heavens!" exclaimed Bjerregrav. "Oh, but I've got it! Could it have come from all the ships that went down? Yes, the sea is truly the power!"

"It's ten o'clock," said Jeppe. "And the lamp is going out—that devilish thing!" Then they hastily broke up, and Pelle put out the lamp.

But long after he had put his head down on his pillow, his mind was still going. He had swallowed everything, and the images swarmed around in his brain like baby birds in a crowded nest, pushing and shoving to find a spot to settle down. The sea was strong; now, in the wintertime, its pounding against the rocks was constantly in his ears. But Pelle wasn't sure that he was afraid of it! He harbored an unconscious unwillingness to set limits on himself, and the power they were quarreling about ultimately dwelled inside him, like a bright feeling of being indomitable despite all defeats.

Sometimes this feeling had to become palpable and carry him through the day. One noontime he was sitting and working after having gulped down his food in five minutes as usual. The journeyman was the only one who allowed himself a short noon break; he was sitting and reading the paper. Suddenly he raised his head and looked at Pelle in amazement. "What on earth is this? Lasse Karlsson—that's your father, isn't it?"

"Yes," replied Pelle in a thick voice, and the blood raced up to his cheeks. Was there something about Papa Lasse in the paper? Not for anything bad, was it? He must have drawn special attention to himself in some way with his farming. Pelle was about to suffocate with excitement but didn't dare ask; and Little Nikas just sat there looking remote. He had assumed Young Master's expression.

But then he read aloud: "Lost! A louse with three tails has run off and can be returned for a good reward to farmer Lasse Karlsson, Heath Farm. Used rye bread available at the same place!"

The others howled with laughter, but Pelle's face turned ashen gray. With one leap he was over the workbench and had Little Nikas under him on the floor. There Pelle lay, crushing his fingers around his neck, trying to strangle him—until he was pulled away. Jens and Peter had to hold him while the strap did its job.

And yet he was proud of himself. What did a couple of beatings matter compared to the fact that he had knocked the journeyman to the ground and punched a hole in the oppressive respect they demanded? Just let them try coming with their lying innuendoes about *that* time— or try to ridicule Papa Lasse! Pelle had no intention of proceeding with caution.

And circumstances proved him right. They showed more consideration for him in the future: they didn't want him and his tools in their faces, even if they could beat him up afterwards.

XI

It was desolate in the skipper's garden: trees and bushes had lost their leaves, and from the workshop you could see right through all of it, across other yards, all the way over to the back of the houses along Østergade. There was no playing there anymore. The paths lay neglected in frost and slush. The coral blocks and the big conch shells, which sang so multifariously with their rosy mouths and fish teeth about the great oceans, had been taken inside because of the frost.

He saw Manna often enough. She would come rushing into the workshop with her schoolbag or her skates; a button had popped off, or a skate heel had worked loose. There was a fresh breeze in her hair and on her cheeks, which the cold turned rosy. "There's some blood there, all right!" Young Master would say, looking his fill at her; he laughed and made jokes whenever she dropped by. But Manna stood by Pelle's shoulder and plopped her foot into his lap so he could button her shoe. Sometimes she pinched him in secret and looked angry; she was jealous of Morten. But Pelle didn't understand a thing. Morten's kind, wise nature had completely subjugated him and taken control. Pelle was unhappy whenever he had an hour to spare and Morten wasn't around. Then he ran all over town, his tongue hanging out of his mouth, searching for him; everything else was unimportant.

One Sunday morning while he was sweeping snow in the courtyard they were on the other side of the wall, building a snowman.

"Oh, Pelle!" they shouted, clapping their mittens. "Come over here, why don't you? Then you can help us build a snow hut. We'll seal up the door and light Christmas candles—we have the stumps of some. Come on, all right?"

"As long as Morten can come too. He'll be here pretty soon."

Manna wrinkled her nose. "No, we don't want Morten to come."

"Why not? He's really very nice," said Pelle, offended.

"Yes, but his father is so nasty—everybody's afraid of him. And he's been in the hole, too."

"Sure, for fighting—that's not so serious. My father was there too, when he was young. It doesn't matter, as long as it's not for stealing!"

But Manna looked at him with an expression like Jeppe himself when he was condemning someone from a petty point of view. "But

Pelle, aren't you ashamed? Only the poorest people think like that, the ones who don't have any shame!"

Pelle turned red at his own simple way of thinking. "Morten can't help it if his father's like that," he objected feebly.

"No, we don't *want* Morten over here. Mother doesn't want him either. She says it's all right for you to come, but nobody else. We aren't rich, after all," she added in explanation.

"My father owns a big farm—that's just as good as a rotten old tub," said Pelle proudly.

"Father's ship isn't rotten at all," replied Manna, insulted. "It's the best one in the whole harbor, and it has three masts."

"You're nothing but a stupid girl!" spat Pelle across the wall.

"Well, you're Swedish!" Manna batted her eyes triumphantly, and Dolores and Aina stood behind her sticking out their tongues.

Pelle had the strongest urge to jump over the wall and slap them silly; but then Jeppe's old woman started yapping from the kitchen, and he went back to his work.

Now, after Christmas, there was nothing at all to do. People went around in worn-out shoes or clogs. Little Nikas was seldom at the workshop; he would show up for meals and then leave again, always in his best clothes. "He's got an easy time of it," said Jeppe. "Up top they don't feed their people in the wintertime, but give them a kick as soon as there's nothing to do."

Several times a day Pelle was sent down to the harbor to check the ships. The masters stood down there with their aprons on and talked about seafaring, or ran to each other's doors for a chat; out of old habit they would have a tool in their hand.

Everywhere people were tightening their belts; the holy ones held meetings every day, since people had plenty of time to come. Now was the time when the town demonstrated what a flimsy foundation it was based on. It wasn't like out in the country where you could go and loaf around, knowing that the earth was working for you. Here everyone had to scrimp and eat less just to squeak by through the dead time.

At the workshops the boys sat slapping together cheap footwear to put in stock. Every spring the shoemakers got together to hire a schooner and ship the shoes to Iceland—that always helped make a living. "Just give it a few whacks," the master had to keep repeating, "we're not getting much for it."

With the lull, serious questions arose. Many workers were already suffering misery, and it was said that the welfare agency would have a hard time giving aid to everyone who applied. Philanthropy was in full swing. "It's nothing compared to over there in Copenhagen. I hear there are tens of thousands out of work," said baker Jørgen.

"I wonder what they're living on, all those thousands of poor souls, since the unemployment is so great?" said Bjerregrav. "The hunger here is bad enough, where every master takes care of feeding his own."

"No one here goes hungry if he doesn't want to," said Jeppe. "We have an efficient welfare agency."

"You must have turned into a socialist, Jeppe," exclaimed baker Jørgen. "You want to turn everything over to the welfare agency!"

Wooden-Leg Larsen laughed: "That's a new explanation, all right!"

"Well, what is it they want then? They sure aren't freemasons. I hear they're sticking their heads out again over there."

"Aw, that's just something that comes and goes with unemployment," said Jeppe. "People have to have *something* to do. One of the sailmaker's sons came home last winter—he was no doubt secretly one of them. But his parents never wanted to admit it, and he was smart enough to pull in his nose again."

"If he were my son, he would have gotten a real whipping," said Jørgen.

"Don't you think it's some of those people getting ready for the Millennium? We've got a few of them here too," said Bjerregrav in jest.

"Do you mean those poor wretches who believe in the clockmaker with his new age? Well, that could very well be," snorted Jeppe in scorn. "But I heard that there's so much evil in them. More likely it's the Antichrist, which the Scripture also prophesies."

"But what do they want?" asked Jørgen. "What's their madness all about?"

"What they want..." said Wooden-Leg Larsen, drawing himself up. "I've been with quite a few of the people over there—and as far as I can tell, they want the right to coin money taken from the Crown and give it to everyone. And they want to overthrow the whole thing, that much is for sure."

"Well," said Master Andrès, "what they want is probably good enough—but they'll never get it. I know a little about them from Garibaldi."

"So what do they want, if not to overthrow the world?"

"What they want? Well, what they want... is for everone to have as much as everyone else, I suppose." Master Andrès wasn't sure.

"Then the cabin boy should have just as much as the captain. No, that's going too far!" The baker slapped his thighs and laughed.

"They want to get rid of the King too," said Wooden-Leg Larsen excitedly.

"Who the hell is going to rule us then? The Germans would be running up here as fast as they could! That's got to be the worst—that Danish citizens would want to turn over their country to the enemy! I wonder why they don't just shoot them down without law or trial. Here on Bornholm they'll never make any headway."

"That's not good to hear," laughed Young Master.

"No, damn it—we'll stand on the beach and fire on them! They'll never make it ashore alive!"

"And they're probably all poor rabble anyway," said Jeppe. "I'd like to know whether there's one real citizen among them."

"The poor are the ones who whine about misery," said Bjerregrav. "That's why there's no end to it."

Baker Jørgen was the only one who had any work to do; times would have to be pretty bad for people to stop buying rye bread. In fact, he almost had more to do than usual; the more people cut back on meat and coldcuts, the more bread they ate. He would often borrow Jeppe's boys to help out with kneading the dough.

But he wasn't in a good mood at all. There was a constant ruckus in public with Søren, who refused to touch his fresh young wife. With his own hands old Jørgen had taken him and put him into bed with her, but Søren cried his way out of it, shaking like a newborn calf.

"Do you think he's bewitched?" the old man asked Master Andrès. "She's young and beautiful; there's not a thing wrong with her. And we've fed him full of eggs all winter. She has to go around hanging her head, and isn't allowed her 'visitation.' 'Marie, Søren!' I shout to put some life into them, 'He's supposed to be such a devil, just like I was, do you hear me!' She laughs and turns red, but Søren just goes off and hides. It's a real shame; she's so lovely in every way. This wouldn't have happened in my day, let me tell you!"

"Uncle Jørgen is still young!" laughed Master Andrès.

"Yes, soon I won't be able to resist . . . Making me go and see such a great injustice committed right before my eyes. Because you know, Andrès, though I've been a swine in many ways, I've also been a merry fellow. People were always glad to be aboard ship with me. And I've had strength enough for a spree, a lass, and the turn of a rope in bad weather. Things haven't been bad at all in the life I've led—I wouldn't mind living it all over again. But Søren, what is he? A miserable cadaver who can't find his way in again. If only you would try to talk to him; you have influence over him, you know."

"I'd be happy to try."

"Thank you. But look here, I think I owe you some money." Jørgen took out a 10-krone bill and put it on the table as he left.

"Pelle, you little devil, can you run an errand for me?" Young Master limped into the cutting room with Pelle at his heels.

Probably a hundred times the master would stand in the street doorway, but he would dash back inside right away—he couldn't stand the cold. In his gaze there were dreams of other lands with milder weather. He talked a great deal about his two brothers, one of whom had disappeared over in South America—murdered, no doubt. But the other was in Australia, herding sheep. He earned more than the town constable was paid, and he was the best boxer for miles around. Then Master knotted up his bloodless hands and let his fists fall on Pelle's back. "That's boxing," he said grandly. "Brother Martin can knock a man out with one blow. He gets paid for it, how disgusting!" Master shuddered. His brother had frequently offered to send a ticket . . . but that blasted leg. "Just tell me how I would manage over there. Just tell me, Pelle!"

Every day Pelle had to get books from the lending library, and he soon learned which authors were the most exciting. He tried to read them himself, but could never get to the end. It was more fun to stand and freeze at the skating rink and watch the others racing across the ice. But from Morten he found out about exciting books, such as *The Flying Dutchman*, and brought them to Master. "Now that's a work of art—God Almighty!" said Master and retold the story to Bjerregrav, who took it all as gospel.

"You should have gone out into the great world, Andrès. I, for my part, am probably better served by staying here around home. But you've been prevented—so that's that."

"Great world!" Master snorted. It wasn't big enough for him, since he couldn't take part in it. "If I went out there, I'd search for the way down into the earth's core. In Iceland there are entrances like that. It might also be fun to take a trip to the moon; but that will probably never come true."

Shortly after New Year's, Crazy Anker came and dictated to Master his letter of proposal to the King's eldest daughter. "This year he'll have to answer," he said, brooding. "Time is passing, and happiness is vanishing without very many people enjoying it. There's a great need for the new age."

"Yes, there certainly is," said Master Andrès. "But if the worst should happen and the King won't do it, then Anker is man enough to carry it out alone."

Things were slow, and in the slowest period of all, shoemaker Bohn went and set himself up in a shop on the market square. He had spent a year abroad and learned newfangled humbug. There was only one pair of boots in his shop window, and they were his own Sunday boots. Every Monday he polished them up and placed them out there again, as if to put on a good front. Whenever he was in the shop talking to someone, his wife would sit in the back and hammer on a boot so that it would sound like he had employees in the workshop.

But work came into Jeppe's shop by Shrovetide. One day Master Andrès came back from Beer Hansen's cellar very excited; he had made the acquaintance of several actors in a company that had just arrived. "Now those were real people!" he said, putting his hands to his cheeks. "They're constantly on the move from place to place giving performances—they get to see the world!" He couldn't sit still.

The next morning they came crowding in and filled the workshop with a deafening din. "Soles and back-heels!" "Back-soles that won't peel!" "A little heeling and two on the snoot!" They kept on this way, pulling a steady stream of footwear out from under their capes or taking shoes out of cavernous pockets and heaping them up on the platform, each with his own ridiculous statement. They called shoes "underlings"; they twisted and turned each word upside down and tossed it like a ball from mouth to mouth until there wasn't any sense left.

The boys forgot everything and surrendered themselves to laughter. Young Master sparkled with wit—he refused to be outdone by anyone. Now it was evident that the luck he had with the ladies wasn't all lies and boasting. The young actress with the hair like the palest straw couldn't take her eyes off him, even though she had all the rest of the men on a string. She motioned to the others to look at Master's magnificent big mustache. Master forgot all about his bad leg and threw aside his cane. He was on his knees taking her measurements for a pair of high boots with patent leather cuffs and accordion pleats on the leg. She had a hole in the heel of her stocking, but she just laughed at it. One of the actors said: "Fried egg!" and then they howled with laughter.

Old Jeppe came rushing in, attracted by the merriment. The fair-haired actress called him "grandfather" and wanted to dance with him, and Jeppe forgot his dignity and laughed along. "Yes, this is the place they come to when they want it done right," he said proudly. "I did my apprenticeship in the King's Copenhagen, and delivered shoes to more than one actor. We sewed for the whole theater. Mademoiselle Pätges, who later made such a name for herself, got her first pair of dancing shoes from us."

"Now those were real people!" said Master Andrès when they had roared off. "Damn it, for once those were real people." Jeppe couldn't imagine how they had found their way to the workshop, and Master Andrès didn't tell him that he had been to a tavern.

"I wonder whether it could have been Mademoiselle Pätges who referred them to me?" he said, staring off into space. "She must have been keeping tabs on me in some way."

There was a plethora of free tickets; Young Master went to the theater every night. Pelle got a ticket for the gallery every time he delivered a pair of shoes. He wasn't supposed to say anything, but the price was clearly written in chalk on the bottom. "Did you get the money?" asked Master tensely. No, Pelle brought their greetings and was supposed to say that they would come and settle accounts in person. "Well, all right, people like that can be trusted," said Master.

One day in the midst of everything, Lasse came stomping into the workshop, just like a real landowner with his fur collar turned up around his ears. His cart was outside with a sack of potatoes; it was a gift to Master because the boy was doing so well. Pelle got the day off and drove out with Lasse. He kept on glancing at his father's fur collar. Finally he couldn't stand it anymore, and he lifted it up to examine it. Then, disappointed, he let it drop again.

"Oh, yes, that . . . no, it's just stitched onto my coat collar! It always looks good, and it's warm around the ears. So you thought I came rolling up with a real fur-lined coat? No, we can't afford that yet, but it'll come! And I could tell you the names of quite a few landowners who don't have anything better than this!"

Well, Pelle *was* a little disappointed. But he had to admit that you couldn't see the difference between this coat and a real bearskin fur coat. "Are things going all right, otherwise?" he asked.

"Oh, yes . . . lately I've been breaking up stones. I have to break up twenty bushels in order to pay everyone his due on the Devil's birthday. If only we can keep our strength and our health, Karna and me . . ."

They drove over to the merchant's house and tied up the horses. Pelle didn't think the merchant's servants jumped up as eagerly for Lasse as for the real farmers, but Lasse was quite jaunty. He stomped right into the merchant's office like the others, filled his pipe from the bin, and poured himself a *snaps*. The air whirled around him as he went back and forth to the wagon with his coat flapping open. His step was so firm on the cobblestones, as if he too had acres of productive land beneath the soles of his boots.

Then they went out to visit the Due family. Lasse was curious to see how they were getting along. "It's not so easy when one of the couple brings an extra burden to the marriage."

Pelle filled him in on how things stood. "Tell Kalle that he should take little Marie back. Anna mistreats her. Otherwise things are going well for them; now they're about to buy horses and a cart and run a delivery business themselves."

"That's probably her doing, isn't it? Yes, the one with no heart is the one who always gets ahead." Lasse sighed.

"Papa," said Pelle suddenly, "there's a theater in town right now, and I know all the actors. I deliver shoes to them, and they give me tickets every night. I've seen everything!"

"That's not a lie, is it?" Lasse had to stop to examine the boy's expression. "So you've been to a real theater, have you? The devil take me if the people who live in town aren't smarter than us farmers—they get to take part in everything!"

"Do you want to go along tonight? I can get tickets."

Lasse scratched himself. He wasn't lacking desire, but... this was something quite out of the ordinary. It was arranged so that he could stay with the Dues that night, and in the evening the two of them went to the theater.

"Is this it?" asked Lasse in amazement as they arrived at an enormous warehouse with a crowd of people standing outside. But inside it was quite fancy; they sat all the way up in the back, as if on a hillside, looking down on everything. Way down in front sat several ladies who were naked, as far as Lasse could tell. "Those are probably the performers, aren't they?" he asked.

Pelle laughed. "No, those are the town's most elegant ladies: the doctor's wife and the mayor's and the inspector's, and others like them."

"Ha, and they're so elegant that they don't even have clothes to wear!" exclaimed Lasse. "That's what we call poverty back home. But where are the people who perform?"

"They're behind the curtain down there."

"You mean it hasn't started yet?"

"No, you should know that—the curtain has to go up first!"

There was a hole in the curtain; a finger poked out and started beckoning to the audience. Lasse laughed. "Hell of a joke!" he said, slapping his thighs when it was repeated.

"It hasn't started yet," Pelle said.

All right, Lasse stifled his humor.

But then the chandelier began rushing up toward the black hole in the ceiling; up there several boys kneeled down and blew out the gas lamps. And the curtain went up on a great, bright room. There were many beautiful young girls in the most wondrous costumes—and they spoke! Lasse was completely astounded that he could understand what they said, because it all looked so oddly foreign; it was like a glimpse into a dreamland. But there was one person sitting all alone and spinning; she was the most beautiful of them all.

"She must be a fine lady," said Lasse.

But Pelle whispered that she was a poor forest girl whom the lord of the castle had kidnapped because he wanted to force her to be his sweetheart. Well—all the others made a great to-do about her, combing her golden hair and kneeling down before her; but she only looked unhappy. And occasionally she would feel so sad that she opened her lovely mouth and let her broken heart bleed in a song that made Lasse gasp deeply for air.

Then a big man with a great red beard came stomping in. Lasse thought he was dressed like someone coming straight from a carnival party.

"He's the one who got the wonderful boots from us," whispered Pelle, "the lord of the castle who wants to seduce her."

"Damn—he sure is ugly!" said Lasse, spitting. "The landowner at Stone Farm was a child of God compared to him."

Pelle shushed him.

The lord of the castle chased all the other women out. Then he paced back and forth, taking great strides and scowling at the forest girl, showing the whites of his eyes. "Well, have you made up your mind?" he roared, inhaling like a mad bull. And suddenly he leapt toward her to take her by force.

But the forest girl stood erect, a shining dagger in her hand. "Ha, don't you touch me," she cried, "or by the living God I'll plunge this dagger into my heart. You think you can buy my innocence because I am poor; but the honor of a poor woman cannot be bought with gold."

"You can say that again," said Lasse aloud.

But the lord of the castle laughed slyly and tugged at his red beard, rolling his *r*'s terribly. "Isn't my offer generous enough? All right, just stay with me tonight, and you shall have a farm with ten cows so that you can go to the altar tomorrow with your hunter."

"Shut up, you whoremonger!" shouted Lasse angrily.

The people around shushed him and someone gave him a poke. "So, isn't a man allowed to open his mouth?" Lasse said to Pelle, offended. "I'm no pastor, but when a girl doesn't want to, he ought to let her go. And he shall not expose his lust unchallenged in the presence of hundreds of people—what a swine!" Lasse was talking loudly, and it seemed as if his words were having an effect on the lord of the castle. He paused for a moment and scowled, then called for a servant and ordered him to take the girl back to the woods.

Lasse sighed with relief as the curtain fell and the boys up in the hole lit the lamps of the chandelier again and lowered it down. "She made it so far," he said to Pelle, "but I don't think I trust that lord of the castle—he's a foul one!" He was quite sweaty, and he didn't seem happy at all.

The next world that was conjured forth on stage was a forest. It was lovely, with geraniums covering the floor, and a spring running out of something green. "It's a covered-up beer keg," whispered Pelle, and now Lasse too could make out the spigot; but it sure did look lifelike. Far in the background a knight's castle on a cliff was visible, and in the foreground was a fallen tree. Two green-clad hunters were sitting astride it, plotting. Lasse nodded—he had experience with the ugliness of the world.

Now they heard something and crept down to hide behind the fallen tree, knife in hand. There was silence for a moment, and then the forest girl and her hunter came strolling along the forest path, hand in hand, in all innocence. They parted at the spring—so tenderly. Then the hunter hurried on toward certain death.

It was impossible to bear. Lasse stood up. "Watch out!" he shouted. "Watch out!" The people behind him pulled at his coat and scolded him. "No, the devil take me if I'm going to keep quiet about this," said Lasse, striking out at them. Then he leaned all the way forward: "Watch out for yourself! It's a matter of life and death! They're behind the fallen tree!"

The hunter stopped and stared. The two assassins stood up and glared. From the wings male and female actors came forward; they laughed and stared out into the audience. Lasse saw that the man was saved, but otherwise he was having trouble because the management wanted to throw him out. "I can walk by myself," he said. "I can see there's no place for an honest man in this company." Out on the street he talked loudly to himself. He was quite upset.

"But it was only a play," said Pelle in disappointment. He was very embarrassed for his father.

"You don't have to teach me about that! I know very well that it all happened a long time ago, and that I couldn't stop it even if I stood on my head. But to think that they should bring up such evil deeds! If the others had felt the way I did, they probably would have taken that lord of the castle and killed him—even though it would be a hundred years too late."

"But that was just actor West who comes to the workshop every day."

"Oh, so it was actor West, was it? Then you're actor Codfish who's letting himself be hoodwinked. I've met people like that before who have the gift to go into a trance and conjure up long-dead people in their place—although not as lifelike as this man, of course! If you had been backstage, you would have seen West lying there like a corpse while the Other—the Devil—took over. I wouldn't wish that gift for myself, because it's a dangerous game. For example, if the others forget the right *word* to call West back to life again, then he's done for, and the Other will take his place."

"That's just superstition! When I know for sure that it was West who was acting. I recognized him, Papa!"

"That's right, you're always the smart one—you could probably have a debate with the Devil any day you want. So it was all just an act? What about the way he showed the whites of his eyes with gluttonous lust? You can be sure that if she hadn't had that knife, he would have jumped on top of her and satisfied his lust right before our eyes. Because if you conjure up the past, the deed must be carried out again, no matter how many people are watching. But to think they do things like that for money! Ugh, how disgusting! And now I want to go home." Lasse would not be dissuaded and harnessed up the horses.

"You shouldn't go to that kind of thing anymore," he said in farewell. "But if it's already gotten power over you, at least take your flatiron with you in your pocket. And we'll send your laundry along with butcher Jensen some Saturday."

Pelle continued going to the theater; he had his wiser conviction that it was all just a play. But there *was* something mysterious about it. Those people must possess some supernatural talent that allowed them to change their skin so completely every evening and become so absorbed in the characters they played. Pelle thought he would probably become an actor when he grew up one day.

They did create a sensation. When they strolled through the streets with their flowing clothes and peculiar headgear, people would run to the windows to look at them, and the old folks spat after them. The town wasn't itself while they were there; everybody's mind was slightly cockeyed. Girls lay whimpering in their sleep, dreaming about abductions; they even propped their windows open. And every young fellow was ready and willing to run away with the company. Those who weren't theater-crazy held religious meetings to combat the evil.

Then one day the actors disappeared as suddenly as they had arrived, leaving behind many debts. "That damned riffraff!" said Master with a glum expression. "They really cleaned us out! But they were splendid people . . . in their own way. And they had seen the world!"

But after that episode, he had a hard time keeping warm. He crawled into bed and stayed there the better part of a month.

XII

It can be cozy enough on these winter evenings when they sit at home in the workshop and loaf because it's dark and cold outside, and they have nowhere else to go. Pelle is tired of standing at the ice-skating rink and watching miserably while the others take a swing around. And it's not much fun wandering back and forth through the streets—heading north, then turning around, south and turning around—back and forth the same stretch until ten o'clock, because he doesn't have nice warm clothes and his arm around a girl. Morten isn't much of a fresh air type either; he gets cold and wants to go inside.

So they tiptoe into the workshop as soon as it grows dark. They take out the key and hang it up on the nail out in the hallway to confuse Jeppe. They cautiously light the stove and put up the screen so that Jeppe won't catch sight of the glow when he makes his rounds past the workshop windows. They crawl up onto the platform together over by the stove with their arms around each other's shoulders, and Morten tells Pelle about the books he has read.

"Why do you want to read all those stupid books?" says Pelle after he has listened for a while.

"Because I want to know about life and the world," replies Morten in the darkness.

"About the world!" says Pelle, snorting scornfully. "No, I want to go out in the world and see something. Everything in those books is nothing but lies. But what else happened?"

And Morten continues goodnaturedly. In the middle of a story he remembers something and pulls out a paper from his breast pocket. "Here's some chocolate from Bodil," he says, cracking it in half.

"Where did she put it?" asks Pelle.

"Under the sheet. I felt something hard when I lay down."

The two boys laugh as they munch on the chocolate.

Suddenly Pelle says: "Bodil—but she seduces children! She was the one who lured Hans Peter away with her from Stone Farm—and he was only fifteen!"

Morten doesn't answer. But after a while his head sinks down onto Pelle's shoulder. He gives a start.

"You're seventeen," says Pelle consolingly. "But it's still just as dumb. She could be your mother—if it weren't for your age." Then they both laugh.

It can be even cozier on weekday nights. Then the fire burns openly in the stove, after eight o'clock as well. The lamp is lit, and Morten is there too. They come dropping in from all directions, and the locked-out cold brings back all the great memories. It's as if the world itself had shrunk to the warm workshop. Jeppe conjures up his apprentice years in the capital and tells them about the great bankruptcy. He takes them all the way back to the beginning of the century, to a quaint old Copenhagen where people wore wigs, where the cat-o'-nine-tails always swung in the air, and the apprentices managed to survive by begging at the citizens' doors on Sunday. Those were the days! And he comes home and wants to set up shop as a master, but the guild won't permit it—he's too young. So he goes to sea as a cook and sails down where the sun is so hot that the tar boils in the seams and the deck scalds your feet. They're a lively bunch, and Jeppe, in spite of his small size, doesn't hold back. In Málaga they storm a tavern, heave all the Spaniards out the windows, and have their fun with the girls—until the whole town gets after them, and they have to flee to their boat. Jeppe can't keep up, and the boat pulls away; he has to jump in the water and swim for it. Knives fall splashing into the water all around him, and one of them sticks in his shoulderblade with a quiver. Whenever Jeppe gets that far in his story, he always starts tearing off his clothes to show them the scar. Master Andrès stops him. Pelle and Morten have heard the story several times, but could listen to it over and over again.

And baker Jørgen, who was a bosun most of the time he spent on the great northern and southern ocean freighters, wrestles with handspikes and polar bears and black-skinned girls from the West Indies. He sets the game in motion so the mighty full-rigger sets sail from Havana harbor, and it sets sail in every listener:

> Heave-ho, men,
> we can't go wrong!
> Leave the girls crying
> and give us a song.

Then they go round and round, twelve men strong, with their breasts pressed against the heavy handspikes. They weigh anchor, and the sail billows—and behind his words they can glimpse the features of a sweetheart in every port. Bjerregrav has to cross himself: he who has never done anything but care for the poor. But Young Master can see the ship sailing—around the world, around the world. And then there's Wooden-Leg Larsen who, in the wintertime, is the well-to-do man living on interest in a blue pea jacket and woolen cap, but every spring flies away from his pretty brick house out into the world as a poor organ-grinder. He tells them about the amusement park at Dyrehavsbakken and the legendary Holmensgade and about strange creatures that live out of garbage cans in the back courtyards of the capital.

But Pelle's body creaks with the slightest movement, his bones are shooting out and demanding to be stretched; he has growing pains and is restless all over. He's the first one that spring touches. One day it announces itself inside him in the form of a question: what does he look like? Pelle has never before asked that question, and the piece of mirror that he begs from the glazier when he goes to get scraping-glass doesn't really tell him anything. He has a feeling about himself that he's somehow impossible.

He starts noticing other people's opinion of his looks. Some girl stares after him, and his cheeks are no longer so chubby that people keep on making fun of them. His blond hair is curly, the cowlick falling over his forehead still evident as a little obstinate streak. His ears are still terribly big, and it doesn't help when he shoves his cap down over them to keep them close to his head. But he is well-developed and big for his age; the workshop air hasn't diminished his vigor. And there is nothing he's afraid of—especially when he's mad. He thinks up hundreds of athletic games to appease the demands of his body, but there aren't enough. Even if he just bends down for a hammer, all his joints start talking.

Then one day the ice breaks up and drifts out to sea. The ships rig up their sails and take on provisions and head out the same way. And the townspeople wake up to visions of a new life and start thinking about leafy forests and summer finery.

And one day the big one-masted sailing ships arrive! They come

racing across the sea from Hällevik and Nogesund and other places over
there along the Swedish coast. Gallantly they steer across the water with
the peculiar Latin sail in tilted flight, like hungry sea birds brushing the
sea with one wingtip in their search for prey. Miles out to sea the town's
fishermen meet them with musket fire; they aren't allowed to put in at
the boat harbor but have to lease a berth at the old ship harbor and
spread their equipment to dry north of town. The craftsmen get together to discuss these foreign robbers who come from a poorer country
and take the bread out of the mouths of the town's own children—
robust as they are, brave enough to go out in the foulest weather, and
with good luck following them! The craftsmen do this every spring, but
when they have to supply themselves with herring, they buy from the
Swedes, who sell it for less than the local people. "Do our fishermen
wear out leather shoes?" asks Jeppe. "Weekdays and Sundays alike they
go around in wooden clogs, that's what they do. So let the clog-maker
do business with them. I buy wherever it's cheapest."

It's as if spring itself makes an appearance in these gaunt, sinewy
figures who walk along the street, singing and provoking the malice of
the small-minded people of the town. Every boat has women along to
clean and repair the equipment, and they wander in groups up past the
workshop, seeking out the old lodgings in the poor quarter near the
Power's house. There's a tumult in Pelle's heart at the sight of these
young women with pretty slippers on their feet, black kerchiefs around
their oval faces, and many beautiful colors in their dresses. So much
wells up in his mind: dim memories from a childhood in which everything lay dormant, as if erased; whispered myths about something he
experienced but cannot remember, like a warm breath of air from another, unknown life.

If one of them happens to have a baby in her arms, the town starts
gossiping. Was it grocer Lund like last year—the one who ever since has
been called nothing but the Herring Dealer? Or was it the sixteen-year-
old apprentice—to the shame of the pastor and teacher who had just
sent him out into the world?

Then Jens takes off with his concertina. Pelle hurries to clean up. He
and Morten tear off to Gallows Hill—hand in hand, because Morten
has trouble running fast. All the young people in town are out there, but
the Swedish girls go first. They're like fire when they dance; you can
swing them so their slippers fly. Minor fights flare up over them. But on
Saturday the Swedes don't go out to sea. Then the men come with
flashing brows and demand their women back, and that's when the big
battles rage.

Pelle takes part in it wholeheartedly. Here is the exercise his body has yearned for so badly in his trade. He has a ravenous need for action and gets so close to the fighters that an occasional punch falls on him too. He dances with Morten and gets up his courage to ask a girl to dance. He's shy and makes the funniest leaps during the dance to overcome it; in the middle of the dance he takes off and leaves the girl high and dry. "What a monkey," say the adults, laughing at him. He has his *own* way of participating in all this frivolity, letting life have its way without a thought for tomorrow or next year. If some man-happy woman tries to capture his youth, he kicks up his heels and is gone in a couple of frisky bounds. But he sings along so heartily when they head homeward in groups, men and women holding each other tight, and he and Morten follow behind with their arms around each other too. Then the moon's path of light stretches out to sea, and in the pine forest where white mist envelops the treetops, the song echoes from every path and accompanies the swaying gait of the strolling couples—its meaning insistently heavy, but carried forth by the lightest of hearts, just the song for singing out your happiness:

> Tie up, tie up your fair yellow hair,
> for you shall bear a son this year—
> neither sobs nor sighs will help you now!
> In forty weeks shall I return
> to see how it's gone with you.
> Those forty weeks slipped calmly by,
> and then the maiden began to cry . . .

And they walk all the way through town, couple after couple. The quiet, crooked streets resound with the songs of death and love, making the old citizens raise their heads from their pillows, shove their nightcaps aside, and shake their heads at all that frivolity. But youth is aware of nothing—it just rushes and dashes along with its boiling blood. And one day the old people will prove to be right: the blood has cooled, and there stand the young men with the consequences and demand reasons and support. "We told you so!" say the old folks. But the young men bow their heads and envision a long, miserable life ahead, with a hasty marriage or perpetual payment to some strange woman, with the eternal blot of debasement and ridicule about them, with marriage and acquaintances beneath their station. They no longer talk of going out into the world to make their own way; if they once dug in their heels against the old people, demanding space for their youth, now they walk meekly in the harness once again with heads bowed, shamefully blinking at their only accomplishment. And the ones who can't bear it have to flee the country by night or falsely deny their paternity.

Young Master discovers spring in his own way. He doesn't take part in the interchange with girls, but when the sun shines quite warm, he sits outside the workshop windows and lets it bake into his back. "Oh, it's so wonderful," he says with a shiver. He makes Pelle feel his leather jacket to see what power the sun already has. "Now, by heaven, it's spring!"

Inside the workshop they whistle and sing to the pounding of the hammers; there are moments when the dingy room seems like a bird-seller's shop. "Now, by God, it's spring," says Master Andrès over and over. "But the harbinger of spring probably won't come this year."

"Maybe he's dead," says Little Nikas.

"Garibaldi dead? He'll never die. As far back as I can remember, he's looked exactly the same and drunk just as much. The quantities that man has drunk in his day—oh, God Almighty! But no shoemaker in the world can match him."

One morning shortly after the arrival of the steamer, a tall, bony-shouldered man appears in the workshop doorway. His hands and face are bluish-gray with the chill of the morning, his cheeks hang like pouches on him, but in his eyes burns an immortal spark. "Morning, comrades!" he says, sweeping his hand in a graceful gesture. "So, how's it going? Is Master well?" He dances in across the floor with his hat crushed flat under his left arm. His jacket and pants flop loosely around his body, revealing that there is nothing underneath; he has bare feet in his shoes and a thick scarf around his neck. But Pelle has never seen anything in a craftsman to match his dignity and carriage. Garibaldi's voice alone is like a prelude.

"Well, son," he says, slapping Pelle lightly on the shoulder, "can you see about getting that half pint? But in a flash, because I'm murder-ously thirsty. Master has credit, of course. Psst, we'll take a pint, then you won't have to run over there twice."

Pelle takes off. In half a minute he is back; Garibaldi knows how to make someone move. He has already put on his apron and is busy evaluating the work in the shop. He takes the bottle from Pelle, slings it over his shoulder and catches it with his other hand, places his fingernail in the middle and drinks. Then he shows the others—right down to the nail, eh?

"What a drinker!" says Little Nikas.

"I can do it when it's pitch dark." Garibaldi gestures arrogantly. "And old Jeppe is still alive? Healthy fellow!"

Master Andrès pounds on the other side of the wall. "He's arrived—he's out there," he says with wide-open eyes. A short time later he's dressed and out in the workshop, talking excitedly, but Garibaldi retains his dignity; he still has his morning hoarseness.

A kind of feverishness has come over everyone, an anxiety not to miss anything. The daily drabness has vanished from the craft, and each of them flexes his abilities. Garibaldi comes from the great world with all the adventure of the wandering life hanging from his thin clothing. "If only he would start talking soon," whispers Pelle to Jens, unable to sit still. Their gaze locks onto his lips; if he's silent it must be because of some stronger will. Even Master doesn't press him but bows to his reticence, and Little Nikas allows himself to be treated like an apprentice.

Garibaldi raises his head. "Well, I don't suppose I've come here just to sit idle," he exclaims cheerfully. "Anything to work on, Master?"

"There's not much, but for you we always have work," replies Master Andrès. "Oh, by the way, we have an order for a pair of bridal shoes—white satin with gold stitching, but we haven't been too eager to get started on them." He glances at Little Nikas.

"Not gold stitching on white satin, Master—white silk, of course, and white stitching!"

"Is that the fashion in Paris now?" asks Master Andrès eagerly.

Garibaldi shrugs. "Let's not bother about Paris, Master Andrès, we have neither the leather nor the tools to make Parisian shoes—nor the legs to put in them."

"Well, I'll be damned! Are they so elegant?"

"Elegant, you say! I can hold a full-grown Parisian woman's foot in the hollow of my hand. And when they walk—God help me if they even touch the pavement! You can make shoes for a Parisian girl out of whipped cream—and they'll hold up! But give her a pair of ordinary Danish maiden's button shoes and she'll jump right into the canal!"

"You don't say!" Master hurries to cut the leather. "I'll be damned!"

No person had ever slipped into something so easily. Garibaldi pulls a three-legged stool over to the workbench and is hard at work. No fumbling around for tools: his hand goes right to where the item is lying, as if there were invisible paths between them. Those hands take care of everything themselves, quietly, with graceful motions, while his eyes are everywhere else: out in the courtyard, on the boys' work, on Young Master. For Pelle and the others who have to look at one thing from ten different angles, this is simply miraculous. And before they know it, Garibaldi has finished everything and is sitting staring at Master, who has taken up the needle himself today.

Then Jeppe comes dashing in, annoyed that no one has announced Garibaldi's arrival. "Hello, Master—hello, Master of the Guild!" says Garibaldi, getting up and bowing.

"Well," says Jeppe uncertainly, "if there were any masters of the guild left, I suppose I'd be it. But things are bad for the craft these days; there's no respect, and where would it come from anyway, when people don't know how to respect themselves."

"That was meant for Young Master, eh?" says Garibaldi, laughing. "But times have changed, Jeppe. That stuff with a strap and respect doesn't work anymore—those were the old days. Start at seven in the morning and done at six at night—period! That's how things are in the big cities now."

"It's probably that socialism, isn't it?" says Jeppe scornfully.

"I don't care what it is—because Garibaldi starts and quits whenever he likes. And if he wants more for his work, he asks for it. And if not—then farewell, Master! There are plenty of girls to go around, as the boy said when he didn't get any food."

The others don't get much done; they have enough to do just keeping up with his method of work. He has emptied the bottle and it's loosened his tongue. Young Master knows how to pump him, and Garibaldi talks on, waving his arms. Not even his hands are a help to his work, but it still progresses swiftly, almost like a revelation—it's as if the shoes give birth to themselves. His attention is on their work, and he steps in at the right moment, corrects their hand position and makes the decisive cut that lends beauty to the arch and heel. It's as if he can feel it when they do something wrong—his spirit is everywhere. "Look, this is how they do it in Paris," he says. "This is the fashion in Nuremberg." He talks of Vienna and Greece so matter-of-factly, as if they lay next door under skipper Elleby's trees. In Athens he went up and shook hands with the King of Greece, because countrymen abroad should always stick together. "Oh, and he was very nice, by the way, but he had already eaten lunch. A bad country to wander around in, though, because there aren't any shoemakers. And then in Italy, there are plenty of shoemakers, but no work—so you can freely loaf around and beg from place to place. They don't come up to you like those officious Germans every time you ask for a handout and say: 'Here, I'll give you work.' And it's warm enough to sleep on the bare ground. Wine flows in all the gutters, but it tastes like dishwater, let me tell you." Garibaldi lifts the empty bottle high in the air and peers under it with amazement. Young Master winks to Pelle, who rushes off at a gallop for a pint.

The hot blood is boiling in Pelle's ears. Out, out, he has to get out and travel like Garibaldi; hide in the vineyards from the gendarmes and steal the ham from the hearth while the people are out in the field. A spirit has come over him and the others, the spirit of the craft. Tools and leather meet lovingly between their fingers when they touch them, and everything has its special texture that tells them something. All the old, familiar things covered with dust have been banished from the workshop. On the shelves the objects are shining with interest; even the most boring things are now scintillating with life.

The world is conjured up like a pale gray wonder, interspersed with endless country roads covered with deep white dust, and Garibaldi wanders down them all. He has sold his itinerant's book to a comrade for a bite of food and has no papers; German police are hounding him. Garibaldi crawls through the vineyards on his hands and knees for fourteen days and has nothing but grapes and an acute colic. Finally his clothes are so alive that he doesn't even have to move by himself; he lies quite still and lets himself be transported along and comes to a little town. "A hostel?" asks Garibaldi. Yes, there is a hostel. Then he makes up a story about being robbed; the good people tuck him into bed and stoke up the fire to dry his clothes. Garibaldi snores and pushes the chair closer to the woodstove, snores and pushes it a little more, and when his clothes are in flames he starts bellowing, scolding, and weeping and is inconsolable. Then Garibaldi gets clean new clothes and new papers and is out on the road once more. The wandering begins all over again: mountains appear and fade into the background, big towns appear, towns on wide rivers. There are towns where the wandering journeyman can't get any money but *has* to work—cursed towns—and German hostels where he's treated like a prisoner: has to take off his clothes in a long passageway, even his shirt, which is inspected by a couple of men, and everything is taken away for safekeeping. Thirty to forty naked men are allowed to pass one by one into the big dormitory.

Paris—it's as if bubbles were bursting in your ears! Garibaldi worked there for two years; he's been through there twenty times. Paris is every imaginable splendor all bundled together, and every imaginable sensible invention turned upside down. Here on Bornholm no decent master would make the "Full Sail's" flopping, elastic-sided shoes. She walks around in downtrodden capes, and when things are really slow with the sea traffic, she wears clogs. Down in Paris there are women who can wear shoes costing 500 francs a pair. They carry themselves like queens, earning a million a year, and yet they're nothing but whores. A million! If anyone but Garibaldi had told them this, they would have thrown all the lasts in his face.

Pelle doesn't hear what the master is saying to him. Jens is busy with the cobbler's wax—he slipped and cut the upper leather of the shoes he's resoling. Everyone is distracted, possessed by that wondrous creature who keeps on gulping down the aquavit, transforming that cursed drink in full view of the motley group into a piece of work that is as miraculous as himself.

The word has already spread, and they come running to see Garibaldi and maybe even take the liberty to shake his hand. Klausen wants to borrow some cobbler's pegs, and Marker sets aside all his pride and shows up in person to borrow the biggest men's lasts. Old cobbler Drejer stands humbly over in a corner, saying "Yes, yes" to the others' words. Garibaldi has shaken his hand, so now he can go back home to his dingy little shop and filthy footwear and his old man's solitude. The genius of the craft has touched him and cast a light upon his pathetic repair work for the rest of his days; he has exchanged a handshake with the man who sewed cork boots for the Kaiser of Germany himself when he went forth and conquered the French. Crazy Anker is there too, but he doesn't come inside—he's shy with strangers. He's pacing out in the courtyard, back and forth in front of the workshop windows, glancing inside. Garibaldi places his finger to his forehead and nods; Anker puts his finger to his forehead too, and nods back. He shakes with silent laughter at a good joke and takes off like a child who's in a hurry, over to a corner to enjoy his glee.

Baker Jørgen stands bent over with his hands on his thighs and his mouth open. "Oh, now I get it!" he exclaims every so often. "Oh, you don't say!" He watches the white silk running through the sole and attaching itself like silver-glistening pearls, pearl next to pearl all along the edge. Garibaldi's arms fly out; he knocks the baker on the thigh. "Am I in your way?" asks old Jørgen.

"Good heavens, no. Just stay where you are." Then his arms fly out again; the awl knob strikes the baker with a bang.

"I think I'm in the way," Jørgen repeats, moving back a little.

"By no means," replies Garibaldi, pulling the stitch tight. Then he pulls again, and this time he turns the awl point outwards.

"Now I really think I'm in the way," says the baker, rubbing his backside.

"Not at all," says Garibaldi affably, making a welcoming gesture with his hand. "Wouldn't Jørgen Kofod like to—?"

"No thank you, no thanks." Old Jørgen winces with a forced smile and lumbers down off the platform.

Otherwise Garibaldi lets them come and go and stare as they please.

What does he care that he's a huge, peculiar creature? He puts the aquavit bottle to his lips without embarrassment and drinks as long as he's thirsty. He sits and plays distractedly with leather and knife and silk, as if he had been sitting here on this three-legged stool all his life and hadn't just plopped down from the moon a few hours ago. And by mid-afternoon the most incomparable results are produced: a pair of lovely satin shoes, slender as calves' tongues, blinding in their white sheen, as if they had stepped right out of a fairy tale and were waiting for the foot of a princess.

"Just look at them, by God," says Master, handing the work to Little Nikas, who passes them around.

Garibaldi tosses his close-cropped, graying head. "You don't have to say who made them—because anyone can see it for themselves. Let's just say that these shoes go to Jutland and get worn and are thrown onto the manure heap. One day several years from now some porridge-eater will be busy plowing. A scrap of shoe shank turns up, and a wandering crafsman who's sitting in the ditch gnawing on his vesper meal drags it over with his stick. 'This shank,' he says, 'well, I'll be damned if it wasn't part of a shoe that Garibaldi made,' he says. 'The devil take me if he didn't!' So that craftsman must be from Nuremberg, or Hamburg, or Paris—it doesn't matter, you understand. Or am I lying, Master?"

No, Master Andrès can assure him it's no lie—he who, from his childhood on, has lived with Garibaldi on the country roads and in the big cities, followed along on his lame leg so intently that he remembers Garibaldi's deeds better than Garibaldi himself. "But now you should stay here," he coaxes him. "Then we'll go into business, and get all the best work from the whole island!" Garibaldi has nothing against it; he's tired of traveling around.

Klausen wants to be part of the company; something is at work in all their eyes, a dream of elevating their craft once again and renewing its grandeur, maybe even competing with those shoemakers in Copenhagen itself.

"How many medals do you have now?" asks Jeppe, holding a black-framed diploma in his hands.

Garibaldi shrugs. "Don't know, Guild Master—a man grows old and unsteady in the hands. But what's that? Did Master Jeppe receive a silver medal?"

Jeppe laughs. "Yes, thanks to a vagabond named Garibaldi. He was here four years ago and got me this silver medal." Oh, Garibaldi had forgotten about that! There are medals strewn all over the place, wherever he has been.

"Yes, there are a hundred masters sitting around, each bragging about his award. First-class workshop. Here, see for yourself: silver medal. But the one who did the work, he got his day's pay and an extra pint, and then—goodbye, Garibaldi! What have I got to show for it, Master Jeppe? There are plenty of trees to change behind—but what about the shirt, Master?" A momentary sadness comes over him. "Lorain in Paris gave me 200 francs for the gold medal I won him. But usually it's always: 'Have a look in my vest pocket!' Or: 'I have a pair of old pants for you, Garibaldi!' But now I'm through with all that. Garibaldi will no longer carry water to the big shots' mill—because now he's become a socialist!"

He pounded on the counter so the broken glass jumped. "The last time was Frantz in Cologne—men's boots with a cork bottom. He was tightfisted, that man, and then Garibaldi got mad. 'I'm afraid this won't get you any medal, Master,' I say, 'there's too much disturbance in the air.' Then he raised my pay and then again. 'This won't get you a medal, by God,' I kept on saying. Finally he sends in his wife with coffee and pastry—she was supposed to butter me up, you see. And she was a lady who usually rode around with a footman on the box. But I was still hopping mad! Well, the boots did get favorable attention after all—for madam's sake, that is."

"Did he have many journeymen?" asks Jeppe.

"Oh, probably about thirty or forty."

"So there must have been something to him." Jeppe is reproachful.

"Something to him? Well, he was a scoundrel, all right! What do I care that he had a lot of journeymen? I'm not going to cheat them out of their pay."

Now Garibaldi is annoyed. He tears off his apron, throws on his hat, and heads into town.

"Now he's going to find himself a sweetheart," says Young Master. "He has a sweetheart in every town!"

Around eight o'clock he comes sailing into the workshop. "What? Are you still sitting here?" he says to the boys. "Other places in the world the workday was over two hours ago. What kind of slaves are you, sitting here and chewing your cud for fourteen hours? Go out on strike, damn it!"

They look at each other stupidly. Strike—what's that?

Then Young Master comes in. "A little nap would sure feel good about now," says Garibaldi.

"We've made up a bed for you in the cutting room," replies Master. But Garibaldi rolls his sweater up under his head and lies down on the platform. "If I start snoring, just tweak me on the nose," he says to Pelle and falls asleep.

The next day he puts the soles on two pair of kidskin shoes with yellow stitching; that's three day's work for Little Nikas. Master Andrès has all the plans worked out. Garibaldi will be part-owner. "We'll add on a cross-timbered wing and have a big shop window put in!"

Garibaldi is willing, but needs to have peace and quiet once in a while. "But we'd better not expand too much," he says. "This isn't Paris, you know." He drinks a little more and doesn't say much; his eyes keep moving to the drifting clouds.

On the third day he starts demonstrating his talents. He doesn't do much work but turns over a heavy walking stick with a swish through the air, and he jumps over a stick that he holds in both hands. "A man needs exercise," he says restlessly. He balances a peg on the head of a hammer and pounds it into a hole on a sole.

And suddenly he throws down his work. "Lend me 10 kroner, Master," he says. "I have to go out and buy myself some decent clothes. Now that I'm an established man and part-owner of a business, I can't go around looking like a pig."

"You'd best finish his work," says Master quietly, giving Garibaldi's work to Little Nikas. "We won't be seeing him anymore!"

Pelle listens. This was almost the strangest thing of all. This was the fairytale part: to go into the little town with the proper intentions of buying something—and then to be seized and whirled out far into the world, any which way. "Right now he might already be on his way to Germany with a skipper," says Master.

"But he didn't even say goodbye!"

Master only shrugs.

It was like a shooting star! But for Pelle and the others it meant something new; they learned more in those three days than in their entire apprenticeship. And they came to see the craft in a different light. It wasn't just some provincial occupation—with Garibaldi it seemed to swing through the whole wonderful world. Pelle's blood burned with wanderlust; now he knew what he wanted. To be skilled like Garibaldi—genius incarnate—and to tramp into the big cities with a walking stick and toolbag like fanfare.

Traces from his fleeting visit remained in all of them. Something had exploded inside them: their hands had acquired freer, bolder technique, and they had seen the craft march past on a larger scale, as a kind of artistic pursuit. The sounds of great birds flying by hung for a long time over the little workshop with its honest mediocrity.

This fresh breath of air in their ears was the spirit of the craft itself passing over their heads, borne by its two mighty wings: genius and application.

But one thing lingered in Pelle like a meaningless fragment—the word "strike." What did that mean?

XIII

People could never feel as happy and secure here in town as they had in the country. Something was always lurking in the background, gnawing, and preventing them from immersing themselves completely in town life. Most people here had come in search of happiness; poverty had lost its ability to surrender to its fate, and people who had grown tired of waiting had taken matters into their own hands. And here they stood, mired for good in misery. They never got away from the place, but just kept working themselves in deeper. But they went on struggling until it closed over their heads; they had gotten a feeling for exodus in their blood.

Pelle was often astounded that there were so many poor people here. Why didn't they just go ahead and become well-to-do? They all had intentions of that sort, which just never came to anything. Why not? They didn't understand why, but silently bowed their heads as if under a curse. And when they raised their heads again, it was to seek the poor man's consolation, liquor, or to join the holy ones.

Pelle didn't understand it. He could vaguely follow along in the happy insanity that arises from need itself, like a misty but mighty dream of reaching the light. Not even he understood why it failed, but he had to keep following the buoyancy inside him and crawl free again. But besides this he knew a great deal: a window stuffed with rags, or the scabby head of a child, was the entrance to the underworlds where he was a born pathfinder and could make his way blindfolded. He paid no more attention to it, but this path gave him knowledge as it broadened; he was on a first-name basis with poor people instantly and knew the sad story of every hut. And everything he saw and heard turned into one long refrain about the same eternal yearning and the same defeats. He didn't worry about it, but it had a depressing effect in his blood, and robbed the pride and fresh excitement from his mind. When he lay his head on his pillow and fell asleep, the pounding of the blood in his ears became an endless procession of weary crowds who went round and round in their blind fumbling for a way out to happiness and the light. His mind could not grasp it, but this too settled with a debilitating effect over his days.

The world of the townsmen remained foreign to him. Most of them were as impoverished as church rats but deftly covered it up and seemed to have no desire but to preserve their skins. "Money!" said Master Andrès. "There's only one 10-krone bill among all the masters in town, and it moves from hand to hand. When it stays for very long with one of them, all the rest of us come to a standstill." The lack of operating means hung over them like exhaustion, but then they would brag about shipowner Monsen's money—there were *some* rich men in town! They each managed to stay afloat by a different tactic: one had sent shoes as far away as the Danish West Indies, another had made the bridal bed for the daughter of the mayor himself. They made their mark as a class by looking down on the common people with contempt.

Pelle had honestly and uprightly decided to follow that path himself, smiling upward and directing his harsh judgment downward, and insinuating himself forward like Alfred. But forces were working in the opposite direction deep inside him and kept pushing him back where he belonged. His fight with the street boys petered out by itself, it was so meaningless; he went in and out of their houses, and the boys became his companions as they gradually reached confirmation age.

The street boys were in irreconcilable war with those who went to private school: they called them "the pigs," from the "trough" they wore on their backs. Pelle had been caught in a crossfire, but took the scorn and the gibes from above with Lasse's temperament, as something that was self-evident. "Some are born to give orders, others to take them," as Lasse said.

But one day he took a swing at one of them. And after he had pickled the postmaster's son so there wasn't a clean spot on him, he discovered that he had a grudge to pay back with all the rich men's sons—even if they weren't taunting him. Something was loosed in his hands by planting them in the face of a boy like that; there was a strange satisfaction associated with stomping those nice clothes into the dirt. After he had thrashed one of the "pigs" he was always in a good mood, and he laughed at the thought of how shocked Papa Lasse would be.

One day he ran into three boys from the Latin school who threw themselves on him at once and whacked him with their schoolbags; each blow said "thanks for last time." Pelle had his back against the wall and was defending himself with his belt but not doing too well; then he gave the biggest of the boys a powerful kick in the gut and ran off. The boy writhed around on the ground and lay there screaming; up at the end of the street Pelle saw the other two boys grappling with him to get him on his feet. Pelle had a black eye.

"Have you been fighting again, you little devil?" asked Young Master.

No! Pelle had just fallen and hit himself.

In the evening he wandered down to the harbor to watch the steamship leave and say goodbye to Peter. He was in a bad mood, and the presentiment of something evil weighed oppressively on him.

Near the steamer there was a crowd of people, and over the railing hung a lot of freshly baked journeymen from this year's crop—all the bravest ones. The rest had already found other kinds of jobs and had become country mailmen or hired hands on farms. "There's no place for us in the trade," they said despondently and gulped. Just turn in your journeyman's piece and then take off! New apprentices all down the line. But the ones here wanted to go to the capital and continue in the trade. All the hundreds of apprentices in town were there, shouting hurrah continually; after all, it was the heroes who were venturing out and conquering the land of happiness for them all. "We'll be coming soon!" they shouted. "Find a place for me! Find a place for me!"

Emil stood over by the shed with some other harbor loafers and watched them—his turn had passed long ago. The indentured apprentice hadn't had the courage to leave town, and now he was a country mailman on the south side of the island, patching shoes at night to survive.

Now Peter was standing up on board. Jens and Pelle stood below and gazed up at him with admiration. "Goodbye, Pelle," he yelled. "Tell Jeppe he can kiss me on Monday!"

A few masters were strutting around down below to make sure that none of the town's apprentices were escaping.

Jens was probably anticipating the time when he would be standing there destitute himself. "Don't forget to send your address," he said. "And find me some work over there."

"And me too!" said Pelle.

Peter spat: "Ptui, that was sour grapes—you can take that home to Jeppe and say thanks for dinner! But greet Master Andrès properly. And then come when I write to you—there's not a damned thing worth staring at in this hole!"

"Don't let the socialists eat you up!" they shouted up to the ones leaving. The word "socialist" was on everyone's lips in those days, but no one knew what it meant—it was used as a swear word.

"If they come up to me with their hocus-pocus, I'll give 'em one on the snoot!" said Peter briskly. Then the steamer pulled away. They received the last hurrah from the outermost jetty. Pelle would gladly have thrown himself into the sea, he was longing so much to get away from it all.

Then he followed the crowd across the harbor square to the circus tent. On the way he overheard part of an exchange that made his ears burn. It was two townsmen talking as they walked.

"He's going to be kicked so he pukes blood," said one of them.

"Yes, that riffraff is appalling! I hope they give the lout a good whipping."

Pelle ducked and slipped back around the tent to the entrance, where he stood every evening taking in the show by smell. He couldn't afford to go in, but it was possible to catch part of the splendor when the curtain was parted for latecomers. Albinus came and went at will—as always when there were entertainers in town. He was familiar with them almost before he saw them. When he had seen a real *tour de force* he would come creeping out under the canvas to show his friends that he could do it too. He was really in his element, walking on his hands along the narrow wharf railing and letting his body hang out over the water.

What Pelle most wanted to do was to go home and sleep through everything. But then a happy couple came walking toward him, a woman taking dance steps and holding an embarrassed young worker tightly under the arm. "Look, Hans," she said, "it's Pelle, the one who brought the two of us together."

Then she laughed out loud in her joy, and Hans stretched out his hand to Pelle with a smile. "Thanks a lot," he said.

"Yes, it was that barn party," she said. "If my dancing shoes hadn't been fixed, then Hans would have flown away with somebody else!" She patted Pelle on the arm. Then the couple left, sincerely happy with each other, and Pelle felt a little playful again. He could do a few good tricks himself.

The next day Pelle was loaned to baker Jørgen to knead dough; the baker had gotten a big order for ship's biscuits for the *Three Sisters* on short notice.

"Let's see you get a move on!" he kept shouting to the two boys, who had taken off their socks and were tramping up in the big kneading trough, with their hands around the molding nailed under the beams. The beamed ceiling was black with dry-rot; vapor and dust and filthy dough dripped down the walls in a slimy mass. When they hung on to the molding too hard, the baker would call up to them: "Put all your weight in it! To the bottom of the dough with you—then you'll have feet like fair maidens! There won't be many calluses left on your feet when we're done."

Søren worked by himself with his head bowed as always, and he sighed now and then. Then old Jørgen nudged Marie, and they both laughed. They were standing up close to each other, and when they rolled out the dough their hands touched; they laughed and flirted incessantly. But the young man didn't see them.

"Are you blind?" his mother whispered to him, poking him hard in the side; she kept her peevish eyes glued on the two of them.

"Oh, leave me alone," said her son, moving away from her a little.

But she followed him. "Go down there and take hold of her the way she wants it! Why do you think she's shoving out her breasts so much? Go and grab her! Let her hips feel your hands, and chuck the old man aside."

"Oh, let me be!" said Søren, moving away wearily.

"Good heavens, you're tempting your father to sin—you know how he is! And she won't control herself much longer, now that she has a right to have her share of things. Do you want to have all that on your head? Go down there and grab her! Hit her if you don't like her—but make her feel that you're a man!"

"Well, are you doing my work?" shouted old Jørgen up to them, turning his smiling face away from Marie. "Step lively, the dough will suck the sickness out of your body! And you, Søren, let's see you get a move on!"

"Yes, let's see you get a move on—don't just stand there like a nitwit!" added his mother.

"Oh, leave me alone! I haven't done anything to anybody, so leave me alone."

"Ptui!" the old woman spat after him. "Are you a man, letting other men paw at your wife? She has to settle for a pitiful, rheumatic old man—ptui! Or maybe you're a woman too? I once gave birth to a girl, but I was always sure that she died—or could it be you? Sure, just go ahead and prick up your ears!" she shouted at the two boys. "You've never seen the likes of what's going on here. Here's a son who lets his old father do all the work!"

"Hey, can you get busy up there!" yelled old Jørgen merrily.

"Mother isn't standing there turning the heads of the young lads, is she?" Marie burst into resounding laughter down below.

Jeppe came to get Pelle. "Now you have to go to the courthouse to be flogged," he said when they reached the workshop. Pelle turned ashen gray.

"What have you done now?" said Master Andrès, looking at him sadly.

"Yes, and it was our customer, on top of it all," said Jeppe. "You deserve it!"

"Can't Father do anything to get him off?" asked Young Master.

"I offered to give Pelle a proper thrashing here at the workshop in the presence of the schoolmaster and his son. But the schoolmaster said no. He wants justice to be meted out properly."

Pelle collapsed. He knew what it meant when a poor boy was taken to the courthouse and was branded for life. His mind searched in despair for some way out. There was only one: death. He could hide the strap under his shirt and go out to the shed and hang himself. He heard a monotonous noise; it was Jeppe giving an admonishing speech, but he didn't hear the words. His soul had already set out to meet death. When the noise stopped, Pelle stood up quietly.

"What? Where are you going?" Jeppe jumped up.

"Out to the courtyard." He spoke like a sleepwalker.

"Do you need to take the strap along out there?" Jeppe and Young Master exchanged knowing looks. Then Master Andrès came over. "You're not stupid, are you?" he said, looking deep into Pelle's eyes. Then he put on his coat and went into town.

"Pelle, you little devil," he said when he came back home, "I've run from Herod to Pilate and fixed it so you'll get off by making an apology. At one o'clock you have to go up to the Latin school. But plan what you're going to say in advance, because the whole class will be there."

"I won't apologize!" It burst out of him like a scream.

Master gave him a long look. "There's no shame in that—when you've done something wrong."

"I didn't do anything wrong. They started it, and they've been beating me up for a long time."

"But you hit them, Pelle, and you can't do that to the rich. They have a doctor's certificate that could ruin you. Does your father have dealings with the town constable? They can dishonor you for the rest of your life. I think you ought to choose the lesser evil."

No, Pelle couldn't do that. "Then they'll have to whip me," he said with his teeth clenched.

"Well, then it's three o'clock at the courthouse," said Master curtly, teary-eyed.

Suddenly Pelle realized how much his stubbornness must hurt Young Master, who had run all over town for his sake, lame and sick as he was.

"All right, I'll do it . . ." he said. "I'll do it!"

"Well, well," replied Master Andrès quietly, "for your own sake. And now I think you'd better get ready."

Pelle took off; he had no intention of giving an apology, so he had plenty of time. He was in a stupor; inside him everything was dead. His thoughts grasped with interest at trivialities and lingered over them as if trying to keep something at bay with chatter. The crazy clockmaker was walking down the street with his sack of sand on his back. His thin legs buckled under him. I should help him carry that, thought Pelle humbly as he passed by. I should help him carry it.

Alfred came strolling along the street. He was carrying a swagger stick and gloves even though it was the middle of the workday. When he sees me, he'll turn down the alley at the coalman's shop, thought Pelle bitterly. Shouldn't I ask him to go with me and speak my case? He's so respectable! And he owes me money for a couple of resolings.

But Alfred headed straight toward him. "Have you seen Albinus? He's disappeared," he said. Something seemed to be twitching in his shiny face. He stood there chewing on his mustache, just like rich people did when they were pondering something.

"I have to go to the courthouse," replied Pelle.

"Yes, I know—you're going to be whipped. But haven't you heard anything about Albinus?" Alfred had pulled him into the coal dealer's doorway so as not to be seen in his company.

"Oh yes, Albinus, Albinus . . ." Something dawned on Pelle. "Wait a minute, he . . . I think he's run off with the circus. Yes, I think so!" Then Alfred did an about-face and ran off—ran in his nice clothes!

Of course Albinus had run away. Pelle understood the whole thing quite well. Last night he had sneaked on board Ole Hansen's sloop, which was going to carry the entertainers over to Sweden during the night. And now he would live a splendid life doing what he liked. Escape was the only clear pathway to life. Before Pelle knew it, he was down at the harbor staring at a docked ship. On impulse he went around and asked about a job on board, but there wasn't any.

He was sitting down on the slip and playing with a wood chip on the water. It was a full-rigged ship, and Pelle loaded cargo onto it; but each time it was supposed to set sail it would capsize, and he had to load it again. All around him carpenters and stonecutters were working on improvements to the new harbor. And over there, a little to himself, stood the Power and worked as usual with some people hanging around him; they stood and stared in morbid anticipation that something might happen. Pelle could feel it as something fateful while he sat sloshing the water to drive his ship out to sea. He would have taken it as a revelation of life's holiest principle if Jørgensen had suddenly started raging like a wild man before his eyes.

But the stonecutter put down his hammer only to pull out his flask of aquavit from under the rock and take a swig; the rest of the time he stood tensed over the granite, as steady as if there were no other forces in the world but he and it. He didn't see the people who stood in gawking anticipation, on tenterhooks, ready to evaporate at the slightest move on his part. He swung so the air sighed, and when he straightened up, his gaze went out past them. Gradually Pelle had put all his expectations into this single man, who bore the town's hatred without blinking and involved himself pensively in all its activities. In the boy's imagination he became a loaded mine; here Pelle stood and didn't know whether it was set, and in an instant the whole thing might blow sky-high. He was a volcano; by his grace the town continued to exist from day to day. And sometimes Pelle let him shake himself a little—just enough so that the whole thing tottered.

But now there was an additional secret between them; the Power had also been punished for committing an offense against the rich! Pelle was not slow in deducing the consequence. Wasn't there already a townsman assigned to stand and watch his game? Pelle too was something of a menace to society. Maybe he would join up with the Power, and then there wouldn't be much left of the rest of the town. In the daytime they would stay hidden up in the rocks, but at night they would come down and plunder the town. They would strike only those who had made their fortune by bloodsucking. People would hide in cellars and attics when they heard that Pelle and the Power were on the rampage. Rich shipowner Monsen would hang dangling from the church spire, as a warning and terror to all. But the poor would come as trusting as lambs and eat from their hands. They would get all they wanted, and then poverty would be banished from the earth, and Pelle could turn, with no feeling of betrayal, toward the bright path upward.

His eyes fell upon the harbor watchman's clock, and it was almost three. He jumped and looked around in bewilderment; out over the sea and down into the harbor's deep water he searched for help. Manna and her sisters: they would contemptuously turn their backs on the defamed Pelle and never look at him again. And people would point—or just stare and think: Look, there he goes, the one who was whipped at the courthouse! Wherever in the world he went, this would follow him like a shadow: that he had been whipped as a child. Something like that would hang invisibly over a person. He knew girls and boys and old taciturn men who came to Stone Farm from regions where no one else had ever been. They could arrive totally unknown, but if there was something in their past it would still rise up behind them and go whispering from mouth to mouth.

He drifted around despondently in his helplessness, and came in his wandering to stonecutter Jørgensen. "Well," said the Power, putting down his hammer, "you seem to have fallen out with the big shots. Do you think you can take it like a man?" Then he grabbed his hammer again. But Pelle had found his bearing and ran toward the courthouse, panting heavily.

XIV

The punishment itself was nothing. It was almost ludicrous: a couple of blows from the cane of the old jailkeeper on the outside of Pelle's clothes. He had endured worse beatings before. But he was branded outside the circles of the poor; he could sense it in people's sympathy whenever he delivered shoes. Dear God, that poor boy, have things gotten that bad for him? said their eyes. Everybody wanted to have a look at him, and when Pelle walked down the street, their faces would appear in the gossip mirrors: There goes the shoemaker's boy! Young Master was the only one who treated him the same as before; Pelle rewarded him with boundless devotion. He bought supplies for the workshop on credit and bore the brunt of things when he could. Whenever there was something that Master had rashly promised to get done, Pelle would sit and slave over it after the workday was over. "What do we care?" said Jens, but Pelle refused to stand by and let the customers tear off Master Andrès's head, or allow him to sit there yearning for whatever kept him going.

He attached himself even more strongly to Jens and Morten—they had a mutual shame, after all—and often went home with them, even though there was little joy to be found in that poor hovel. They were among the most impoverished; even though everyone in the household worked, it wasn't enough.

"It doesn't make any difference," the Power himself said when he was feeling talkative. "Poverty is like a sieve—everything goes right through it. While we're plugging up one hole, ten more appear in the meantime. They say I'm a pig, and why shouldn't I be? Sure, I can do the work of three men, but do I get paid for three? I get my daily pay and the rest goes into the pocket of the man who exploits me. Even if I behaved properly, what would that accomplish? Does a family get proper living quarters, proper food, and proper clothes for 9 kroner a week? Can a worker afford to live anywhere else but the dump, which is normally only a home to swine? Why should I live and dwell like a pig and not be a pig? Is there any meaning in that? Can I release my wife and children from working if I want to live properly? And can I live properly when my wife and children have to go out and take care of strangers? No, half a pint of aquavit will take care of all that, and if it's not enough, then a whole pint." That's the way he would sit and jabber when he had a headful; usually he was silent.

Pelle knew the Power's story from all the daily gossip among the townspeople, and his path seemed to Pelle sadder than that of all the others. It was the myth of happiness itself that had been knocked to the ground.

From the peevish gossip that constantly nagged at stonecutter Jørgensen and would never let up, it appeared that in his youth he had come wandering down from the cliffs wearing patched canvas pants and cracked clogs, but with a swagger as if everything was already his. He never touched aquavit; he had better uses for his powers, he said. He was full of great thoughts about himself and refused to be satisfied with the ordinary. And he had excellent talents—quite meaningless talents for a poor man.

He wanted to get busy right away, turning all concepts on their heads. Simply because he had been conceived up in the cliffs by an old stonecutter, bent with toil, he immediately appointed himself the master of the stone, sweeping aside ancient, well-tested knowledge and hauling new procedures out of his own head. The stone seemed to be released beneath his hands; just place a drawing in front of him and he could carve out demon heads, subterranean creatures, and the great sea serpent—everything that normally had to be done by the artisans over in Copenhagen. Old, hard-working stonecutters suddenly saw themselves set aside, and they might just as well switch over to breaking up rocks—

a vagrant fellow was leaping right over their many years of experience. So they turned to the oldest method of all for teaching youth humility, but even this failed. Peter Jørgensen had the strength of three men and the courage of ten. It was impossible to cope with someone who had stolen skills from God Himself and might even be in cahoots with the Devil. So they gave up and sought revenge by calling him the Power—and put their faith in misfortune.

Following his path meant venturing out into recklessness; no matter how many times respectable citizens made this journey, there was always a good deal of dizziness left behind. At night he would sit and draw and figure, so that no one knew when he got any sleep. And on Sunday when decent people went to church, he would stand there carving the most fantastic things out of stone without getting an øre for it. It was about this time that the world-famous sculptor came from the capital of Germany itself to carve an enormous lion out of granite—in honor of freedom, no less! But he couldn't do a thing with his butter-paddle tool; the stone was too hard for someone who was used to chipping at marble. If he finally managed to bite into it, it was in the wrong place.

Then the Power turned up and started carving the lion based on the clay model the other man had slapped together! Everyone was sure he would crack from that piece of work, but he was so bold in his talent that he completed it to the utmost satisfaction. He received a nice sum of money for it, but that wasn't enough for him—he wanted half the honor too, and a mention in all the papers like the artist himself. When nothing came of it, he threw down his tools and refused to work for anyone anymore. "Why should I do the work and let others take the credit?" he said, showing up when there was an invitation for bids for stone work. With his intractable pride he wanted to push aside those who were born to stand at the forefront of things. But pride goeth before a fall; his punishment was already lying in wait for him.

He had put in the lowest bid for the south bridge, and they couldn't get around him. So they tried to place every possible obstacle in his way, luring the workers away from him, and preventing him from obtaining materials. The town constable, who was in on it, demanded that he finish the contract; and the Power had to work day and night with his few remaining men in order to get done in time. No one had ever seen a more beautiful bridge, but he had to sell the shirt off his back to cover his obligations.

At that time he lived in a pretty little house that he owned. It was out near the East Road and had a spire on the roof—Jens and Morten had spent their earliest childhood there. There was a little garden in front with neat pathways and a grotto that looked like a whole rockery. Jørgensen had built it himself. The house was taken away from him, and they had to move out to the poor people's section of town where they belonged and rent a place. But that didn't break him; he was just as cheerful and even more arrogant than before. He wasn't easy to knock down!

But then he made a bid on the new slipway. They could have disqualified him since he didn't have the capital, but now they were going to get him! He got credit from the savings bank to get started, and the materials and workers were placed at his disposal. Then in the middle of the project, it started all over again, and this time they *were* going to break his neck. Rich and poor alike, the entire town stood together on this one thing. Now they demanded their collateral back; the order established by God Himself—of high and low, wretched and distinguished—had to be upheld. The Power came from the poorest background; he ought to go back calmly to the station he was born to!

He was ruined. The rightful contractor took over a good piece of work for nothing, and stonecutter Jørgensen was left with a pair of cracked clogs and a debt he would never be able to pay. Everybody was happy to see him return to the day-laborer's existence, but he didn't go peacefully. He turned to drink, and occasionally he would flare up and rage like a devil. They couldn't get rid of him; he hovered over everyone's mind like an evil growling. Even when he went soberly about his work, they were preoccupied with him. In this way he squandered the last remnants, and they moved out to the hut near the dump where no one else would live.

He had been a changed man ever since the allocation for the great harbor project had been approved. He didn't touch liquor; whenever Pelle came over, he would be sitting under the window, puttering with drawings and figures. His wife went around weeping, and the old woman scolded, but Jørgensen turned his broad back to them and minded his own business in silence. Once again it was impossible to tear him out of his self-confidence.

The mother would receive them out in the kitchen whenever she heard them come roaring in. "You have to be a little quieter—Father is figuring and figuring, the poor man. He hasn't had a moment's peace in his head since the harbor project was accepted. Ideas are constantly at work in him. 'That's how it should be!' he says. 'Like that!' If only he'd settle down among his peers and leave the big shots to themselves."

He sat over by the window in the midst of the Sunday sunshine, adding up some complicated figures. He was whispering to himself, moving his cracked forefinger, from which the tip had been blown off, down along the numbers. Then he banged on the table. "Oh—to think they haven't learned a thing!" he groaned. The sun played in his dark beard. The hard labor hadn't managed to stiffen his joints or wear him down; the drinking hadn't affected him. He sat there looking like strength personified. His great forehead and neck were completely sunburned.

"Take a look here, Morten," he exclaimed, turning toward them. "Just look at these numbers."

Morten looked at them. "What is it, Father?"

"What is it? Our earnings for the past week! You can see for yourself that the numbers are big!"

"No, what's this?" Morten put his thin hand on his father's beard.

The Power's eyes grew gentle at this caress. "It's a suggestion for a change. They want to keep the entrance at the old place, but that's all wrong; the harbor won't be accessible in an onshore storm. The entrance has to be out here and the outer jetty should curve like this." He showed them on his drawings. "Any fisherman or sailor would say I'm right—but the big gentlemen engineers think they're so smart."

"Are you going to put in a bid—again?" Morten looked at him in horror.

His father nodded.

"But they won't take you seriously, you know that! They'll just laugh at you."

"This time it's my turn to laugh," replied Jørgensen, frowning a little at the memory of all the scorn that had been heaped on him.

"Of course they'll laugh at him," said the old woman over in the corner by the stove, turning her bird-of-prey head toward them. "But then he'll have something to play at. Peter is going to play the big-shot."

Her son didn't answer.

"You're supposed to be good at drawing, Pelle," he said calmly. "Couldn't you fix this a little? There's the breakwater, if we imagine the water gone, and this is the harbor—in cross-section, you understand! But I can't get it to look natural, though the measurements are accurate enough. Here, above the water line, there are supposed to be big headers, and down below is the fracture surface."

Pelle tried his hand at it, but he was too meticulous.

"Not so exact," said Jørgensen, "just put in the general idea!"

"Yes, just put in the general idea," repeated the old woman.

That's the way he was always sitting when they came in. Through his wife they found out that he didn't put in a bid after all, but wanted to take his plans to the man who was in charge of the work and make him a partnership offer. She had lost faith in his plans now and was always uneasy. "He's so strange, constantly obsessed with this one thing," she said, shivering. "He never drinks or rages at the world, like before."

"But that's all well and good," said Morten reassuringly.

"Sure, you talk about good—what do you know? When he's acting normal, a woman knows what's what; but the way he is now... I'm so afraid of a relapse when he's defeated. Don't believe for a minute that he's changed—it's just asleep inside him. With Karen he's the same as always; he can't stand to see her disfigurement. It reminds him of too many things that aren't the way they should be. He says she shouldn't go to work, but how can we do without her help? We have to live, after all! I hardly dare let him catch sight of her. He's angry at himself, but the child suffers under it. He's almost the only one she cares for."

Karen hadn't grown at all in the past few years but had become even more deformed. Her voice was dry and sharp, as if it had passed through desolate and frozen fields before it came out. She liked to sit and watch Pelle and listen to him talk. When she thought he was coming over in the evening, she would hurry home from work. But she never took part in the conversation or anything else; no one knew what she was thinking. Sometimes her mother would suddenly give a shudder and burst into tears when she happened to look at her.

"She should get out of that job soon," her mother would often say. "But the doctor and his wife keep having children, and they plead so earnestly for her to stay just six more months. They're so pleased with her because she's so good with the children."

"Yes, if it was Pelle, he's probably drop them," Karen cackled. She didn't say another word. She never begged to get out of work, and never complained either. Her silence was like a mute accusation that stripped away all comfort whenever she was present.

But one evening she came home and tossed several small coins on the table.

"Now I won't have to go to the doctor's anymore," she said.

"What do you mean? Did you do something wrong?" asked her mother in horror.

"The doctor gave me a box on the ear because I wouldn't carry Anna over the gutter. She's so heavy."

"You weren't sent away because he hit you, were you? You must have answered him back—you're so stubborn!"

"No, but then I happened to turn over the baby buggy with little Erik in it, and he fell out. His head is like a rotten apple." Her expression didn't change.

Her mother burst into tears. "Oh, how could you do that? Dear child!" Karen stood there looking insolent. Suddenly her mother grabbed hold of her.

"You didn't do it on purpose, did you? Did you, Karen?" Karen pulled away with a jerk and went up to the attic without saying good night. Her mother wanted to run after her.

"Let her go," said the old woman softly. "You'll never be able to talk any sense into her. She was conceived in adversity."

XV

All winter long Jens had been rubbing his upper lip with chicken manure. Now his mustache was appearing, and he got himself a sweetheart. She was a nursemaid at the consul's house. "It's so much fun," he said. "You should get yourself one too. When she kisses me, she sticks out her tongue like a little baby."

But Pelle didn't want any sweetheart. First, probably no one would have him—branded as he was—and second, he was feeling melancholy.

Whenever he lifted his head up from his work and looked straight across the manure heap and the pigsty, he had the dim green light beneath the apple trees to dream in. It was like an enchanted world with green shadows and silent movements: countless yellow caterpillars hung there swinging back and forth from their thin threads; the yellowhammers and finches kept flitting from branch to branch, snapping up a caterpillar at every turn, but there were still just as many left. They rolled down from the branches incessantly, hung there, an appetizing yellow, and swayed in the soft breezes of the day, waiting to be eaten.

And deeper inside the green light—as if at the bottom of a pool— were the three girls in bright dresses, playing. Once in a while the two younger ones would glance over, but they averted their eyes at once whenever he looked at them. Manna walked around, so grown-up and poised, as if he didn't even exist.

Manna had been confirmed long ago. She wore her dresses longer

and promenaded demurely along the street, arm in arm with her girl-
friends. She didn't play anymore either; quite some time ago she had
realized with an almost adult sensibility that, God knows, it just
wouldn't do. In a matter of days she leapt from Pelle's side over to the
adult camp. She no longer came to see him at the workshop, and when
he greeted her on the street, she looked the other way.

Manna no longer came dashing in like a wildcat and tore Pelle out of
his chair when she needed something done, but walked primly up to
Young Master's place with her shoe wrapped up in paper. Secretly she
still acknowledged her playmate; when no one was looking, she would
sometimes pinch his arm quite hard and then clench her teeth as she
walked past.

But Pelle was too melancholy to understand this transformation and
too much a child to make the leap along with her into furtiveness. He
stayed behind alone, brooding uncomprehendingly about the new state
of things.

And then she refused to acknowledge him even in secret; he didn't
exist at all for her. And Dolores and Aina had washed their hands of
him; when he looked outside, they turned their heads the other way and
tossed their shoulders: Ugh! They were ashamed that they had ever had
anything to do with the likes of him. He knew very well why.

It had been a special, gentle pleasure to be tumbled around by such
fine, tender fingers—he had many wonderful memories from over
there. It had been so nice to sit with his mouth open and be filled with
delicacies by all three of them until he was just about to suffocate! He
wasn't supposed to swallow; they wanted to see how much they could
stuff in his mouth. Then they would laugh and dance around him, and
the chubby girl-hands would take hold of both sides of his head to press
his mouth shut. Well, Pelle had gradually grown a full yard in understanding society. He knew quite well that he was made of much simpler
stuff than they were, and that it would have to come to an end—even
without the courthouse incident.

But it still hurt. It was like being left behind and defrauded, and he
really ought to refuse to take sustenance. Because Manna—wasn't she
his sweetheart, when it came right down to it? He had just never thought
about it before! It was lovesickness—so that's how it looked! Did the
ones who took their own lives in unrequited love feel any different? But
his sadness wasn't really all that great. When Young Master told a joke
or cursed in his Malabarian way, Pelle could laugh just fine. But the
shame was much worse.

"You should get yourself a sweetheart," said Jens. "Mine's as soft as a baby bird, and she warms me right through my clothes and everything."

But Pelle had other things on his mind. He wanted to learn to swim. He wanted to be able to do everything the town boys could do and win back his place among them. He no longer dreamed of any leader position. So he kept to the pack, moved off a bit if they taunted him too badly—and then came back. At last they got used to him.

Every evening he would set off at a run toward the harbor. South of the big basin, which was now being pumped dry, it was always full of apprentices in the twilight. They jumped around naked among the rocks and swam in splashing groups out toward the west where the sky was still glowing with the sunset. Some distance out there was an underwater rock where they could just touch down; there they would rest before they made the trip back. Their dark heads bobbed on the red water like splashing sea birds.

Pelle made the trip out with them to get used to the depths, which still kept nipping at his legs. When the sea was in bloom, it was like swimming among roses; all the slightly slimy flora, flung up to the surface by the plants from the deep, glowed in the evening light and glided softly against his shoulder. And far out to the west lay the land of happiness in a magnificent gateway of light, or with golden plains stretching all the way to infinity. It lay there shining with its own unique attraction, so that he forgot the limits of his own abilities and swam farther out than his strength could actually manage. And when he turned around, shoving the flowering layer aside with much too violent movements, the water stared darkly at him and the terror of the deep closed around him.

One evening the boys were mean to him; one of them claimed that he could still see marks on Pelle's back from the flogging. "Pelle's never been flogged!" shouted Morten furiously. Pelle didn't answer but merely followed the "squadron"; there was something rather desperate about him.

The sea was a little choppy, which may have confused their sense of direction, or maybe the tide was abnormally high—they couldn't find the resting spot. They splashed around for a while, searching for it valiantly, then they headed back to shore. Pelle looked at them with an odd expression.

"Lie on your back and rest!" they shouted in passing. Then they steered for shore; they were all a little panic-stricken. Pelle tried to rest but wasn't experienced enough—the waves came crashing over his face—and then he struggled after the others. On shore there was a great commotion; he wondered what it was all about. Morten, who never took part in the swimming, had jumped up on a rock and was standing there yelling.

Some of the first boys had reached safety. "You can touch bottom here!" they called, standing with outstretched arms in water up to their mouths. Pelle steadfastly kept on going, but he was certain that it was hopeless; he was making only slight headway and was sinking deeper and deeper. Swells were constantly washing over him and filling him with water. The strongest of the boys had come out again; they swam around him and tried to help but it just made things worse. He saw Morten run screaming into the water with his clothes on, and that gave him a little strength. But then his arms grew numb again; he lay thrashing in place, with only his eyes above water.

Pelle had flown so often in his dreams, and there was always something that held on to his legs and hindered his flight. But this was reality; he was hovering up in the blue sky and floating with outspread wings. And from down there in the darkness he heard a voice: "Pelle!" it called. "Pelle, lad!" — "Yes, Papa Lasse!" he replied, folding his tired wings with relief; he sank with breathtaking speed and a roaring in his ears.

Then he suddenly felt a sharp pain on his shinbone and his hands grabbed onto some seaweed growing on the bottom. He stood straight up with a jolt, and light and air poured over him as if from a new life. On shore the boys were running around in terror with one leg in their pants, and here he stood on an underwater rock in water to his chest, gulping up sea water by the quart. Around him boys were swimming and splashing, in the midst of diving attempts to pull him up from the bottom. The whole thing was almost ludicrous, and Pelle raised his arms high over his head like a greeting to life and took to the sea with a great dive. A good way in he popped up again and lunged over the waves like an acrobat, with bold leaps. But up on shore he fell asleep the way Our Lord had created him — with only one sock pulled over his big toe.

From that day on, the boys accepted him again. He hadn't exactly accomplished any great deed, but for a moment fate had hovered over his head — that was enough. In the future Pelle always took a flatiron along with him and placed it on the shore with the point toward land; he did want to live a little longer. But he refused to be scared off and charged onward.

When it was stormy weather and they couldn't swim out through the surf, they would lie on the beach and let the waves roll them around.

Then the entire ocean comes sweeping in from the west to crash over them; it races like hordes of wild horses with their gray manes flying straight out behind. They come rearing up, sweeping the sea with their white tails, kick wildly at the air with their hooves, and then go under. Others leap forward over them in closed ranks; they lie flat in the water and hurtle forward. The wind tears the white foam from their muzzles and carries it in over the shore where it catches in the bushes and sparkles away into nothingness. On the beach they explode and sink down dead. But out there new hordes storm forward as if the land were going to be trampled down. They rear up, foaming, and flail at each other, leaping with a whinny and a shudder up into the air, bursting with panic—it never ends. In the distance the sun goes down in fire-red smoke; a strip of clouds lies out there, spreading far into infinity. Like a glowing fire on the steppes, the horizon closes in, chasing the hordes before it in panic-stricken terror; and on the shore the naked group of boys hoots and howls. Back and forth they leap with outspread arms, shouting and chasing the wild horses back into the sea!

XVI

Out at the boys' house, things were not going well. Jørgensen hadn't gotten anywhere with his plans; everyone but him knew that's how it would go. People also knew that the engineer had offered him 100 kroner for his plans, and when he refused to take the money and demanded a share in the management and the credit, they showed him the door.

He had never accepted anything this calmly before. He didn't fly into a rage with loud words and commotion but settled down to his daily work at the harbor just like any other worker. He didn't mention his defeat, and no one was allowed to touch on it either; to his wife he acted as if nothing had happened. But once again she had to watch him lock himself away in his silence, without knowing what was going on inside him. She suspected something terrible and complained of her fears to the boys. He never made any scenes, even though he was sometimes drunk; he ate in silence and went to bed. When he wasn't at work, he was sleeping.

But when his plans had been carried out to such an extent that they were evident to everyone, his working days were over. The engineer had taken what he could use from Jørgensen's plans—everybody could see that—and there stood the Power with an empty mouth, just because he had piled so much on the spoon that his mouth wasn't big enough. Most people meant him well and spent a great deal of time discussing the matter; the town was used to neglecting its own affairs to throw all its weight onto that stubborn neck. But now he was down in the dust; everyone had been to the harbor to see the Power moving dirt in a wheelbarrel like any ordinary laborer for his own great project. They were astonished only at how quietly he took it. It was somewhat disappointing that he wasn't writhing under the dead weight and raging in his impotence.

He made do with drinking, but he did it for his own benefit. He was constantly in a haze of liquor, working the bare minimum to maintain his drunken state.

"He's never been like this before," wept his wife. "He's not out on the streets raving, but he's so mean all the time that I can't stand being in the house. He touches everything with his meanness and chases after poor Karen something terrible. He has no respect for anyone except his old mother, and God knows how long that will last. He doesn't work but just drinks; he steals my hard-earned *skillings* out of my dress pocket and spends them on booze. There's no shame in him anymore—he had so much self-respect before. And he can't hold his liquor like he used to. He keeps on falling down. He came home a few days ago all bloody, with a cut on his head. What have we done to Our Lord that He should afflict us this way?"

The old woman didn't say a thing but shifted her sharp gaze from one to the other, keeping her thoughts to herself.

That's how things went week after week. The boys grew tired of hearing their mother's whining and stayed away from home.

One day when Karen was supposed to run an errand for her mother, she didn't come back. She didn't come back the next day either. Pelle heard about it down by the boat harbor, where she had last been seen. They were dragging the bottom for her, but no one dared tell Jørgensen about it. Later that afternoon they came carrying her past the workshop. Pelle knew what it was when he heard all the heavy footsteps out in the street. She was lying on a litter, and two men were carrying her. In front of her the autumn wind was rolling the first rustling leaves along, and her thin arms hung down to the cobblestones, as if she wanted to grab them. Her limp hair hung down too, and the water dripped off her. Behind the litter walked the Power, dead drunk. He was holding his hand in front of his eyes and muttering as if in prayer, and he kept raising his forefinger. "She has found peace," he said thickly, trying to look soulful. "That peace which surpasses..." He couldn't find the right words.

Jens and Pelle relieved the men at the litter and carried her home. They were afraid of what was going to happen.

But the mother was standing in the doorway and received them in silence, as if she had been expecting them. She was simply white in the face. "She couldn't stand it anymore," she whispered to them and knelt down by the child.

She lay with her head against the tiny, worn-out body, whispering inaudibly; now and then she would stuff the child's fingers into her mouth to stifle her sobs. "And you were supposed to run an errand for Mother," she said, smiling as she shook her head. "You're a fine girl, can't even buy two spools of thread. And what about the money you took along—you threw it away, didn't you?" Her words came between smiles and tears, and they sounded like humming. "Did you throw it away? It doesn't matter. You couldn't help it. Little girl, little girl." Then she fell apart. Her tightly pressed lips broke open and then closed again, and she kept doing that as she rocked her head back and forth while her hand dug eagerly into the child's pockets. "Didn't you go on an errand for Mother?" she whimpered. She needed to have something confirmed in the midst of all this—just some unimportant thing—and she dug in the coin purse. There were a few øre and a strip of paper.

Suddenly she stood up, her expression terrifyingly stern, and turned toward her husband, who was standing there swaying against the wall. "Peter!" she shrieked in fear. "Peter! Don't you know what you've done? Forgive me, Mother. You stand here and she spent 4 øre of the 13 to buy candy! Look at this—her hand is still sticky!" She opened the child's fist, which was clenched around some sticky paper. "Oh that poor, persecuted child; she needed to sweeten her life! For 4 øre—and then into the brink! That's how much joy is given to a child in this house. Forgive me, Mother," she said again as if she had committed some offense. "And everything she did was wrong! So she had to leave! Karen, Karen, I'm not mad at you—it was all right—what do a few *skillings* matter? I didn't mean it when I reproached you for staying home. But I didn't know any other way to get food; he drank up the little we had—that man over there!" She turned the face of the corpse toward the father and pointed.

That was the first time the Power's wife uttered accusations against him, but he didn't comprehend it. "She has found peace," he muttered, trying to straighten himself up a bit. "The peace which . . ."

But then the old woman in the corner stood up—she hadn't moved until then. "Shut up!" she said sternly, poking her cane into his chest, "or your old mother will curse the day she brought you into the world."

He stared at her, light dawning; the fog seemed to lift from his gaze. For a moment he stood there, unable to take his eyes off the corpse. He seemed about to throw himself down next to his wife, who was again bent over, whispering. Then, stooped, he went upstairs and lay down.

XVII

When Pelle got home the workday was over, but he didn't feel like running down to the beach to swim. The image of the drowned girl continued to haunt him, and for the first time death appeared to him with its sinister "Why?" He could find no answer, and gradually he forgot about it and thought of other things. But the dread kept on hovering over him and made him afraid for no reason at all, so that he became suspicious of the dusk itself. The secret powers that emanate from heaven and earth, where light and darkness meet, seized him as well with their mysterious agitation. Restlessly he moved from one thing to another, as if he had to be everywhere in order to deal with the incomprehensible, which stood menacing behind everything. For the first time he experienced the inexorable without the disguise of something that he himself had committed; never before had life itself settled down on him with its heavy weight.

Pelle thought that something was calling, but couldn't figure out from where. He crept from his window out onto the roof and up along the ridge—maybe it was the world. The hundreds of tile roofs in the town lay absorbing the purple of the evening sky, blue smoke rose up, and voices drifted up from the hot darkness beneath the houses. He heard Crazy Anker's shouts too; this perpetual warning of something meaningless was like the complaint of a sick animal. The sea out there and the dense evergreen forests to the north and south—it had all been long familiar to him.

Then there was singing in his ears—and far out in the distance; and behind him someone was standing and blowing hot air at his neck. He turned around slowly—he wasn't afraid of the dark anymore—and he knew beforehand that nothing would be there. Into his bright soul the twilight had slipped, with its mysterious bustling of creatures that could not be perceived with any ordinary senses.

He went down to the courtyard and wandered around. It was quiet everywhere. Peers the cat was sitting on the rain barrel and mewing feebly at a sparrow on the clothesline. Young Master was coughing in his room; he was already in bed. Pelle hung over the edge of the well and peered vacantly at the gardens. He was hot and dizzy, but cool air rose up from the well and wafted soothingly over his head. Bats glided like ghosts through the air, coming so close to his face that he could feel the flapping of their wings, and then they turned away with a little snap. He had the strangest urge to weep.

Up in the tall black-currant bushes something was moving, and Miss Shermanna's head came into view. She moved cautiously, looking around, but when she caught sight of Pelle, she came over quickly.

"Good evening," she whispered.

"Good evening!" he replied loudly, delighted at seeing a person again.

"Hush! You mustn't shout like that!" she pleaded.

"Why not?" Pelle was whispering now too. He was scared.

"Because you shouldn't—stupid! Come here and I'll whisper something to you—no, come closer!"

Pelle stuck his face into the elder bush. Suddenly both her hands were around his head; she kissed him violently and pushed him back. Dazed, he searched for a foothold, but she stood there laughing, her face glowing in the dark. "You didn't hear me," she whispered. "Come here, and I'll tell you!"

This time he laughed heartily and stuck his face eagerly into the elder bush. But all of a sudden he had her fist in his face. She laughed with contempt.

He stayed in that position, paralyzed; he held his mouth out as if still expecting a kiss. "Why did you hit me?" he asked, staring at her with glazed eyes.

"Because I can't stand you! You're a perfectly hideous boy—you're so simple."

"I've never done anything to you."

"Is that right? Well, that's all fine and good—you could have not kissed me!"

Pelle stood there, stammering helplessly, and his entire world of experience collapsed around him. "It . . . it wasn't my fault," he finally managed to say. He looked incredibly stupid.

Manna imitated his expression. "Boo! Moo! Watch out you don't freeze solid to the ground and turn into a lamppost. Over here at the wall there's nothing for your mind to shine on."

In a flash Pelle was over the wall. Manna seized him swiftly by the hand and pulled him into the bushes. "Aina and Dolores are coming any minute—then we'll play," she said.

"I didn't think they were allowed outside at night," said Pelle, permitting himself to be pulled along.

She didn't answer but looked around for something to offer him, like in the old days. In her rush she tore off a handful of raspberry leaves and stuffed them in his mouth. "Here, take these and shut up!" She was the old Manna again, and Pelle laughed.

They had reached the gazebo. Manna swabbed his swollen cheek with wet mulch while they waited.

"Did it hurt much?" she asked sympathetically, putting her arm around his shoulder.

"It doesn't matter at all. It was just a slap," he replied manfully.

"That's not what I'm thinking about. You know what I mean—did it hurt much?"

Pelle looked at her darkly. She seemed curious. "Was it here?" she said, letting her hand glide down over his back.

He stood up silently to leave, but she grabbed his wrist. "I'm sorry," she whispered.

"Aren't they coming soon?" asked Pelle harshly; he was intending to be stern like in the old days.

"No, they're not coming at all—I was teasing you. I wanted to talk to you!" Manna gasped for breath.

"I didn't think you wanted anything to do with me anymore."

"I don't either. I just wanted to . . ." She couldn't find the words and stamped angrily on the ground. Then she said slowly and emphatically, with all the gravity of a child: "Do you know what I think? I think I love you."

"Then we can get married when we're old enough," exclaimed Pelle happily.

She looked at him for a moment, appraising him. The courthouse, the cane! thought Pelle. He realized that now he was going to hit her. But then she laughed.

"Oh, what a precious fool you are," she said and, as if in thought, she let the wet mulch trickle down his back.

Pelle cogitated for a brief moment too, then boldly stuck his hand down to her breast. It landed on softness, touching with amazement; a new realization welled up inside him and made him grab her.

She looked at him in terror and tried gently to remove his hand, but it was too late. The boy had made the great leap over to her.

When Pelle sneaked home, he was overwhelmed but not happy. His heart was pounding wildly, and his brain was in chaos. Out of pure instinct he walked very quietly. He lay tossing and turning for a long time, unable to sleep. His soul had opened itself to the mysterious, and now he had discovered the living blood inside him. It was singing its song in his ears, rushing in and out of his heart and cheeks, chattering around in countless pulses so his body vibrated. Powerful and secretive it made its way all through him, filling him with profound wonder— never before had he known all this.

In the following days his blood was his secret conspirator in every- thing. He felt it like a caress when it filled his limbs and brought a round, taut feeling to his throat and wrists. He had his own secret now and didn't betray by a single look that he had ever known Shermanna. All of a sudden his bright days had been transformed into bright nights. He was still enough of a child to long for the old days with their open, daytime games, but something made him listen to the future and bend his soul in search of the mysterious. The night had made him a partici- pant in its secrets.

He didn't speak to Manna any more often than before. She never came into the garden, and if he encountered her, she would turn down a different street. On her face there was constantly a red flame, as if it had been burned in. Soon afterwards she went to stay on a farm on the east side of the island where an uncle of hers lived.

But Pelle felt nothing and regretted nothing. He walked around in a stupor; everything seemed hazy and veiled to him. He was completely bewildered by all that was happening within him. There was pounding and activity everywhere inside him; ideas that were too fragile were destroyed, and stronger ones were put in their place that could support a man. His limbs grew harder, his muscles turned to steel, he had a general feeling of breadth in his back and hollow strength. Occasionally he would awaken from his lethargy to a moment of astonishment— whenever he felt himself a man in some way. So it was that he heard his own voice one day. It had a deep resonance that sounded quite foreign to his ear and made him listen as if it were someone else talking.

XVIII

Pelle was struggling against decline at the workshop. A new boy had arrived, but Pelle still took care of the most difficult things, handled the borrowing, and scraped together a living on credit. He had to go to the impatient customers and try to placate them. He got lots of exercise but never learned anything properly. "Run down to the harbor right now," the master might say. "Maybe there's some work we can nab." But Master was more interested in the news from down there.

Pelle also went there on his own. Everybody in town went down to the harbor as often as they could; it was the heart of the town. Everything came and went through it: money and fantasies and the fulfillment of dreams. Every man had been to sea and had his best memories from out there, and his hardest tasks. Their dreams turned in that direction. Beyond lay the sea, sucking in their thoughts: of the young who wanted to get out and get moving, and of the old who were reminiscing. It was like a song in everyone's mind, and like God deep inside their souls. The abundance of life moved in that direction—all that was mysterious and unexplained. The sea had drunk the blood of thousands without changing its color, and the riddle of life brooded in its restless waters.

From the bottom of the depths, fate rose up and gave her man short notice. He might become a landlubber like baker Jørgen, who never went to sea again after it had once warned him off; or he might get up in his sleep and walk right out over the side of the ship like bosun Jensen. Down there where the drowned men wandered, ships sank to bring them what they needed. The bloodless children of the sea drifted up to the beach now and then, to play with children born on Sunday and bring happiness and death to them.

Three times a week the steamer came across the sea, bringing word from the King's Copenhagen. And ships came in covered with ice; others were completely waterlogged or had corpses on board. And big schooners arrived that ran to the hot countries and had real Negroes in their crews.

Down here stood the old men who had left the sea, staring out all day long over the playground of their manhood until death took them. The sea had breathed rheumatism into their limbs; they had been banged around until they were warped and crooked, and on winter nights you could hear them howling like wild animals from the pain.

Down here all the riffraff hung around—the invalids and the decrepit and the lazy. And those who were ambitious would rush back and forth across the harbor with sheets whipping to ferret out some profit.

Young people were always playing around down here—it was like meeting the future to play here by the open sea. Many never went any further; but many others were gripped and let themselves be whirled out into uncertainty—like Nilen. When the ships were rigged, he couldn't stand it any longer; he sacrificed two years' apprenticeship and ran off aboard a long-haul freighter. Now he was far out in the trade winds, on his way south around the Horn after redwood.

And with every steamship there was someone who emigrated. The girls were the most undaunted about resigning their jobs; they steamed off briskly and dragged heavy men along after them in heady infatuation. And men left to try something that paid more than work here at home.

Pelle had seen this all once before—this same urge—and felt the pull in himself. Out in the countryside it was the dream of all poor people to fight their way into town, and the boldest of them would actually try it one day, their cheeks hot, while the old folks warned of the town's corruption and told them not to venture there. And in the town there was the dream of the capital: Copenhagen, that was happiness! Those who were brave would one day hang over the side of the ship, waving goodbye, with that uneasy glaze in their eyes at playing for such high stakes. Over there they would be vying with the cleverest people. But the old folks shook their heads and spoke of the capital's temptations and corruption.

Now and then someone would come home and tell them they were right. Then the old people would run gloating from door to door—what did we tell you! But others came home for the holidays, and there was no end to their elegance. And for some girls, things went so well that they had to ask for Wooden-Leg Larsen's advice.

Those who got married over there—well, they were provided for. They came home to see their parents at long intervals with many years in between, traveling on deck among the livestock and giving the cabin stewardess 50 øre in order to be listed among the cabin passengers in the newspaper. Their clothes were nice enough, but their faces revealed their gauntness. "Looks like there isn't enough food over there," said the old women.

But Pelle wasn't interested in those who returned home. All his thoughts were with those who went away. The urge for flight was so strong in him that his heart ached painfully in his chest. The sea, whether it was churning or lazily becalmed, constantly filled his head with the roar of the world out there—a hollow, enigmatic song of happiness.

One day when he was on his way down to the harbor, he met old thatcher Holm from Stone Farm. Holm was walking along looking the houses up and down; he lifted his legs high out of sheer amazement and muttered to himself. On his arm he had a split basket with sandwiches and *snaps* and beer.

"So, here's somebody at last," he said, sticking out his hand. "I was just wondering what happens to everybody who heads over here year after year—and whether they ever amount to anything. Mother and I have often said it would be nice to know how the future has shaped up for one or another of you. And then this morning she thought it was time I took the bull by the horns before I completely forgot my way around. I haven't been here in ten years. And from what I've seen so far, Mother and I have no cause to regret that we stayed at home. Nothing grows here but lampposts, and Mother doesn't know anything about cultivating those. I haven't seen any thatched roofs either—here in town they couldn't support a thatcher. But I want to see the harbor before I go home."

"Then we can go there together," said Pelle. It put him in a good mood to meet people from his home district; in his mind the country-side around Stone Farm would always be his childhood home. He chattered on, pointing things out.

"Yes, I've been to the harbor two or three times before," said Holm, "but I've never been lucky enough to see the steamship. People say great things about it though. They say it carries all our products to the capital now."

"It's in port today," exclaimed Pelle eagerly. "It's leaving tonight."

Holm's eyes lit up. "So I'll get to see that rascal too! I've seen the smoke drifting over the sea often enough from the hills back home, and it really made me think. They say it eats coal and is made of iron." He looked at Pelle uncertainly.

He was fascinated by the great empty harbor basin where a couple of hundred men were at work. Pelle pointed out the Power, who was now slaving away like any idiot, letting them give him the heaviest work.

"So that's him, is it," exclaimed Holm. "I knew his father. Now there was a man who wanted to do something extraordinary, but he never managed it. And how are things with your father? Not the best, I've heard."

Pelle had been home not too long ago; things weren't going very well, but he kept quiet about it. "Karna's feeling a little poorly," was all he said. "She's probably been working too hard and overstrained herself."

"There's a rumor that they're having a hard time getting by; they've probably taken on too much," Holm went on. Pelle didn't answer. And then the steamship took all their attention. Holm completely forgot to use his mouth, talkative though he usually was.

The steamer was busy taking on crates of cargo; at both hatches the winches sang, wheezing each time they were pulled in a new direction. Holm grew so light-footed; he was standing on pins and needles when the boom swung in over the dock and the chain rattled down, and he retreated in under the warehouse roof. Pelle wanted to take him on board, but that was out of the question. "It's like a vicious beast," he said, "the way it's sneezing and carrying on."

Over on the dock near the forward hatch a pile of poor household goods was heaped up every which way. A man was standing there holding a mahogany mirror—the only object of value—in his arms; his expression was gloomy. You could tell by the way he blew his nose (with his knuckles instead of his fingers) that this was an unfamiliar situation for him. His eyes were fixed on the humble possessions, anxiously following every pitiful item on its journey up into the air and then down into the belly of the ship. His wife and children were sitting on the edge of the dock eating food from a basket. They had probably been sitting there for hours; the children were whimpering and tired. Their mother comforted them and lay them down to sleep on the stones.

"Aren't we going to leave soon?" they asked constantly, whining.

"Yes, the ship is going soon, but you must be good—or else they won't take you along. And you're going to the capital where they eat white bread and wear leather shoes all the time. That's where the King himself lives, and they have everything in the shops there." She put her shawl under their heads.

"But that's Per Anker's son from Blåholt!" exclaimed Holm after he had stood and stared at the man for a while. "So . . . are you going to leave the countryside?"

"Yes, I think so," replied the man quietly, his hand fumbling over his face.

"I thought things were going so well for you. Didn't you go to the east side of the island to take over an inn?"

"They lured me into it—and now I've lost everything."

"You should have looked into it beforehand. That doesn't cost anything but the trouble."

"But when they presented me with false books that showed a bigger profit than there really was . . . Shipowner Monsen was probably behind it, along with a brewer from over there who had taken over the hotel as payment for debts."

"But how did the big shots sniff *you* out?" Holm scratched his head. He didn't understand it at all.

"Oh, they probably heard about the 10,000 kroner I inherited from my father; people like that have their nets out. So then one day they sent a commissioner after me. Ten thousand—that was exactly the right amount—and now they've taken over the hotel again. Out of kindness they let me keep this junk here. But I don't care about any of it." He turned his face away suddenly and wept. Then his wife came quickly over to him.

Holm pulled Pelle away with him. "I think they'd like to be left alone," he said quietly.

He kept on walking, chattering about the man's sad fate as they moved along the jetty, but Pelle wasn't listening. A little schooner sailing far out at sea had caught his eye, and he grew more and more restless.

"I think that's the Iceland schooner," he said at last. "I've got to go home!"

"Sure, run along," said Holm. "Thanks for the good tour. And say hello to Lasse and Karna!"

Up on the harbor hill Pelle met Master Jeppe, and farther up were Drejer and Klausen and Blom. The Iceland skipper had been expected for months. Word had already spread that he was approaching, and all the town's shoemakers took off—to hear, even before the gangplank had been put down, whether business had been good.

"The Iceland ship has arrived," said the grocer and the leather dealer when they saw the shoemakers running. "We'd better get busy and write up the bills, because now the shoemakers are coming into money."

But the skipper had most of the shoes in the hold and brought the terrible news that they wouldn't be able to sell any more shoes in Iceland. The winter trade was ruined for the shoemakers.

"What does this mean?" asked Jeppe bitterly. "You've certainly taken your time about it. Did you use some new approach up there? Other years you've been able to sell it all—lock, stock, and barrel."

"I did what I could," replied the skipper gloomily. "Offered the customers larger lots, lay at anchor and sold small amounts from the ship. I tried the whole west coast, but there's not a thing to be done about it."

"Why not?" asked Jeppe, horrified. "Are the Icelanders going to walk around with no shoes on?"

"It's the factories," replied the skipper.

"Factories, factories!" Jeppe laughed contemptuously but with a tinge of uncertainty. "You're not trying to make me think that they can make shoes by machine, are you? Cut out and tie up and bind the edges, sew the soles and all that? No, only a human hand controlled by a human mind can do that, damn it all. Making shoes is human work. You can't replace me with a machine—a couple of wheels whirring around, and that's all! A machine is dead—I know that. And it can't think or take any extra effort: this is how it has to be for *that* foot because it has tender toes! Or: I'll give this sole that particular shape in the arch because it looks so pretty! Or: now I have to be careful not to cut the upper leather!"

"There are machines that can make shoes, and they do it cheaper than you do. That's a fact," snapped the skipper.

"I'd like to see that! Why don't you show me a shoe that wasn't made by a human hand," laughed Jeppe snidely. "No, there's something else behind this; someone is trying to trick us."

Insulted, the skipper went on his way.

Jeppe kept on claiming that there was some kind of cheating behind it, but the story about the machines continued to haunt him anyway; he kept coming back to it. "Pretty soon they'll be making people by machine too," he bellowed angrily.

"No, there I think the old-fashioned way will survive," said baker Jørgen.

One day the skipper stepped in through the workshop door, threw a pair of shoes onto the platform, and departed. They had been bought in England and belonged to the first mate of a three-masted bark that had just come in. Young Master looked at them, turned them over in his hands, and looked again. Then he called Jeppe. The sole, edge, and upper leather had been sewn together at the same time—a grownup man's shoe and sewn together all at once! And to top it all off, the factory stamp was on the arch.

Jeppe didn't have a good word to say about them, but there was still no getting around it.

"So we're of no use anymore," he said, shaking; all his boasting had vanished. "Because if they can make one thing with machines, they can make other things too! Our craft is doomed, and we'll all be out of a job someday. Well—thank God I don't have much time left!" That was the first time Jeppe admitted that he too owed Our Lord a death.

Every time he came out to the workshop he would slip into the same topic and stand there turning over the disdained shoes in his hands. Then he would criticize them. "We have to make a bigger effort next winter."

"Father is forgetting that it's all over for us," replied Young Master wearily.

Then the old man fell silent and shuffled off, but a little while later he was back, fingering the shoes to find mistakes. His mind was constantly preoccupied with the New; praise for the craft no longer crossed his lips. When the young master came and asked for his help with a difficult task, he would refuse; he felt no need to triumph over youth with the old skills but went around in a state of collapse. "What about everything we valued so highly?" he might ask. "Because machines don't make masterpieces or win any medals, do they? What's happened to all the skill?"

Young Master didn't look that far ahead. He was thinking mostly about the money they didn't have right now. "How the devil are we going to get by, Pelle?" he asked sadly.

Little Nikas looked around for something else; they couldn't afford to keep a journeyman. He decided to get married and settle down as a master up north. The Baptists' shoemaker had just died, and he could probably get customers by joining the sect—he was already going to their meetings. "But be careful," said Jeppe, "or it won't work out."

It was a powerful blow to them all. Klausen went bankrupt and had to go to work at the new harbor. Blom left town, leaving his wife and children behind; they had to go live with her parents. Things had been going downhill at the workshop for a long time; now this happened and made the decline tangible in everyone's eyes. But Young Master pushed it aside. "Soon I'll be healthy once more," he said, "then just watch me build up the business again." He stayed in bed more often and was sensitive to all kinds of weather. Pelle had to take care of everything.

"Run out and borrow it!" Master would say. And when Pelle came home with a "no," he would look at him with his big, astonished eyes. "What a bunch of Plimsolls!" he exclaimed. "Then we'll have to put the soles on with pegs."

"On a lady's patent-leather shoe? That won't do," said Pelle firmly.

"It'll be all right—we'll polish the bottom with black wax."

But when the black had worn off, Miss Lund and the others showed up, and they were angry—they weren't used to wearing pegged shoes. "It must be a misunderstanding," said Master, beads of sweat on his forehead; or else he would hide and send Pelle to placate them. When it

was over, he panted with exhaustion and reached up to the shelf.
"Could you get me something, Pelle?" he whispered.

One day when they were alone, Pelle gathered up his courage and
said that it probably wasn't healthy with all that liquor since Master was
throwing up so much.

"Healthy?" said Master. "No, God help me, it's not healthy; but
the beasts have their demands, you know! At first I could hardly get the
liquor down—especially beer—but now I've gotten used to it. If I
didn't feed them, they would soon pounce on me and start gnawing
away."

"Do they digest it?"

"Do they! Just as much as you can pour into them. Or have you ever
seen me drunk? I can't get drunk—the tubercles take it all, and it's pure
poison to them. The day I get drunk again I'll thank God, because then
the beasts will have croaked, and liquor can have its way with me again.
Then the trick is to stop or else your mind will go."

The food had gotten even worse since the journeyman had left.
Master couldn't afford to buy a pig in the spring, so there was no one to
take the garbage; they had to eat everything themselves. Master Andrès
never came to the table. He ate almost nothing: a couple of sandwiches
now and then was all. They ate breakfast alone at seven-thirty. It consisted of salt herring, bread and drippings, and gruel. The gruel was
made from all kinds of bread scraps and leftover porridge mixed with
cheap beer; it was yeasty and inedible. Whatever was left over from
breakfast was put into a big crock standing in the corner of the kitchen,
then warmed up the next day with a little fresh beer added; this is how it
went all year round. The contents were only renewed whenever someone happened to kick the crock and break it. The boys stuck to the salt
herring and bread and drippings; the gruel they just used for fishing in.
They had their fun by throwing something into the gruel and discovering it again six months later.

Jeppe was still asleep in the alcove with his nightcap askew over one
eye. In his sleep he still had that comical air of self-confidence. The
room was thick with fumes. The old man had an odd way of breathing—inhaling the air with a long snore and then letting it run rumbling
through his body. When it got too bad, the boys would make a commotion; then he'd wake up and scold them.

They longed wildly for dinner. As soon as Jeppe shouted "Come
and get it!" in the doorway, they dropped everything, lined up accord-
ing to age, and tumbled after him. They pinched each other in the
behind and made faces in silence. At the head of the table Jeppe reigned,

in his skullcap, trying to maintain strict table etiquette; no one was allowed to start before he did or keep eating after he stopped. They would pick up their spoons, put them down again with a frightened glance at him, and were about to die with suppressed laughter. "Yes, I'm very hungry today, but you don't have to pay attention to that," he liked to warn them after they had dug in. Pelle winked at the others, and they kept on eating, emptying dish after dish, and kept right on. "There's no respect," roared Jeppe, pounding on the table. But when he belched, discipline descended upon them at once, and they all belched in turn. Master Andrès sometimes had to make a trip through the dining room if they got too rowdy.

The long workday, the food, and the bad workshop air left their mark on Pelle. His kindness to Master Andrès knew no bounds; he could sit and work until midnight without compensation when something had been promised. But otherwise he slipped unconsciously into the others' rut and acquired their view of the day as something endlessly bitter that you had to make your way through. It was physically necessary to work at half-power, and he grew sluggish in his movements, less quick to act in general, more brooding. The dimness in the sun-forsaken workshop made his skin pale and filled him with unhealthy fantasies.

On his own he didn't earn much, but he had learned to keep house with very little. Every time he got hold of 10 øre, he would buy a savings stamp with it, and in this way he kept track of his *skillings* so that they would add up to something. Now and then he would also get a little help from Lasse, but he had a more and more difficult time finding anything to spare. And Pelle had also learned to resign himself to his poverty.

XIX

The crazy clockmaker threw open the workshop door. "Bjerregrav is dead," he said solemnly. "Now there's only one person left to grieve over all the misery!" Then he walked on, shouting his news in the door at baker Jørgen's; they heard him going from house to house along the street.

Bjerregrav dead? Only last night he was sitting here on that chair beneath the platform, and his crutches were over in the corner by the door! He came and shook hands all around in his usual naive way—that much-too-soft hand that they felt uncomfortable touching because it was so intimate, almost skinless in its warmth, as if a person had been inadvertently caught in the nude or had exposed something. Pelle was reminded of Papa Lasse, who had never learned to armor himself either, but who continued to be the same trusting, good-natured soul and remained unaffected by harsh experiences.

The big baker had, as usual, started in on him; he grew crude at the touch of Bjerregrav's childlike vulnerability that allowed his heart to burn all the way into his handshake. "Well, Bjerregrav, have you tried out you-know-what since last time we saw you?" he asked, winking at the others.

Bjerregrav blushed bright red. "I'm content with the experience Our Lord has granted me," he replied, blinking.

"Do you believe it! He's over seventy and doesn't even know how a woman's made!"

"Since I've always felt best when I was alone . . . and besides, I have a clubfoot."

"That's why he goes around asking all kinds of questions that any child could answer," said Jeppe jauntily. "Bjerregrav has never gotten rid of his childhood innocence."

Even on his way home, with Pelle helping him over the gutter, he stopped in his perpetual amazement. "I wonder what star that is?" he said. "It has a different kind of light than the others. It looks so red—I hope we're not in for a harsh winter with frozen ground and expensive fuel for the poor people." Bjerregrav sighed. "You shouldn't stare too hard at the moon. Skipper Andersen was done in just by lying on the deck and sleeping with the moon right on his face. Now he's an idiot!"

Last night just the same as always—and now dead! And no one had suspected or imagined it, so that they could have been a little kind to him in the end. He died in his bed with their last jeers on his mind, and it wouldn't help to send a messenger to say: "Pay no attention to it, Bjerregrav, we didn't mean any harm!" Maybe it had made his last hours bitter. Here they stood, at any rate, Jeppe and his brother Jørgen, unable to look each other in the eye, oppressed by what was now irreparable.

And there was an emptiness—as if the clock had stopped in the parlor. The steadfast thumping of his crutches would no longer approach the workshop at six o'clock. Young Master grew uneasy at that hour; he couldn't get used to the idea. "Death is a nasty thing," he said when the truth finally dawned on him. "A wretchedly disgusting thing.

Why should someone disappear and leave nothing behind? Now I listen for Bjerregrav's crutches and have only emptiness in my ears; and when some time has passed, there won't be even that. Then he'll be forgotten, just as the next person after him will be too—and that's how it will continue. What kind of real meaning is there in all this? Damn it, Pelle! 'Heaven,' they would probably say, but what do I care about going up to a wet cloud and sitting and singing Hallelujah? I would much rather walk around here and have a dram—especially if I had a good leg."

The boys followed him to the grave from the workshop. Jeppe wanted them to do it in order to make amends. Jeppe and baker Jørgen walked closest to the coffin, wearing top hats; otherwise only poor women and children showed up, out of curiosity. Teamster Due drove the hearse. He had gotten a couple of horses now, and this was his first ceremonial duty.

Life moved on, sluggish and uneventful. Winter had arrived again with its doldrums, and the Iceland trade had been ruined. The shoe-makers didn't work by lamplight anymore; there wasn't enough work to cover the cost of the kerosene. The hanging lamp was put away, and the old tin lamp was taken out again; it was good enough for sitting around to gossip. Neighbors often came over at dusk. When Master Andrès had gone to bed, they would tiptoe out, or loaf around until Jeppe announced that it was bedtime. Pelle had taken up his carving work again. He would sit as close to the lamp as possible and listen to the conversation while he worked on a bone button that was supposed to be carved to look like a 25-øre piece. Morten was going to get it as a humbug pin.

The talk was about the weather, and how lucky it was that the frost hadn't come and stopped the big harbor project. Then it turned to the Power and from him to Crazy Anker and then on to poverty and dissatisfaction. The socialists over in Copenhagen had been occupying their minds for a long time; disturbing news had been arriving all summer. It was quite clear that they were making progress—but in what? It wasn't anything good, that was for sure. "It's always the poorest ones who make trouble," said Wooden-Leg Larsen, "so their numbers must be great." It was like hearing the roar of something out on the horizon and not knowing what was going on. The echo of the revolt of the lower class reached them in distorted form. They understood only that those on the bottom wanted to turn God's lawful order on its head and see about getting on top—and they involuntarily stole a glance at the poor people here in town. But they went along in their usual lethargy, working when there was work, and otherwise accepting their lot.

"That's all we need," said Jeppe. "Here, where we have such a well-organized welfare system."

Baker Jørgen was the most eager of them all; every day he would arrive with something new to tell. Now they had threatened the life of the King himself! And now the military had been called out!

"The military!" snorted Young Master. "That'll be a big help! All they have to do is throw a fistful of dynamite among them, and there won't be a whole pants button left. No, now they'll probably take the capital." His cheeks burned—he was already imagining the event.

"And then what? Then they'll plunder the royal treasury, won't they?"

"Then . . . no, then they'll come over here—the whole flotilla!"

"Here? No, by Satan! We'll call out the entire militia and shoot them down on the beach. I've cleaned out my musket."

One day Marker came running. "The pastry chef on the square just got himself a new journeyman from over there—and he's a socialist!" he shouted, out of breath. "He arrived with the steamship last night." Baker Jørgen had heard about it too.

"Well, now you'll have them on top of you," shouted Jeppe ominously. "You've all gone around playing with the new spirit of the times. This would have been something for Bjerregrav—him with his pity for the poor."

"Let the tailor have peace in his grave," said Wooden-Leg Larsen in a conciliatory voice. "He shouldn't bear the blame for the evil forces that may be at work today. He only meant well! And maybe these people mean well too."

"Mean well!" Jeppe was full of scorn. "They want to throw out law and order and sell their fatherland to the Germans. Rumor has it the amount has been agreed on and everything."

"The Germans are going to be let into the capital at night when our own people are asleep," said Marker.

"Yes," said Master Andrès solemnly, "they gave away the secret that the key is under the mat—those little devils!"

Then baker Jørgen burst out laughing; he filled the whole workshop once he got started.

They wondered what kind of fellow the new journeyman was; no one had seen him yet. "He probably has red hair and a beard," said baker Jørgen. "That's Our Lord's way of marking those people who have sold their souls to the Evil One."

"God only knows what the pastry chef wants with him," said Jeppe.

"People like that don't do any work, they just make demands! I've heard they're supposed to be freethinkers, to boot."

"What devilish nonsense!" Young Master shook with amusement. "I don't think he'll be growing old here."

"Old?" The baker raised his heavy body. "Tomorrow morning I'm going straight to the pastry chef and demand that he get rid of him. I'm the chairman of the militia, and I'm sure all the citizens feel the same way I do."

Drejer thought that it might be wise to make the request from the pulpit—just like during the plague and that terrible year with the field mice.

The next morning Jørgen Kofod walked past on his way to see the pastry chef. He had put on his old militia coat; at his belt still hung the leather pouch in which he had carried pieces of flint for his flintlock musket many years ago. He filled out his clothes quite impressively, but he came back without accomplishing his mission. The pastry chef praised his new journeyman to the skies and wouldn't hear of parting with him. "He was completely bewitched. So we just won't buy anything there anymore—we all have to agree on that. And no decent family ought to associate with him in the future. That traitor!"

"Did Uncle Jørgen see the journeyman?" asked Master Andrès eagerly.

"Yes, of course I saw him—from a distance, that is. He had hideous, piercing eyes. But he won't bewitch *me* with his lizard look."

In the evening Pelle and the others strolled over to the square to catch a glimpse of the new journeyman. There were a lot of people loitering around there for the same reason. But he stayed indoors.

But one day toward evening Master came limping in. "Hurry up, damn it!" he shouted breathlessly. "He's going past!" They dropped everything and stormed through the hallway into the good parlor that they were normally not supposed to enter. He was a tall, powerful man with full cheeks and a big, rakish mustache just like Master's. He had flaring nostrils and he thrust out his chest; his vest and coat were open, as though he needed a lot of air. Behind him slunk the street urchins, hoping for some adventure; they had lost their usual intrepid manner and were walking in silence.

"He's striding around as if the whole town were already his," sneered Jeppe. "But he'll soon be finished here."

XX

Someone ran by out on the street, and then another, and another; it turned into a whole stampede of footsteps. Young Master scratched at the wall. "What on earth is going on, Pelle?" He didn't intend to get out of bed that day.

Pelle ran to find out. "It's Jens's father having a delirious fit," he said. "He's cleared out the entire harbor and is threatening to kill everybody."

Master raised his head. "I think, by God, I'll get up." His eyes shone. In no time he was all dressed and limped off. They heard him coughing hideously in the cold.

Old Jeppe shoved his witness's skullcap into his pocket before he ran out—they might need an official present. The boys sat there for a moment, staring at the door like sick birds; then they took off too.

Outside, everything was in an uproar. The wildest rumors were circulating about what stonecutter Jørgensen had already done. The excitement couldn't have been any greater if an enemy fleet had dropped anchor and proceeded to fire on the town. Everyone dropped whatever they had in their hands and dashed down to the harbor. The narrow lanes were one big swarm of children and women and shopkeepers wearing aprons. Old, rheumatic sailors crept out of their old-age hibernation and lumbered along with one hand on the small of their backs, their faces grimacing with pain.

> Footy, footy, footy, fie
> for the waxy snouts!

A couple of street boys permitted themselves this little digression as Pelle and his apprentice comrades came running by. Aside from that, all attention was fixed on one thing: the Power had let loose again!

There was almost a kind of festiveness on everyone's face as they ran—a sense of bright expectation. The stonecutter had been silent for a long time. He went about pushing his wheelbarrow like any other giant oaf, dull and dead in appearance, slaving like a bear and quietly taking home his 2 kroner a day. It was almost embarrassing to watch, and there was an air of silent disappointment about him. And now he had suddenly exploded so everybody squawked!

They raked him up one side and down the other as they hurried along. They had all forseen that something like this would have to happen; he had been going around brooding for a long time, storing up bad feelings. It was simply a wonder that it hadn't happened earlier. People like him shouldn't be allowed to go free; they ought to be locked up for life! And they went over his life in town for probably the hundredth time: from the day he arrived, young and bold, pushing his way forward in his rags, wanting to make his powers felt, until he drove the child into the sea and fell apart like some kind of idiot.

Down by the harbor there was a big crowd. Everyone who could crawl or walk had shown up. People were in a good mood, in spite of the cold and the hard times; they stamped their feet and told jokes. With one stroke the town had shaken off its winter doldrums. People crept up onto the boulders and, in a crowd, clung to the timber caissons that were going to be sunk to make jetties. They craned their necks nervously, as if something might catch them unawares and chop off their heads. Jens and Morten were there too, standing huddled together off to one side. They looked pitiful with their shy, anxious faces. And over where the big slipway slanted down toward the bottom of the basin, the workers were standing in groups, aimlessly tugging at their pants, glancing stupidly at each other, and cursing.

But down at the bottom of the great basin the Power was puttering around alone. He seemed as unconscious of his surroundings as a child absorbed in play; he had his own plans, but it was hard to say what they were. In one hand he was holding a bunch of dynamite sticks; with his other he leaned on a heavy iron bar. His movements were slow and steady like a lumbering bear. Whenever he straightened up, his comrades would shout biliously at him: they were going to tear him into little pieces, rip open his stomach so he could smell his own guts, cut him with their sheath knives, and rub lunar caustic into the wounds—if he didn't throw down his weapon and let them get back to their work.

The Power didn't deign to reply; maybe he didn't hear them at all. Whenever he raised his face, his gaze was far away, heavy with a strange gravity that was not human. His terrible, deadly-tired face revealed his sorrow more deeply than anyone could comprehend. "He's crazy," they whispered. "Our Lord has taken his mind." Then he bent to his work again. He seemed to be placing the dynamite sticks underneath the big jetty, the one he himself had designed. He pulled sticks of dynamite from all his pockets—that's why they were bulging so strangely!

"What the devil is he planning to do? He's not going to blow up the jetty, is he?" they said, trying to slip behind the skids and sneak up on him. But his eyes were everywhere; if they made the slightest movement, he was there with his iron bar!

The entire project was at a standstill. Two hundred men stood idle hour after hour; they growled and threatened him with death and the Devil, but didn't dare step forward. The foremen ran around aimlessly, and even the engineer had lost his head. Everything was in chaos. The town constable paced back and forth in full uniform looking inscrutable; his mere presence was comforting, of course, but he didn't do a thing.

One wild suggestion followed the other: they should make a huge shield and push it in front of them, or mighty tongs of long timbers to catch him with. But no one tried to carry them out. They ought to be happy that he even allowed them to stand where they were. The Power could sling a stick of dynamite with such force that it would explode and sweep everything away.

"The dump cars!" someone shouted. Finally here was something sensible. In an instant they were filled with armed workers, and they released the brake. But the cars didn't budge. The Power, with his devilish mind, had anticipated them. The endless chain wouldn't move; he had jammed it. And now he knocked out the supports from a couple of struts so they couldn't send the cars down on him by manual force.

This was no delirium—at least no one had ever seen delirium manifest itself like this before. And he hadn't touched any liquor since the day they carried home his daughter. No, this was the result of the calmest decision in the world. When they got up from their morning break and headed down toward the slipway, he was standing there with his iron bar and calmly told them to keep away—the harbor was his! A couple of punches fell before they realized that he was serious. Yet he wasn't mean; it was quite evident that he didn't want to hit them. It had to be the Devil riding him—against his own will.

But no matter what the reason was, enough was enough! Now the big harbor bell was ringing for the noon meal; it sounded quite ridiculous, like an insult to decent people who wanted nothing more than to take up their work again. They had no desire to waste the whole day, but they didn't want to risk life and limb for a madman's shenanigans either. Even strong Bergendal had left his scorn for death at home today and was content to grumble just like the others.

"We should punch a hole in the dike," he said. "Let the beast drown in the waves!"

They picked up their tools to begin at once. The engineer threatened them with the authorities and the law; it would cost thousands to pump out the harbor again. They didn't listen to him. What did he matter when he couldn't even assure them the peace they needed to do their work?

They wandered over to the harbor entrance with pickaxes and crowbars to knock a hole in the dike. The engineer and police officers were pushed aside. Now it was no longer a question of the work; it was a matter of how long two hundred men would permit themselves to be made fools of by a crazy devil. Now Belisarius would have to step aside; the Power would be allowed to come up out of there—or perish in the waves!

"I'll give you a full day's pay!" yelled the engineer, trying to stop them. They didn't hear a thing. But when they came around the bend, there stood the Power at the foot of the dike swinging his pickaxe so that it crashed against the dike wall. He beamed with helpfulness at every blow; he had chosen the weak spot where the water seeped in, and they watched in horror at the progress of his blows. What he was doing was sheer madness.

"He's going to fill the harbor for us, that devil!" they shouted, pelting him with stones. "And think of all the work it took to empty it!"

The Power took cover under a strut and kept on hammering away.

So there was nothing they could do but shoot him down before he reached his goal. A load of buckshot in the legs, if nothing else, so at least he would be put out of action. The town constable was at his wits' end, but Wooden-Leg Larsen had already gone home for his musket. There he came now, clumping along in a crowd of boys. "I've loaded it with rock salt," he said so the constable could hear him.

"Now you're going to be shot!" they yelled down. In reply the Power swung the pickaxe at the foot of the dike so the packed clay gave a sigh and shot a stream of water all the way up to their feet. A long groan announced that the first plank had burst.

The decision had been made. Everybody was talking about shooting him down as if it were a legal sentence and they longed to see it carried out. They hated the man down there with a concealed hatred that needed no explanation. With his stubbornness and fierce will he was a slap in the face of them all; they would have gladly lent their own heel to crush him if they could.

They rained abuse down over him, let him hear about the home he had destroyed with his arrogance, the child he had driven to death— and his crude attack on the town's philanthropist, wealthy shipowner Monsen! For a moment they tore themselves out of their lethargy to

take part in bringing him down. And now it was going to be done
thoroughly; they had to have peace from this one man who refused to
bear his shackles quietly but made them clank beneath poverty and
oppression.

The town constable balanced his way out along the dock to pro-
nounce sentence on the Power. It had to be proclaimed three times in
order to give him the chance to surrender. He was deathly pale, and at
the second proclamation, he gave a great shudder. But the Power didn't
throw any dynamite at him; he simply touched his hand to his head as if
in greeting and made a few stabbing motions in the air with two fingers
sticking out from his forehead like a pair of horns. Over where the
pharmacist was standing in a circle of elegant ladies there was muted
laughter. Everyone's face turned toward the mayor's wife, who was
standing tall and buxom on a rock, but unmoved she stared down
toward the Power as if she had never seen him before.

For the mayor the gesture had the force of an explosion. "Shoot him
down!" he bellowed so he was blue in the face, rushing excitedly along
the jetty. "Go ahead and shoot, Larsen."

But no one paid any attention to his shouts. Everybody was crowding over by the slipway, where a shriveled-up old woman was busy
fumbling her way down along the incline to the bottom of the basin.
"It's the Power's mother," went from mouth to mouth. "Look how old
and tiny she is! You can hardly believe that she could have brought such
a giant into the world."

They followed her intently with their eyes as she tottered across the
jagged bottom, which with its pressure cracks looked like broken pack
ice. She made slow progress, and she constantly seemed on the verge of
breaking her legs. But the old woman kept going, bent over and shriv-
eled up as she was, looking straight ahead with her nearsighted eyes.

Then she caught sight of her son, standing there hefting the iron bar
in his hand. "Put down that stick, Peter!" she shouted hoarsely, and
mechanically he dropped the bar. He slowly stepped back from her
until she had him backed into a corner and was about to grab hold of
him; then he cautiously swept her aside, like some kind of pest.

A sigh went through the crowd and passed around the harbor like a
roving shudder. "He hits his own mother," they said, shivering. "He
must be crazy."

But the old woman was on her feet again. "So you hit your own
mother, Peter?" she exclaimed in a voice full of amazement, reaching up
for his ear. She couldn't reach it, but the Power bent down as if gravity
itself were pulling him and let her grab it. And she walked off with him

like that, up the sloping slipway where the people were standing like a wall. He walked bent over, looking like a huge animal in the tiny woman's hands.

Up there the police stood ready to jump on him with ropes, but the old woman turned peppery when she saw what they intended. "Get away or I'll set him loose on you again!" she hissed. "Can't you see that he's lost his mind? Are you going to assault the one God has stricken?"

"Yes, he's crazy," said people in a conciliatory tone. "Just let his mother punish him—she's the best one to do it."

XXI

Pelle and the youngest boy were alone in the workshop now. Jens finished his apprenticeship in November and was fired at once. He didn't have the courage to go to Copenhagen and try his luck, so he rented a room in the poor section of town and moved in with his sweetheart. They couldn't get married since he was only nineteen. Whenever Pelle had errands on the north side of town, he liked to look in on them. The workbench stood between the bed and the window; there Jens sat and scraped by, doing occasional repair work for the poor. Whenever he had a piece of work to do, she would stand over him, waiting tensely for it to be done so they could get something to eat. Then she would cook the food in the woodstove while Jens sat and watched her with burning eyes until he got another piece of work in his hands. He had become gaunt and had grown a thin goatee; lack of nourishment shone from both of them. But they loved each other and helped each other with everything, awkward as two children playing house.

They had chosen the dreariest neighborhood. The lane, which went straight down to the sea, was full of garbage; scabby dogs and cats ran around and dragged fish guts over to the stoops, leaving them there. In front of each doorway filthy youngsters were rolling in the dirt. One Sunday morning when Pelle had been out to visit them, he heard screams from one of the hovels and the sound of chairs overturning. He stopped in bewilderment. "That's just One-Eyed Johan beating up his wife," said an eight-year-old girl. "He does that almost every day."

Outside on a chair sat an old man, staring unperturbed at a little boy who kept running around in a circle. Suddenly the child stopped trotting, put his hands on the old man's knee, and said with delight: "Papa runs around the table, Mama runs around the table. Papa hits Mama, Mama runs around the table—screaming." He imitated her scream, laughed with his little idiot face, and drooled down his shirt.

"Yes, that's right," the old man said. The boy had no eyebrows; his forehead receded over his eyes. He ran around delightedly, stamping and imitating the commotion inside. "Yes, that's right," said the old man unperturbed. "Yes, that's right!"

In the window of one of the hovels sat a woman staring pensively outside, her forehead pressed against the windowpane. Pelle recognized her and greeted her cheerfully. She waved him over to the street door; her bosom was still just as bold, but her face seemed rather careworn. "Look, Hans!" she shouted uncertainly. "Here's Pelle, who's the reason why the two of us found each other!"

The young worker rushed into the room. "Then he'd better get out of here, and be quick about it!" he said menacingly.

Master Andrès stayed in bed most of the time, in spite of the mild winter. Pelle had to receive all the orders and take Master's place as best he could. They didn't make anything new anymore, they only did repairs. And Master was constantly scratching at the wall to start up a conversation.

"Tomorrow I'll get up," he said, his eyes flashing. "Yes I will, Pelle! Order us some sunshine for tomorrow, you little devil! This is the turning point—now nature is turning over inside me. When this is over, I'll be completely well! I can feel how it's raging in my blood, because now the daggers are drawn—but the good fluid will win! Then you'll see me . . . if only the shop could get on its feet, because it's all going to hell. You'll remember to borrow the list of lottery winners for me, won't you?"

He wouldn't admit it, but things were going downhill for him. He didn't curse the pastors anymore either, and one day Jeppe quietly sent for one. When the pastor had gone, Master Andrès pounded on the wall.

"It's a damned strange thing," he said, "because what if there's something to it, after all? And he's an old man, that pastor . . . He ought to be thinking about himself instead." Master lay there looking pensive, staring up at the ceiling. He could lie that way all day; he didn't feel like reading anymore.

"Jens was actually quite a nice fellow," he might suddenly say. "I never did like him, but he had a good heart. Do you think I'll ever be myself again?"

"Yes, when it gets warm," replied Pelle.

Now and then Crazy Anker would come over and ask about Master Andrès. Then the master would pound on the wall. "Let him come in here," he said to Pelle. "I'm so shamefully bored."

By now Anker had completely given up on the marriage to the King's eldest daughter and had taken matters into his own hands. Now he was working on a clock that would be the new age incarnate and keep time with people's happiness. He had gears and a pinion shaft—the whole works—with him, and he explained it all as his gray eyes leapt from one thing to another around him; they were never fixed on what he was showing them. Like everyone else he had a blind faith in Young Master, and he explained everything in detail. The clock was going to be designed so that it only told the time when everybody in the country had what they needed. "Then you can always tell if someone is in need—and there's no way of getting around it! Because time passes and passes and they're not getting any food; and one day she'll start chiming for them, and they'll go hungry to their grave." His temples throbbed incessantly; to Pelle it looked like the pecking of a restless soul that was locked inside. And his eyes bulged with their gray, indescribable expression.

Master would be totally swept up in the story as long as it lasted. But as soon as Anker was out the door, he would shake the whole thing off. "It's just a bunch of madman's babble," he said, astonished at himself.

Then Anker came over again with something new to show them. It was a cuckoo—every ten millennia it would pop out over the clock and cuckoo. It was no longer time that was going to be shown, but rather the long, long stretch of time that had no end—eternity. Master looked at him in bewilderment. "Get him out of here, Pelle," he whispered, wiping the clear sweat from his brow. "I feel dizzy. He's making me crazy with his jabbering."

Pelle was actually supposed to spend Christmas at home, but Master didn't want to let him go. "Who's going to talk to me in the meantime? And take care of everything?" he said. Well, Pelle didn't resist much either; there wasn't much joy in going home. Karna was feeling poorly, and Papa Lasse had enough to do with keeping up her spirits. Lasse was brave enough, but Pelle couldn't help noticing that, from one visit to the next, he was sinking deeper and deeper into difficulties. He hadn't been able to come up with his annual payment, and the winter stonecutting which, year after year, had helped him through the worst periods didn't amount to much anymore—he didn't have the strength for all the burdens he had to bear. But he was still feisty. "What does it matter if I'm a few hundred kroner short when I've improved the property by several thousand?" he said.

Pelle had to agree. "Take out a loan," he said.

Lasse did try. Every time he came to town, he would run around to lawyers and saving banks. But he couldn't get any loan on the property. On paper it belonged to the county until after he had accomplished what he was supposed to do for a certain number of years.

Around Shrovetide he was in town again, and this time he had lost his spirit. "We might as well give up pretty soon," he said despondently, "because Ole Jensen has sent an omen—you know, the man who had the place before me and hanged himself when he couldn't meet his obligations. He appeared to Karna last night."

"That's stupid," said Pelle. "You shouldn't believe in things like that." Pelle wasn't completely immune to believing it either.

"Is that so? But you can see for yourself how it's getting harder and harder for us—and just when we've improved everything and ought to be able to enjoy the fruits of our labor! And then there's Karna, who can't seem to get well." Lasse was quite disheartened. "Oh, what the devil—maybe it *is* just superstition!" he exclaimed suddenly; he had the gumption to try it one more time.

Master Andrès kept to his bed. But he was still cocky enough; the more downhill things went, the friskier was his tongue. It was quite strange to listen to his boasting words and see him lying there, emaciated and ready to expire at any moment.

At the end of February the weather was so mild that people cautiously began to look for the first signs of spring. Then, in one night, winter came sailing down from the north on an enormous expanse of pack ice. Seen from the coast, it looked as if all the sailing ships in the world had gotten new white sails and were on their way down to Bornholm to greet them before continuing on their voyage after their winter rest. But they weren't allowed to rejoice over the thaw for very long; within twenty-four hours the island was locked in ice on all sides and there wasn't a single spot of open water in sight.

And then it started to snow. "Here we were just starting to think about tackling the soil," people said. But they didn't worry about it; there was plenty of time. They set about struggling with the snow and fixing up the sleighs; there hadn't been the right snow for sleighs all winter. Soon the snow was ankle-deep and there was enough for sleighing. Now it could stop—and stay for a week or two so they could have some proper sleigh parties out of it. But the snow kept on coming down, reaching up to their knees, to their waists; by the time people went to bed, it was impossible to work their way through it. And whoever didn't have to get up at daybreak might not get out of bed at all, because during the night it had turned into a blizzard, and by morning the snow was up to the eaves and covered all the windows. They could hear the storm raging in the chimney, but inside it was warm. The boys had to go through Jeppe's house to reach the workshop; there was a heavy blanket of snow blocking all the outer doors.

"What the hell is this?" asked Master Andrès, looking at Pelle in horror. "Is the world going under?"

The world—it might very well have ended already. They didn't hear a sound from outside and couldn't tell whether their fellow townspeople were dead or alive. All day long they burned candles, but the coal supply gave out; they had to see about going out to the shed. With all of them shoving, they managed to get the top half of the kitchen door pushed open enough that Pelle could crawl out. But it was impossible to make any headway outside; he disappeared in the snowdrifts. They had to dig tunnels to the well and the coalshed. As for food, they had to make do as best they could.

In the early afternoon the heat of the day melted the snow so much on the south side that the uppermost part of the windows let in a little daylight; it shone through the snow in a weak milky glow. But they saw no signs of life outside. "I think we're going to starve to death like the North Pole explorers," said Master, creeping around with excitement, his eyes burning like candles; he was in the midst of a world adventure.

Along toward evening they dug and burrowed halfway over to baker Jørgen's house; they had to secure access to bread, at the very least. Jeppe walked along with a lamp. "Watch out that it doesn't slide down on top of you," he kept on saying. The lamp glistened on the snow and the boys were enjoying themselves. Young Master lay in bed, shouting at every sound from outdoors, so his cough tore at his chest; he couldn't contain his curiosity. "By heaven, I want to get up and watch the bandits," he insisted. Jeppe scolded him, but he refused to give in. He won the battle and put on his pants and leather shirt. A blanket was wrapped around him. But his legs wouldn't hold him, and he fell back on the bed with an exclamation of despair.

Pelle looked at him until his chest began to ache. Then he took Master in his arms and carried him carefully into the snow tunnel. "You're certainly strong—good heavens!" Master held one of his arms tightly around Pelle's neck; with the other he chopped at the air, provocative as the strongman in a circus. Hip! Hip! He was infected with Pelle's strength. He rummaged around cautiously in the glittering vault, his eyes flashing like ice crystals. But in his gaunt body burned the fire; Pelle could feel it against him, through all his clothes, like a consuming blaze.

The next morning they dug the tunnel all the way over to baker Jørgen's steps, and with that the connection to the outside world was complete. Over there great things had happened during the past twenty-four hours. Marie had been so frightened by the thought that the end of the world was near that she had rushed to bring Little Jørgen into the world. Old Jørgen was in seventh heaven; he had to come over at once to tell them about it. "He's a real devil, the spitting image of me."

"I can believe that," exclaimed Master Andrès with a laugh. "Is Uncle Jørgen content now?" But Jeppe took the news quite coolly; he didn't approve of the relationships over at his brother's.

"Is Søren happy about the boy?" Jeppe asked cautiously.

"Søren!" The baker burst out laughing. "All he thinks about is Judgment Day and praying to Our Lord!"

Later in the day they heard the clanging of shovels; the workers were out. They were shoveling along one of the sidewalks so people could make their way through. The path hung up near the eaves.

Then they could get down to the harbor. It was just like catching your breath again after a choking fit. The ice lay as far as the eye could see, piled up in big chunks and with long embankments where the surf had moved. A hurricane was blowing up. "Thank God," said the old sailors. "Now the ice will get a move on!" But it didn't budge. Then they knew that the entire sea was frozen; there couldn't be a single open spot as big as a tabletop for the storm to seize hold of. But it was an eerie sight to see the ocean lying dead and lifeless like a stone desert in the midst of that raging storm.

And one day the first farmer came to town with news from the countryside. The farms out there were snowed in; they had to dig a path out to the open fields and lead the horses out one by one. But he didn't know of any mishaps.

All commerce stood still; no one could bring themselves to do anything. And they had to save too—especially on coal and kerosene, which were threatening to run out. The shopkeepers had already warned of this at the beginning of the second week. Then people set about doing useless tasks; they built peculiar things out of snow or took to wandering across the ice from town to town. And one day half a dozen brave men got ready to take the iceboat over to Sweden to get the mail; they couldn't live without news from the outside world any longer. On Christiansø the people had raised the emergency flag. They gathered provisions—a little here, a little there—and prepared to send an expedition over.

Now deprivation arrived, growing out of the closed earth, and became the only topic of conversation. Those who were reasonably well off talked of nothing else; those in need were silent. There was an appeal for public charity: Bjerregrav's 5,000 kroner were still in the treasury. But no, they weren't, after all. Shipowner Monsen claimed that Bjerregrav had gotten the money back by the deadline, and in Bjerregrav's papers there was no evidence to the contrary. Nobody knew for sure what had happened, and it was always good material for a conversation. No matter how things stood, however, Monsen still got to play the big shot, as always. Out of his own pocket he gave 1,000 kroner to the needy.

Many people turned their eyes to the sea, but the men in the iceboat didn't come back—the mysterious "out there" had swallowed them up. It seemed as if the world had sunk into the sea; beyond the bumpy surface of ice that stretched to the horizon there now lay an abyss.

The holy people were the only ones who were busy. They held crowded meetings about the end of the world. Everything else lay dead; who cared about the future under these conditions? At the workshop they sat and froze with their coats and hats on. What little coal was left had to be saved for Master. Pelle was constantly in Master's room. He didn't say much but just lay there, tossing, with his eyes on the ceiling. But as soon as Pelle left he would pound on the wall again. "I wonder how it's going?" he said, wearily. "Run down to the harbor and see if the ice will break up soon—it's making things so cold. The whole world is going to turn into a lump of ice if this keeps up. Tonight they're supposedly having a meeting about Judgment Day. Run over and hear what they say about it."

Pelle would run off and come back with news, but when he returned Master had often forgotten all about it. Now and then Pelle could report that the sea looked like a blue clearing far out in the ice; then Master's eyes would light up. But with his next report the whole thing had turned to ice again. "The sea eats the ice," said Master with a faraway look. "But maybe it can't handle so much. Then the cold will take over and we'll be done for!"

But one morning the sheet of ice drifted out to sea, and a hundred men set about clearing the ice from the harbor entrance with dynamite. It had been three weeks since they had had any mail from the outside world, and the steamship went out for a run to Sweden for news. It was grabbed by the ice out there and rolled toward the south. From the harbor every few days they could see it wandering past in the ice floe, first north and then south.

At last the heavy shackles burst completely, but it was hard for the earth and the people to pull themselves together again. Everything had received a blow. Master couldn't recover from the change when it switched from bitter cold to thaw in the air. When his cough wasn't wracking him, he lay quietly. "Oh, I'm suffering so damned much, Pelle," he complained in a whisper. "It doesn't hurt, but oh how I'm suffering."

Then one morning he was in a good mood. "Now I'm past the turning point," he said in a feeble but cheerful voice. "Just you wait and see how fast I get better! What day is today? Thursday? Hell and damnation, then we'd better get my lottery ticket renewed. I feel so light! All night long I floated through the air, and I only have to close my eyes to fly again. It's the power in the new blood, Pelle. By summer I'll be well. Then I'm going out to see the world! But what the devil— you never can experience the best: outer space and the stars and all that! Then you'd have to be able to fly! But last night I was there."

Then a coughing fit seized him. Pelle had to bend him over; it sounded like a wet slapping inside him at every cough. He held one of his hands on Pelle's shoulder and rested his forehead against his chest. Suddenly the coughing stopped; his gnarly white hand clenched burning hot at Pelle's shoulder. "Pelle, Pelle!" gasped Master, turning his bulging eyes toward him in terrified horror.

I wonder what he sees now? thought Pelle, shivering, and lay him back down again.

XXII

Pelle often regretted that he had signed up for an apprenticeship of five years. During his apprenticeship he had seen between a hundred and two hundred boys move up to the ranks of journeyman. They were put out on the street at once, while new boys from the countryside and the town took the positions vacated. So there they stood and were now supposed to start on their own; in most cases they hadn't acquired any proper skills, but had just sat there toiling for their master's bread. Now they suddenly had to be responsible for the craft itself. Emil had gone to the dogs. Peter was a country mailman, earning one krone a day by walking thirty miles. When he came home he could sit down with his awl and shoemaker's cord and earn the rest of his living at night. Many of them left the craft entirely; they had toiled away the flower of their youth for nothing.

Jens didn't fare much better than most; he sat and struggled to make a living as a cobbler, and they were literally starving. His sweetheart had just miscarried, and they had no food in the house at all. When Pelle went out there they would sit staring at each other, red-eyed. The law hung over their terrified heads like a threat because they weren't married. "If only I knew something about farming," said Jens, "then I'd go out to the country and work for a landowner."

Carefree as he was, Pelle couldn't help seeing his own fate in that of all the others; it was only his devotion to Master Andrès that had kept him from leaving and looking for some other kind of work.

Now the whole thing suddenly dissolved all by itself: old Jeppe sold the workshop, boys and all. But Pelle wouldn't let himself be sold. Now his chance had come, and he intended to close this chapter with one swift stroke.

"You are *not* leaving!" yelled Jeppe menacingly. "You have a year left of your apprenticeship! I'll turn you in to the authorities—you've tried that before, I suppose." But Pelle left, and they could run to the authorities as much as they wanted to.

Happy and in a buoyant mood he rented an attic room over on the harbor hill and moved his odds and ends down there. It was like standing up straight after years of bondage. He had no one above him, no burden, no obligation. He had struggled for years against constant decay. It had not strengthened his youthful courage that day in and day out he had used all his strength in a vain effort to stem the workshop's decline. The most he could do was to slow the pace a little and then slide along with it. A good dose of resignation and a little too much patience in view of his eighteen years: that was his immediate gain from his downhill slide.

Now everything lay at the foot of the hill, and he could step to one side and straighten up a bit, with his conscience in order and a slightly shabby joy over freedom in abundance. He had no money to travel, and his clothes were in a bad way, but for the time being it didn't concern him. He just took a deep breath and faced the times. Master's death had left so much emptiness inside him. He missed the soulful gaze that had made him feel as if he were in the service of an idea. His surroundings had become so oddly godforsaken now that the master's eyes no longer rested on him, half clear and half unfathomable. And that voice, which had always pierced him to the heart, either when it was angry or exceedingly gentle and playful! In its place his ear now found loneliness.

He did nothing to pull himself together, but only lazed around. One or two masters had their fingers out after him: they knew he was a clever and reliable worker and wanted to have him indentured for one krone a week plus board. But Pelle wasn't interested. He felt that his future lay elsewhere. Beyond that he was sure of nothing, but just waited, with a strange dullness, for something to happen—anything. He had been ejected from his safe existence and felt no urge to intervene. From his window he could see down to the harbor; the big project was under way again after the hard winter. A hum rose up to him from the work down there. They were chopping, drilling, and blasting; the dump cars moved up the tracks in long lines, dumped their contents onto the shore, and returned. His limbs were craving hard work with pick and shovel, but still his mind did not seek that way out.

When he went out on the street the industrious townspeople turned their heads after him and exchanged remarks, loudly enough for him to hear. "There goes Master Jeppe's boy, loafing," they would say to each other. "He's young and strong, but he doesn't really want to do anything. He'll probably turn into a drunk, you'll see!"

"Wasn't he the one who got the whipping at the courthouse for his rough behavior? Well, what can you expect?"

So Pelle stayed home. He got a piece of work now and then from his friends and the poor people he knew, muddled his way through it with no tools, and went out to Jens when it couldn't be done. Jens had a few lasts and forms. The rest of the time he sat freezing by the window and staring out over the harbor and the sea. He watched the ships tacking and pitching on the sea, and with every ship that glided out of the harbor and vanished over the horizon, it seemed as if one last opportunity slipped away from him. That's how it felt, but it didn't affect him. He withdrew completely from Morten and didn't go out among people anymore. He was ashamed of walking around when everyone else was working.

He had figured out a practical arrangement for his food: he lived on milk and bread and only spent a few øre a day. He was just able to keep the worst hunger at bay, but there was never any money for fuel. When he sat idle he enjoyed his rest with a certain sense of shame, but otherwise nothing much was alive inside him.

On sunny mornings he got up early and sneaked out of town. All day he would prowl around in the big conifer forests or lie on the slopes by the beach and let the murmur of the sea seep into his half-doze. He ate like a dog whatever he stumbled on that was edible, without thinking about what it was. The glitter of the sunlight on the water and the powerful scent of the firs and pines and the incipient ebullience of spring made him giddy and filled his mind with half-wild imaginings. The animals weren't frightened by him, but would merely stop for a moment and take a sniff; then they went on living without a care and unfolded their daily life before his eyes. It didn't bother him in his half-doze, but when human beings approached he would slink away and hide with an inimical, almost hostile feeling. He felt a kind of well-being out here. Often he had an urge to give up his room in town and creep in under a fir tree for the night.

He didn't return home until darkness concealed him, and then he flung himself on the bed with his clothes on and lay there unmoving. Far off he could hear his neighbor, Strøm the diver, come up across the attic, staggering, and start rummaging in his food supplies. The smell of food, mixed with the odor of sleep and tobacco smoke that always penetrated through the thin lath wall and hung nauseatingly thick above his head, grew even stronger; it made his mouth water. He closed his eyes and forced himself to think of something to quell his hunger. Then the familiar light footsteps sounded on the attic stairs and someone knocked on his door. It was Morten. "Are you there, Pelle?" he asked. But Pelle didn't move.

Pelle could hear how Strøm would bite off a big hunk of food and chew it, smacking his lips. And in the midst of the chewing there was suddenly an odd sound, a stifled roar that was cut off each time he took a mouthful. It sounded like a child eating and wailing at the same time. The sound of another person crying melted something inside Pelle and gave him a little feeling of life; he raised up on one elbow and listened. As one cold chill after another crept up his spine, he lay there listening to Strøm wrestling with the horror.

People said that Strøm was here because of something he had done back home in his youth. Pelle forgot his own problems and listened, rigid with fear, to this fight with the powers of evil, which began when Strøm, his speech mixed with sobs, patiently intoned the words of the Bible against the writhing demons. "Maybe that'll make you put your tails between your legs, eh?" he exclaimed after he had read a passage. There was a peculiar broadness to his voice, a need for peace and quiet. "Aha!" he shouted a little later. "So you want more, you rascals of Satan? What do you think of this? 'I am the Lord thy God, the God of Abraham, Isaac, and Jacob'..." Strøm spat out the words, and there was a nasty catch in his voice. And suddenly he lost his patience, threw down the book, and stomped across the floor. "Then may the Foul One take you!" he shrieked, throwing things around the room.

Pelle lay there and started to sweat at the gripping struggle. With a sense of relief he heard Strøm bang open the window and chuck the devils out over the roofs below. The diver performed the last part of the fight with some humor; he went and lured them into the corners with flattery: "Ah, you little demon, what soft fur you have . . . You have to let Strøm pet you a little! Aha, you weren't expecting that! Are we too smart for you, eh? So, you're trying to bite, demon breed? There you go, don't bust your eyebrows!" Strøm slammed the window shut with a heartfelt chuckle.

He went around gloating for a while. "Strøm is just the man to clean out the joint by himself," he said contentedly.

Pelle heard him go to bed and dropped off himself. But in the middle of the night he awoke when he heard Strøm in bed, banging his head rhythmically against the lath wall, weeping and singing "By the rivers of Babylon . . ."

In the middle of the song the diver broke off and got up. Pelle heard him fumble around and go out in the attic. Horror-struck he jumped out of bed and lit his candle. Out there stood Strøm, busy hanging a noose over the rafter beam. "What do you want?" he snapped. "Can't *you* leave me in peace either?"

"Why do you want to do yourself harm?" Pelle asked sadly.

"There's a woman and a little child crying inside my ear all the time—I can't stand it anymore!" replied Strøm, still tying the rope.

"But think of the little child," said Pelle firmly, pulling down the rope. Then Strøm let himself be led inside, his will gone, and crept into bed. But Pelle had to stay in there with him. He didn't dare put out the light and lie alone in the dark.

"Is it the devils?" asked Pelle.

"What devils?" Strøm didn't know about any devils. "No, it's the regret," he replied. "The child and its mother keep blaming me for my faithlessness."

But the next moment he might jump up and whistle under the bed as though trying to coax out a dog. In one quick motion he had something by the neck, opened the window, and tossed it out. "So, that's that," he said with relief. "Now there aren't any more of those devil's spawn!" He reached for the liquor bottle.

"Leave it alone," said Pelle, taking the bottle from him. The other man's misery gave him the will.

Strøm crept back into bed. He lay there tossing around with his teeth chattering. "If only I could have one swallow," he pleaded. "What harm will that do—since you're the only one who'll help me? Why do I have to go and torment myself and pretend I'm Peter Proper, when I could have peace in my soul for such a bargain? Come on, give me a swig."

Then Pelle handed him the bottle.

"You should take a dram too, it'll give you a lift! Don't you think I can see that you're shipwrecked too? The poor man has such an easy time walking on the bottom, there's so little water under his keel. And who do you think will help him out when he spurns his only good friend? Take a swig, it'll wake up the devil in you and liven up your life."

No, Pelle wanted to go to bed.

"Why do you have to go? Stay here, we're having such a good time. If you could just tell me something that could chase this cursed sound out of my ears for a while! There's a young woman and a little child who keep crying in my ears all the time."

Pelle stayed and tried to amuse the diver. He reached up into his own empty soul and didn't know what to think up, so he told about Papa Lasse and their life at Stone Farm—this and that all mixed up together, wherever he happened to start in. But the memories welled up in him during the telling, and stared at him so sadly that they awoke the paralyzed life of his soul. Suddenly he felt pain about himself and broke down.

"What's this?" said Strøm, raising his head. "Are you going to take the trip too? Have you done mean things that you regret? Or what's wrong?"

"I don't know."

"You don't know? That's just like when women cry—it's part of their amusement! But Strøm is no stick-in-the-mud. He'd sure let his joy be fulfilled if there weren't a pair of child's eyes always reproaching him. And the accusation of a young woman! The two of them are sitting at home in Småland wringing their hands for a crust of bread, and here their provider goes and spends his earnings at the taverns. Maybe they're dead, because he left them. See, this is real, there isn't any baby drool to this! But you might just as well have a *snaps*."

Pelle wasn't listening, but sat staring blindly into space. All at once he started swaying on the chair; he was ready to faint from hunger. "Give me a *snaps* then—I haven't had a thing to eat today!" He smiled, embarrassed at his confession.

With a leap Strøm was out of bed. "No, you're going to have something to eat," he said eagerly, dragging out food. "Has anyone seen the like of this desperate devil—he wants to pour aquavit into an empty stomach! Now eat, then you can get drunk somewhere else! Strøm has enough on his conscience already. He can drink his *snaps* himself. So, it was hunger that made you cry? I had a feeling it sounded like a child's crying."

Pelle had many nights like this, and they deepened his world in the direction of the darkness. When he came home late and fumbled his way across the attic, he had a secret fear of bumping into Strøm's dead body. He breathed easily only when he heard Strøm snoring or rustling around in his room. He liked to look in on him before he went to bed.

Strøm was always glad to see him and would offer him food, but he didn't want to give him aquavit. "That's nothing for a young boy like you to drink," he said. "There'll be plenty of time for you to acquire a taste for it."

"But *you* drink," Pelle insisted.

"Sure, I drink to deaden the pain. But you don't need to do that."

"I feel so empty inside," said Pelle. "Maybe the *snaps* could wake up something inside me. I don't really feel like a human being, but something dead, like a table."

"You have to find something to do, or else you'll turn into a slob! I've seen so many people like us go to the dogs. We don't have much to resist with."

"I don't care what happens to me," said Pelle dully. "To hell with all of it!"

XXIII

It was Sunday and Pelle felt like doing something out of the ordinary. First he went over to visit Jens, but the couple got in a fight and came to blows. Jens's sweetheart happened to tip the skillet into the fire with their dinner in it, and Jens had given her a box on the ear; she was still pale and weak after the miscarriage. They sat in separate corners, scowling like two children. They were both sorry, but neither of them wanted to say the first word. Pelle got them to make up, and they wanted him to stay for dinner. "We still have potatoes and salt," said Jens, "and I can borrow a pint from the neighbors." But Pelle left. He couldn't stand to watch them hanging all over each other, half-blubbering and slobbering and endlessly begging forgiveness.

Then he went over to see the Due family. They had moved out to an old merchant's house where there was room for Due's team of horses, and things seemed to be going well for them. People said that the old consul had taken a liking to them and had helped them get ahead. Pelle never went into the house but headed over to the stable to see Due. If he wasn't home, he would leave—Pelle wasn't welcome to visit Anna. But Due received him kindly. Whenever he wasn't out driving he liked to go out to the stable and fuss over the horses; he didn't like being indoors. Pelle gave him a hand at cutting chaff or whatever else needed to be done, and they would go into the house together. Due seemed like a different person when he had Pelle at his side—his step was firmer. Anna was getting the upper hand over him more and more. She was as clever as always and kept the house neat and clean. She no longer had little Marie at home. She kept her two boys nicely dressed and had put them in a private school for young children. She looked lovely and knew how to dress well, but she had nothing good to say about anyone else. Pelle wasn't fine enough for her; she wrinkled her nose at his simple clothes. In order to deride him, she would always talk about Alfred's wonderful engagement to grocer Lau's daughter. "He's not going around wasting his time—and sniffing at people's doors for a meal," she would say. Pelle merely smiled; nothing really stung him anymore.

The little boys were outside, bored in their nice clothes. They weren't allowed to play with the poor children on the street or get their clothes dirty. "Come and play with us for a while, Uncle Pelle," they said, clinging to him. "Aren't you our uncle? Mother says you're not. She wants us to call the consul 'Uncle,' but then we just run away. His nose is so red and ugly."

"Does the consul come over to visit you?" asked Pelle.

"Yes, he does—he's inside right now!"

Pelle peered into the courtyard. The nice wagon was gone. "Father has gone to Åkirkeby," said the boys. Then Pelle sneaked off home. He stole a mouthful of bread and a *snaps* from Strøm, who wasn't home, and threw himself on the bed.

When darkness fell he wandered outside and hung around, freezing, on the streetcorners; he had a dull urge to take part in something. People were strolling up and down the streets, dressed in their finery.

Several of his acquaintances were out with their sweethearts. He avoided saying hello to them but caught some muttered remarks and heard them laughing. As listless as he was, his ears were still alert; this stemmed from the time he was branded at the courthouse. People usually had something to say to each other whenever he went by; their laughter could still make his knees tense nervously with a hidden impulse for flight.

He slipped down a side street. He had buttoned his thin jacket all the way up and turned up the collar. In the dimness of the doorways stood young men and girls whispering confidentially. Waves of warmth emanated from the girls and their white aprons shone in the dark. Pelle crept around in the cold and knew even less what to do with himself. He fantasized about finding a sweetheart.

At the market square he met Alfred arm in arm with Miss Lau. He was wearing foppish shoes and brown gloves and a top hat. That scoundrel, he owes me two and a half kroner, and I'll never see it again, thought Pelle. For a moment he felt like throwing himself at Alfred and rubbing all his finery in the mud. Alfred turned his head away. He only acknowledges me when he needs something repaired and doesn't have any money, thought Pelle bitterly.

He trotted along the street to keep warm, with his eyes on the windows. There sat the bookbinder's family singing songs about Jesus. The man kept his head tilted even at home—this could be seen clearly in the silhouette on the shade. And at the woolen dealer's house they were busy eating supper.

Farther along at the Sow's place it was as lively as ever; noise and clouds of smoke were billowing out of the open windows. She kept a tavern for seamen on leave and earned good money. Pelle had often been invited to visit them, but always felt he was too good for that—and he couldn't stand Rud. But tonight he eagerly recalled these invitations and went inside. Maybe a scrap of food would fall his way.

Several groggy sailors were sitting around a table, shouting at each other at a deafening pitch. The Sow was sitting on the knee of a young fellow. She was leaning halfway across the big table, her finger playing in some spilled beer. Once in a while she would screech right into the face of the one who was shouting the loudest. She hadn't gotten any less hefty in the past few years.

"Hey look, is that you, Pelle?" she said, standing up to give Pelle her hand. She wasn't completely sober and had a hard time finding his hand. "It's nice of you to come—I thought you sort of looked down on us. Sit down and have a drink. It won't cost you a thing." She forced him to sit down.

The sailors had fallen silent. They sat and stared dully at Pelle; their heavy heads moved uncontrollably. "So, is this a new customer?" one of them asked, and the others laughed.

The Sow laughed too, but suddenly grew serious. "You keep him out of your mischief," she said. "He's much too good to be roped into anything. So now you know." She dropped into a chair near Pelle and sat there looking at him as she stroked her fat face. "How big and handsome you've grown, but I can't say much for your clothes. And you don't look like you've been overfed either. I can still remember you from the time you and your father came to this country. You were a little lad—and Lasse had the hymnbook along from my mother!" She suddenly stopped short and her eyes welled up.

One of the sailors whispered something to the others, who started to laugh.

"Stop laughing, you pigs!" she shouted angrily, going over to them. "You won't get to corrupt this one. He comes as a reminder from the days when I too was a decent human being. His father is the only one who can testify that I was once a pretty and innocent girl who was treated badly. He held me on his lap when I was little and sang lullabies to me." She glared at them aggressively, her red face trembling.

"You probably didn't weigh as much as you do now, did you?" said one of them, putting him arm around her.

"Don't tease the little one," exclaimed another. "Can't you see that she's crying? Take her on your lap and sing her a lullaby. Then she'll think you're Lasse-Basse!"

Furiously she grabbed a bottle. "Shut up with your wisecracks," she screamed, "or you'll get this in your face!" Her obese features melted in tears.

They left her in peace, and she sat there sniffling with her hands over her face. "Is your father still alive?" she asked. "Then say hello to him from me. Just send him greetings from the Sow; it's all right for you to call me the Sow. And tell him he's the only one on earth that I have to thank for anything. He thought well of me and brought me my mother's dying wishes."

Pelle sat and listened tensely to her tearful speech with a hollow smile. His guts were burning inside him with emptiness, and the beer was going to his head. He remembered all the details from that day at Stone Farm when he saw this person for the first time, and Papa Lasse brought back memories of her childhood home for her. But Pelle didn't associate anything with it. That was long ago, and . . . I wonder if she'll give me any food? he thought, listening indifferently to her sniffles.

The sailors sat and stared at her anxiously; there was a solemn silence in their groggy faces. They looked like drunken people around a grave. "So, that's enough of your washing down the deck—let's get something to drink," said an old fellow at last. "Everybody's had a visit from those innocent days of childhood, and I say: give them credit for wanting to peek inside to an old devil! But let the water stay overboard, I say. The more you scrub at an old tub, the more its faults come out! So give us a round and a deck of cards, Madam."

She got up and poured them a drink. Her emotions had subsided but her legs still felt heavy.

"That's good—and let's have a little show today, since it's Sunday. Show us your art, Madam!"

"It costs a krone, you know that," she replied with a laugh.

They pooled together their *skillings,* and she went behind the counter and took off her clothes. She came out with only her shift on and with a lighted candle in her hand. Pelle noticed lazily how her fat body quivered under the black linen, and he heard the sailors' hoarse shouts and laughter. Inside his left ear an endless sound was boiling, and underneath that his blood was pounding like a piston. A sound from another world seemed to fill his head and rob him of his very sense of balance; he had to hold on to the table in order not to fall. Far away and irrelevant, he saw the Sow climb onto a chair and stretch her shift across her behind. A sailor held the candle up to her backside, and she showed them how winds could burn with a bluish flame.

Pelle sneaked out while they were so preoccupied. He was weak with hunger and rawness and a deafening sense of shame; he wandered around aimlessly, not knowing where he was going. He had only one feeling: that of the indifference of all things. Either life went on in such and such a manner, either he continued to live in wearisome respectability, or he wallowed in drink, or he perished . . . did it matter at all? What difference did it make? No one paid any attention, not even himself. Not a soul would shed a tear if he went to the dogs—oh yes, Lasse, old Papa Lasse! But to go home now and reveal his wretchedness, after they had futilely expected so much of him . . . he couldn't do it. The last remnants of his sense of shame rose up. And what about work—why? His dream was dead, and he stood there with that hollow feeling of the nearness of the bottom, which is so fateful for those down there. Year after year he had kept himself afloat by never releasing the tension, and with the insane idea that things were going upward. Now he found himself very close to the bottom of life—and he was tired. Why not let himself sink down the rest of the way too and let fate sweep him away? There would be sweet repose in it after such a mad fight with superior forces.

He woke up a little at the sound of hymns. He had come into an alley, and right in front of him lay a big, broad building with a gable and a cross on top. Over the course of time hundreds of voices had tried to lure him here, but he hadn't had any need for it in his boldness—what was there for a bold boy to find here? And now he had ended up outside this building anyway! He was in need of a little caring, and he felt that a hand had led him here.

The hall was full of poor families. They sat so oddly crammed together on the benches, each family separate. The men were sleeping, for the most part; the women were busy making the children keep still and sit nicely with their legs sticking straight out. They were people who had come to get a little free light and warmth in their dreary existence; they felt they could at least demand something from a Sunday. The most wretched of the town's poor were there, seeking refuge in a place where they were not judged but received promises about the Millennium. Pelle knew them all, both those he had seen before and the others with the same drowned expressions. He felt immediately at home among all those disheveled little birds, who had allowed themselves to be carried across the sea on the strong wind and now came drifting ashore on the waves.

A large man with a full beard and kind childlike eyes stood up between the benches and proposed a hymn—it was Dam the blacksmith. He started off, standing there and keeping time by bobbing at the knees, and everyone sang along, their voices quavering, with their own sound of what had swept over them. The notes forced their way painfully out of the dry, haggard throats. They were pitifully born of layers of rust and cracks and scrapes, huddling together, frightened at emerging into the light. Hesitantly they unfurled a couple of fragile net-veined wings and vibrated from the trembling lips out into the room. And up near the ceiling the notes joined with hundreds of siblings and brushed their exhaustion aside. They grew into a jubilation, vast and wondrous, about some unknown, rich land of happiness that was near. For Pelle it was as if the air were full of butterflies, glittering in the sunshine:

> Blessed, blessed will that meeting be,
> when our soul from grief and loss is free,
> and we, with Jesus, are gathered up
> in heaven, our rightful home.

"Mother, I'm hungry," said a child's voice as the hymn ended.

The mother, a worn-out woman, hushed the child with annoyance and looked around in amazement—what a nonsensical idea that was. "But you just ate," she said, louder than necessary.

But the child kept on crying, "Mother, I'm hungry."

Then baker Jørgen's son Søren came up and gave the child a roll; he had a whole basket full of baked goods. "Are there any other children who are hungry?" he asked aloud. He looked everyone directly in the eye and was quite a different person than he was at home. And here nobody laughed at him either, even though it was said that he was the brother of his own son.

And a white-bearded old man stepped up to the podium in the back of the hall. "That's him," they whispered to each other, and hurried to finish up their coughing and get the children to finish chewing. He took the little child's tears as his starting point: Mother, I'm hungry! That was the voice of the world—that great, terrible shout—placed in a child's mouth. He didn't see one person who hadn't cringed under that cry from his neighbors, and, afraid to hear it again, wanted to secure bread for the rest of his life—and was rebuffed. They simply didn't see God's hand when he lovingly transformed naked hunger into a hunger for happiness. They were poverty-stricken, and the poor were God's chosen people! That's why they had to wander in the desert and ask blindly: Where is the land? But the light which the faithful continued to follow was not earthly happiness! It was God Himself who led them around and around until their hunger was purified into the proper hunger—the soul's hunger for eternal bliss.

They didn't understand much of what he said, but his words released something inside them so that they fell into lively chatter about little, everyday things. Suddenly the heated buzzing stopped; a short, hunchbacked man had crawled up onto a bench and was surveying them with shining eyes. It was Sort, the itinerant shoemaker from out near the town meadow.

"We want to be happy," he said, putting on an odd expression. "God's children are always happy, no matter what evil they're struggling with, and no harm can come to them—God is joy!" He started laughing, as unrestrained as a child; and everybody laughed along with him, one person infecting another. They couldn't control themselves. An enormous sense of amusement seemed to have come over everyone. The little children looked at the adults and laughed so that their throats filled with mucus and coughs. "He's a real clown," said the men to their wives, their faces one big smile. "But there's a good heart in him."

On the bench next to Pelle sat a quiet family, a man with his wife and three children, who were sniffing politely up into their chafed little noses. The parents were small people, and they had an air about them as if they were constantly trying to make themselves even smaller. Pelle knew them slightly and fell into conversation with them. The husband was a potter, and they lived in one of the most wretched hovels out near the Power's house.

"Yes, that's true—that part about happiness," said the wife. "Once we dreamed about getting ahead too, so we would have some security. We scraped together a little money by borrowing and opened a tiny shop that I took care of while Father went to work. But it didn't work out; no one would support us. We got bad supplies because we were poor, and who wants to buy from the likes of us, anyway? We got out of it with a debt that we have to keep paying back—50 øre a week! And we'll be doing that for as long as we live, because it keeps collecting interest. But we're honest folks, thank God!" she concluded. Her husband took no part in the conversation.

Her last remark may have been brought on by a man who had quietly stepped inside and squeezed onto a bench in the background; because *he* was not an honest man. He had been sentenced to bread and water for theft. It was Jacob the thief, the man who knocked in the windowpane to Master Jeppe's good parlor about ten years ago and stole a pair of patent-leather shoes for his wife. He had heard about a rich man who had given his sweetheart a pair like that; he wanted to see how it felt to give someone a nice gift for once, a gift that was equal to two weeks' pay, he explained to the court. "Codfish," Jeppe always said whenever he dwelled on the subject, "a pitiful louse goes and gets grand ideas and wants to give expensive presents! If only they were intended for a sweetheart—but for his wife! But he got the punishment he deserved, in spite of Andrès."

Yes, he'd been punished, all right—even here no one wanted to sit next to him! Pelle looked at him and was amazed that he himself had managed to get off relatively easy. There was just a look in people's eyes when they talked to him. But now blacksmith Dam went over and sat down next to Jacob the thief; they sat there whispering.

And over there someone was nodding so kindly at Pelle. It was the woman with the dancing slippers. The young man had left her, and now she had ended up here—her dance was over. But she was still grateful to Pelle. The sight of him had brought back sweet memories for her, which was apparent in her mouth and eyes.

Pelle sat there, feeling more gentle; something melted inside him. A quiet, shabby feeling of happiness crept over him. There *was* one person who still felt indebted to him, even though everything had fallen apart for her.

When the congregation parted around nine-thirty, she was standing outside, talking to another woman. She came over and gave Pelle her hand. "Shall we walk together part of the way?" she suggested. She probably knew about his situation; he read sympathy in her gaze. "Come home with me," she said when their ways diverged. "I have a piece of medister-sausage that *has* to be eaten—and, after all, we're both alone."

He followed her hesitantly, a little hostile toward this new and foreign situation, but as soon as he was sitting in her little room, he felt at home. Nice and white the bed stood against the wall, and she moved around, cooking the sausage in the woodstove as she chattered away with an unabashed heart. Things probably don't fall apart easily for her, thought Pelle, looking at her quite happily.

They had a pleasant meal, and Pelle wanted to give her a hug out of gratitude, but she pushed his hands away. "Save yourself the trouble," she said with a laugh. "I'm a middle-aged widow, and you're no more than a child. If you want to make me happy, see about finding yourself! It's a shame the way you're going around wasting your time—you're so young and handsome! And now you'd better go home because I have to get up early for work tomorrow."

Pelle went to visit her almost every evening. She was always prodding him about his laziness. On the other hand, she was refreshing in her even-keeled manner of looking at everything. She got him repair work now and then and was always glad to share her poor meal with him. "Someone like me needs to have a man at the head of the table once in a while," she said. "But keep your fingers to yourself—you don't owe me anything." She criticized his clothes too. "They're going to fall off you pretty soon. Why don't you put something else on and let me fix those for you?"

"I don't have anything else," said Pelle, and felt ashamed again.

Saturday night he had to take off his clothes and crawl into her bed completely naked—there was no getting around it. She took his shirt and everything and put them in a basin of water. She spent half the night going over them. Pelle lay in bed with the comforter all the way up to his chin and watched her; he felt so strange. She hung everything up to dry on the woodstove and then made up a bed for herself on some chairs. When he woke up late in the morning she was sitting at the window mending his clothes.

"How did you sleep last night?" asked Pelle anxiously.

"Fine. Do you know what I was thinking about this morning? You should give up your room and move in here until you straighten things out for yourself. You have to get your rest sometime!" she laughed, teasing him. "That room is an unnecessary expense, and as you can see, there's room enough for two here."

But Pelle didn't want to. He didn't want any part of letting a woman support him. "Then people will think there's something between us—and think badly of us," he said.

"Go ahead and let them," she replied with her hearty laugh. "As long as I have my life in order, I don't care about other people."

While she chattered away, she worked industriously on his underclothes and tossed piece after piece over to him. Then she ironed his clothes. "Now you look quite nice," she said after he had put them on, and she gazed at him kindly. "You look almost like a new person. I'd like to walk down the street with you at my arm, if only I were ten or fifteen years younger. But you'll have to give me a kiss—I've taken care of you as if you were my own child." She kissed him swiftly and turned toward the woodstove.

"Now I don't know what else to do except eat a cold dinner and then each go our own way," she said, her head turned away. "I used up all my fuel last night drying your clothes, and we can't stay here in this cold. I'm thinking of finding someone to visit and then the day will pass. You'll find someplace to go too."

"It doesn't matter where I am," said Pelle indifferently.

She looked at him with a peculiar smile. "I wonder if you're going to keep on loafing around like this," she said. "You men are some strange devils, all right. As soon as something crosses you just a little bit, you have to drink yourself silly or pickle your brain in some other way—you're not much better than babies! But we have to work just as hard, no matter how things have gone!"

She stood there with her coat on, hesitating. "Here's 25 øre for you," she said. "It's enough for a cup of coffee to warm you up."

Pelle wouldn't take it. "What do I need your money for?" he muttered. "Keep it yourself!"

"Oh, just take it! I know it's not much, but that's all I have. And the two of us shouldn't have to be ashamed in front of each other." She put the coin in his jacket pocket and rushed out.

Pelle wandered around in the woods. He had no desire to go home and have another futile round with Strøm. He wandered around on the desolate paths, taking a faint pleasure in noticing that spring was breaking forth. Underneath the old, moss-gray fir trees there was still snow, but down among the needles mushrooms were already poking up their heads, and the earth was as spongy as dough rising.

He stopped himself as he walked around, busy with his own thoughts, and suddenly woke up out of his semi-dream state. He had a feeling of something quite pleasant—oh, yes, it was the idea of moving in with her after all, and setting himself up like Jens. He could get some lasts and sit at home and work. He could always make do until better times. She earned some money too, and she had a generous nature.

But as soon as his mind latched onto this idea, it turned sour for him. He had preyed enough off her poverty and good nature; he had taken her last piece of firewood so she had to humble herself for a little heat and food. This kept bothering him once he realized it. It accompanied him home and into bed, and behind all her kindness he felt her contempt because he did not counter the misery and work like a decent person.

The next morning he got up early and signed up for work down at the harbor. He didn't really see the necessity of it, but he didn't want to owe a woman anything. On Saturday she would get her *skillings* back.

XXIV

Pelle was standing at the bottom of the harbor basin, loading rocks into the dump cars. When a car was full, he and his partner would push it forward to the main track. Then they would hang on to the empty car and coast back. Now and then the others would let their tools drop and glance over at him: he certainly worked hard for a shoemaker! He sure knew how to handle the stone! Whenever he had to get a big boulder up into the car, he would lift it onto his knee, swear once, and then push it up with his whole body. Then he wiped the sweat from his brow and had himself a dram and a drop of beer—he wasn't going to be outdone by anyone!

He didn't let himself think, just took each day as it came, and enjoyed the toil and weariness. The hard labor broke down something in his body and filled him with pure animal well-being. I wonder whether my beer will last through the afternoon? he might think; there was nothing else on his mind. The future didn't exist, but neither was

there any painful feeling about it not existing. There was no rancor in
him over something he had lost or something he had neglected; the hard
labor took over everything. There was only this rock that had to be
moved—and then the next one, this car that had to be filled—and the
next one too! When the rock wouldn't budge at the first shove, he
gnashed his teeth; he was obsessed with his work. "He's still so new at
it," said the others. "He'll probably burn himself out!" But Pelle
wanted to show his strength; that was his only ambition. His partner let
Pelle strain himself, taking it easy and praising him now and then to
keep him fired up.

It was the most wretched work at the harbor; anyone could do it
without training. Most of Pelle's fellow workers were men who had left
their homes and allowed themselves to be pulled wherever the current
took them. And he felt comfortable among them. No words reached
down here to the bottom that might bring dead fantasies to life or
merely haunt an empty mind. The iron curtain had fallen on the future,
and happiness lay so close you could trip over it—the day's toil was
instantly transformed into cheerful rounds of beer.

He spent his free time with his work comrades. They were free souls
who had been drawn here by rumors of the big project. Most of them
were unmarried. Some may have had a wife and children somewhere,
but they either didn't speak of them or didn't remember them anymore.
They didn't have any real place to live but took up lodgings in teamster
Køller's abandoned barn near the harbor. They never took off their
clothes but slept in the hay and washed in a bucket of water that was
seldom changed. Their diet consisted mainly of crusts of bread and eggs
that they fried over a fire between two stones.

Pelle felt comfortable in this life and liked their company. On Sunday they would eat and drink all day long, burrowing down into the hay
in the smoke-filled barn, and tell stories. Tragic stories about youngest
sons who took up the axe and murdered their fathers and mothers and
all their siblings because they felt cheated out of the inheritance. Stories
about children who were studying with the pastor and fell in love with
each other and became pregnant—and that's why they were going to be
beheaded. And about women who refused to bring the children into the
world that they should—and that's why they had their bellies closed up
as punishment!

He hadn't been out to visit Marie Nielsen since he started working
there. "She's putting on a show for you," said the others whenever he
mentioned her. "She wants to play the proper woman to get you to bite.
Women always have something up their sleeve—the main thing is to

stay on your toes. They'd take two sooner than one, and the young widows are always the worst. It takes a tough devil to resist them."

But Pelle was a man and wasn't going to be led by the nose by some woman. Either they were friends and didn't make a fuss about it—or they weren't! That's what he would tell her on Saturday night, and toss 10 kroner onto the table in front of her—then they'd be even! And if she stirred up a ruckus he'd give her one on the noggin! He couldn't forgive her for the episode with the firewood that ran out so she had to spend her Sunday on the street; it sat inside him somewhere, stinging like a nasty spark. She made herself a martyr for his sake!

One day at noon he was standing near the slipway along with the demolition crew. He and Emil had been over to the barn to gulp down a little food. They were giving up their midday nap to observe a huge explosion that was going to take place during the noon break while the harbor was empty. The whole place was deserted, and people in the nearby houses had opened their windows so they wouldn't shatter from the concussion. The dynamite had been lit. They had taken shelter beneath the timberwork and were chatting as they waited for the explosion. The Power was there too. He was standing nearby, as usual, glaring with that dull expression on his face, without taking part in anything. They paid no attention to him, just let him come and go as he pleased.

"Take better cover, Pelle," said Emil. "It's going to go off now!"

"Where are Olsen and Strøm?" someone said suddenly. They looked at each other in confusion.

"They're probably taking their noon nap," said Emil. "They had a lot of *snaps* this morning."

"Where are they sleeping?" roared the foreman, leaping out from cover. Everybody knew, but no one wanted to say. A ripple went through them as if they were about to do something, but nobody made a move.

"Dear Jesus," said Bergendal, pounding his hand against the rock wall. "Oh, dear Jesus!"

The Power jumped out from cover and raced down the slipway; he ran across the floor of the basin, taking great leaps from rock to rock, his enormous wooden clogs ringing. "He's going to rip off the fuse!" shouted Bergendal. "He won't make it. It must have burned down by now!" It resounded like a cry of terror—far over their heads. Then, they breathlessly followed his progress; they had come all the way out from cover. Something meaningless tugged at Pelle; he leapt after him but was grabbed by the scruff of his neck. "One is enough," said Bergendal, pulling him back.

The Power was all the way over there and was stretching out his hand to grab the fuse. Suddenly he was lifted away from it by an invisible hand; he floated softly backward through the air like a balloon person and fell on his back. In an instant the explosion made everything vanish.

When the last rocks had fallen, they ran over to him. The Power lay stretched out on his back, looking calmly up at the sky. He had a little blood in the corner of his mouth, and blood was trickling out of a tiny hole behind one ear. The two drunks hadn't come to any harm; they got up in a daze a few paces beyond the explosion site. The Power was carried up to the barn. While someone went to get the doctor, Emil tore off a strip of his shirt and put some aquavit on it, which they placed behind his ear.

The Power opened his eyes and looked at them; his gaze was so wise that everyone knew he didn't have long. "It smells of *snaps*," he said. "Can anybody give me a dram?" Emil handed him the bottle, and he emptied it. "It still tastes good," he said quietly. "I haven't touched liquor for I don't know how long—but what good is it? A poor man has to drink or he's not good for anything—it's no joke being a poor man! He has no other salvation. You saw that with Strøm and Olsen— drunk people come to no harm. They didn't, did they?" He tried to raise his head. Strøm stepped forward.

"Here we are," he said in a thick voice. "But I'd give anything if we'd shot straight to hell, both of us, rather than have this happen. None of us have ever wished you any good." He put out his hand.

But the Power couldn't lift his head; he lay there and stared up at the straw roof full of holes. "It's sure been hard belonging to the poor," he said. "And it's good that it's over. But there's nothing to thank me for! Why should I leave you in the lurch and take it all for myself? Does that sound like the Power? Of course it was my plan, but could I have done it alone? No, keep all the money. You've earned it honestly! The Power shouldn't get any more than anyone else if we all share the work equally." He lifted his hand with difficulty, making a generous gesture.

"Oh, he thinks he's the harbor contractor," said Strøm. "He's delirious. Don't you think something cold on his head would help?" Emil took the bucket and went after fresh water. The Power lay with his eyes closed and a faint smile; he looked like a blind man listening.

"Do you remember," he said without opening his eyes, "how we toiled and toiled and could hardly make enough for food? The rich sat and ate up everything we could produce; when we put down our tools and wanted to quell our hunger, there was nothing left. They stole our ideas, and if we had a pretty sweetheart or daughter, they could use her too. Not even our cripples did they spurn. But now that's all past, and let's be glad that we can experience this; it could have taken a very long time. Mother even refused to believe it when I told her that the evil days would soon be over—but just look! Don't I get just as much money for my work as the doctor does for his? And I can provide for my wife and daughters and own books and a piano just like he does. Isn't it important to do manual labor too? Karen is taking music lessons; I've always wanted her to, because she's so feeble and can't stand hard work. You should come home with me and hear her play—she's a quick learner! A poor man's child has talents too. It's just that no one has ever noticed them before."

"Dear Lord, how he's talking," said Strøm, weeping. "It's almost as if he has the delirium."

Pelle bent down over the Power. "You should be good and keep quiet now," he said, placing a wet compress on his forehead. The blood was trickling out fast behind the wounded man's ear.

"Just let him talk," exclaimed Olsen. "He hasn't said a word in months and needs to let it out. And he probably doesn't have long, either."

The Power could only move his lips feebly now; life was bleeding swiftly out of him. "Did you get wet, little Karen?" he muttered. "Don't worry, it'll dry again. And you can't complain, now that things are going well for you. Is it fun being a lady? Just tell me everything you want—it's no use being modest. We've been modest long enough! Gloves for your chapped fingers—all right. But then you have to play a little for me. Play that pretty piece: about the happy wandering... through the kingdoms of the earth. The one about the Millennium!" He began softly humming along. He couldn't move his head in time so he blinked his eyes instead; now and then his humming broke into words.

Something made the others awkwardly join in—maybe because it was a hymn. Pelle led with his clear voice; he was also the one who knew the words by heart:

> Lovely is the earth,
> magnificent is God's heaven,
> splendid is the souls' pilgrimage!
> Through the fair
> kingdoms on earth
> we go to Paradise with song.

The Power sang louder as if he wanted to drown out Pelle. One of his feet had started keeping time. He lay with his eyes closed, his head lolling blindly to the song, looking like someone who is putting in his last words in a hazy drinking bout before he goes under the table. Bloody fluid was running out of the corners of his mouth.

> Times will come,
> times will pass,
> generation will follow generation.
> The sounds from heaven
> will never be silenced
> in the soul's joyous pilgrim song.

The Power fell silent; his head slumped to one side. The others stopped at once.

They sat in the hay and stared at him. His last words were still hanging in their ears like some foolish dream blending strangely with the victory cry of the hymn. They all felt the same mute reproach from the dead man and directed it at themselves in the eeriness of the moment.

"Yes, who knows what a man might have made of it," a ragged fellow pondered at last, chewing on a piece of straw.

"I'll never make a go of it," replied Emil despondently. "Things have always gotten worse for me. I was an apprentice, and when I became a journeyman, they kicked me out. I wasted five years of my life and had nothing to show for it. But that Pelle will probably make something of himself."

Pelle raised his head in amazement and looked at him, puzzled.

"What good is it for a poor devil to try getting ahead—he'll just be struck down again!" said Olsen. "Just look at the Power. Did anyone have greater prospects than he did? No, the rich won't allow the rest of us to get ahead!"

"And did we allow it ourselves?" muttered Strøm. "We're afraid that one of our own will fly past us."

"I don't understand why all the poor don't join forces against the others—we're all suffering the same," said Bergendal. "If we all stuck together and stopped having anything to do with the ones who want to hurt us, it would probably show them that poverty as a whole is what determines the others' prosperity. That's what they're trying to do over in Copenhagen, I've heard."

"We'll never be able to agree on anything," said an old stonecutter sadly.

"No, because if one of the gentlemen just scratches our neck a little, we roll right up at his feet and let ourselves be set loose on our own kind. If we were all like the Power, then maybe everything might look different."

They fell silent and sat looking at the dead man; there was something of an apology in every man's attitude. "No, it won't happen anytime soon," said Strøm with a sigh. Then he felt under the hay and pulled out a bottle.

A few still sat there, pondering something that maybe ought to be said; but then the doctor arrived, and they withdrew into themselves. They picked up their beer bottles and went off to work again.

Pelle silently gathered up all his belongings, went over to the foreman, and asked for his wages. "This is sudden," said the foreman. "And you were just starting to make good progress. What are you going to do now?"

"I just want my wages," said Pelle. Other than that, he didn't know.

Then he went home and straightened up his room. It looked like a pigsty; he couldn't understand how he could have stood the mess. Sullenly he thought about alternatives. It had been quite pleasant to be part of the rabble and know that he couldn't get any lower, but there still might be some other possibility! Emil had uttered those stupid words—what had he meant by them? "That Pelle will probably make something of himself!" Sure, but did Emil know anything about other people's misery? He probably had plenty of his own.

He went down to buy a little milk, and then he wanted to go to sleep. He needed to suppress everything that was suddenly starting to muddy up his mind again.

Down on the street he ran into Sort, the itinerant shoemaker. "So, there you are!" exclaimed Sort. "I was just going around wondering how I could best have a talk with you. I wanted to tell you that tomorrow I'm starting my trip, if you'd like to come along. It's a splendid life going around from farm to farm now that spring is here—and you'll go to the dogs if you keep on this way! So now you know, and you can decide for yourself. I'm leaving at six o'clock. I can't put it off any longer."

Sort had noticed Pelle that night at the prayer meeting, and had been after him a couple of times to get him going. He's put off his trip for two weeks for my sake, thought Pelle with a hint of self-confidence. But he wasn't going to trudge around begging for work from farm to farm! Pelle was a workshop apprentice, and he looked down on the itinerant shoemaker who made his rounds like any pauper, getting his leather and cord at each place and gulping down food from the same dish as the servants. He still had that much pride in his craft! From his time at the workshop, he was used to regarding Sort as a pitiful remnant of the past, an inheritance from the days of serfdom.

"You'll go to the dogs!" said Sort, and Marie Nielsen thought the same thing with all her ambiguous hints. But so what? Maybe he had already gone to the dogs, if there wasn't any other way out! But now he wanted to go to sleep—and be free of all that.

He drank his bottle of milk, ate some bread, and went to bed. He heard the church clock strike—it was the middle of the afternoon and beautiful weather. But Pelle needed to sleep, just sleep. His mind felt like lead.

He woke up early the next morning and was out of bed with a leap. Sunshine filled the room, and he was full of a robust feeling. He jumped into his clothes—there was so much he had to do! Then he threw open the window and inhaled the spring morning in a great breath that spread all through his body like a feeling of profound joy. Out across the sea the ships were heading toward the harbor. The morning sun fell on the slack sails, making them glow, and each ship was working its way slowly forward with oars. He had slept like a rock from the moment he lay down, and his sleep was like a chasm between yesterday and today. Humming, he packed up his things and set off with a little bundle under his arm. He headed over toward the church to have a look at the clock—it wasn't much past five. Then he steered toward the outskirts of town, striding swiftly, as happy as if he were heading toward his good fortune.

XXV

Two men emerged from the woods and crossed the road. One of them was short and hunchbacked. He had a shoemaker's bench tied onto his back; its edge was resting against his hump, and a little cushion was stuck in between so it wouldn't chafe. The other was young and well-built, rather thin but with a healthy, robust complexion. He had a big bunch of lasts on his back; they were balanced by a box in front which, from the sound of it, might contain tools. He flung off his burden at the side of the ditch and then untied the bench from the hunchback. They threw themselves down on the grass and lay there staring up at the blue sky. It was a beautiful morning, the birds were busy, and the cattle were walking through the dewy clover, leaving long streaks behind them.

"And yet you're always happy," said Pelle. Sort had just told him the story of his sad childhood.

"Well, you know, it often bothers me that I take everything so easy—but I don't know anything I should be sad about! If I examine things, I always find something that makes me even happier—like your company, for example. You're young and the picture of health; the girls are so nice wherever we go. It's as if *I* were the cause of their happiness."

"Where did you get all your knowledge about everything?" asked Pelle.

"Do you think I know so much?" Sort laughed joyfully. "I wander around and see many different kinds of homes, where husband and wife live in harmony—and where they fight like cats and dogs. I come into contact with all sorts of people. I also find out a lot because I'm not shaped like other people—more than one girl has confided her misery to me! And I also think about everything during the winter when I'm sitting alone. The Bible is a good place to find knowledge too. There you learn to get behind things; and as soon as you realize that everything has its back side, you learn to use your mind. You can go behind anything you like, and they all lead to one place—to God. Everything comes from Him, after all. That's the connection, you see; and as soon as you know that, you will always be happy. It would be fun to follow things forward too—to where they separate; and show that, in the end, they still run together into God again. But I don't have the talent for that."

"We ought to see about moving on," yawned Pelle, beginning to stir.

"Why? This is a good spot—and we'll achieve whatever we're supposed to! If there's a pair of boots that Sort and Pelle don't manage to get soled before they die, someone else will do it."

Pelle threw himself down on his back and pulled his cap over his eyes; there was no hurry as far as he was concerned. He had been traveling with Sort for almost a month now, and had spent practically as much time on the road as on his work stool. Sort was always restless; whenever he'd been in one place for a couple of days, he had to move on! He liked the edge of the forest and the ditches and could spend half his days there. And Pelle had some sense of attachment for this fresh-air lolling; he had his entire childhood to draw on. He could lie there for hours, chewing on a blade of grass—slowly, like someone convalescing—while the sun and the air did their work on him.

"Why don't you ever preach at me?" he asked suddenly, squinting merrily from under his cap.

"And why should I preach—because I'm holy? But you are too; everybody who's happy and content is holy."

"I'm far from content," replied Pelle, rolling on his back with all four limbs in the air. "But you . . . I don't understand why you don't get yourself a congregation! You have the word in your power."

"If I was shaped like you, I probably would. But I'm a hunchback."

"So what? You don't care about women, anyway."

"No, but without them nothing can get done. They're the ones who pull the men and the children along after them. And it's odd that they should be the ones—because women don't care about God! They have no talent for going behind things; they make their choices based on the surface. They have to hang everything on the outside as decoration— even men. Yes, and preferably Our Lord too. They can use it all."

Pelle lay still for a moment, reviewing his own scattered experiences. "Marie Nielsen wasn't like that," he said thoughtfully. "She would gladly give the shift from her body and she never demanded a thing for herself. I've acted shamefully toward her! I didn't even tell her goodbye before I set out."

"Then you should seek her out and admit your error when we get to town. You weren't sweethearts, were you?"

"She looked on me as a child—I already told you that."

Sort lay still for a while. "If you would join us, then we could get together a congregation! I can see in their eyes that you would have power over them if you wanted to—like the farmer's daughter at Willow Farm. We could get thousands to join us."

Pelle didn't reply. His thoughts had drifted curiously back to Willow Farm, where he and Sort had last worked. He was once again in that clammy room with the much-too-large bed in which the pale girl's face almost disappeared. She lay there holding on to her thick braid with a transparent hand—and gazed at him. And behind him they pulled the door gently shut. "That was a strange idea," he said, taking a deep breath—"someone she had never even laid eyes on before. I could cry just thinking about it."

"Her parents told her we were there and asked whether she wanted me to speak God's Word with her—they're holy, you know. But she wanted to see you instead. Her father was angry and wouldn't permit it.

'She's never had young men on her mind before,' he said. 'She must be able to stand utterly pure before the throne of God and the Lamb.' But I said: 'Are you sure that Our Lord cares about what you call purity, Ole Jensen? Just let them meet if it will make her happy!' Then we closed the door on the two of you and . . . well, how was it?" Sort turned toward him.

"You know quite well," replied Pelle sullenly, "that she just lay there and looked at me, as if she were thinking: Is that how he looks, and he's been so far down? I could see from her eyes that you had told her about me and that she knew about all my wretchedness."

Sort nodded.

"Then she stretched out her hand toward me. How she looks like one of God's angels already, I thought. But it's still a shame for someone so young. And then I went over and took her hand."

"And what happened then?" Sort moved closer, his eyes fixed expectantly on Pelle's lips.

"Then she pursed up her mouth a little. And at that moment I forgot all about what a pig I've been—and I kissed her!"

"Didn't she say anything to you—not a word?"

"She just looked at me with those inscrutable eyes. Then I didn't know what else to do, so I saw about getting out of there."

"Weren't you afraid that she would bring death down upon you?"

"No, why? I didn't think about that. She wouldn't think of doing anything like that. She was such a child."

For a moment they both lay there without speaking. "There's something about you that has power over them," said Sort at last. "If you wanted to join me . . . I would take up the Word."

Pelle stretched lazily. He felt no need to establish any religions. "No, I want to go abroad," he said. "There are supposed to be places in the world where they've started slaughtering the rich—that's where I want to go."

"Nothing good comes of getting help from the Devil—stay here instead! Here you know what's what. And if we went in together . . ."

"No, there's nothing to be had here for anyone who's poor. If I stay here, I'll end up in the dirt again. I want my share, even if I have to kill a bloodsucker to get it—and that can't be a very big sin. But don't you think we should see about moving on? For a whole month we've been trudging around the farms in the south, and you keep promising me that we would go inland to the *heath*. I haven't heard anything about Papa Lasse and Karna for months. When things started going bad for me, I seemed to have completely forgotten about them."

Sort got hastily to his feet. "It's good you have thoughts about something other than killing bloodsuckers. How far is it to Heath Farm?"

"About six miles, more or less."

"We'll go there at once. I don't feel like doing anything today anyway!"

They hefted their things onto their backs and trudged off, talking happily. Sort pictured their arrival. "I'll go in first and ask whether they have any old shoes or harnesses they need repaired. And then right in the middle of things, you'll come in."

Pelle laughed. "Shall I carry the bench for you? You can tie it right onto the lasts."

"You're not sweating for my sake, are you?" replied Sort, laughing. "Because then you should try taking off your pants."

They were tired of talking and trudged in silence. Carefree, Pelle walked in front, taking in the brisk day. He felt an abundance of strength, like a kind of pleasure inside him. Otherwise he wasn't thinking of much, just looking forward—quite unconsciously—to his visit home. He constantly had to slow his stride so that Sort wouldn't be left behind.

"What are you thinking about now?" Pelle asked suddenly. It was so irritating that Sort should walk along thinking as soon as he was silent. You could never tell beforehand where he would end up.

"That's just the way children ask," answered Sort, laughing. "They want to see what's inside."

"So tell me. You can tell me, can't you?"

"I was thinking about life, Pelle. Here you are, walking at my side, strong and confident as young David, and a month ago you were an outcast."

"Yes, that's strange, isn't it?" said Pelle, growing thoughtful.

"But how did you get sucked into all that? You could have saved yourself if you wanted to."

"I don't know. It was like someone hitting you on the head—and then you walk around not knowing what you're doing. And it's not that bad once you're in it. You slave away and get drunk—and hit each other over the head with bottles."

"You say it so gleefully—you're not getting behind things, that's the problem! I've seen so many people fall by the wayside; all it takes is just a tiny step to the side for the poor man, and he goes to the dogs. And he thinks he's a hell of a fellow. But it was still good that you got out of it, so regret didn't make your whole life bitter."

"If regret came up, there was always liquor," said Pelle with the voice of experience. "That will drive out everything else."

"And in a way, that's a good thing too—it helps them through the waiting period."

"Do you really believe the Millennium will come? With good times for everyone, poor and miserable?"

Sort nodded. "God has promised—we have to believe His word. Something like that is being prepared over in Copenhagen; but I don't know whether it's the real thing."

They strode briskly onward. The road was stony and uneven; alongside the road the rocks with their tough growth were beginning to stick up from the fields. In front of them the blue, rocky landscape of the heath rose up. "As soon as we've been home, I'm leaving. I have to go across the ocean and see what's going on," said Pelle.

"I have no right to hold you back," replied Sort in a low voice, "but the wandering will be lonely for me. I will always feel as if it was my son who had left me. But you'll probably have other things to think about than remembering a poor hunchback! For you the world stands open, and as soon as you've found your place, you probably won't think about little Sort."

"I'll remember you, all right," replied Pelle. "And as soon as I've gotten ahead, I'll come home and visit you—but not before. Papa will probably oppose the idea of me leaving. He wants me to take over Heath Farm from him—but you'll have to take my side. I have no desire to be a farmer."

"All right, I will."

"Just look at this—bare stone on top of stone with heather and tough weeds in between! That's the way Heath Farm was only four years ago. And now it's quite a nice place. That's what those two have accomplished—without any outsiders' help!"

"There's solid timber in your family," said Sort. "But who's that poor old man up there on the ridge? He has a big sack on his back and walks as though he's going to fall over at every step."

"He's . . . why, that's Papa Lasse! Hello!" Pelle waved his cap.

Lasse came stomping down toward them. He let the sack drop and stuck out his hand without looking at them.

"What are you doing here?" exclaimed Pelle happily. "We were just coming over to see you."

"Well, you can save yourself the trouble! Your feet were aching, so now you can spare them completely!" said Lasse tonelessly.

Pelle stared. "What's the matter? Have you moved?"

"Yes, we've moved!" Lasse laughed hollowly. "Moved—yes, yes, we have—and parted ways too. Karna is where there are no sorrows . . . and here is Lasse and everything he owns!" He kicked the sack with his foot, half turned away from them, staring at the ground.

All life had vanished from Pelle's face. He stared in horror at his father, but he couldn't get a word out.

"Here I go and run into my own son by accident, in the middle of this wilderness! And how I've looked and searched—no one could tell me anything about you. Your own flesh and blood has turned away from you, I thought. But I had to tell Karna that you were sick. She waited so steadfastly to see you before she passed on. 'You'll have to give him my greetings,' she said. 'God willing that things go well for him!' She thought more about you than many a mother would—no matter how little you deserved it. It's been a long time since you set foot in our house."

Pelle didn't reply. He stood there, swaying. Every word struck him like the blow of a club.

"You mustn't be too hard on him," said Sort. "He's not to blame—as sick as he's been."

"So, you've had hard times to fight with too? Then I should be the last one to chastise you, since I'm your father." Lasse stroked his sleeve, and Pelle got back his breath at this caress. "Go ahead and cry, my boy, it helps the soul! The tears have dried up inside me long ago, so I have to resign myself to the agony. It's been a rough time for me, let me tell you. Many a night I've watched over Karna and didn't know what I was going to do. I couldn't leave her and run off, and everything collapsed around our heads. I wasn't far from wishing you ill; you were the one who should have had a kind thought for us. And you could have always sent a message. But now it's all over."

"Are you going to leave Heath Farm, Papa?" asked Pelle softly.

"They've taken it away from me," replied Lasse, whimpering. "I couldn't come up with the annual payment because of everything, and their patience was exhausted. I was allowed to stay out of sheer mercy until Karna found peace and was put to rest in the earth. Anybody could see that it was only a matter of days."

"If it's only the interest . . ." said Sort, "I have a few hundred kroner that I've been saving for my old age."

"Now it's too late. The property is already being transferred to another man. And even if it weren't . . . what would I do without Karna? I'm not good for anything anymore."

"We'll take off together, Papa," said Pelle, raising his head.

"No, I'm not going anywhere but to the churchyard. I'm not worth anything anymore! They've taken my farm, and Karna worked herself to death on it, and I put my last ounce of strength into it. And then they just took it away!"

"I'll work for both of us. You'll have an easy time of it and go around enjoying your old age." Pelle looked ahead brightly.

Lasse shook his head. "I can't shrug off anything else—and just let it lie and go on!"

"I suggest we head for town," said Sort. "Up at the church we should be able to find a man who will give us a ride." They gathered up their possessions and set off. Lasse stayed behind the others, muttering to himself as he walked, now and then breaking into a complaint. Then Pelle would go over to him and take his hand.

"No one takes care of us or gives us good advice! On the contrary— they like to see us squander our lives and happiness as long as they can earn a couple of *skillings* from it. Even the authorities don't look out for the poor man; he just exists so everybody can hack at him and make off with whatever they can! What do they care that they subject us to misery and unhappiness and ruin—as long as they get their taxes and interest. In cold blood I'd like to stick my knife into the throats of every one of them!" That's the way he carried on for a while, rising up—and then collapsing like a little child.

XXVI

They lived with Sort, who owned his own little house up by the town meadow. There was no end to all the good the little itinerant shoemaker wanted to do for them. Most of the time Lasse shuffled around aimlessly; he couldn't sit still or concentrate on anything. Every once in a while he would break out in a complaint. He had become quite decrepit, and couldn't lift a spoon to his mouth without spilling his food. When they wanted to bring him along to do something that would amuse him, he was stubborn.

"Now we'll have to see about clearing out your things," the others would say time after time. "There's no point in giving all your possessions to the parish."

But Lasse refused. "As long as they've plundered everything else from me, then let them have that too," he said. "I'm not going there anymore . . . to be pitied by one and all."

"But you'll have to start from scratch," said Sort.

"That's what they wanted anyway, so let them have their way. They'll have to be held accountable for it someday."

So Pelle got hold of a wagon and drove up after the things himself; there was a full wagonload. He found Mama Bengta's green chest up in the attic, full of skeins of yarn. It was so strange to see it again. He hadn't thought of his mother in many years. I want this for a traveling chest, he thought, and took it along.

Lasse was standing outside when he came driving up. "Look what I'm bringing you, Papa!" Pelle shouted, cracking his whip cheerfully, but Lasse went inside without a word. When they had unloaded the wagon and went to look for him, he had crawled into bed with his face to the wall and refused to speak.

Pelle told him the news from home to liven him up a little. "Now the parish has transferred Heath Farm to the farmer on the hill for 5,000 kroner, and they say he made a good deal—it's supposed to be worth twice as much. He wants to live there himself and let his son take Hill Farm."

Lasse turned his head halfway round. "So, now there's a good crop, now thousands of kroner will be harvested—and it's the *landowner* who gets it!" he said bitterly. "But it's well fertilized soil too: Karna overstrained herself and died and left me alone, and we were so used to each other, and her thousand kroner went too. And now I'm a poor wreck! I put it all into that desolate rock so it turned into good, fertile land. And then the landowner moves in, now he likes living there—we poor lice have prepared the way for him. Do we exist for anything besides this? Anyone who wants to make a fuss about something like this is crazy! But I sure did take a liking to that spot!" Lasse suddenly burst into tears.

"Now you have to be sensible and be happy again," said Sort. "The bad times for poor people will soon be over, and a time will come when nobody has to wear himself out for other people, but each man will reap what he himself has sown! What injury have you suffered? Now you're on the right side and have thousands of kroner to draw on. It would have been worse if it was you who stood there owing money!"

"I don't think I'll live to see that day," said Lasse, raising up on his elbow.

"Maybe you and I won't, for those who are on the migration must die in the desert. All the same, we are God's chosen ones, we poor people! And Pelle there, he'll get to see the promised land!"

"Now you should come in the other room, Papa, and see how we've fixed it up for you," said Pelle.

Lasse got up wearily and followed them in. They had arranged his furniture in one of Sort's empty rooms, and it looked quite cozy. "We thought you ought to live here until Pelle gets on his feet in Copenhagen," said Sort. "No, don't bother thanking me—I'm happy to have the company, as you must realize."

"Our Lord will pay you back for this," said Lasse in a quivering voice. "We poor folks have no one but Him to turn to."

Pelle was restless and couldn't control his mind any longer because of the wanderlust. "If you would give me the money for the ticket, since I helped you," he told Sort, "then I could leave tonight."

Sort gave him 30 kroner.

"This is half of what we took in—I don't deserve this much," said Pelle. "You're the master, and have kept us in tools and everything."

"I don't want to live from others' work, but from my own," Sort replied, shoving the money across the table to him. "Do you want to leave town with nothing but the shirt on your back?"

"Now I've got plenty of money," said Pelle happily. "I've never had so much money at once! I could buy a lot of clothes with this money!"

"But you mustn't touch it! You can spend 5 kroner for the journey, but you have to save the rest to meet the future with."

"In Copenhagen—I'll probably make plenty of money there!"

"He's always been a careless devil when it comes to money," worried Lasse. "He had 5 kroner the time he came to town to start his apprenticeship, and he had a hard time telling me what he spent it on."

Sort laughed.

"Then I'll go with just the shirt on my back," exclaimed Pelle resolutely.

But that was wrong as well. There was no way to please those two—they were like two worried hens.

There was a good supply of underwear now, when Lasse remembered his possessions; Karna had taken good care of him. "But they'll probably be too short on your lanky body. It's not like when you took off from Stone Farm—then we had to take up my shirts for you."

His shoes were all wrong too. It wouldn't do for a journeyman shoemaker to show up with feet looking like that when he applied for a job. Sort and Pelle had to sew a pair of nice boots. "We have to take our time," said Sort. "Remember that they have to pass muster in the capital." Pelle was impatient and wanted to get to work.

Then there was just one new suit of clothes. "You'll take it ready-made on credit," said Sort. "Lasse and I will just have to stand surety for a suit of clothes."

The night before Pelle was going to leave, he and Lasse went out to visit the Dues. They chose a time when they would be sure to meet Due himself; neither of them liked Anna much. When they came down toward the house, they saw an elegantly dressed old man going in the front door.

"It's the consul," said Pelle. "He's been helping them out. Due must be out on a long haul, and we're probably not welcome."

"So that's the way things are," exclaimed Lasse, stopping abruptly. "Then I feel sorry for Due when he figures it all out. He'll probably find that he paid too much for his independence! Ah yes, the price is hard for those who want to get ahead! May it go well for you over there, lad."

They had come down by the church. A wagon stood outside full of green plants; two men were carrying them into the entryway. "What's all the fancy commotion here for?" asked Pelle.

"There's going to be a fine wedding here tomorrow," answered one of the men. "Grocer Lau's daughter is going to marry that pompous ass—Karlsen, I think his name is. He's a poor fellow like the rest of us, but do you think he even gives us a look? When filth rises to the top, it doesn't know where to stop! Now he's gone into the family business too."

"I'd like to go to that wedding," said Lasse eagerly as they wandered on. "It's always amusing to see that someone from your own family can be successful." Pelle took it as something of a reproach, but didn't answer.

"Shall we walk down a ways and take a look at the new harbor?"

"No, the sun's going down, and now I want to go home and go to bed. I'm old, Pelle! But you go ahead, I'll find my way home all right."

Pelle started down there but then turned off and headed north—he wanted to go out and say goodbye to Marie Nielsen. He owed her a friendly word for all her kindness, and she'd probably like to see him in some nice clothes for a change. She had just come home from work and was busy making supper.

"I don't believe it! Are you coming to see me, Pelle?" she exclaimed happily. "And look how handsome you've become—you look just like a prince." Pelle had to stay and have some supper.

"I just stopped by to thank you for your kindness—and to say goodbye. I'm leaving for Copenhagen tomorrow."

She gave him a serious look. "You must be really happy."

Pelle had to tell her what had happened since they last saw each other. He sat there gazing gratefully around the poor room, where the bed stood so chastely by the wall, covered with a snow-white blanket. He would never forget this aroma of lye and cleanliness and her fresh, even-tempered nature. Here she had taken him in, in the midst of his misery, and hadn't spared her white bed as she scrubbed the dirt from him. When he got to the capital he would have his picture taken and send it to her.

"How are you getting along these days?" he asked gently.

"The same as last time you were here—just a little lonelier," she replied solemnly.

Then he had to go. "Goodbye, and take care of yourself," he said, shaking her hand. "And thanks for everything!"

She just stood there and looked at him silently with a vague smile. "Oh well, I'm just a human being after all!" she burst out suddenly, and she threw her arms tightly around him.

Finally the great day arrived. Pelle woke up with the sun and had packed the green chest before the others got up. Then he went around not knowing what to do with himself, he was so restless and excited. He answered in a daze and his eyes were far off in bright dreams. He and Lasse carried the chest down to the steamer in the morning so they would have their hands free that evening. From there they went up to the church to watch Alfred's wedding. Pelle didn't really want to; he had enough excitement of his own, and felt no sympathy with Alfred's doings. But Lasse insisted.

The sun was high, baking the crooked streets so that the half-timbering sweated out its tar and the gutters stank. Down by the harbor they could hear the drummer yelling about herring and an auction. People were dashing toward the church in breathless conversation about Alfred, this child of fortune who had made such a good match.

The church was full of people. It was festively decorated, and up around the organ stood eight girls in white dresses who were going to sing "It is so lovely to walk together." Lasse had never seen such a fancy wedding. "I feel so proud, Pelle," he said.

"He's a windbag," said Pelle. "He's just taking her for the glory."

Then the bridal couple approached the altar. "It's really nasty, the way Alfred has greased up his hair," whispered Lasse. "He looks like a calf who's just been licked. But she's beautiful! I just wonder why they haven't put the myrtle wreath on her head... There isn't anything wrong with them, is there?"

"She's got that kid," Pelle whispered back, "otherwise he never would have gotten her."

"Ah yes! Still, it's quite a catch he made, nabbing such a rich man's daughter."

Now the girls were singing. They sounded almost like angels from heaven itself come down to seal the pact.

"We have to find a spot so we can congratulate them," said Lasse, starting to push his way out to the aisle, but Pelle held him back.

"I'm afraid he won't recognize us today. But look—there's Uncle Kalle!"

Kalle stood squeezed into the back row, and he had to wait there until all the others had gone out. "Well, I had to take part in this great day too, after all," he said. "I wanted to bring Mother along, but she didn't think she had a presentable dress to wear." Kalle was wearing a new gray linsey-woolsey; he had become even smaller and crookeder with the years.

"Why did you stay back here in the corner where you couldn't see anything? You should have been in the front row as the bridegroom's father," said Lasse.

"I was, too—didn't you see me sitting next to grocer Lau? We were reading the psalm book together. I was just pushed in here by the crowd. Now I'm supposed to go over and eat with them—I got a formal invitation to the reception—but I don't know." He looked down at himself. Suddenly he tossed his head and laughed in his own desperate way. "Satan should be standing here telling stories to people who won't believe lies! No, it's probably not for pigs to go into the chancellery. I might bring in a bad smell, you see—people like us haven't learned how to sweat perfume."

"So that's it! He's too fancy to acknowledge his own father—phooey! Just come home with us and have something to eat."

"No, I'm so full of roast pork and wine and cakes that I couldn't hold any more this time. Now I have to go home and tell Mother about all the splendor. And I've got twenty miles to go!"

"You walked all the way into town too. Forty miles is a little too much for your years!"

"I'd counted on being able to stay the night. I didn't think—oh, the hell with it! Can your children rise any higher than to the level where they don't know you anymore? Anna is well on her way to getting fancy ways too. I wonder if I'll even recognize myself much longer! Damn it, Kalle Karlsson, I'm from a fine family! Well, so long, you two."

He started off wearily on his homeward trek, looking quite pitiful in his disappointment. "I've never seen him so miserable," said Lasse as he stood staring after him. "It takes a lot before brother Kalle gives up."

That evening they walked down through town to the steamship. Pelle took long, robust strides, and his own solemn mood made him silent. Lasse toddled along beside him, bent over; a whining tone had come up in him again. "You're not going to forget your old father, too, are you?" he kept repeating.

"There's no danger of that," said Sort. Pelle heard nothing; his senses were out wandering.

The hearth smoke sank blue into the narrow street. The old folks were sitting outside on the stoops discussing the day's news, and the evening sun glinted off their round glasses so their wrinkled faces stared out with great fiery eyes. A deep evening peace hovered over the street. But down the dark alleys there was a rustling, with the eternal muffled restlessness of a large animal that turns around and around and can't settle down. Now and then it flared up in a shout or a child's cry and then began again, like heavy, labored breathing. Pelle knew this ghostly rustle that always emerged from the weary den of the poor. It was the worries of poverty collecting the bad dreams for the night. But he let this impoverished world, bleeding away its life so unnoticed in the silence, die away in his thoughts like a sad song—and he stared down toward the sea, which lay reddening at the end of the street. Now he was venturing out into the world!

Crazy Anker was standing up on his high stairway. "Farewell!" shouted Pelle. But Anker didn't notice; he turned his face up to the sky and uttered his demented cries.

Pelle cast a last glance at the workshop. I spent a lot of pleasant hours in there, he thought, remembering Young Master. Old Jørgen was standing outside his window and playing with Little Jørgen, who was sitting inside on the windowsill. "Peekaboo, baby," he shouted in his high falsetto, hiding and then popping out. The young wife was holding on to the child, and she was flushed with motherly joy.

"You'll write sometime, won't you?" said Lasse once again as Pelle hung over the ship's railing. "Don't forget your old father!" He was completely helpless in his worry.

"I'll write for you to join me as soon as I get settled," Pelle replied for what had to be the twentieth time. "You don't have to worry." He smiled, confident of victory, down at the old man. Then they just stood silent, looking at each other.

Finally the steamship departed. "Goodbye now!" he shouted for the last time as the ship swung around the jetty, and he kept waving his cap as long as he could see them. Then he went forward and sat down on a roll of hawser.

Behind him he had left everything, and he just kept staring forward—as if the great world might appear at any moment before the bow. He didn't bother to think about what was to come or how he would grapple with it—he simply longed for it!

AFTERWORD

One fine day the usual toil and boredom in the shoemaker's workshop is interrupted by the arrival of a talented itinerant shoemaker, appropriately nicknamed Garibaldi. He calls himself a socialist and advocates that the apprentices *strike*. With Garibaldi, Nexø foreshadows Pelle's future and asserts his novel's message.

Both Pelle and his author seem obsessed with the word *lykke*, which can only approximately be translated as "happiness." When phrases such as "the dream of happiness" or "the land of happiness" appear, however, the kind of happiness implied is that of the Biblical "Millennium," or the kind of happiness in a folktale that concludes with the marvelous words: "and they lived happily ever after."

In short, social realism and myth-making are interwoven, and it is this combination that gives *Pelle the Conqueror* its breathtaking perspective. The amalgamation of social anger and mythical imagination in Nexø's novel gives his sweeping story its uniqueness. Stark realism— revealing the social, physical, or mental misery of the poor—is combined with a depiction of a world that has a palpable sense of Providence.

Volume Two: Apprenticeship was published in 1907. It pictures Pelle as he works as an apprentice in an old-fashioned shoemaker's shop in Rønne, the largest town on the island of Bornholm. During those five years Pelle undergoes the throes of puberty, experiencing sexuality and the sense of listlessness that haunts the young, who cannot fathom their future. Eventually he sets out, as he did at the end of the first volume, to conquer new worlds.

Early in this century *Pelle the Conqueror*, Nexø's epic autobiographical novel, became a bestseller in many countries because the working class identified with its hero and his struggle for justice. In the second volume Nexø, inspired by the socialist dream of justice for the poor, has young Pelle confront a world against which he has to react if he is to survive, and in this phase of his life he has to be on his own. In the first volume the reader's heart goes out to gutsy Pelle and his father, lovable old Lasse, who knows he is weak, but whose unvanquished spirit gives Pelle the support the boy needs.

Lasse and the feudal farming culture—of which he is an integral and sad part—are only glimpsed briefly in Volume Two. That near omission reflects not only Nexø's own departure from the farming culture, but also a historical process. In the late nineteenth century, farmhands left the countryside for the city—a development not fully registered in *Pelle the Conqueror* until the third volume. Pelle's refusal to stay at Stone Farm and share his father's lot implies a change of consciousness, inspired by the industrial revolution, that typified the mindset of the rural work force of that era.

This mindset and this historical change can be placed in sharper focus if we look at the difference between Lasse's and Pelle's perceptions of the world. Lasse is simultaneously a fatalist and an optimist, for he knows that life can deal harsh blows, but they are blows that he has come to expect. Pelle, on the other hand, tends to believe that he is the master of his own destiny, so he has trouble dealing with the adversity he meets. Lasse is a representative of the old rural working class, which accepted its social position and conditions—even though Lasse's parting shots show him to be an embittered man who finally sees he has been exploited by the ruling class—and Pelle emerges as a young rebel who refuses to accept the lowly position allotted to him by the feudal culture.

The second volume makes it clear that Pelle's arbitrary decision to become a shoemaker is hardly appropriate to his dreams and desires, for he is not destined to join the petit bourgeoisie in the socially stratified provincial town. Pelle, whose lust for life is made so evident in Volume One through his audaciously foolhardy yet brave behavior, remains himself, but at the price of an inner struggle. He is caught between the temptation to conform to the rigid, numbing norms of the town and his instinctive desire to maintain his integrity. He may waver in making his decision, but his integrity wins out. Without realizing it, he establishes his solidarity with the poor and with all those who are despised and feared by the bourgeoisie. He remains a conqueror, but at this period in his life, his conquests have to be in his interior world—a necessary part of his psyche. Young Pelle, who is quite physical and not very reflective, barely grasps its significance. The reader, however, sees the contours of the traditional coming-of-age novel emerging—the novel of a quest for self-understanding and a conquest of both the internal and external worlds.

Pelle is a disarmingly charming hero, and part of his charm is that, unlike Hamlet, he is not inclined toward self-doubt. The major Danish authors immediately preceding Nexø had dwelt on such doubt-ridden figures, and their protagonists often turned out to be failures in life. Nexø's Pelle, a man of instinct and action, is headed in the opposite direction, but he is not yet a thinker. His youthful high hopes for an exciting life in the town are soon frustrated; he is alone and lonely. Even though he is warmly supported by the consumptive Young Master, it soon becomes clear that Pelle must fend for himself and that Andrès's protection has only limited powers. The pubescent Pelle is so isolated with his feelings and problems, and so listless at times, that he appears to be heading for the same subsistence existence of many of his proletarian peers.

Like the hero of a folktale, however, he encounters not only opponents but helpers. The opponents are imbued with the feudal spirit of the small town; they look askance at anyone who does not fit in or attempt to move upward in society by conforming to its norms. The personal antagonists of Pelle's childhood have now given way to impersonal forces. The powers opposing Pelle's lust for life are ideological, the repressive thinking of a class-structured society. But several individuals come to Pelle's aid: Andrès, who has a tolerance that far transcends the outlook of the town; the girls next door, who permit Pelle to be a playful child even as he grapples with his sexuality; and Morten, the friend who finally breaks the ice of Pelle's loneliness. Through him Pelle meets the helper, Morten's father, who sets him on the road to his destiny.

"The Power" is a brilliant, self-taught engineer whose plans for a new harbor were stolen by the town. That theft has left the Power destitute, lonely, and seething with anger. He has been reduced to virtual slave labor, and when he tries to escape his pitiful life in drunken binges, he succeeds only in persecuting his family. He resists being broken by the town and eventually gives his life to save two other workers from being blown up. In spite of his degradation, his integrity remains intact.

At that point, Pelle is at the nadir of his youthful life. Following Andrès's death, Pelle can see no purpose anywhere. But after seeing the self-sacrifice of the Power, he soon resolves to set out for new shores. Pelle survives and, along with Morten, becomes heir to the Power's legacy of directed anger, the harbinger of a world in which the proletariat will experience the rays of the sun.

Such a story could easily ring false: tendentiousness could lead to oversimplification. But in *Pelle the Conqueror* Nexø did not resort to crude black-and-white portrayals, but wrote with compassion about characters who would never live to share his socialist dream. More importantly, Nexø admits to those darker sides of reality that the fervent reformists or revolutionaries tend to suppress to further their causes. Pelle is a hero for both the author and the reader, as well as for many of the characters in the book: he is roundly applauded, and great deeds are expected of him. Those feats are accomplished in the third and fourth volumes of the novel. Still, Nexø allows the reader to see Pelle's shortcomings, darkening the vision of the novel and enhancing its realism.

It is quite natural for the young boy now to be on his own, but the reader is inclined to share Papa Lasse's indignation at Pelle's scant attempts to stay in touch with him, after he has seen the boy through his years at Stone Farm. Pelle may fervently wish to be with Lasse and may seek him out, but on the whole he keeps his own counsel—a pattern that will be repeated ominously in the following volumes. Only reluctantly will Pelle allow others to help him. Nexø did not make life falsely idyllic in his optimistic novel. Lasse's bitterness, the suffering and death of Andrès, the mental torment and insecurity of many secondary characters, and Pelle's own dark moments—and they are many—all suggest that Nexø refused to be simplistic and wisely admitted the shortcomings of his hero.

Nevertheless, Pelle remains a heroic figure. The fact that Nexø presents him as a complex, even flawed character grants him the verisimilitude that many literary heroes have lacked. Pelle is compassionate, yet unwittingly thoughtless to the point of being ruthless—traits characteristic of both a successful crusader and a man of destiny and vitality who can lead his people to a promised land.

This realistic novel with a socialist message is richly interwoven with allegory, symbolism, and myth, but in such a way that the realism of the story is never undercut. Nexø knew how to entice an audience that wanted social justice. He did it with language that appealed to them through its Biblical overtones and echoes of folklore—language that the working class had known for centuries.

Finally, Fjord Press should be thanked for reviving *Pelle the Conqueror* in a new translation that retains the frank, earthy realism of the Danish. Sadly, that was not the case when this masterpiece was first translated into English over seventy-five years ago—one reason why Nexø is scarcely known in the English-speaking world today. May he regain his former stature. *Pelle the Conqueror* proves that he deserves it.

Niels Ingwersen
University of Wisconsin − Madison

Fjord Modern Classics

*Works that have stood the test of time in other languages,
now in graceful and accurate American translations*

No. 1
Pelle the Conqueror, Volume 1: Childhood
by Martin Andersen Nexø
Translated from the Danish by Steven T. Murray
$9.95 trade paperback

No. 2
Niels Lyhne
by Jens Peter Jacobsen
Translated from the Danish by Tiina Nunnally
$19.95 clothbound

No. 3
Katinka
by Herman Bang
Translated from the Danish by Tiina Nunnally
$8.95 trade paperback

No. 4
Pelle the Conqueror, Volume 2: Apprenticeship
by Martin Andersen Nexø
Translated from the Danish by Steven T. Murray & Tiina Nunnally
$9.95 trade paperback

No. 5
Selma Berg
by Victoria Benedictsson
Translated from the Swedish by Eric O. Johannesson
$10.95 trade paperback (forthcoming)

No. 6
Mogens and Other Stories
by Jens Peter Jacobsen
Translated from the Danish by Tiina Nunnally
$10.95 trade paperback (forthcoming)

Other translations from Fjord Press

Night Roamers and Other Stories by Knut Hamsun
Translated from the Norwegian by Tiina Nunnally
$9.95, trade paperback (forthcoming)

Love & Solitude: Selected Poems, 1916–1923 by Edith Södergran
Translated from the Finland-Swedish by Stina Katchadourian
$10.95, trade paperback, Third bilingual edition (forthcoming)

Titles now available:

The Faces by Tove Ditlevsen
Translated from the Danish by Tiina Nunnally
$9.95, trade paperback

Idealists by Hans Scherfig
Translated from the Danish by Frank Hugus
$9.95, trade paperback

Peasants and Masters by Theodor Kallifatides
Translated from the Swedish by Thomas Teal
$8.95, trade paperback

Another Metamorphosis and Other Fictions by Villy Sørensen
Translated from the Danish by Tiina Nunnally & Steven T. Murray
$8.95, trade paperback

The Missing Bureaucrat by Hans Scherfig
Translated from the Danish by Frank Hugus
$8.95, trade paperback

Stolen Spring by Hans Scherfig
Translated from the Danish by Frank Hugus
$7.95, trade paperback

Witness to the Future by Klaus Rifbjerg
Translated from the Danish by Steven T. Murray
$8.95, trade paperback

The First Polka by Horst Bienek
Translated from the German by Ralph R. Read
$7.95, trade paperback

Laterna Magica by William Heinesen
Translated from the Danish by Tiina Nunnally
$7.95, trade paperback

Please write for a catalog: Fjord Press, P.O. Box 16501, Seattle, WA 98116

This book was typeset by Fjord Press
in 10/12½ Stempel Garamond,
a modern adaptation by the
Stempel foundry, Frankfurt,
of the classic French typeface
designed by Claude Garamond
in the 16th century.

DATE DUE

HIGHSMITH   # 45220